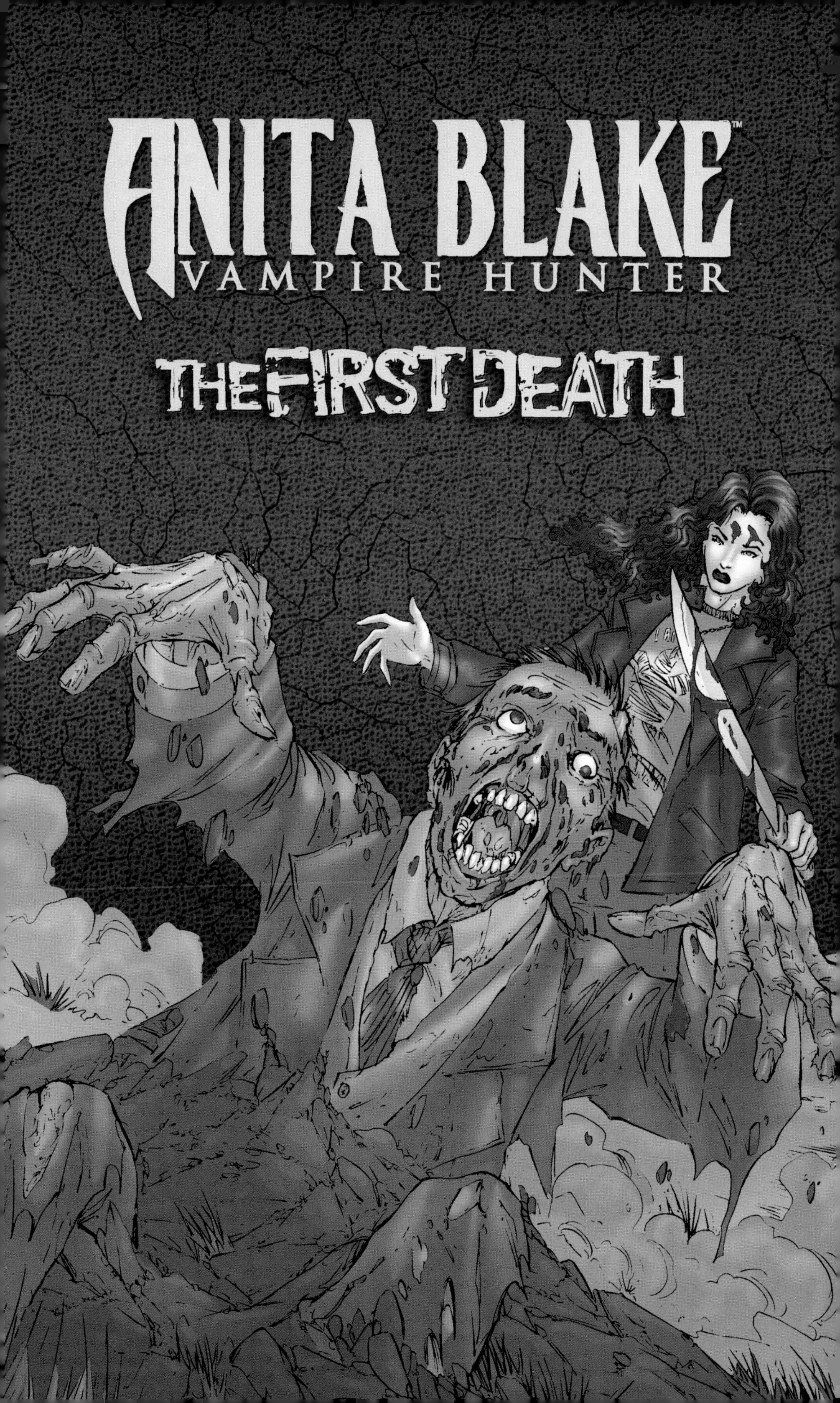
ANITA BLAKE™
VAMPIRE HUNTER
THE FIRST DEATH

ANITA BLAKE
VAMPIRE HUNTER

THE FIRST DEATH

WRITERS: **LAURELL K. HAMILTON & JONATHON GREEN**
ARTWORK: **WELLINTON ALVES**
COLORS: **COLOR DOJO**
LETTERS: **BILL TORTOLINI**

ASSISTANT EDITOR: **JORDAN D. WHITE**
EDITORS: **MIKE RAICHT & MARK PANICCIA**

GUILTY PLEASURES HANDBOOK

HEAD WRITER/COORDINATOR: **STUART VANDAL**
WRITERS: **RONALD BYRD, MICHAEL HOSKIN, CHRIS BIGGS & AVE CULLEN**
ARTWORK: **BRETT BOOTH**
COLORS: **IMAGINARY FRIENDS**
SPECIAL THANKS TO **MELISSA MCALISTER, ANN TREDWAY, JASON & DARLA COOK**

COVER ARTISTS: **BRETT BOOTH & RON LIM**

COLLECTION EDITOR: **CORY LEVINE**
ASSISTANT EDITOR: **JOHN DENNING**
EDITORS, SPECIAL PROJECTS: **JENNIFER GRÜNWALD & MARK D. BEAZLEY**
SENIOR EDITOR, SPECIAL PROJECTS: **JEFF YOUNGQUIST**
VICE PRESIDENT OF DEVELOPMENT: **RUWAN JAYATILLEKE**
SENIOR VICE PRESIDENT OF SALES: **DAVID GABRIEL**
VICE PRESIDENT OF CREATIVE: **TOM MARVELLI**
DUST JACKET DESIGN: **PATRICK MCGRATH & DAYLE CHESLER**
PRODUCTION: **JERRON QUALITY COLOR**

EDITOR IN CHIEF: **JOE QUESADA**
PUBLISHER: **DAN BUCKLEY**

LAURELL K. HAMILTON'S ANITA BLAKE, VAMPIRE HUNTER: THE FIRST DEATH. Contains material originally published in magazine form as LAURELL K. HAMILTON'S ANITA BLAKE, VAMPIRE HUNTER: THE FIRST DEATH #1-2 and ANITA BLAKE: GUILTY PLEASURES HANDBOOK. First printing 2008. ISBN# 978-0-7851-2941-7. Published by MARVEL PUBLISHING, INC., a subsidiary of MARVEL ENTERTAINMENT, INC. OFFICE OF PUBLICATION: 417 5th Avenue, New York, NY 10016. Copyright © 2007 and 2008 Laurell K. Hamilton. All rights reserved. $19.99 per copy in the U.S. and $32.00 in Canada (GST #R127032852); Canadian Agreement #40668537. Anita Blake: Vampire Hunter and all characters featured in this issue and the distinctive names and likenesses thereof, and all related indicia are trademarks of Laurell K. Hamilton. No similarity between any of the names, characters, persons, and/or institutions in this magazine with those of any living or dead person or institution is intended, and any such similarity which may exist is purely coincidental. Printed in the U.S.A. ALAN FINE, CEO Marvel Toys & Publishing Divisions and CMO Marvel Entertainment, Inc.; DAVID GABRIEL, Senior VP of Publishing Sales & Circulation; DAVID BOGART, VP of Business Affairs & Editorial Operations; MICHAEL PASCIULLO, VP Merchandising & Communications; JIM BOYLE, VP of Publishing Operations; DAN CARR, Executive Director of Publishing Technology; JUSTIN F. GABRIE, Managing Editor; SUSAN CRESPI, Production Manager; STAN LEE, Chairman Emeritus. For information regarding advertising in Marvel Comics or on Marvel.com, please contact Mitch Dane, Advertising Director, at mdane@marvel.com.

10 9 8 7 6 5 4 3 2 1

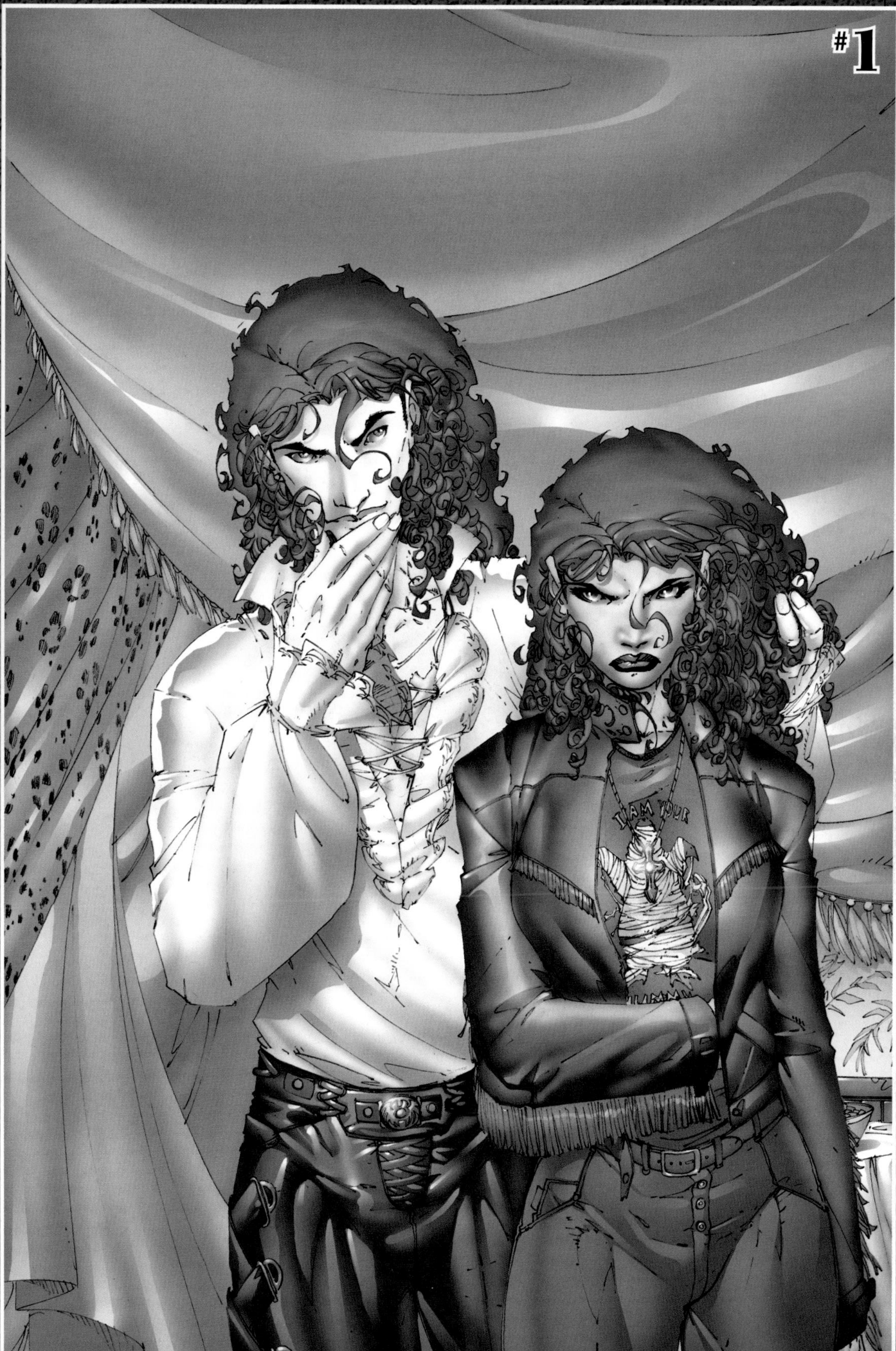
#1

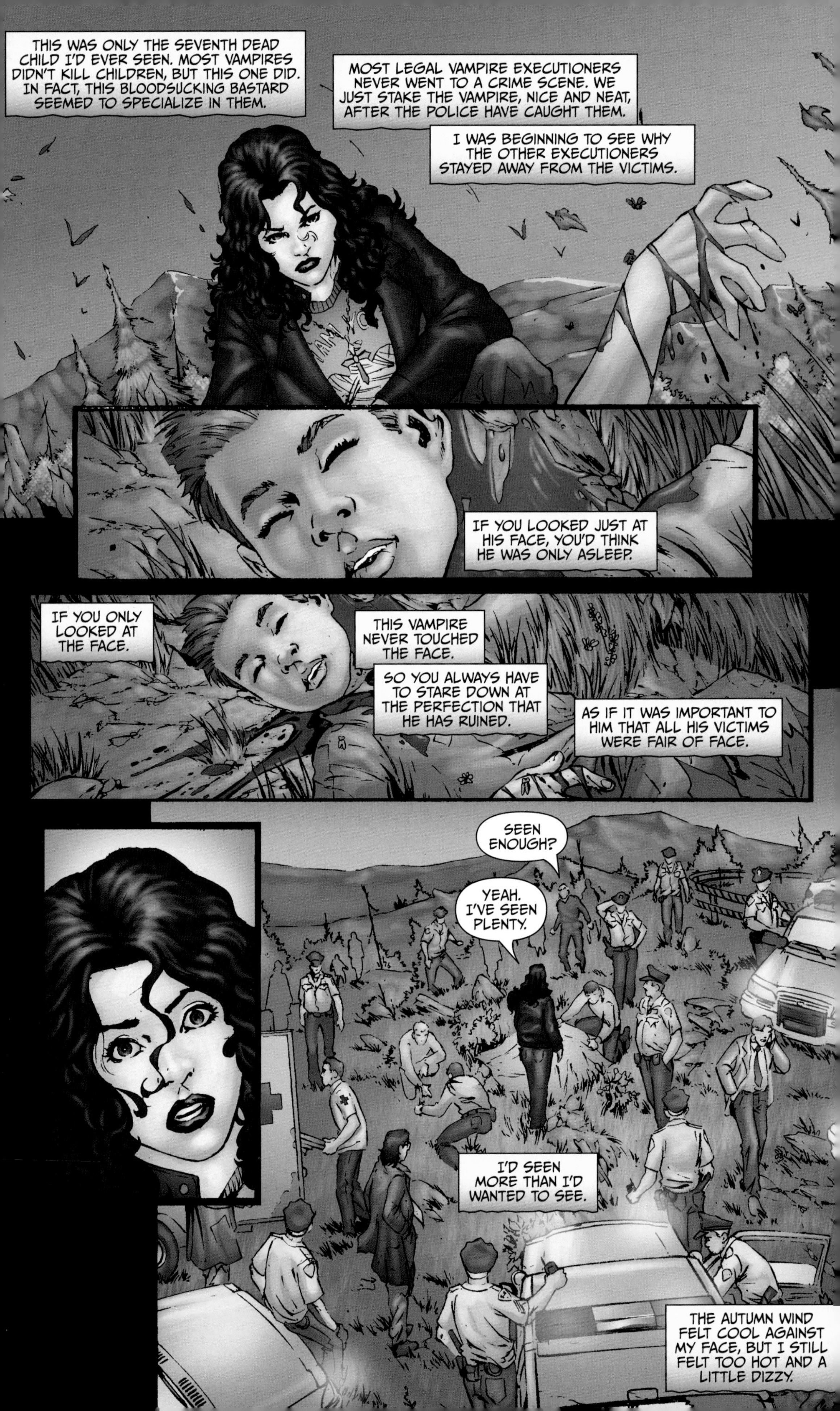
THIS WAS ONLY THE SEVENTH DEAD CHILD I'D EVER SEEN. MOST VAMPIRES DIDN'T KILL CHILDREN, BUT THIS ONE DID. IN FACT, THIS BLOODSUCKING BASTARD SEEMED TO SPECIALIZE IN THEM.
MOST LEGAL VAMPIRE EXECUTIONERS NEVER WENT TO A CRIME SCENE. WE JUST STAKE THE VAMPIRE, NICE AND NEAT, AFTER THE POLICE HAVE CAUGHT THEM.
I WAS BEGINNING TO SEE WHY THE OTHER EXECUTIONERS STAYED AWAY FROM THE VICTIMS.
IF YOU LOOKED JUST AT HIS FACE, YOU'D THINK HE WAS ONLY ASLEEP.
IF YOU ONLY LOOKED AT THE FACE.
THIS VAMPIRE NEVER TOUCHED THE FACE.
SO YOU ALWAYS HAVE TO STARE DOWN AT THE PERFECTION THAT HE HAS RUINED.
AS IF IT WAS IMPORTANT TO HIM THAT ALL HIS VICTIMS WERE FAIR OF FACE.
SEEN ENOUGH?
YEAH. I'VE SEEN PLENTY.
I'D SEEN MORE THAN I'D WANTED TO SEE.
THE AUTUMN WIND FELT COOL AGAINST MY FACE, BUT I STILL FELT TOO HOT AND A LITTLE DIZZY.

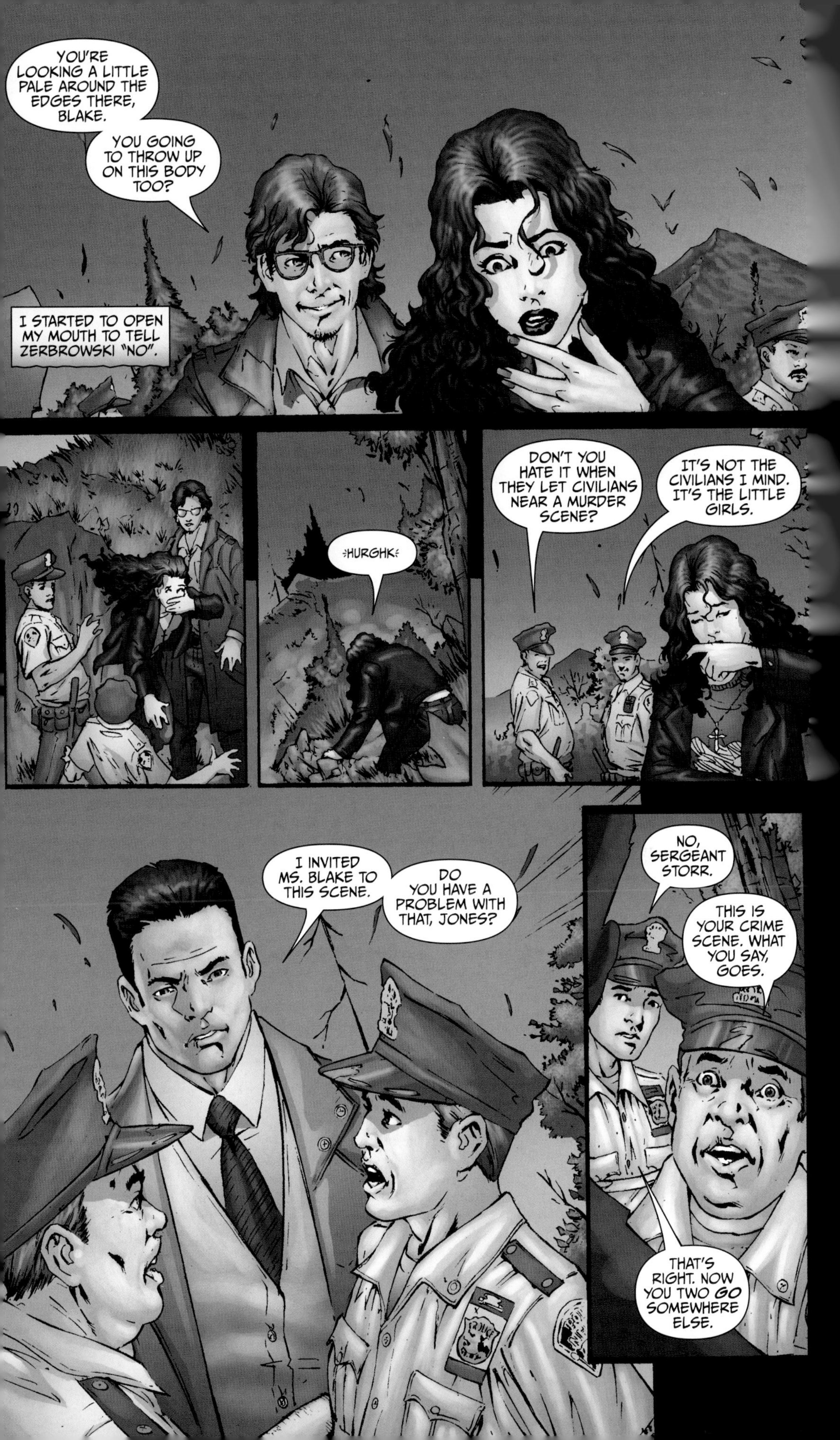
YOU'RE LOOKING A LITTLE PALE AROUND THE EDGES THERE, BLAKE.
YOU GOING TO THROW UP ON THIS BODY TOO?
I STARTED TO OPEN MY MOUTH TO TELL ZERBROWSKI "NO".
HURGHK
DON'T YOU HATE IT WHEN THEY LET CIVILIANS NEAR A MURDER SCENE?
IT'S NOT THE CIVILIANS I MIND. IT'S THE LITTLE GIRLS.
I INVITED MS. BLAKE TO THIS SCENE.
DO YOU HAVE A PROBLEM WITH THAT, JONES?
NO, SERGEANT STORR.
THIS IS YOUR CRIME SCENE. WHAT YOU SAY, GOES.
THAT'S RIGHT. NOW YOU TWO GO SOMEWHERE ELSE.

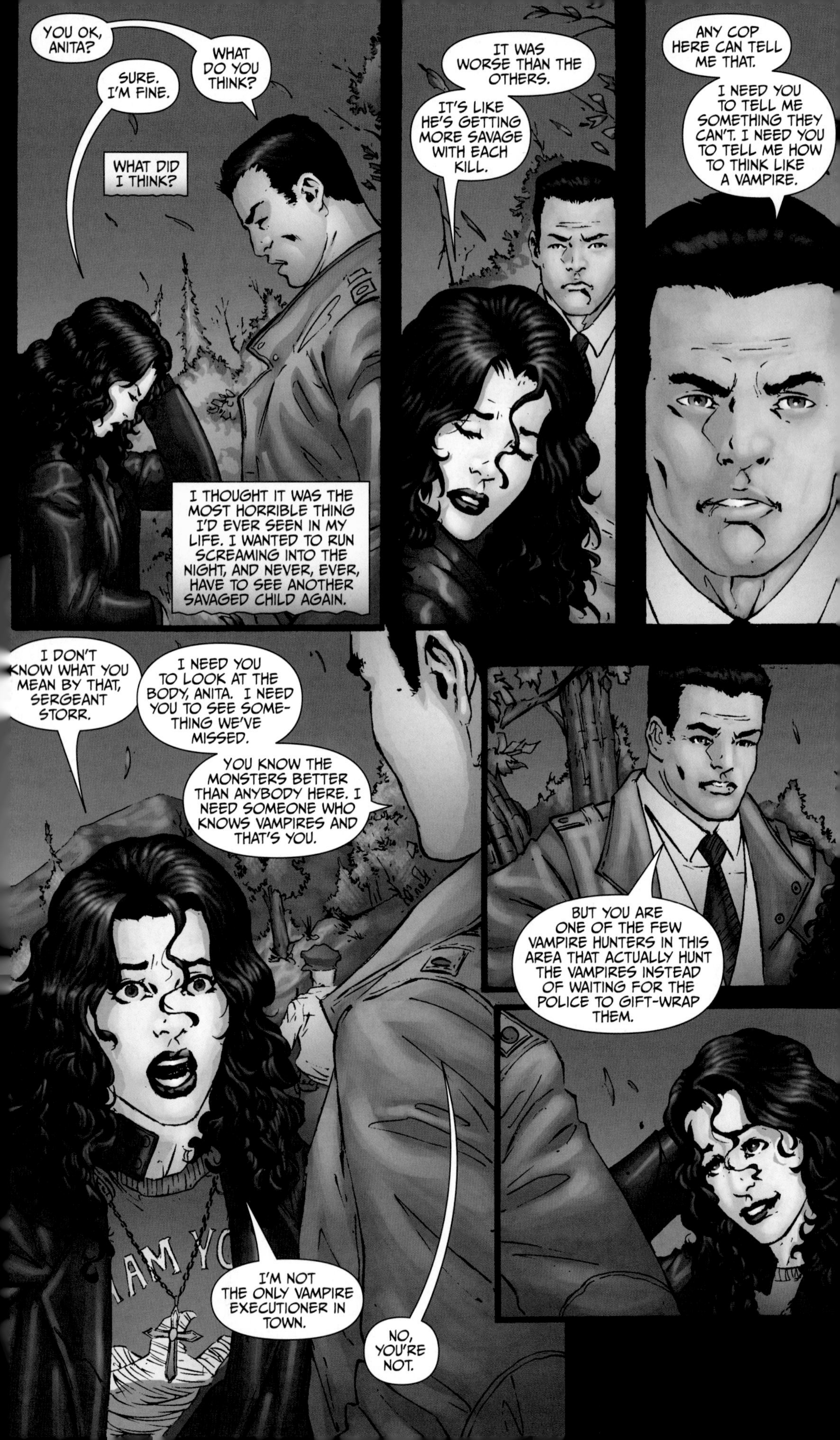

YOU OK, ANITA?
WHAT DO YOU THINK?
SURE. I'M FINE.
WHAT DID I THINK?
I THOUGHT IT WAS THE MOST HORRIBLE THING I'D EVER SEEN IN MY LIFE. I WANTED TO RUN SCREAMING INTO THE NIGHT, AND NEVER, EVER, HAVE TO SEE ANOTHER SAVAGED CHILD AGAIN.
IT WAS WORSE THAN THE OTHERS.
IT'S LIKE HE'S GETTING MORE SAVAGE WITH EACH KILL.
ANY COP HERE CAN TELL ME THAT.
I NEED YOU TO TELL ME SOMETHING THEY CAN'T. I NEED YOU TO TELL ME HOW TO THINK LIKE A VAMPIRE.
I DON'T KNOW WHAT YOU MEAN BY THAT, SERGEANT STORR.
I NEED YOU TO LOOK AT THE BODY, ANITA. I NEED YOU TO SEE SOME-THING WE'VE MISSED.
YOU KNOW THE MONSTERS BETTER THAN ANYBODY HERE. I NEED SOMEONE WHO KNOWS VAMPIRES AND THAT'S YOU.
I'M NOT THE ONLY VAMPIRE EXECUTIONER IN TOWN.
NO, YOU'RE NOT.
BUT YOU ARE ONE OF THE FEW VAMPIRE HUNTERS IN THIS AREA THAT ACTUALLY HUNT THE VAMPIRES INSTEAD OF WAITING FOR THE POLICE TO GIFT-WRAP THEM.

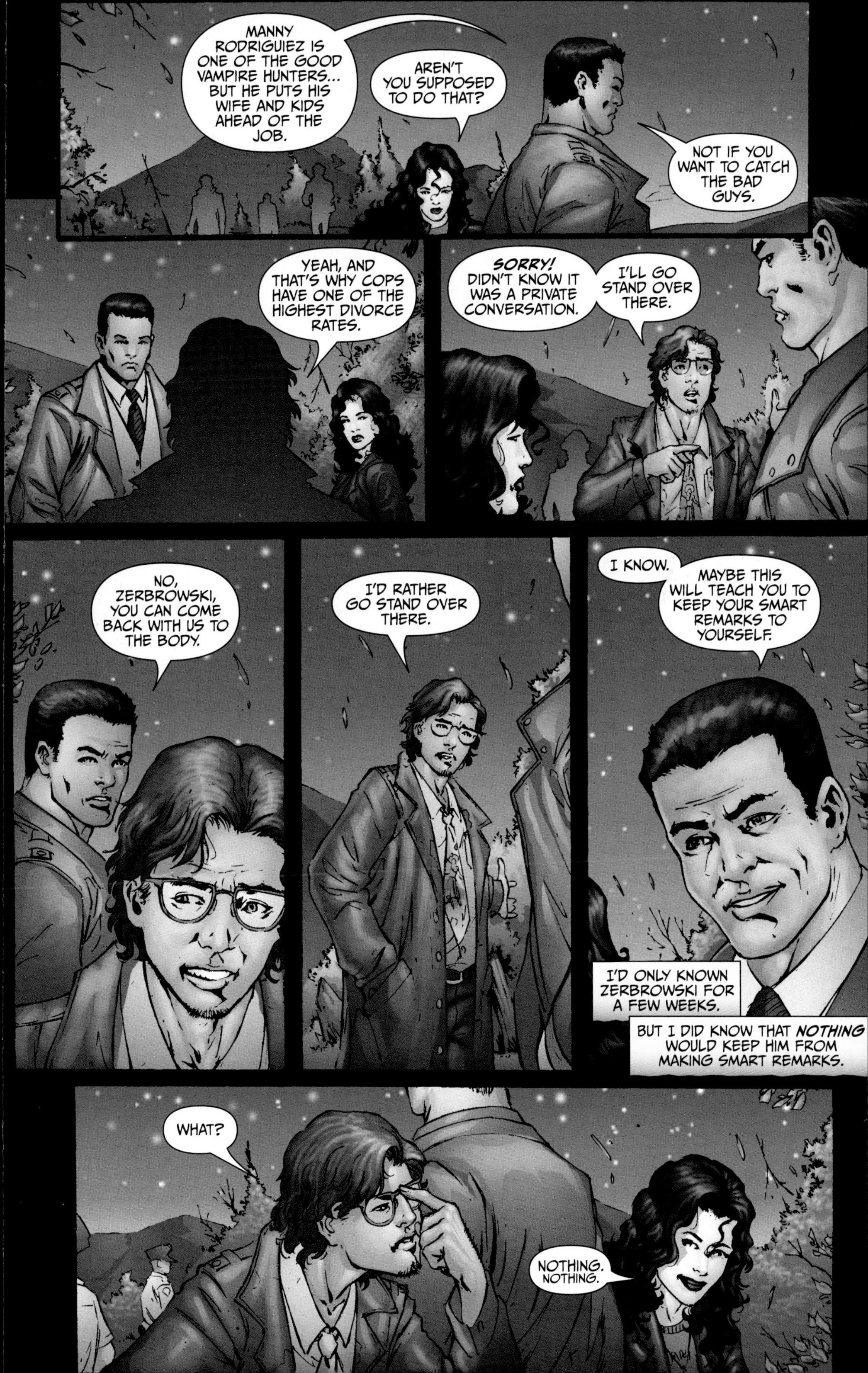
MANNY RODRIGUIEZ IS ONE OF THE GOOD VAMPIRE HUNTERS... BUT HE PUTS HIS WIFE AND KIDS AHEAD OF THE JOB.
AREN'T YOU SUPPOSED TO DO THAT?
NOT IF YOU WANT TO CATCH THE BAD GUYS.
YEAH, AND THAT'S WHY COPS HAVE ONE OF THE HIGHEST DIVORCE RATES.
SORRY! DIDN'T KNOW IT WAS A PRIVATE CONVERSATION.
I'LL GO STAND OVER THERE.
NO, ZERBROWSKI, YOU CAN COME BACK WITH US TO THE BODY.
I'D RATHER GO STAND OVER THERE.
I KNOW.
MAYBE THIS WILL TEACH YOU TO KEEP YOUR SMART REMARKS TO YOURSELF.
I'D ONLY KNOWN ZERBROWSKI FOR A FEW WEEKS.
BUT I DID KNOW THAT NOTHING WOULD KEEP HIM FROM MAKING SMART REMARKS.
WHAT?
NOTHING. NOTHING.

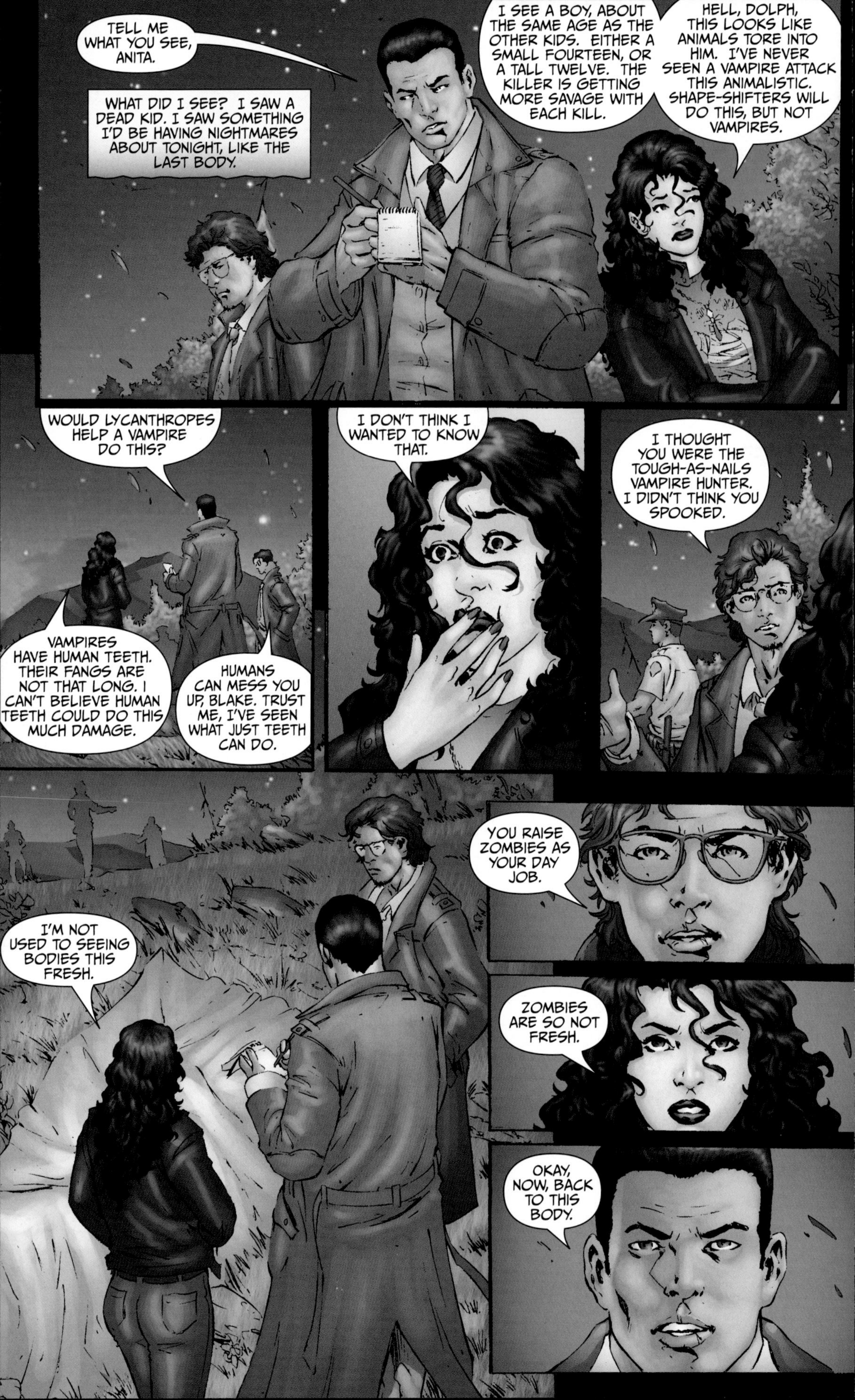
TELL ME WHAT YOU SEE, ANITA.
WHAT DID I SEE? I SAW A DEAD KID. I SAW SOMETHING I'D BE HAVING NIGHTMARES ABOUT TONIGHT, LIKE THE LAST BODY.
I SEE A BOY, ABOUT THE SAME AGE AS THE OTHER KIDS. EITHER A SMALL FOURTEEN, OR A TALL TWELVE. THE KILLER IS GETTING MORE SAVAGE WITH EACH KILL.
HELL, DOLPH, THIS LOOKS LIKE ANIMALS TORE INTO HIM. I'VE NEVER SEEN A VAMPIRE ATTACK THIS ANIMALISTIC. SHAPE-SHIFTERS WILL DO THIS, BUT NOT VAMPIRES.
WOULD LYCANTHROPES HELP A VAMPIRE DO THIS?
VAMPIRES HAVE HUMAN TEETH. THEIR FANGS ARE NOT THAT LONG. I CAN'T BELIEVE HUMAN TEETH COULD DO THIS MUCH DAMAGE.
HUMANS CAN MESS YOU UP, BLAKE. TRUST ME, I'VE SEEN WHAT JUST TEETH CAN DO.
I DON'T THINK I WANTED TO KNOW THAT.
I THOUGHT YOU WERE THE TOUGH-AS-NAILS VAMPIRE HUNTER. I DIDN'T THINK YOU SPOOKED.
I'M NOT USED TO SEEING BODIES THIS FRESH.
YOU RAISE ZOMBIES AS YOUR DAY JOB.
ZOMBIES ARE SO NOT FRESH.
OKAY, NOW, BACK TO THIS BODY.

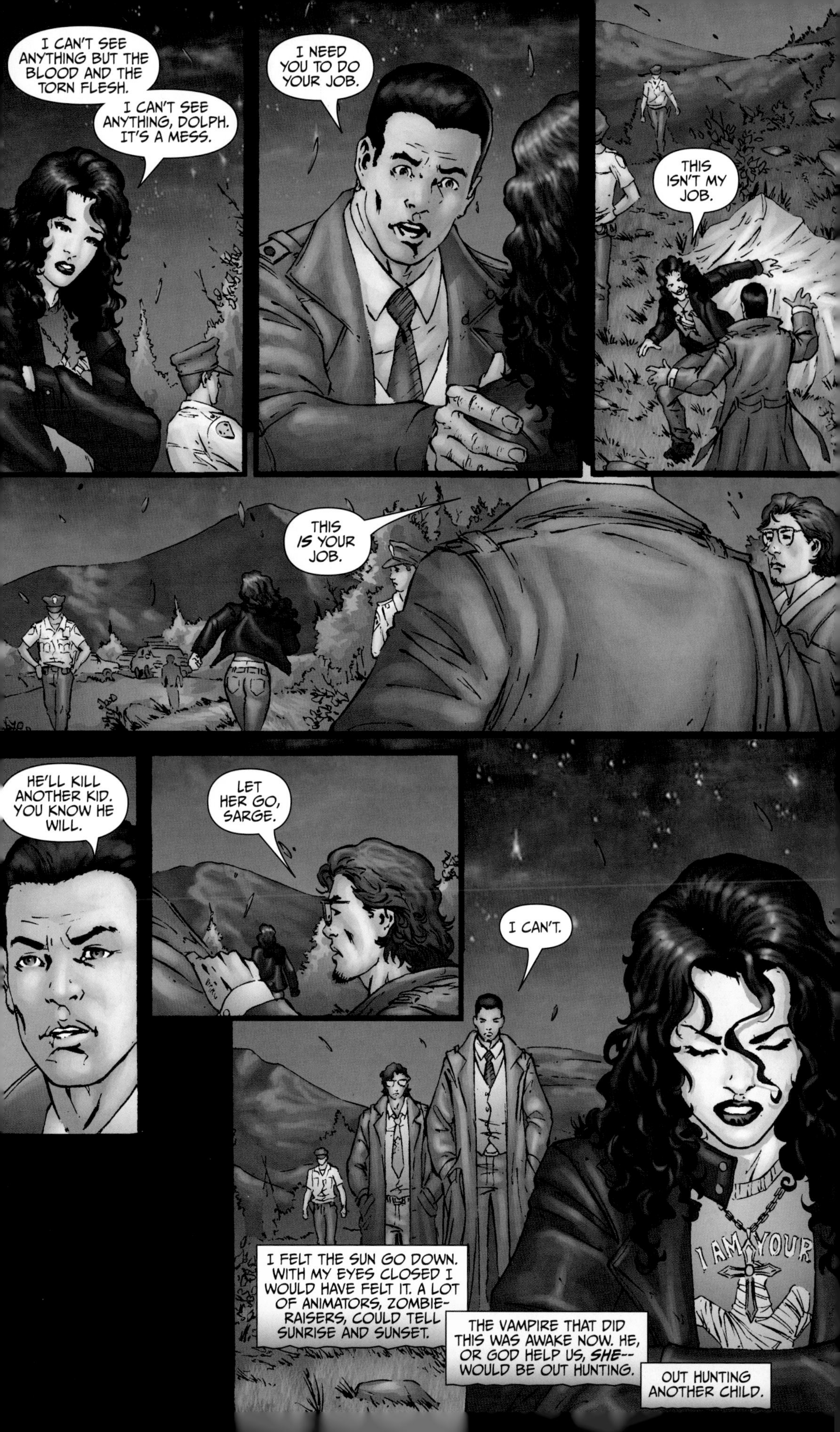

I CAN'T SEE ANYTHING BUT THE BLOOD AND THE TORN FLESH.
I CAN'T SEE ANYTHING, DOLPH. IT'S A MESS.
I NEED YOU TO DO YOUR JOB.
THIS ISN'T MY JOB.
THIS *IS* YOUR JOB.
HE'LL KILL ANOTHER KID. YOU KNOW HE WILL.
LET HER GO, SARGE.
I CAN'T.
I FELT THE SUN GO DOWN. WITH MY EYES CLOSED I WOULD HAVE FELT IT. A LOT OF ANIMATORS, ZOMBIE-RAISERS, COULD TELL SUNRISE AND SUNSET.
THE VAMPIRE THAT DID THIS WAS AWAKE NOW. HE, OR GOD HELP US, *SHE*-- WOULD BE OUT HUNTING.
OUT HUNTING ANOTHER CHILD.
I AM YOUR

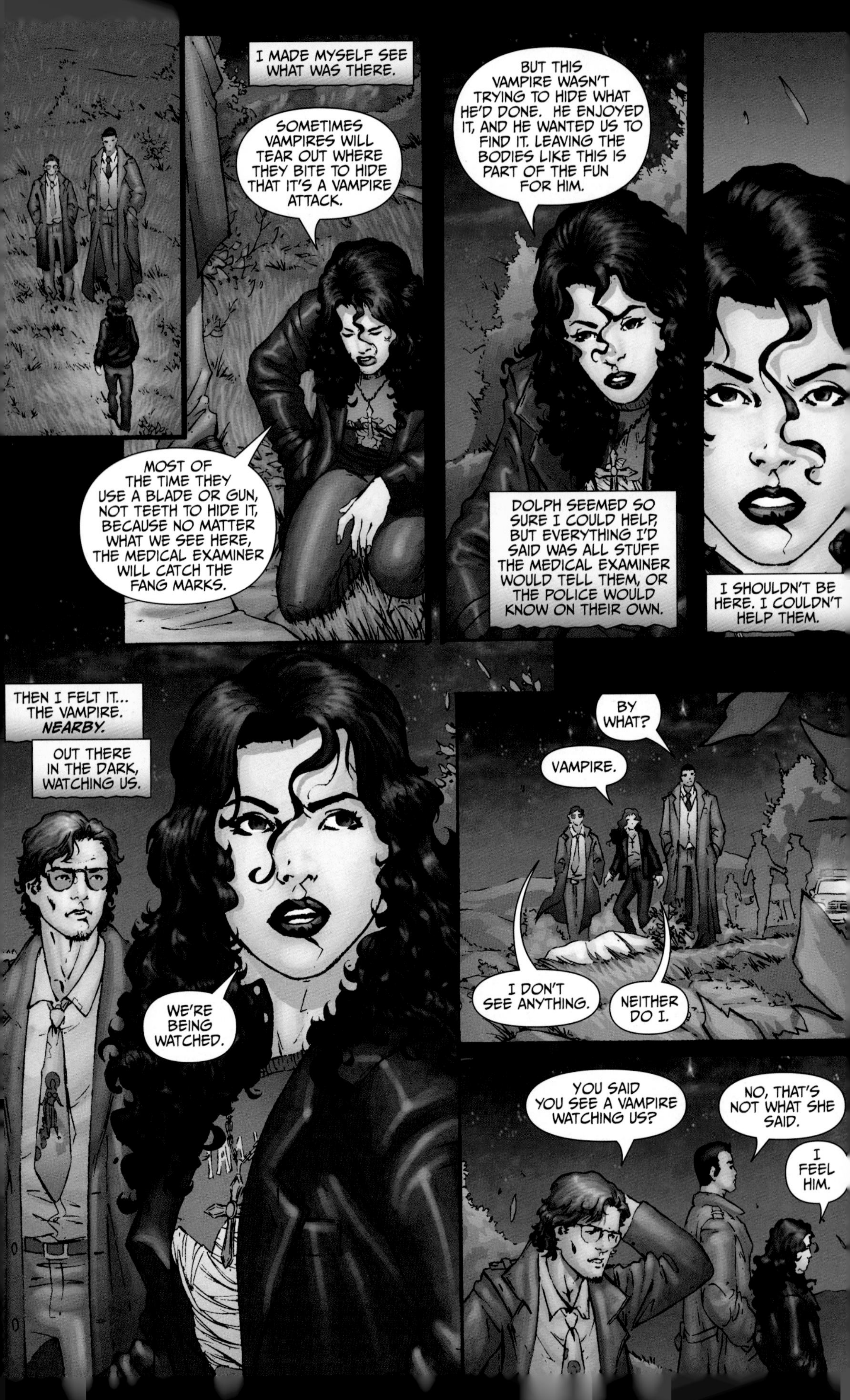
I MADE MYSELF SEE WHAT WAS THERE.
SOMETIMES VAMPIRES WILL TEAR OUT WHERE THEY BITE TO HIDE THAT IT'S A VAMPIRE ATTACK.
MOST OF THE TIME THEY USE A BLADE OR GUN, NOT TEETH TO HIDE IT, BECAUSE NO MATTER WHAT WE SEE HERE, THE MEDICAL EXAMINER WILL CATCH THE FANG MARKS.
BUT THIS VAMPIRE WASN'T TRYING TO HIDE WHAT HE'D DONE. HE ENJOYED IT, AND HE WANTED US TO FIND IT. LEAVING THE BODIES LIKE THIS IS PART OF THE FUN FOR HIM.
DOLPH SEEMED SO SURE I COULD HELP, BUT EVERYTHING I'D SAID WAS ALL STUFF THE MEDICAL EXAMINER WOULD TELL THEM, OR THE POLICE WOULD KNOW ON THEIR OWN.
I SHOULDN'T BE HERE. I COULDN'T HELP THEM.
THEN I FELT IT... THE VAMPIRE. *NEARBY.*
OUT THERE IN THE DARK, WATCHING US.
WE'RE BEING WATCHED.
BY WHAT?
VAMPIRE.
I DON'T SEE ANYTHING.
NEITHER DO I.
YOU SAID YOU SEE A VAMPIRE WATCHING US?
NO, THAT'S NOT WHAT SHE SAID.
I FEEL HIM.

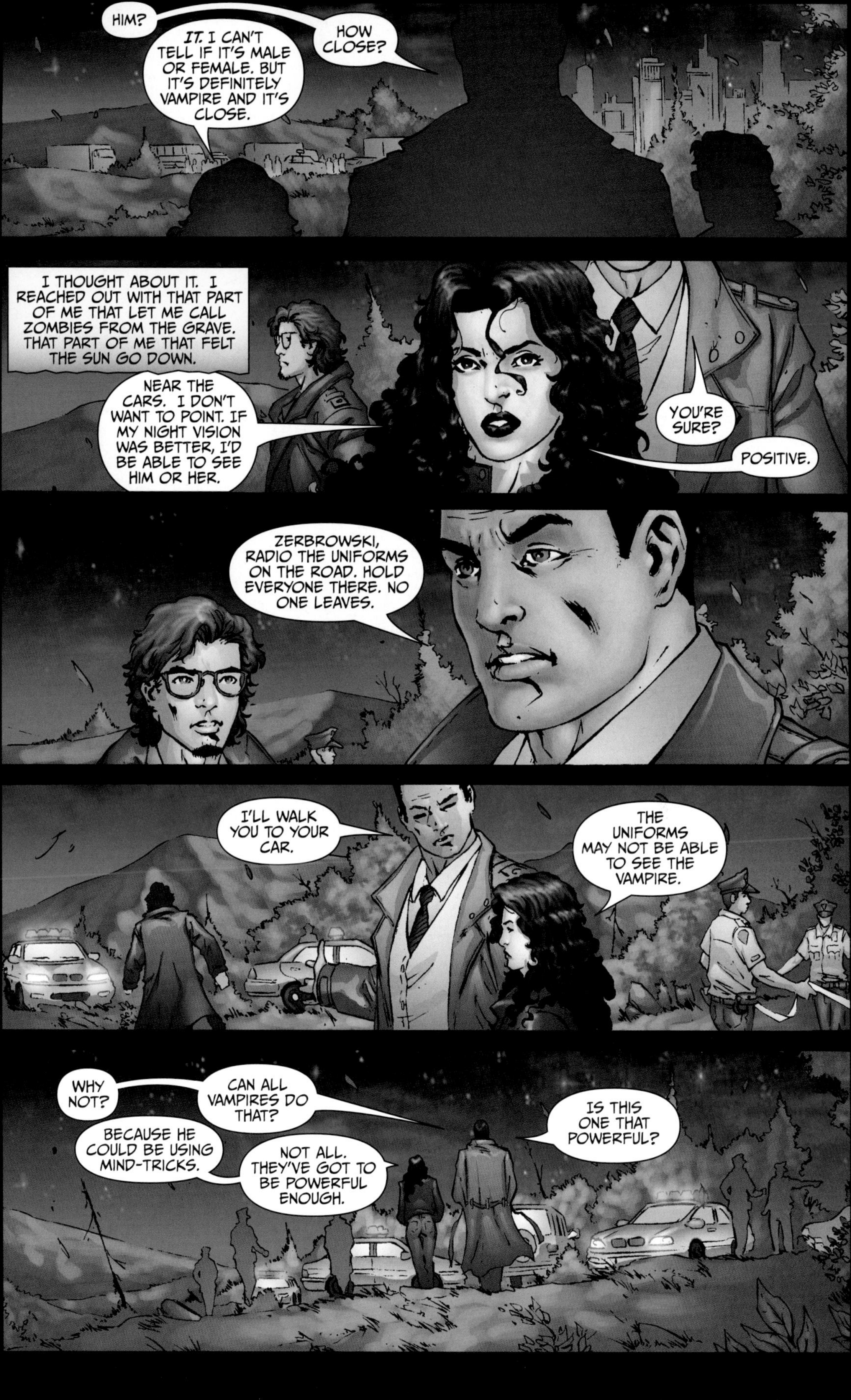
HIM?
IT. I CAN'T TELL IF IT'S MALE OR FEMALE. BUT IT'S DEFINITELY VAMPIRE AND IT'S CLOSE.
HOW CLOSE?
I THOUGHT ABOUT IT. I REACHED OUT WITH THAT PART OF ME THAT LET ME CALL ZOMBIES FROM THE GRAVE. THAT PART OF ME THAT FELT THE SUN GO DOWN.
NEAR THE CARS. I DON'T WANT TO POINT. IF MY NIGHT VISION WAS BETTER, I'D BE ABLE TO SEE HIM OR HER.
YOU'RE SURE?
POSITIVE.
ZERBROWSKI, RADIO THE UNIFORMS ON THE ROAD. HOLD EVERYONE THERE. NO ONE LEAVES.
I'LL WALK YOU TO YOUR CAR.
THE UNIFORMS MAY NOT BE ABLE TO SEE THE VAMPIRE.
WHY NOT?
BECAUSE HE COULD BE USING MIND-TRICKS.
CAN ALL VAMPIRES DO THAT?
NOT ALL. THEY'VE GOT TO BE POWERFUL ENOUGH.
IS THIS ONE THAT POWERFUL?

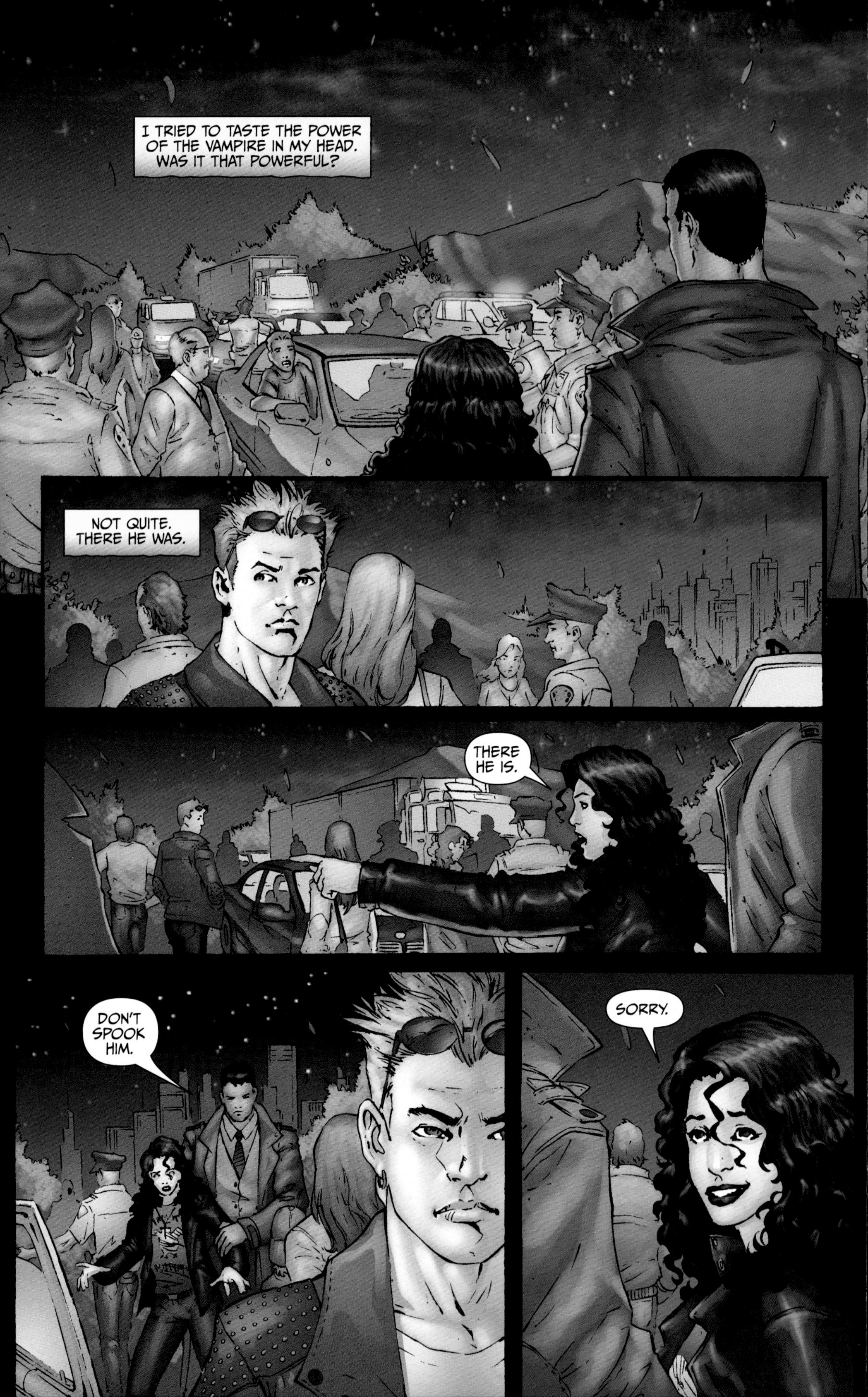
I TRIED TO TASTE THE POWER OF THE VAMPIRE IN MY HEAD. WAS IT THAT POWERFUL?
NOT QUITE. THERE HE WAS.
THERE HE IS.
DON'T SPOOK HIM.
SORRY.

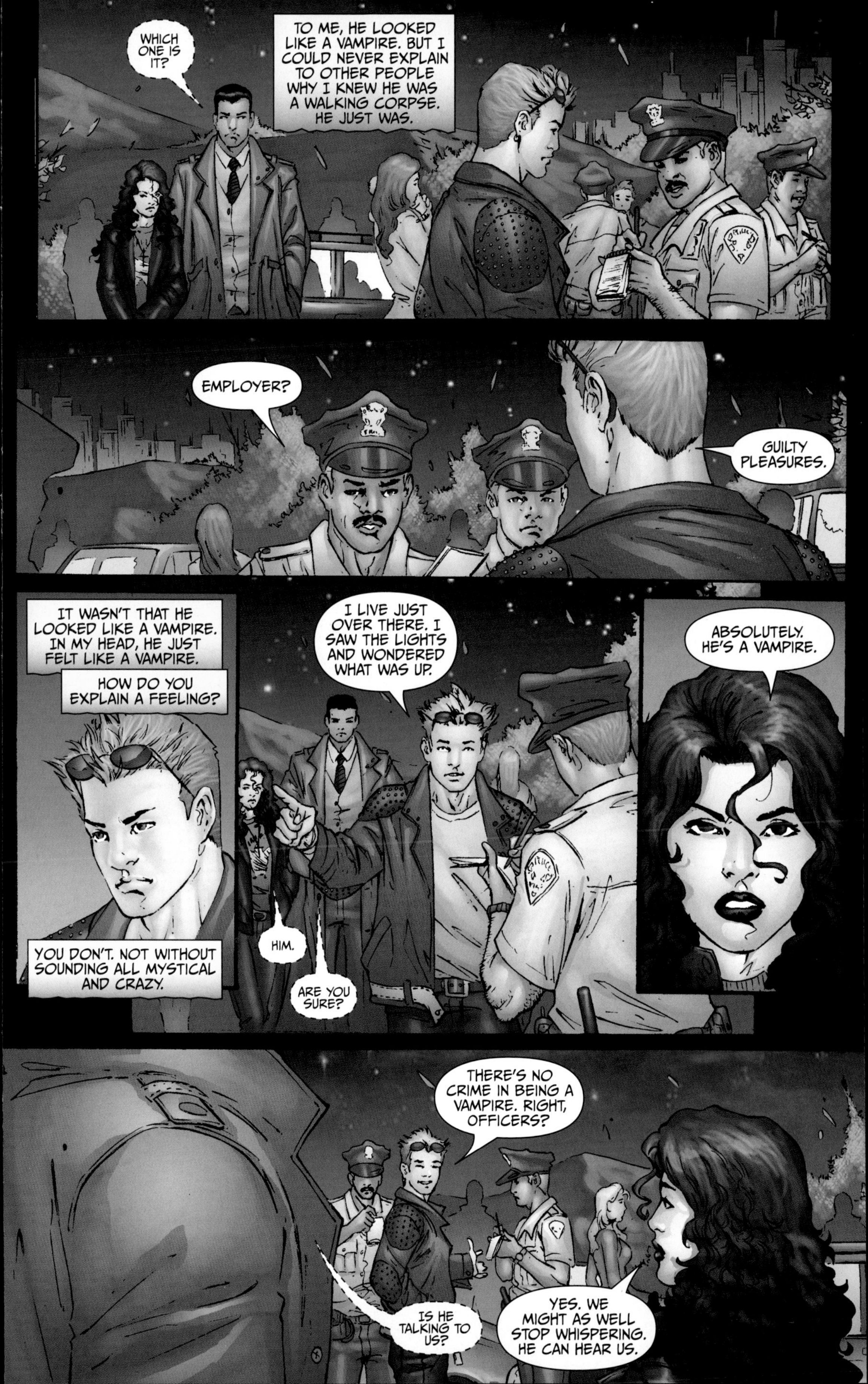
WHICH ONE IS IT?
TO ME, HE LOOKED LIKE A VAMPIRE. BUT I COULD NEVER EXPLAIN TO OTHER PEOPLE WHY I KNEW HE WAS A WALKING CORPSE. HE JUST WAS.
EMPLOYER?
GUILTY PLEASURES.
IT WASN'T THAT HE LOOKED LIKE A VAMPIRE. IN MY HEAD, HE JUST FELT LIKE A VAMPIRE.
HOW DO YOU EXPLAIN A FEELING?
YOU DON'T. NOT WITHOUT SOUNDING ALL MYSTICAL AND CRAZY.
I LIVE JUST OVER THERE. I SAW THE LIGHTS AND WONDERED WHAT WAS UP.
HIM.
ARE YOU SURE?
ABSOLUTELY. HE'S A VAMPIRE.
THERE'S NO CRIME IN BEING A VAMPIRE. RIGHT, OFFICERS?
IS HE TALKING TO US?
YES. WE MIGHT AS WELL STOP WHISPERING. HE CAN HEAR US.

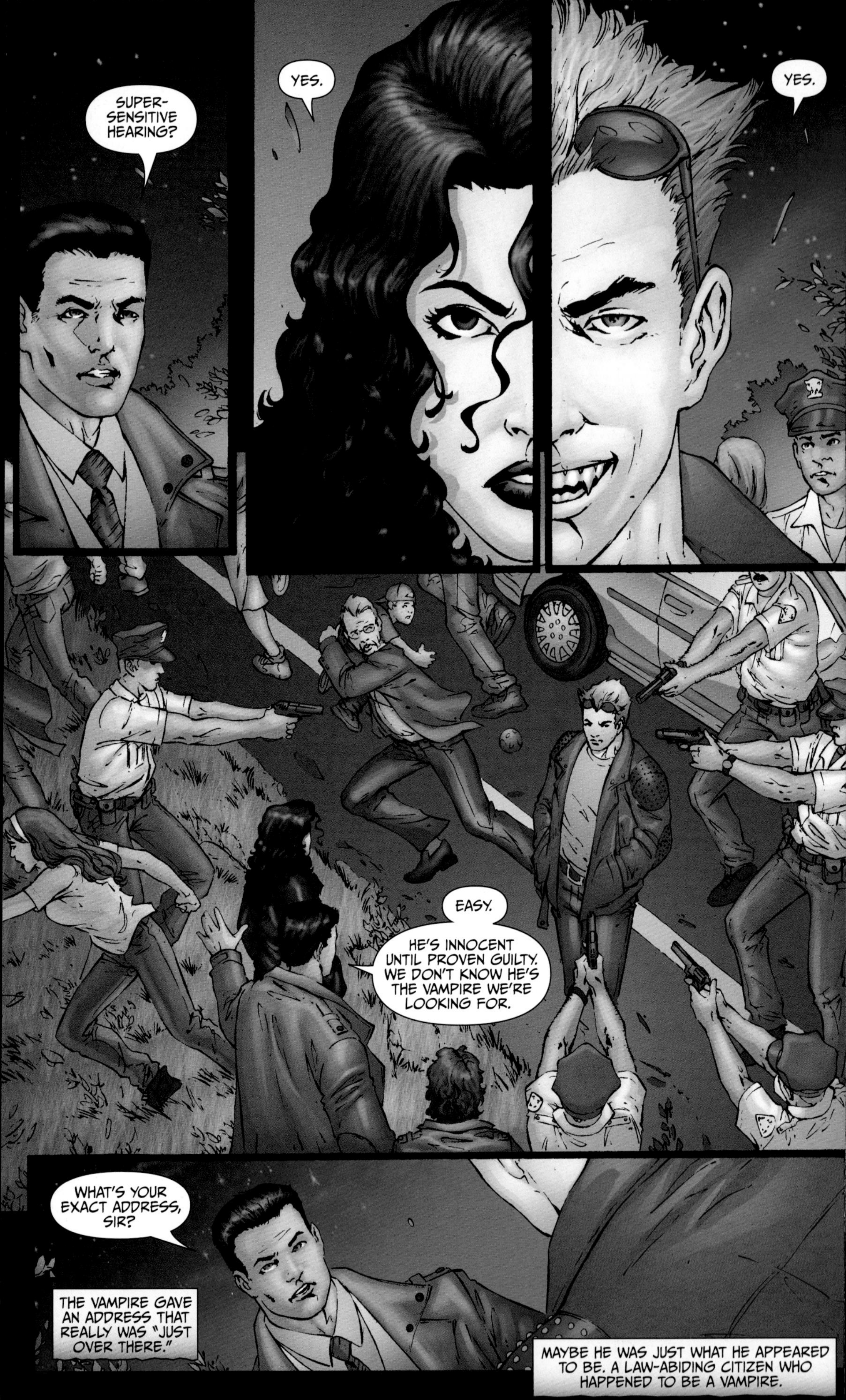
SUPER-SENSITIVE HEARING?
YES.
YES.
EASY.
HE'S INNOCENT UNTIL PROVEN GUILTY. WE DON'T KNOW HE'S THE VAMPIRE WE'RE LOOKING FOR.
WHAT'S YOUR EXACT ADDRESS, SIR?
THE VAMPIRE GAVE AN ADDRESS THAT REALLY WAS "JUST OVER THERE."
MAYBE HE WAS JUST WHAT HE APPEARED TO BE. A LAW-ABIDING CITIZEN WHO HAPPENED TO BE A VAMPIRE.

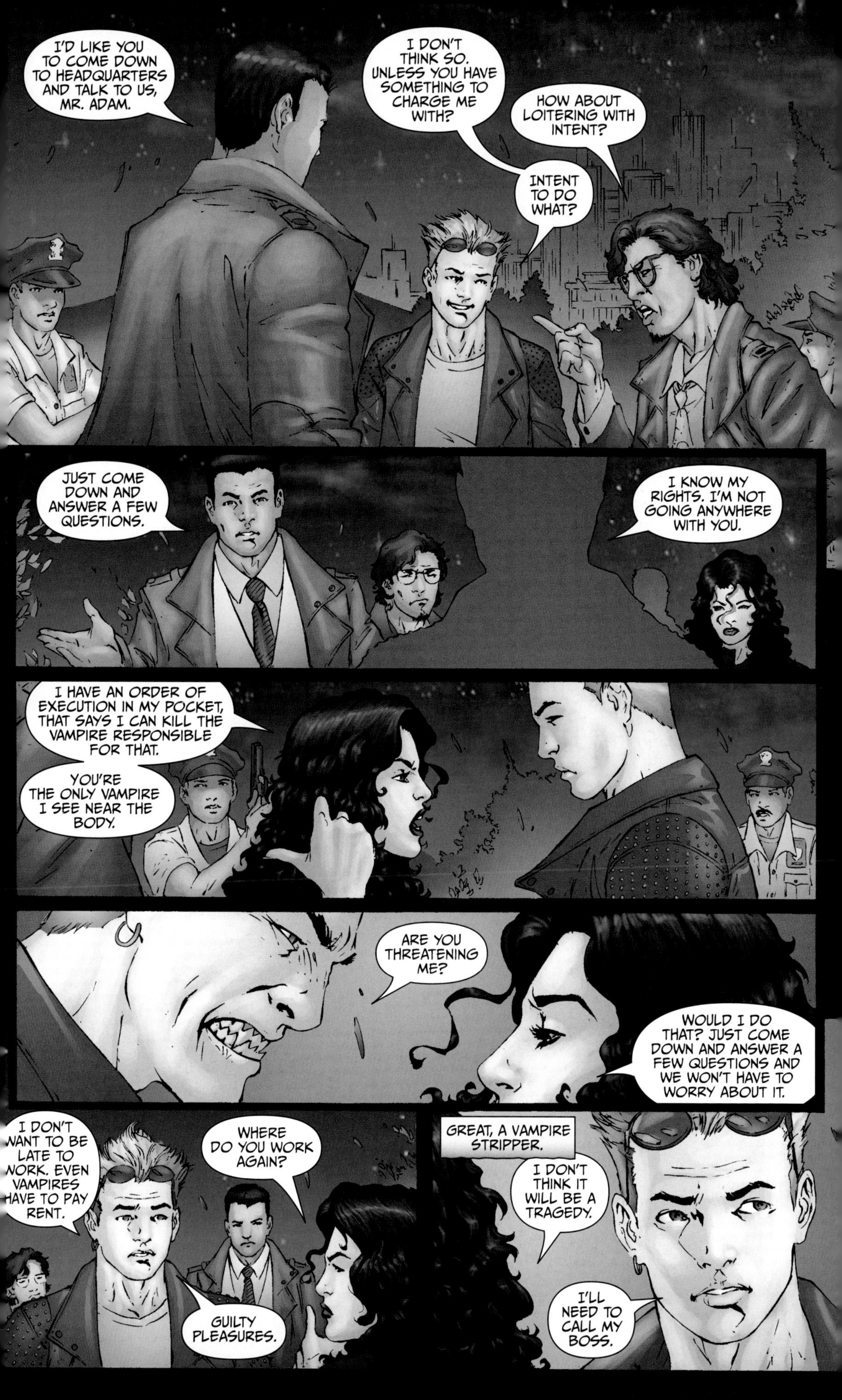
I'D LIKE YOU TO COME DOWN TO HEADQUARTERS AND TALK TO US, MR. ADAM.
I DON'T THINK SO. UNLESS YOU HAVE SOMETHING TO CHARGE ME WITH?
HOW ABOUT LOITERING WITH INTENT?
INTENT TO DO WHAT?
JUST COME DOWN AND ANSWER A FEW QUESTIONS.
I KNOW MY RIGHTS. I'M NOT GOING ANYWHERE WITH YOU.
I HAVE AN ORDER OF EXECUTION IN MY POCKET, THAT SAYS I CAN KILL THE VAMPIRE RESPONSIBLE FOR THAT.
YOU'RE THE ONLY VAMPIRE I SEE NEAR THE BODY.
ARE YOU THREATENING ME?
WOULD I DO THAT? JUST COME DOWN AND ANSWER A FEW QUESTIONS AND WE WON'T HAVE TO WORRY ABOUT IT.
I DON'T WANT TO BE LATE TO WORK. EVEN VAMPIRES HAVE TO PAY RENT.
WHERE DO YOU WORK AGAIN?
GUILTY PLEASURES.
GREAT, A VAMPIRE STRIPPER.
I DON'T THINK IT WILL BE A TRAGEDY.
I'LL NEED TO CALL MY BOSS.

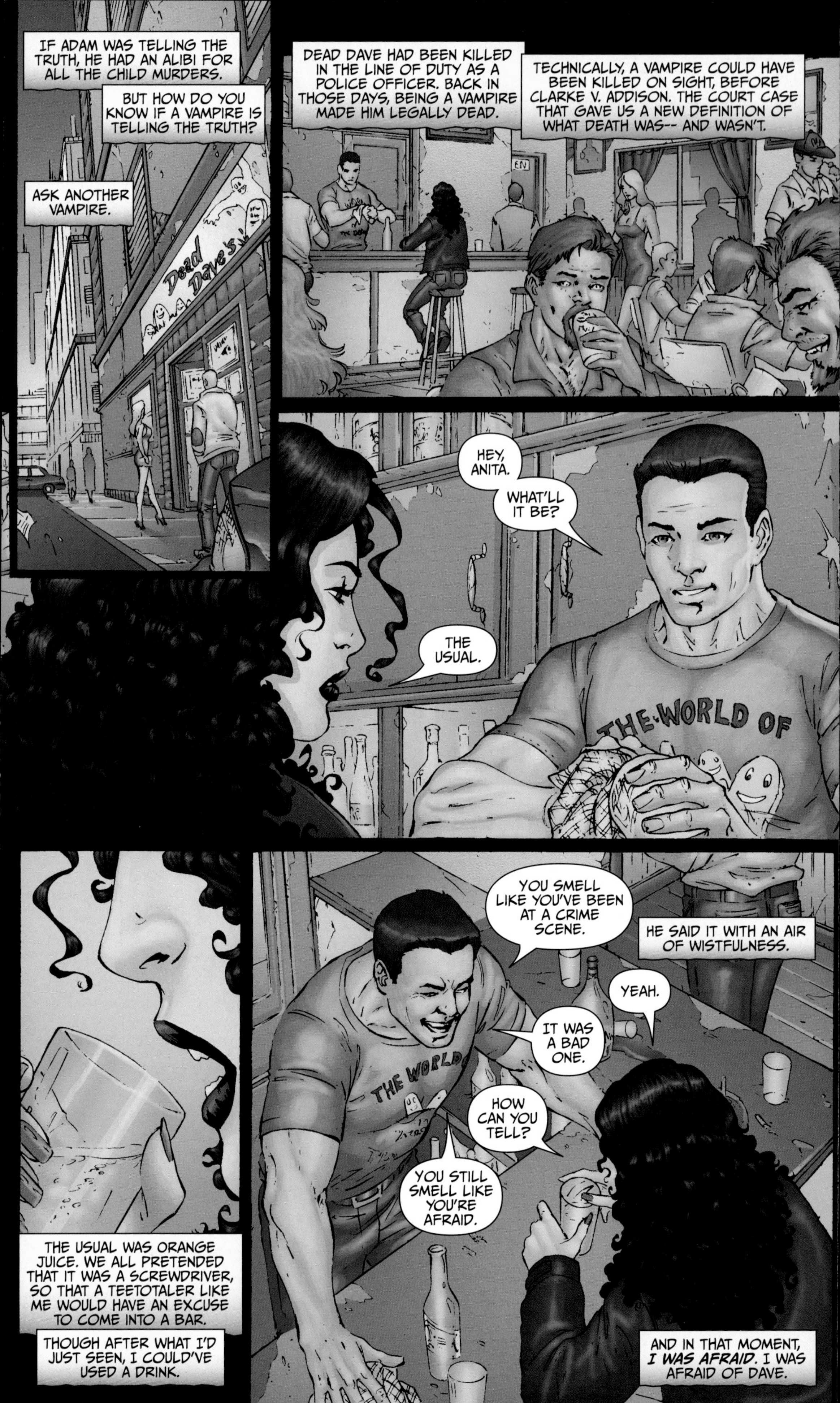
IF ADAM WAS TELLING THE TRUTH, HE HAD AN ALIBI FOR ALL THE CHILD MURDERS.
BUT HOW DO YOU KNOW IF A VAMPIRE IS TELLING THE TRUTH?
ASK ANOTHER VAMPIRE.
Dead Dave's
DEAD DAVE HAD BEEN KILLED IN THE LINE OF DUTY AS A POLICE OFFICER. BACK IN THOSE DAYS, BEING A VAMPIRE MADE HIM LEGALLY DEAD.
TECHNICALLY, A VAMPIRE COULD HAVE BEEN KILLED ON SIGHT, BEFORE CLARKE V. ADDISON. THE COURT CASE THAT GAVE US A NEW DEFINITION OF WHAT DEATH WAS-- AND WASN'T.
HEY, ANITA.
WHAT'LL IT BE?
THE USUAL.
THE WORLD OF
THE USUAL WAS ORANGE JUICE. WE ALL PRETENDED THAT IT WAS A SCREWDRIVER, SO THAT A TEETOTALER LIKE ME WOULD HAVE AN EXCUSE TO COME INTO A BAR.
THOUGH AFTER WHAT I'D JUST SEEN, I COULD'VE USED A DRINK.
YOU SMELL LIKE YOU'VE BEEN AT A CRIME SCENE.
HE SAID IT WITH AN AIR OF WISTFULNESS.
YEAH.
IT WAS A BAD ONE.
HOW CAN YOU TELL?
YOU STILL SMELL LIKE YOU'RE AFRAID.
AND IN THAT MOMENT, *I WAS AFRAID*. I WAS AFRAID OF DAVE.

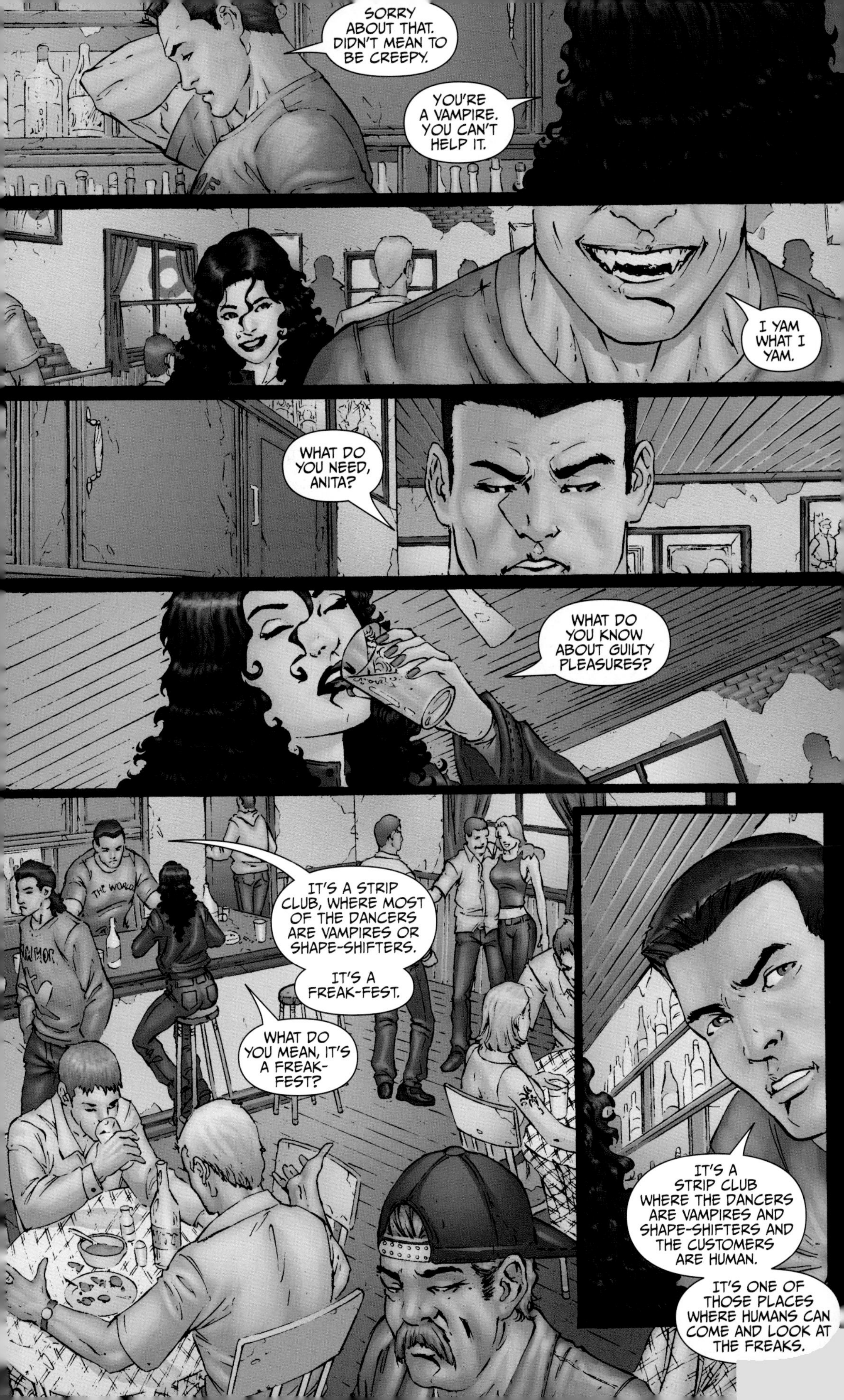
SORRY ABOUT THAT. DIDN'T MEAN TO BE CREEPY.
YOU'RE A VAMPIRE. YOU CAN'T HELP IT.
I YAM WHAT I YAM.
WHAT DO YOU NEED, ANITA?
WHAT DO YOU KNOW ABOUT GUILTY PLEASURES?
IT'S A STRIP CLUB, WHERE MOST OF THE DANCERS ARE VAMPIRES OR SHAPE-SHIFTERS.
IT'S A FREAK-FEST.
WHAT DO YOU MEAN, IT'S A FREAK-FEST?
IT'S A STRIP CLUB WHERE THE DANCERS ARE VAMPIRES AND SHAPE-SHIFTERS AND THE CUSTOMERS ARE HUMAN.
IT'S ONE OF THOSE PLACES WHERE HUMANS CAN COME AND LOOK AT THE FREAKS.

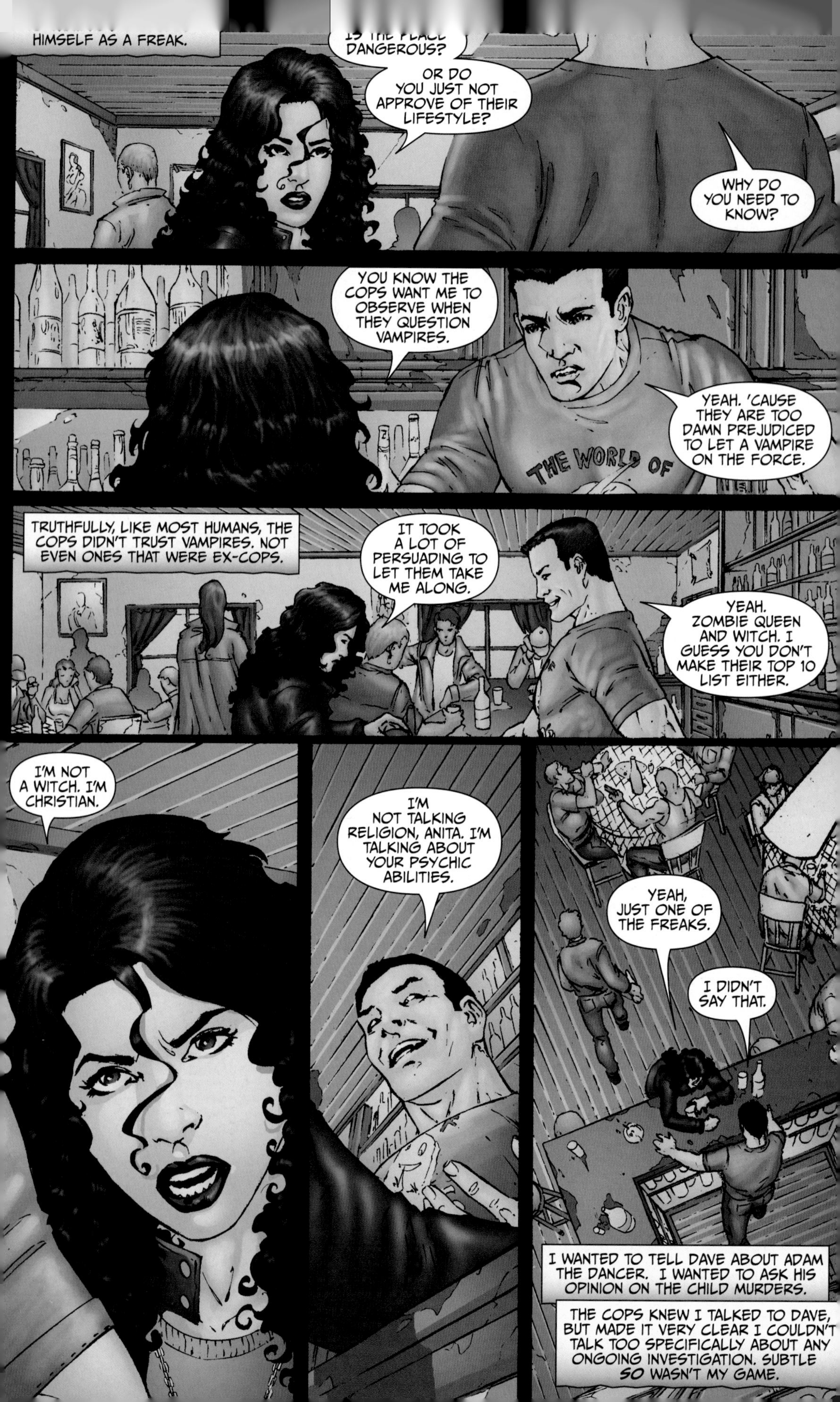
HIMSELF AS A FREAK.
DANGEROUS?
OR DO YOU JUST NOT APPROVE OF THEIR LIFESTYLE?
WHY DO YOU NEED TO KNOW?
YOU KNOW THE COPS WANT ME TO OBSERVE WHEN THEY QUESTION VAMPIRES.
YEAH. 'CAUSE THEY ARE TOO DAMN PREJUDICED TO LET A VAMPIRE ON THE FORCE.
THE WORLD OF
TRUTHFULLY, LIKE MOST HUMANS, THE COPS DIDN'T TRUST VAMPIRES. NOT EVEN ONES THAT WERE EX-COPS.
IT TOOK A LOT OF PERSUADING TO LET THEM TAKE ME ALONG.
YEAH. ZOMBIE QUEEN AND WITCH. I GUESS YOU DON'T MAKE THEIR TOP 10 LIST EITHER.
I'M NOT A WITCH. I'M CHRISTIAN.
I'M NOT TALKING RELIGION, ANITA. I'M TALKING ABOUT YOUR PSYCHIC ABILITIES.
YEAH, JUST ONE OF THE FREAKS.
I DIDN'T SAY THAT.
I WANTED TO TELL DAVE ABOUT ADAM THE DANCER. I WANTED TO ASK HIS OPINION ON THE CHILD MURDERS.
THE COPS KNEW I TALKED TO DAVE, BUT MADE IT VERY CLEAR I COULDN'T TALK TOO SPECIFICALLY ABOUT ANY ONGOING INVESTIGATION. SUBTLE *SO* WASN'T MY GAME.

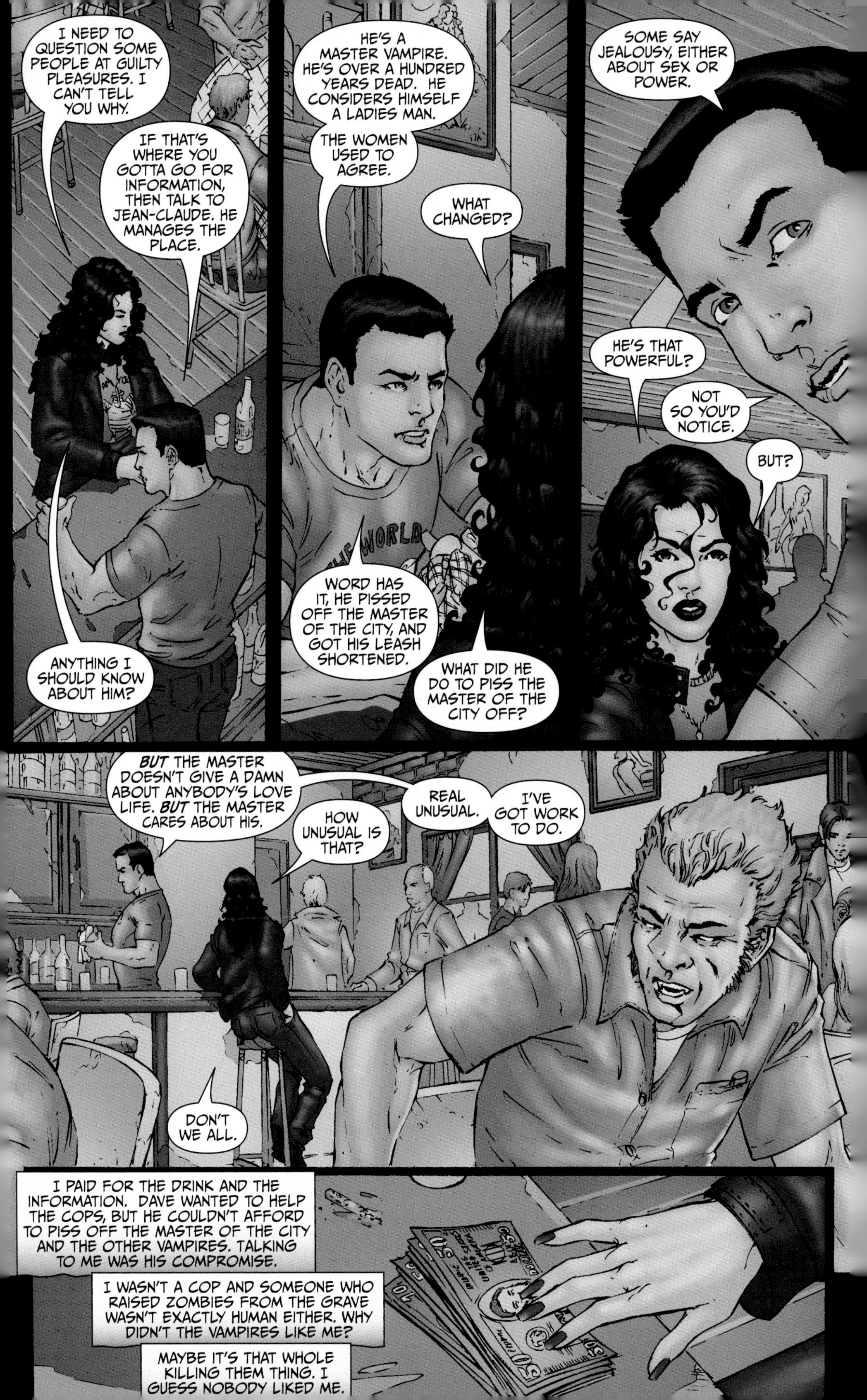
I NEED TO QUESTION SOME PEOPLE AT GUILTY PLEASURES. I CAN'T TELL YOU WHY.
IF THAT'S WHERE YOU GOTTA GO FOR INFORMATION, THEN TALK TO JEAN-CLAUDE. HE MANAGES THE PLACE.
ANYTHING I SHOULD KNOW ABOUT HIM?
HE'S A MASTER VAMPIRE. HE'S OVER A HUNDRED YEARS DEAD. HE CONSIDERS HIMSELF A LADIES MAN.
THE WOMEN USED TO AGREE.
WHAT CHANGED?
WORD HAS IT, HE PISSED OFF THE MASTER OF THE CITY, AND GOT HIS LEASH SHORTENED.
WHAT DID HE DO TO PISS THE MASTER OF THE CITY OFF?
SOME SAY JEALOUSY, EITHER ABOUT SEX OR POWER.
HE'S THAT POWERFUL?
NOT SO YOU'D NOTICE.
BUT?
BUT THE MASTER DOESN'T GIVE A DAMN ABOUT ANYBODY'S LOVE LIFE. *BUT* THE MASTER CARES ABOUT HIS.
HOW UNUSUAL IS THAT?
REAL UNUSUAL.
I'VE GOT WORK TO DO.
DON'T WE ALL.
I PAID FOR THE DRINK AND THE INFORMATION. DAVE WANTED TO HELP THE COPS, BUT HE COULDN'T AFFORD TO PISS OFF THE MASTER OF THE CITY AND THE OTHER VAMPIRES. TALKING TO ME WAS HIS COMPROMISE.
I WASN'T A COP AND SOMEONE WHO RAISED ZOMBIES FROM THE GRAVE WASN'T EXACTLY HUMAN EITHER. WHY DIDN'T THE VAMPIRES LIKE ME?
MAYBE IT'S THAT WHOLE KILLING THEM THING. I GUESS NOBODY LIKED ME.

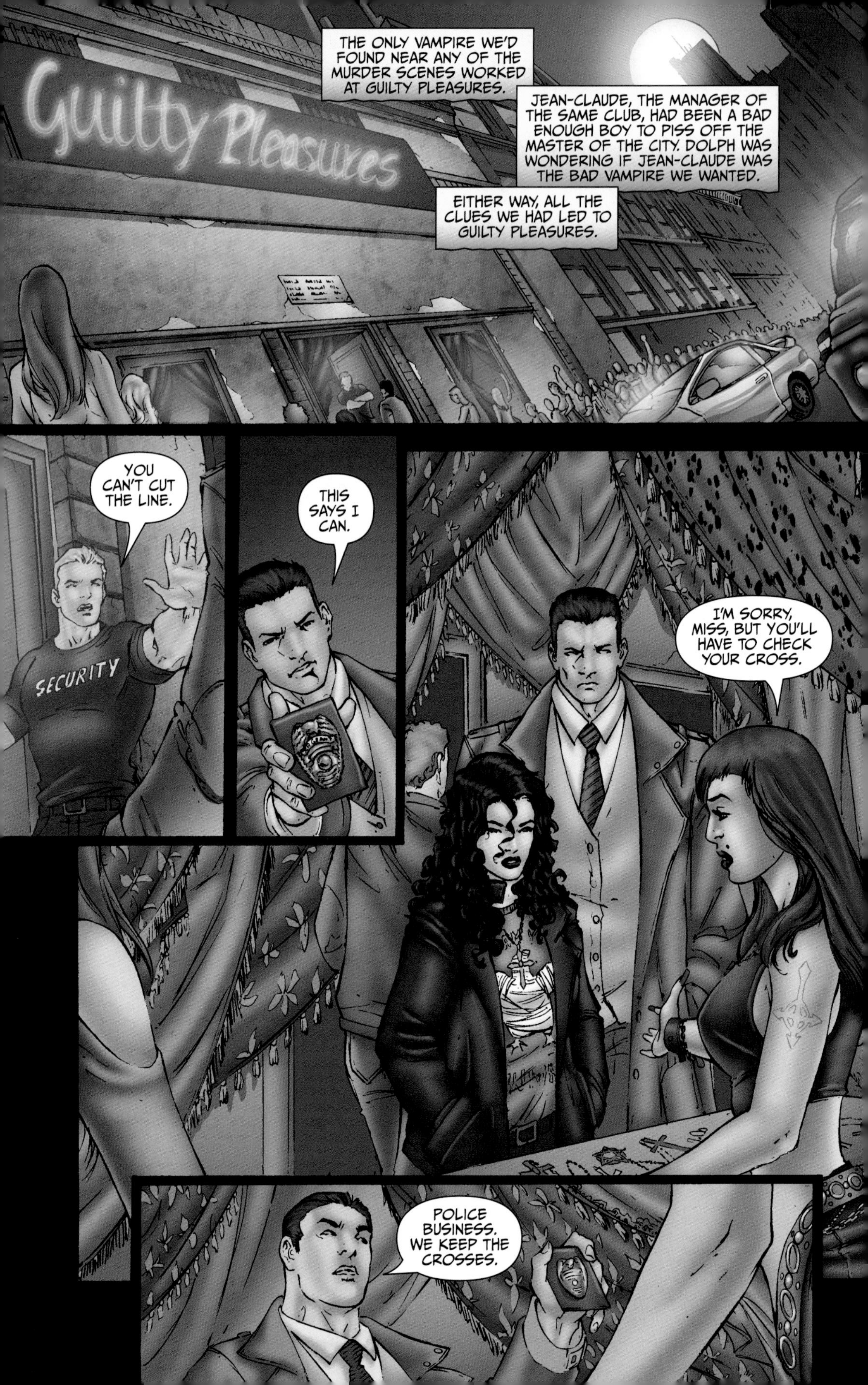
Guilty Pleasures
THE ONLY VAMPIRE WE'D FOUND NEAR ANY OF THE MURDER SCENES WORKED AT GUILTY PLEASURES.
JEAN-CLAUDE, THE MANAGER OF THE SAME CLUB, HAD BEEN A BAD ENOUGH BOY TO PISS OFF THE MASTER OF THE CITY. DOLPH WAS WONDERING IF JEAN-CLAUDE WAS THE BAD VAMPIRE WE WANTED.
EITHER WAY, ALL THE CLUES WE HAD LED TO GUILTY PLEASURES.
YOU CAN'T CUT THE LINE.
SECURITY
THIS SAYS I CAN.
I'M SORRY, MISS, BUT YOU'LL HAVE TO CHECK YOUR CROSS.
POLICE BUSINESS. WE KEEP THE CROSSES.

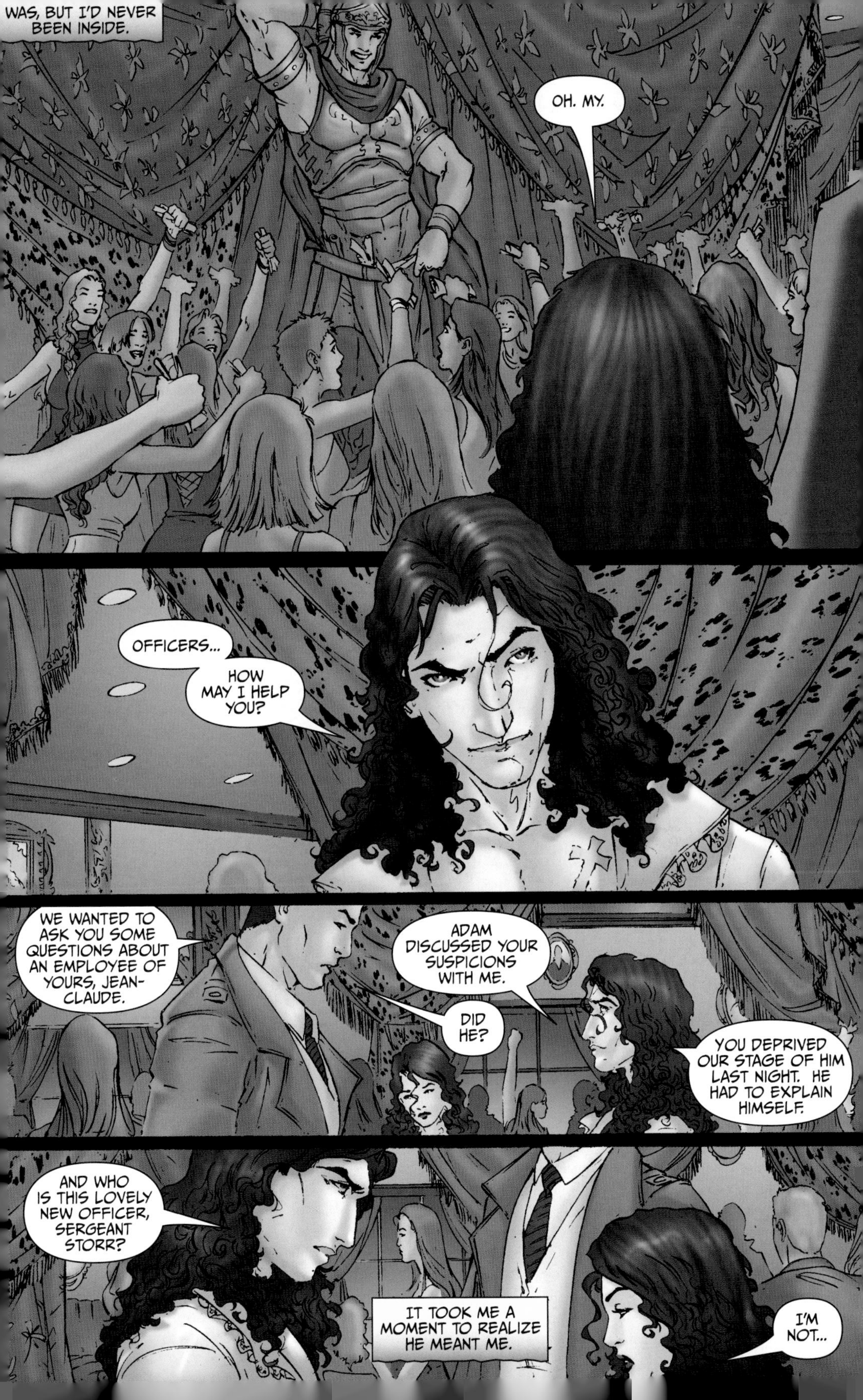
WAS, BUT I'D NEVER BEEN INSIDE.
OH. MY.
OFFICERS...
HOW MAY I HELP YOU?
WE WANTED TO ASK YOU SOME QUESTIONS ABOUT AN EMPLOYEE OF YOURS, JEAN-CLAUDE.
ADAM DISCUSSED YOUR SUSPICIONS WITH ME.
DID HE?
YOU DEPRIVED OUR STAGE OF HIM LAST NIGHT. HE HAD TO EXPLAIN HIMSELF.
AND WHO IS THIS LOVELY NEW OFFICER, SERGEANT STORR?
IT TOOK ME A MOMENT TO REALIZE HE MEANT ME.
I'M NOT...

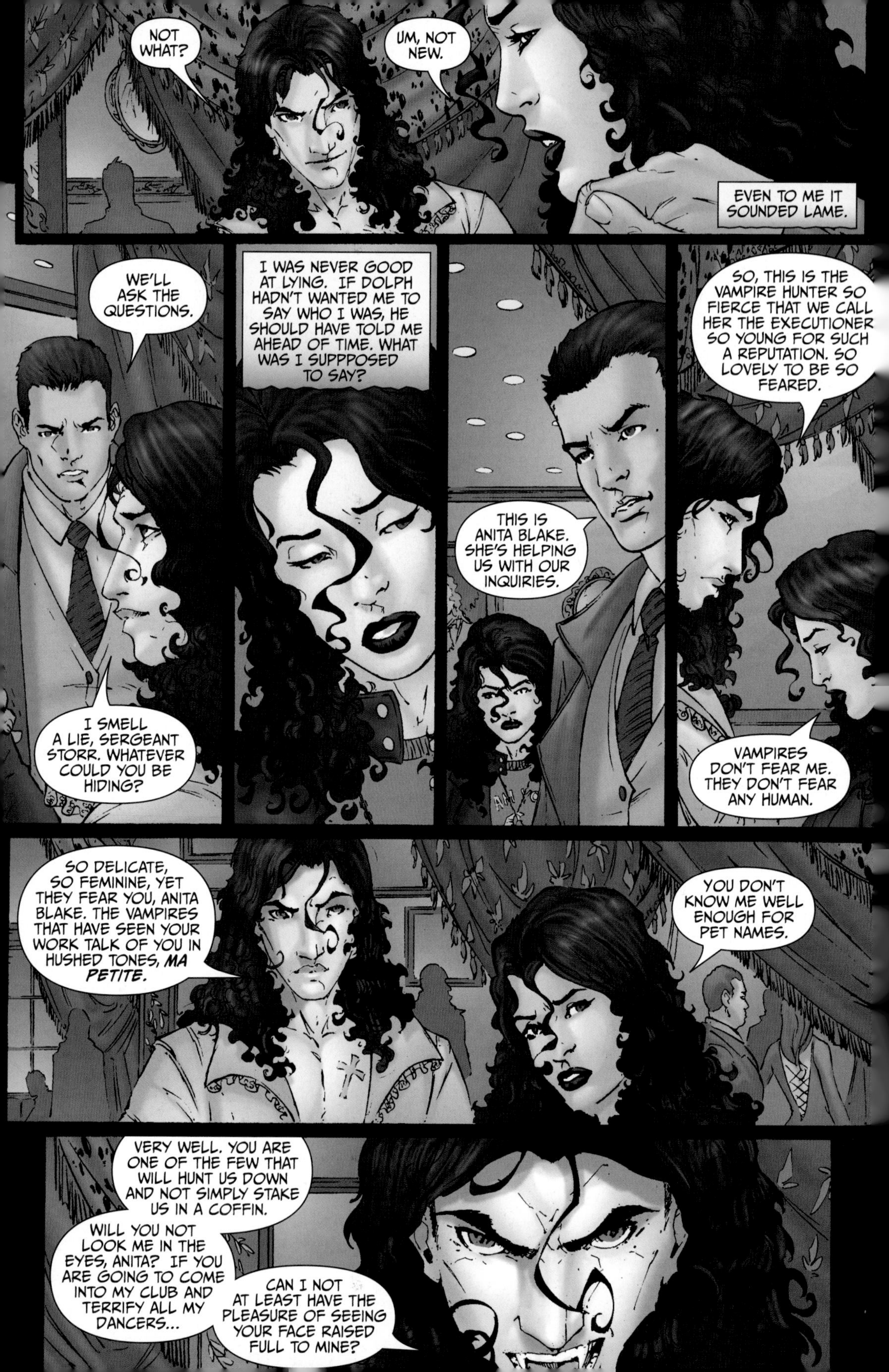
NOT WHAT?
UM, NOT NEW.
EVEN TO ME IT SOUNDED LAME.
WE'LL ASK THE QUESTIONS.
I SMELL A LIE, SERGEANT STORR. WHATEVER COULD YOU BE HIDING?
I WAS NEVER GOOD AT LYING. IF DOLPH HADN'T WANTED ME TO SAY WHO I WAS, HE SHOULD HAVE TOLD ME AHEAD OF TIME. WHAT WAS I SUPPPOSED TO SAY?
THIS IS ANITA BLAKE. SHE'S HELPING US WITH OUR INQUIRIES.
SO, THIS IS THE VAMPIRE HUNTER SO FIERCE THAT WE CALL HER THE EXECUTIONER SO YOUNG FOR SUCH A REPUTATION. SO LOVELY TO BE SO FEARED.
VAMPIRES DON'T FEAR ME. THEY DON'T FEAR ANY HUMAN.
SO DELICATE, SO FEMININE, YET THEY FEAR YOU, ANITA BLAKE. THE VAMPIRES THAT HAVE SEEN YOUR WORK TALK OF YOU IN HUSHED TONES, *MA PETITE*.
YOU DON'T KNOW ME WELL ENOUGH FOR PET NAMES.
VERY WELL. YOU ARE ONE OF THE FEW THAT WILL HUNT US DOWN AND NOT SIMPLY STAKE US IN A COFFIN.
WILL YOU NOT LOOK ME IN THE EYES, ANITA? IF YOU ARE GOING TO COME INTO MY CLUB AND TERRIFY ALL MY DANCERS...
CAN I NOT AT LEAST HAVE THE PLEASURE OF SEEING YOUR FACE RAISED FULL TO MINE?

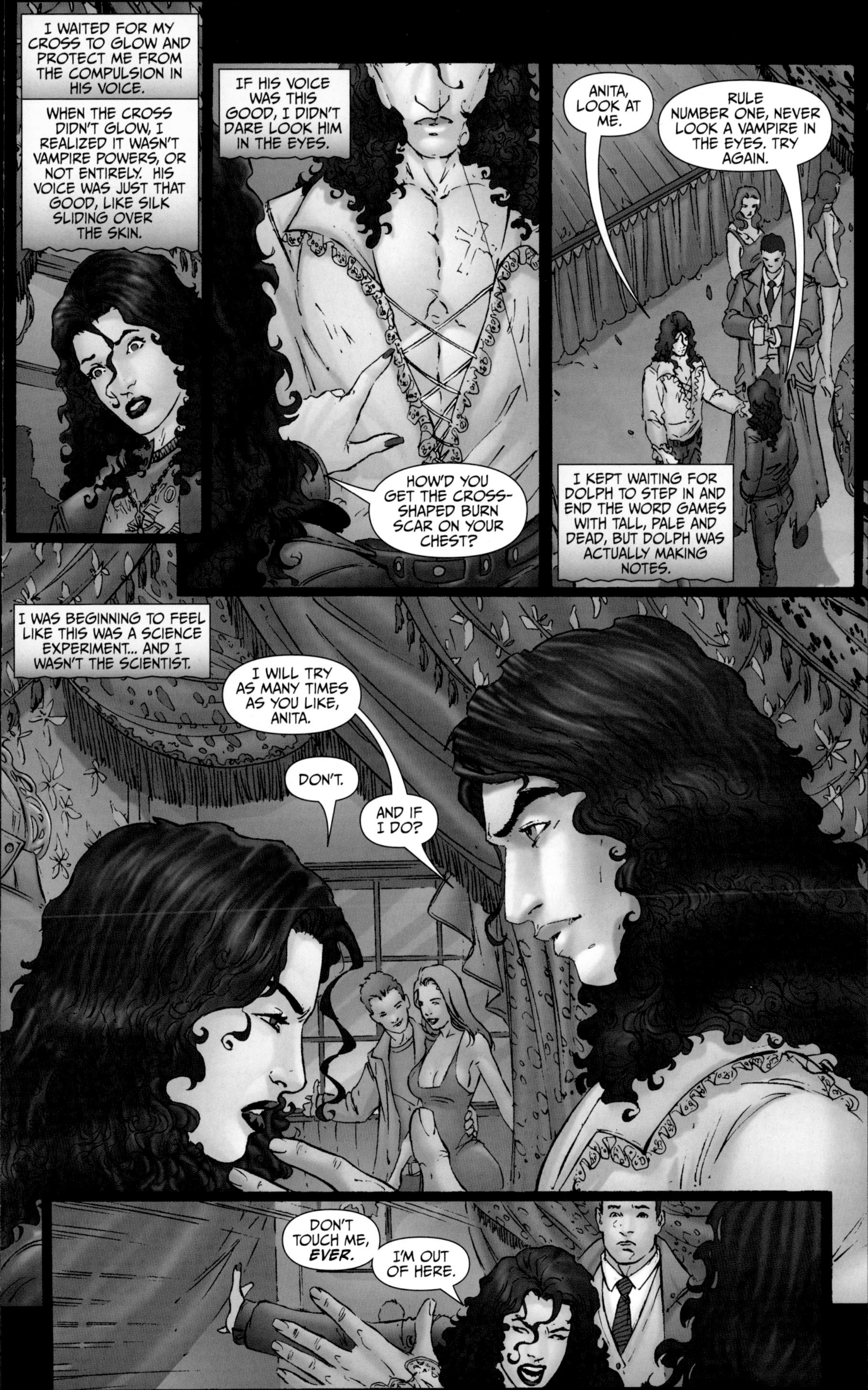
I WAITED FOR MY CROSS TO GLOW AND PROTECT ME FROM THE COMPULSION IN HIS VOICE.
WHEN THE CROSS DIDN'T GLOW, I REALIZED IT WASN'T VAMPIRE POWERS, OR NOT ENTIRELY. HIS VOICE WAS JUST THAT GOOD, LIKE SILK SLIDING OVER THE SKIN.
IF HIS VOICE WAS THIS GOOD, I DIDN'T DARE LOOK HIM IN THE EYES.
HOW'D YOU GET THE CROSS-SHAPED BURN SCAR ON YOUR CHEST?
ANITA, LOOK AT ME.
RULE NUMBER ONE, NEVER LOOK A VAMPIRE IN THE EYES. TRY AGAIN.
I KEPT WAITING FOR DOLPH TO STEP IN AND END THE WORD GAMES WITH TALL, PALE AND DEAD, BUT DOLPH WAS ACTUALLY MAKING NOTES.
I WAS BEGINNING TO FEEL LIKE THIS WAS A SCIENCE EXPERIMENT... AND I WASN'T THE SCIENTIST.
I WILL TRY AS MANY TIMES AS YOU LIKE, ANITA.
DON'T.
AND IF I DO?
DON'T TOUCH ME, EVER.
I'M OUT OF HERE.

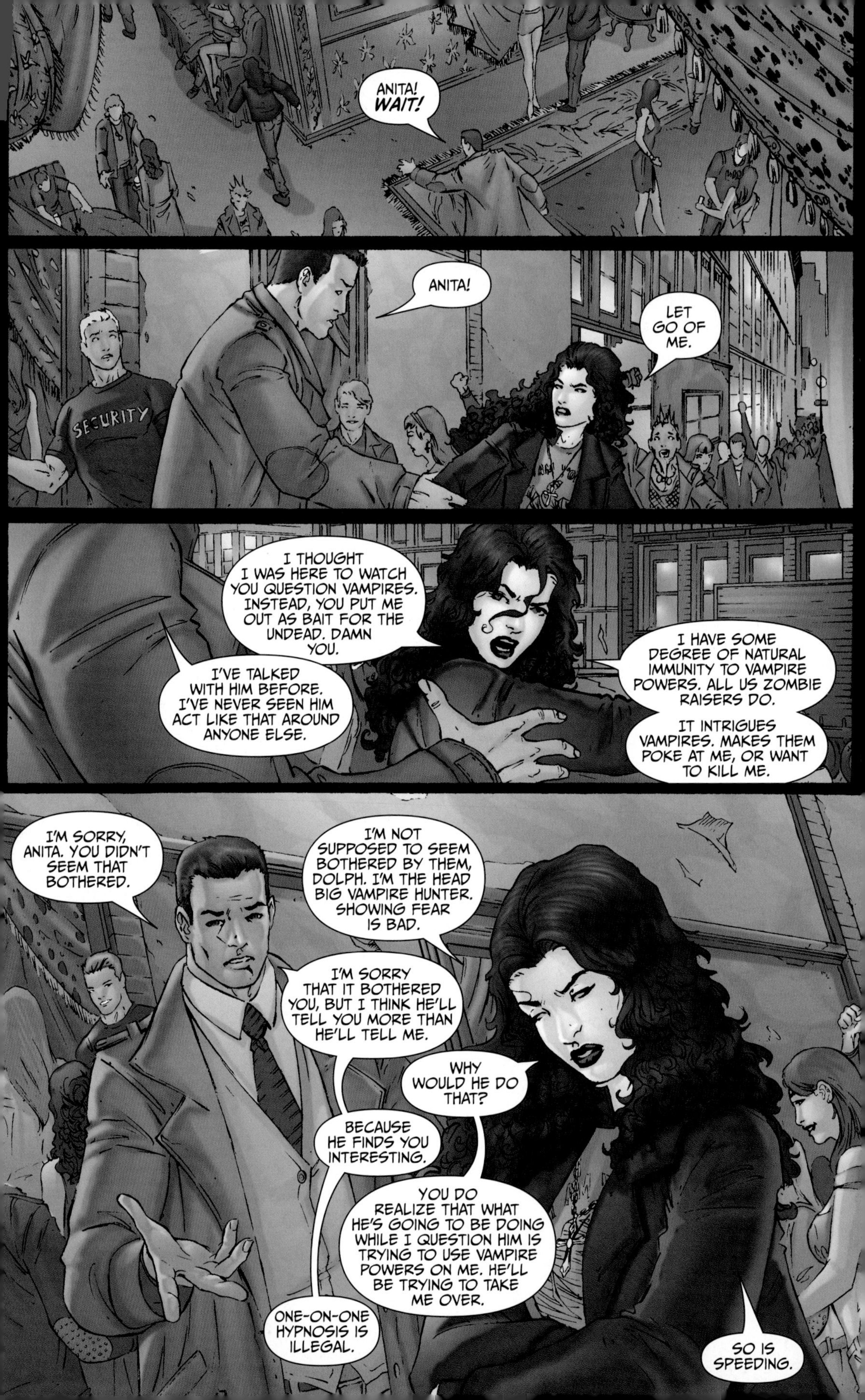
ANITA! WAIT!
ANITA!
LET GO OF ME.
I THOUGHT I WAS HERE TO WATCH YOU QUESTION VAMPIRES. INSTEAD, YOU PUT ME OUT AS BAIT FOR THE UNDEAD. DAMN YOU.
I'VE TALKED WITH HIM BEFORE. I'VE NEVER SEEN HIM ACT LIKE THAT AROUND ANYONE ELSE.
I HAVE SOME DEGREE OF NATURAL IMMUNITY TO VAMPIRE POWERS. ALL US ZOMBIE RAISERS DO.
IT INTRIGUES VAMPIRES. MAKES THEM POKE AT ME, OR WANT TO KILL ME.
I'M SORRY, ANITA. YOU DIDN'T SEEM THAT BOTHERED.
I'M NOT SUPPOSED TO SEEM BOTHERED BY THEM, DOLPH. I'M THE HEAD BIG VAMPIRE HUNTER. SHOWING FEAR IS BAD.
I'M SORRY THAT IT BOTHERED YOU, BUT I THINK HE'LL TELL YOU MORE THAN HE'LL TELL ME.
WHY WOULD HE DO THAT?
BECAUSE HE FINDS YOU INTERESTING.
YOU DO REALIZE THAT WHAT HE'S GOING TO BE DOING WHILE I QUESTION HIM IS TRYING TO USE VAMPIRE POWERS ON ME. HE'LL BE TRYING TO TAKE ME OVER.
ONE-ON-ONE HYPNOSIS IS ILLEGAL.
SO IS SPEEDING.

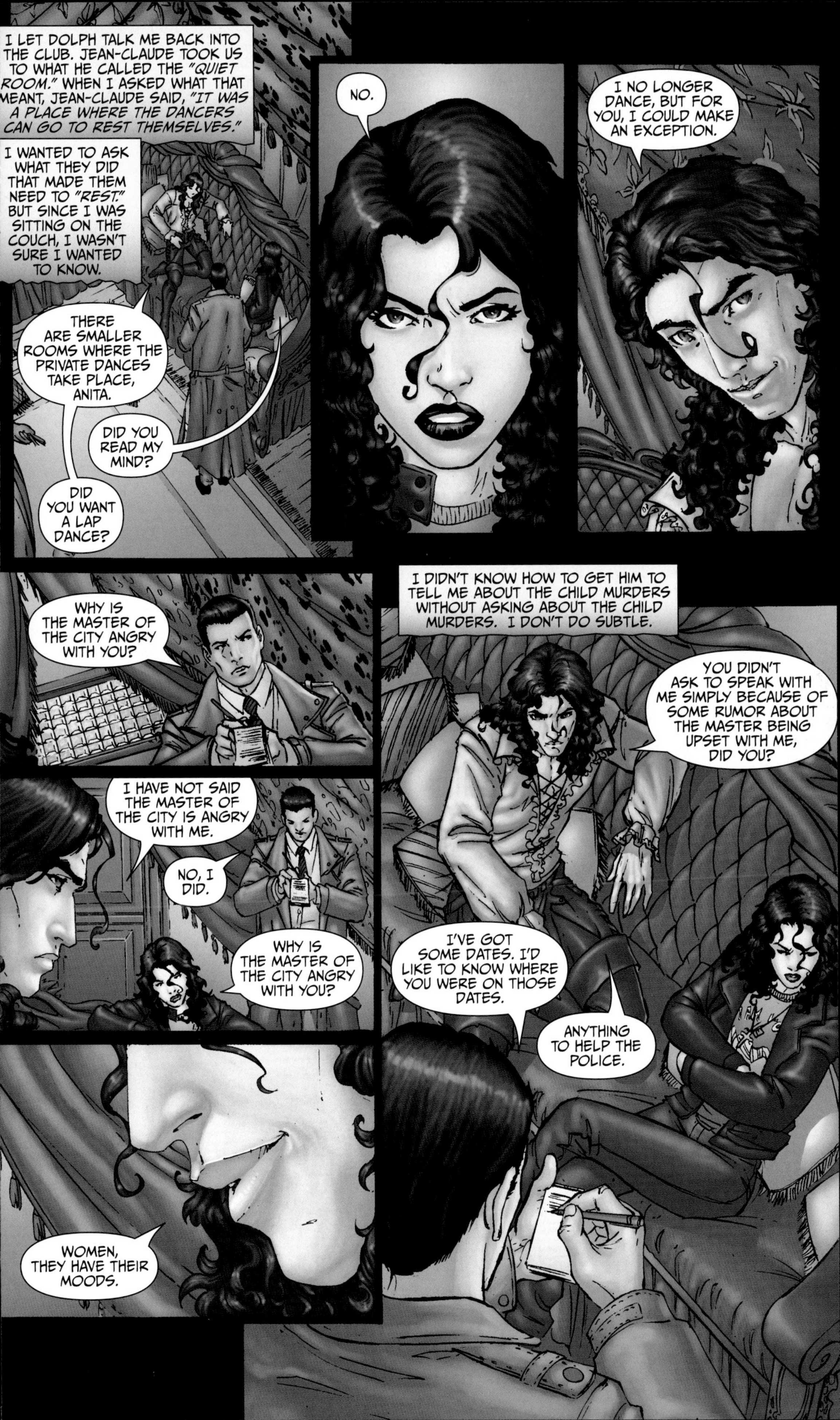
I LET DOLPH TALK ME BACK INTO THE CLUB. JEAN-CLAUDE TOOK US TO WHAT HE CALLED THE "QUIET ROOM." WHEN I ASKED WHAT THAT MEANT, JEAN-CLAUDE SAID, "IT WAS A PLACE WHERE THE DANCERS CAN GO TO REST THEMSELVES."
I WANTED TO ASK WHAT THEY DID THAT MADE THEM NEED TO "REST." BUT SINCE I WAS SITTING ON THE COUCH, I WASN'T SURE I WANTED TO KNOW.
THERE ARE SMALLER ROOMS WHERE THE PRIVATE DANCES TAKE PLACE, ANITA.
DID YOU READ MY MIND?
DID YOU WANT A LAP DANCE?
NO.
I NO LONGER DANCE, BUT FOR YOU, I COULD MAKE AN EXCEPTION.
WHY IS THE MASTER OF THE CITY ANGRY WITH YOU?
I HAVE NOT SAID THE MASTER OF THE CITY IS ANGRY WITH ME.
NO, I DID.
WHY IS THE MASTER OF THE CITY ANGRY WITH YOU?
WOMEN, THEY HAVE THEIR MOODS.
I DIDN'T KNOW HOW TO GET HIM TO TELL ME ABOUT THE CHILD MURDERS WITHOUT ASKING ABOUT THE CHILD MURDERS. I DON'T DO SUBTLE.
YOU DIDN'T ASK TO SPEAK WITH ME SIMPLY BECAUSE OF SOME RUMOR ABOUT THE MASTER BEING UPSET WITH ME, DID YOU?
I'VE GOT SOME DATES. I'D LIKE TO KNOW WHERE YOU WERE ON THOSE DATES.
ANYTHING TO HELP THE POLICE.

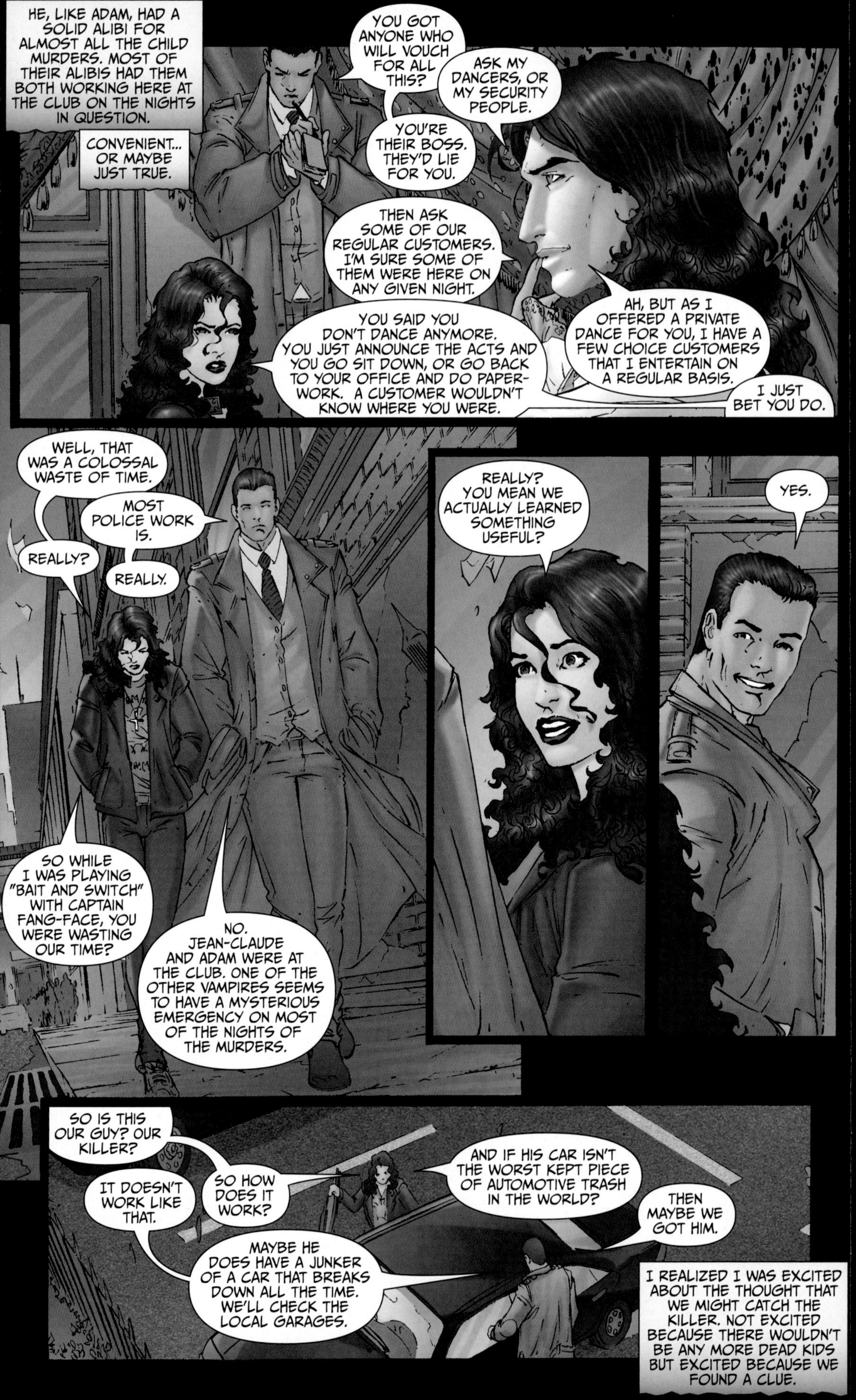
HE, LIKE ADAM, HAD A SOLID ALIBI FOR ALMOST ALL THE CHILD MURDERS. MOST OF THEIR ALIBIS HAD THEM BOTH WORKING HERE AT THE CLUB ON THE NIGHTS IN QUESTION.
CONVENIENT... OR MAYBE JUST TRUE.
YOU GOT ANYONE WHO WILL VOUCH FOR ALL THIS?
ASK MY DANCERS, OR MY SECURITY PEOPLE.
YOU'RE THEIR BOSS. THEY'D LIE FOR YOU.
THEN ASK SOME OF OUR REGULAR CUSTOMERS. I'M SURE SOME OF THEM WERE HERE ON ANY GIVEN NIGHT.
YOU SAID YOU DON'T DANCE ANYMORE. YOU JUST ANNOUNCE THE ACTS AND YOU GO SIT DOWN, OR GO BACK TO YOUR OFFICE AND DO PAPER-WORK. A CUSTOMER WOULDN'T KNOW WHERE YOU WERE.
AH, BUT AS I OFFERED A PRIVATE DANCE FOR YOU, I HAVE A FEW CHOICE CUSTOMERS THAT I ENTERTAIN ON A REGULAR BASIS.
I JUST BET YOU DO.
WELL, THAT WAS A COLOSSAL WASTE OF TIME.
MOST POLICE WORK IS.
REALLY?
REALLY.
SO WHILE I WAS PLAYING "BAIT AND SWITCH" WITH CAPTAIN FANG-FACE, YOU WERE WASTING OUR TIME?
NO. JEAN-CLAUDE AND ADAM WERE AT THE CLUB. ONE OF THE OTHER VAMPIRES SEEMS TO HAVE A MYSTERIOUS EMERGENCY ON MOST OF THE NIGHTS OF THE MURDERS.
REALLY? YOU MEAN WE ACTUALLY LEARNED SOMETHING USEFUL?
YES.
SO IS THIS OUR GUY? OUR KILLER?
IT DOESN'T WORK LIKE THAT.
SO HOW DOES IT WORK?
MAYBE HE DOES HAVE A JUNKER OF A CAR THAT BREAKS DOWN ALL THE TIME. WE'LL CHECK THE LOCAL GARAGES.
AND IF HIS CAR ISN'T THE WORST KEPT PIECE OF AUTOMOTIVE TRASH IN THE WORLD?
THEN MAYBE WE GOT HIM.
I REALIZED I WAS EXCITED ABOUT THE THOUGHT THAT WE MIGHT CATCH THE KILLER. NOT EXCITED BECAUSE THERE WOULDN'T BE ANY MORE DEAD KIDS BUT EXCITED BECAUSE WE FOUND A CLUE.

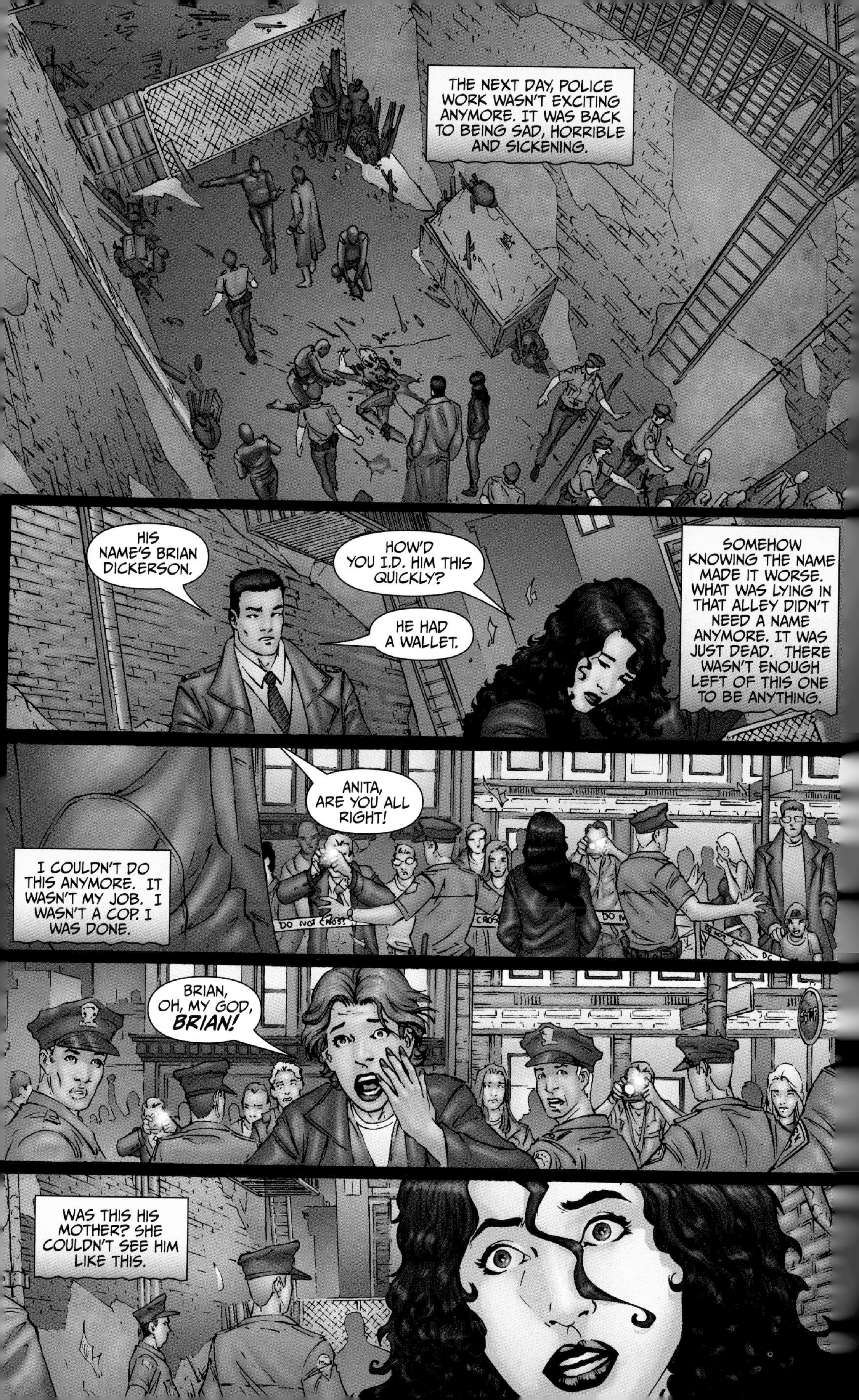
THE NEXT DAY, POLICE WORK WASN'T EXCITING ANYMORE. IT WAS BACK TO BEING SAD, HORRIBLE AND SICKENING.
HIS NAME'S BRIAN DICKERSON.
HOW'D YOU I.D. HIM THIS QUICKLY?
HE HAD A WALLET.
SOMEHOW KNOWING THE NAME MADE IT WORSE. WHAT WAS LYING IN THAT ALLEY DIDN'T NEED A NAME ANYMORE. IT WAS JUST DEAD. THERE WASN'T ENOUGH LEFT OF THIS ONE TO BE ANYTHING.
ANITA, ARE YOU ALL RIGHT!
I COULDN'T DO THIS ANYMORE. IT WASN'T MY JOB. I WASN'T A COP. I WAS DONE.
BRIAN, OH, MY GOD, ***BRIAN!***
WAS THIS HIS MOTHER? SHE COULDN'T SEE HIM LIKE THIS.

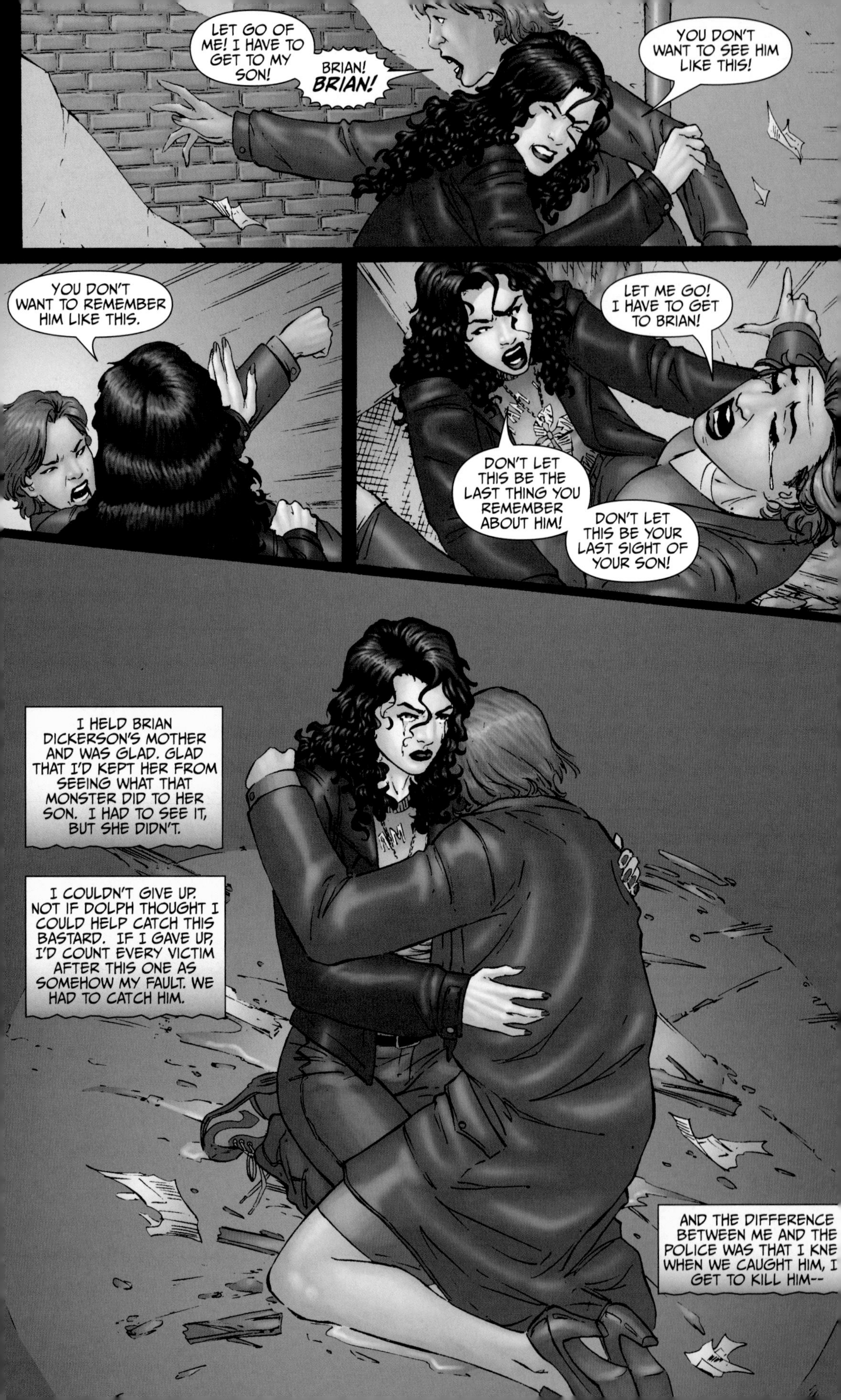

LET GO OF ME! I HAVE TO GET TO MY SON!
BRIAN! BRIAN!
YOU DON'T WANT TO SEE HIM LIKE THIS!
YOU DON'T WANT TO REMEMBER HIM LIKE THIS.
LET ME GO! I HAVE TO GET TO BRIAN!
DON'T LET THIS BE THE LAST THING YOU REMEMBER ABOUT HIM!
DON'T LET THIS BE YOUR LAST SIGHT OF YOUR SON!
I HELD BRIAN DICKERSON'S MOTHER AND WAS GLAD. GLAD THAT I'D KEPT HER FROM SEEING WHAT THAT MONSTER DID TO HER SON. I HAD TO SEE IT, BUT SHE DIDN'T.
I COULDN'T GIVE UP. NOT IF DOLPH THOUGHT I COULD HELP CATCH THIS BASTARD. IF I GAVE UP, I'D COUNT EVERY VICTIM AFTER THIS ONE AS SOMEHOW MY FAULT. WE HAD TO CATCH HIM.
AND THE DIFFERENCE BETWEEN ME AND THE POLICE WAS THAT I KNE WHEN WE CAUGHT HIM, I GET TO KILL HIM--

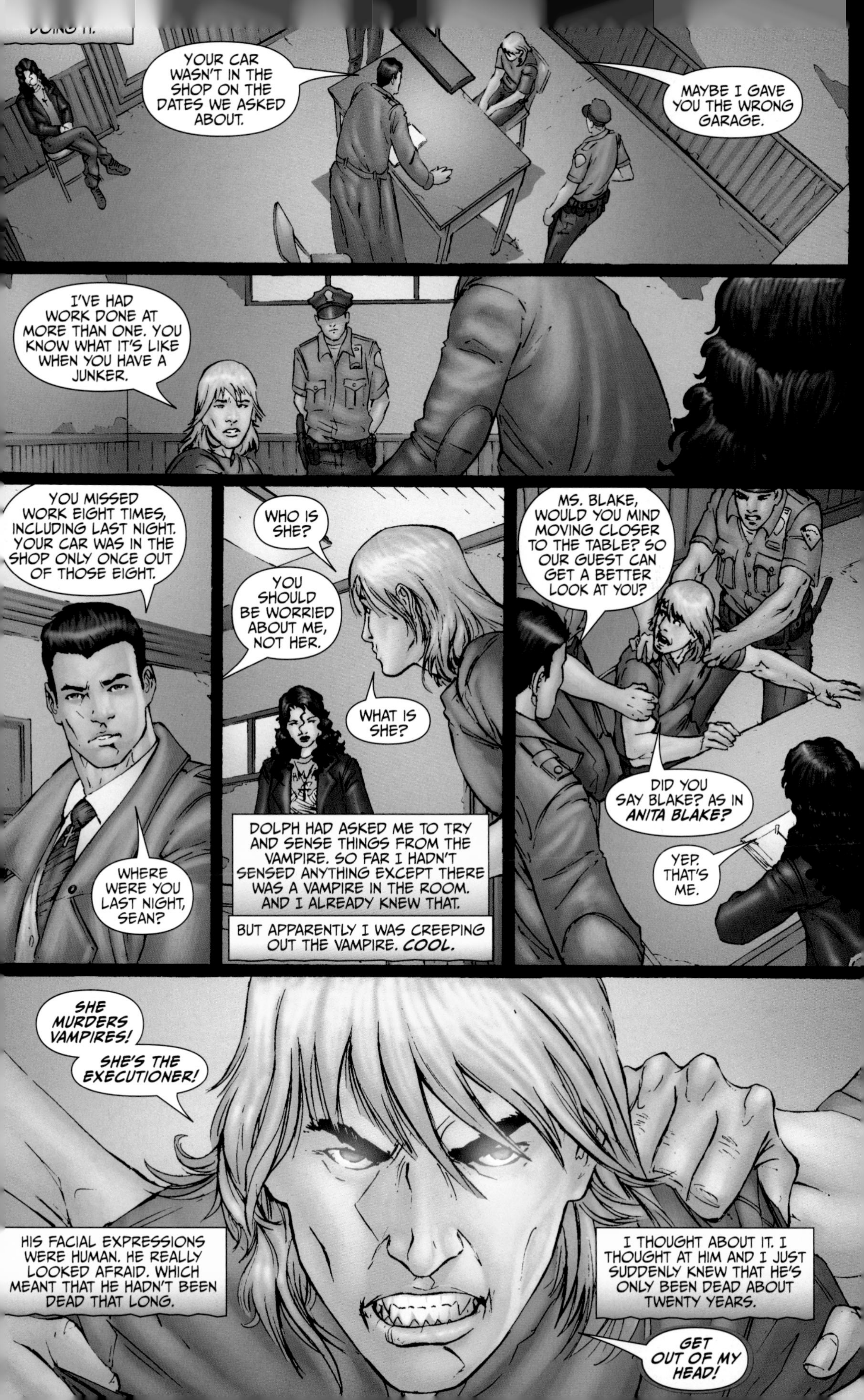
DOING IT.
YOUR CAR WASN'T IN THE SHOP ON THE DATES WE ASKED ABOUT.
MAYBE I GAVE YOU THE WRONG GARAGE.
I'VE HAD WORK DONE AT MORE THAN ONE. YOU KNOW WHAT IT'S LIKE WHEN YOU HAVE A JUNKER.
YOU MISSED WORK EIGHT TIMES, INCLUDING LAST NIGHT. YOUR CAR WAS IN THE SHOP ONLY ONCE OUT OF THOSE EIGHT.
WHERE WERE YOU LAST NIGHT, SEAN?
WHO IS SHE?
YOU SHOULD BE WORRIED ABOUT ME, NOT HER.
WHAT IS SHE?
DOLPH HAD ASKED ME TO TRY AND SENSE THINGS FROM THE VAMPIRE. SO FAR I HADN'T SENSED ANYTHING EXCEPT THERE WAS A VAMPIRE IN THE ROOM. AND I ALREADY KNEW THAT.
BUT APPARENTLY I WAS CREEPING OUT THE VAMPIRE. *COOL.*
MS. BLAKE, WOULD YOU MIND MOVING CLOSER TO THE TABLE? SO OUR GUEST CAN GET A BETTER LOOK AT YOU?
DID YOU SAY BLAKE? AS IN *ANITA BLAKE?*
YEP. THAT'S ME.
SHE MURDERS VAMPIRES!
SHE'S THE EXECUTIONER!
HIS FACIAL EXPRESSIONS WERE HUMAN. HE REALLY LOOKED AFRAID. WHICH MEANT THAT HE HADN'T BEEN DEAD THAT LONG.
I THOUGHT ABOUT IT. I THOUGHT AT HIM AND I JUST SUDDENLY KNEW THAT HE'S ONLY BEEN DEAD ABOUT TWENTY YEARS.
GET OUT OF MY HEAD!

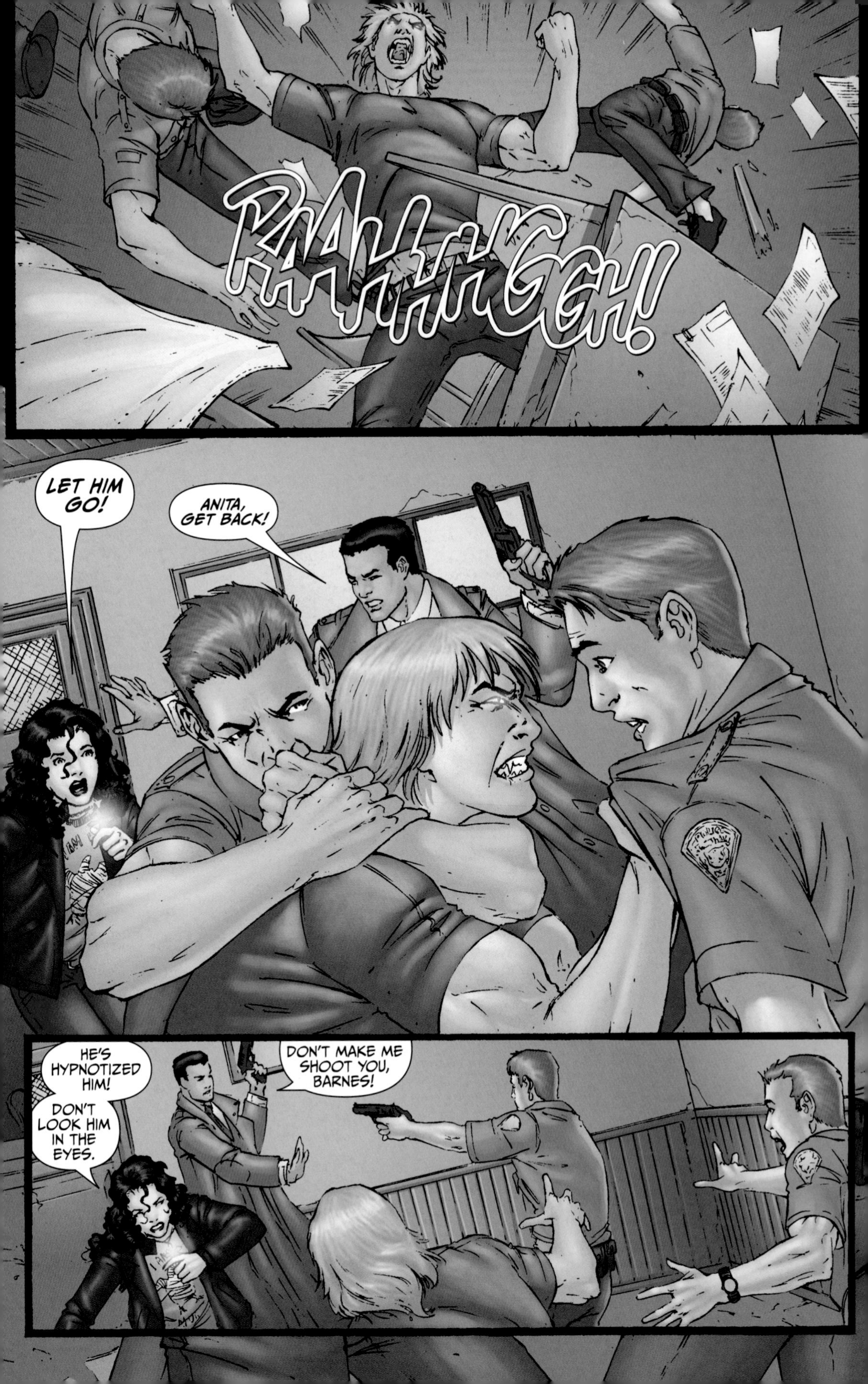
RAAAHHHGGH!
LET HIM GO!
ANITA, GET BACK!
HE'S HYPNOTIZED HIM!
DON'T LOOK HIM IN THE EYES.
DON'T MAKE ME SHOOT YOU, BARNES!

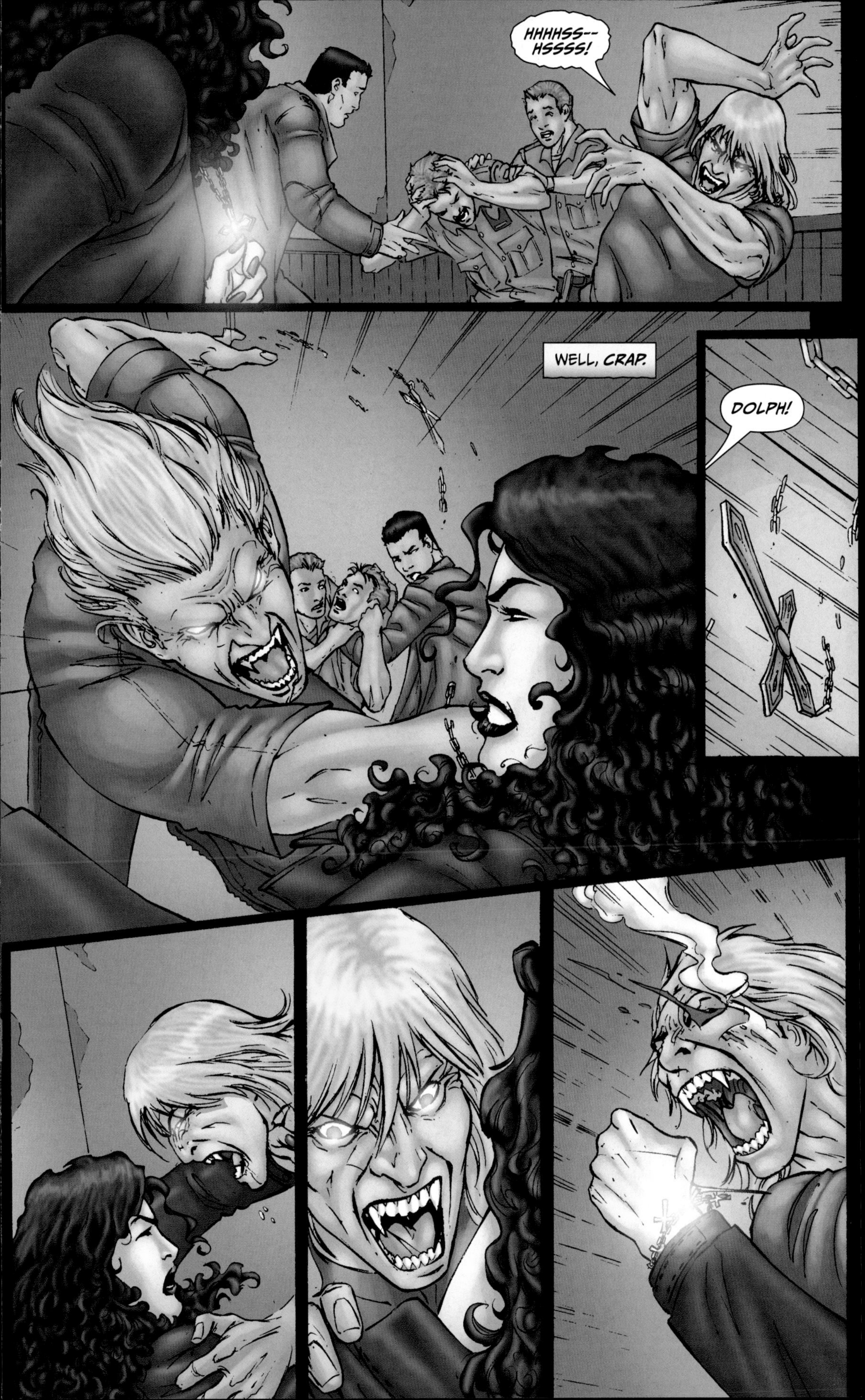
HHHHSS--
HSSSS!
WELL, CRAP.
DOLPH!

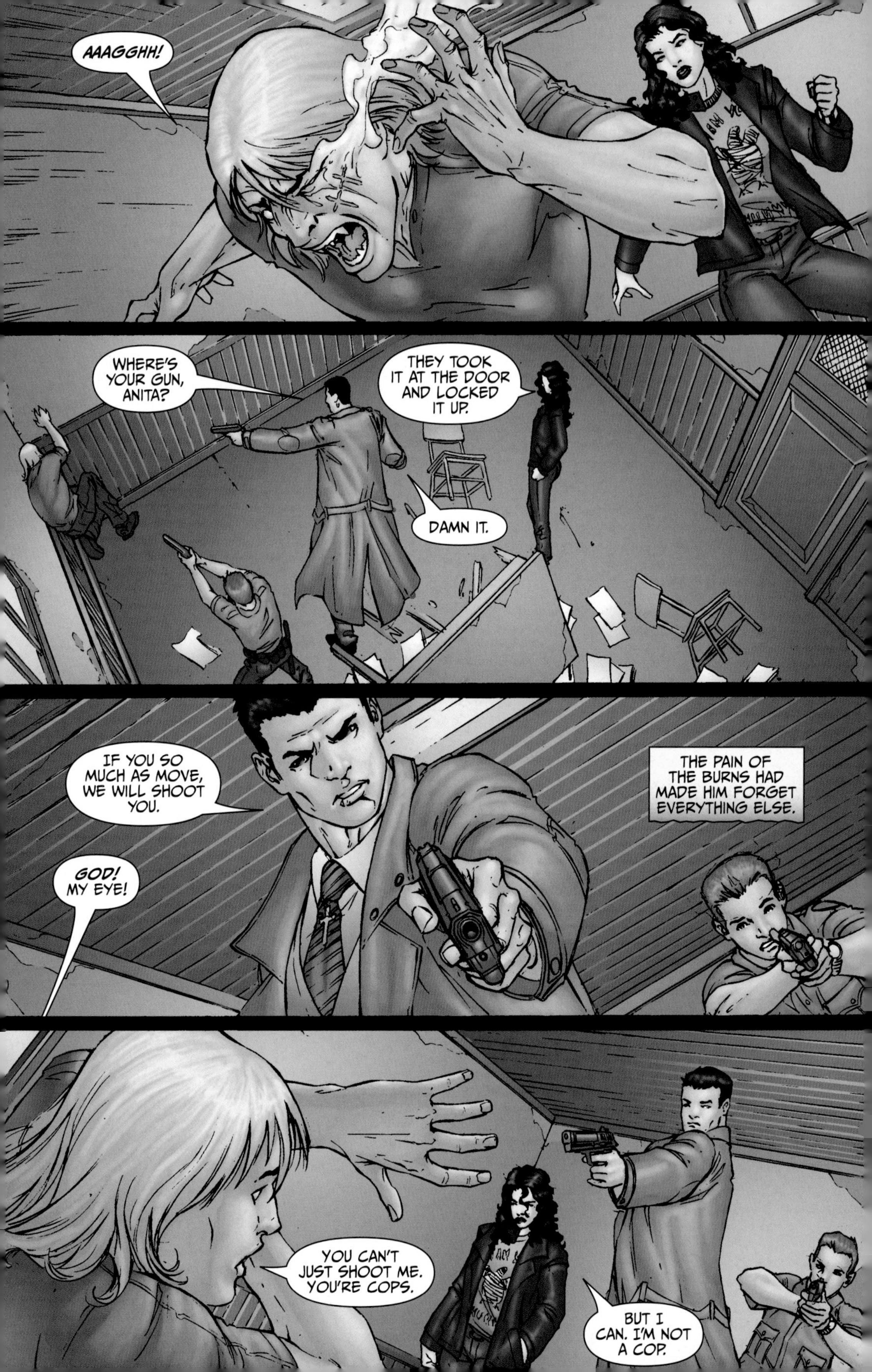
AAAGGHH!
WHERE'S YOUR GUN, ANITA?
THEY TOOK IT AT THE DOOR AND LOCKED IT UP.
DAMN IT.
IF YOU SO MUCH AS MOVE, WE WILL SHOOT YOU.
THE PAIN OF THE BURNS HAD MADE HIM FORGET EVERYTHING ELSE.
GOD! MY EYE!
YOU CAN'T JUST SHOOT ME. YOU'RE COPS.
BUT I CAN. I'M NOT A COP.

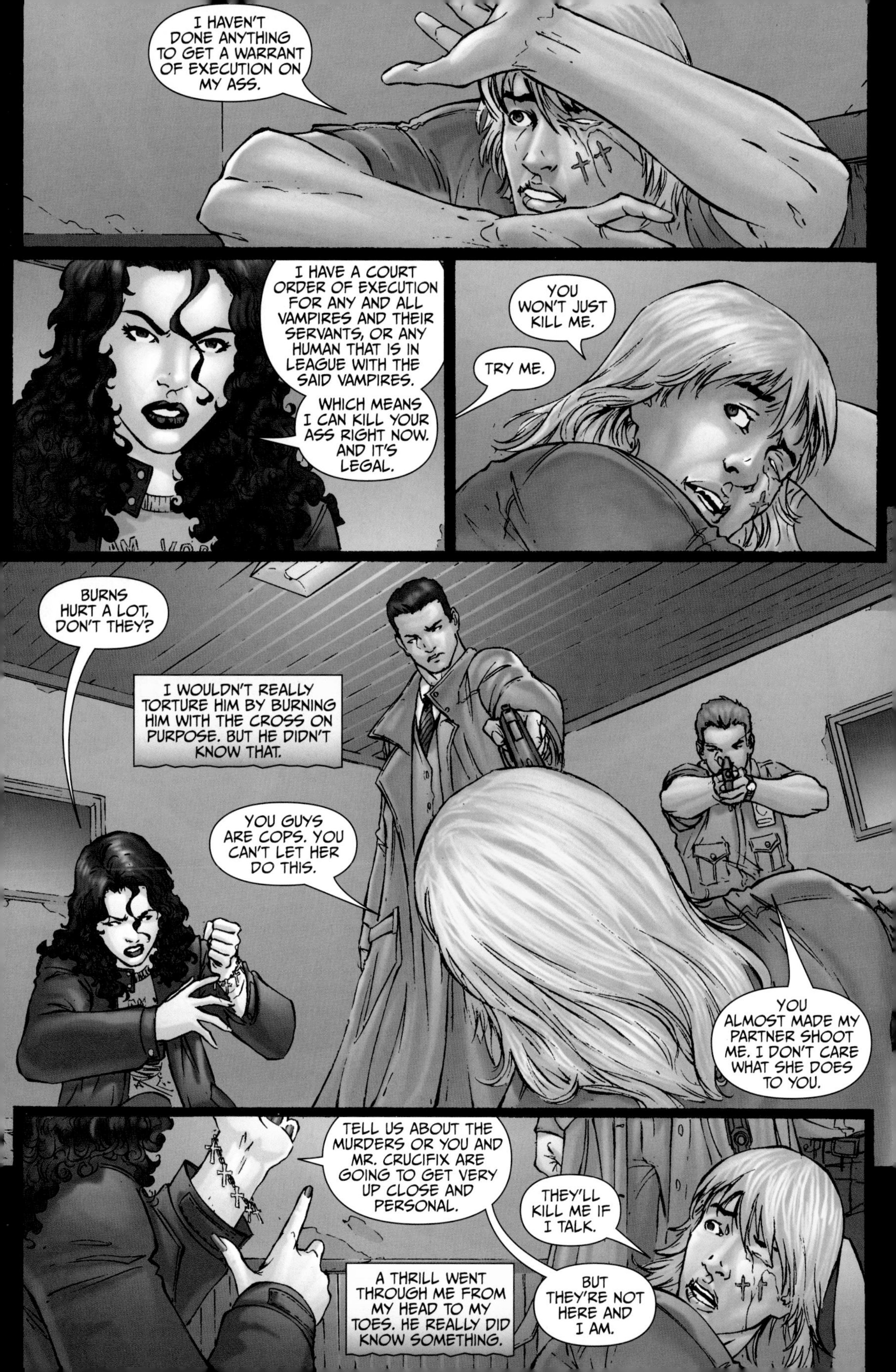

I HAVEN'T DONE ANYTHING TO GET A WARRANT OF EXECUTION ON MY ASS.
I HAVE A COURT ORDER OF EXECUTION FOR ANY AND ALL VAMPIRES AND THEIR SERVANTS, OR ANY HUMAN THAT IS IN LEAGUE WITH THE SAID VAMPIRES.
WHICH MEANS I CAN KILL YOUR ASS RIGHT NOW. AND IT'S LEGAL.
YOU WON'T JUST KILL ME.
TRY ME.
BURNS HURT A LOT, DON'T THEY?
I WOULDN'T REALLY TORTURE HIM BY BURNING HIM WITH THE CROSS ON PURPOSE. BUT HE DIDN'T KNOW THAT.
YOU GUYS ARE COPS. YOU CAN'T LET HER DO THIS.
YOU ALMOST MADE MY PARTNER SHOOT ME. I DON'T CARE WHAT SHE DOES TO YOU.
TELL US ABOUT THE MURDERS OR YOU AND MR. CRUCIFIX ARE GOING TO GET VERY UP CLOSE AND PERSONAL.
THEY'LL KILL ME IF I TALK.
BUT THEY'RE NOT HERE AND I AM.
A THRILL WENT THROUGH ME FROM MY HEAD TO MY TOES. HE REALLY DID KNOW SOMETHING.

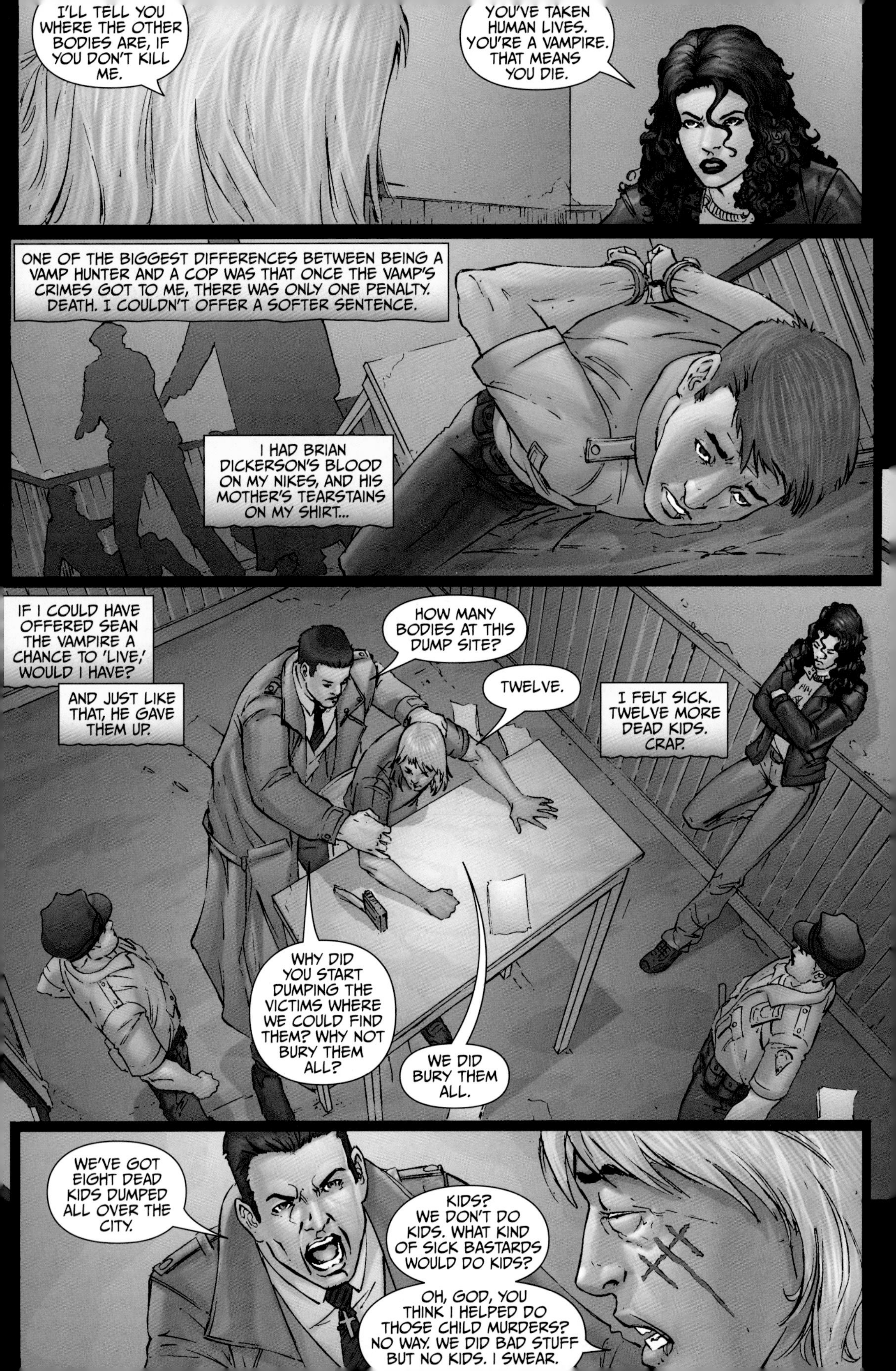
I'LL TELL YOU WHERE THE OTHER BODIES ARE, IF YOU DON'T KILL ME.
YOU'VE TAKEN HUMAN LIVES. YOU'RE A VAMPIRE. THAT MEANS YOU DIE.
ONE OF THE BIGGEST DIFFERENCES BETWEEN BEING A VAMP HUNTER AND A COP WAS THAT ONCE THE VAMP'S CRIMES GOT TO ME, THERE WAS ONLY ONE PENALTY. DEATH. I COULDN'T OFFER A SOFTER SENTENCE.
I HAD BRIAN DICKERSON'S BLOOD ON MY NIKES, AND HIS MOTHER'S TEARSTAINS ON MY SHIRT...
IF I COULD HAVE OFFERED SEAN THE VAMPIRE A CHANCE TO 'LIVE,' WOULD I HAVE?
AND JUST LIKE THAT, HE GAVE THEM UP.
HOW MANY BODIES AT THIS DUMP SITE?
TWELVE.
I FELT SICK. TWELVE MORE DEAD KIDS. CRAP.
WHY DID YOU START DUMPING THE VICTIMS WHERE WE COULD FIND THEM? WHY NOT BURY THEM ALL?
WE DID BURY THEM ALL.
WE'VE GOT EIGHT DEAD KIDS DUMPED ALL OVER THE CITY.
KIDS? WE DON'T DO KIDS. WHAT KIND OF SICK BASTARDS WOULD DO KIDS?
OH, GOD, YOU THINK I HELPED DO THOSE CHILD MURDERS? NO WAY. WE DID BAD STUFF BUT NO KIDS. I SWEAR.

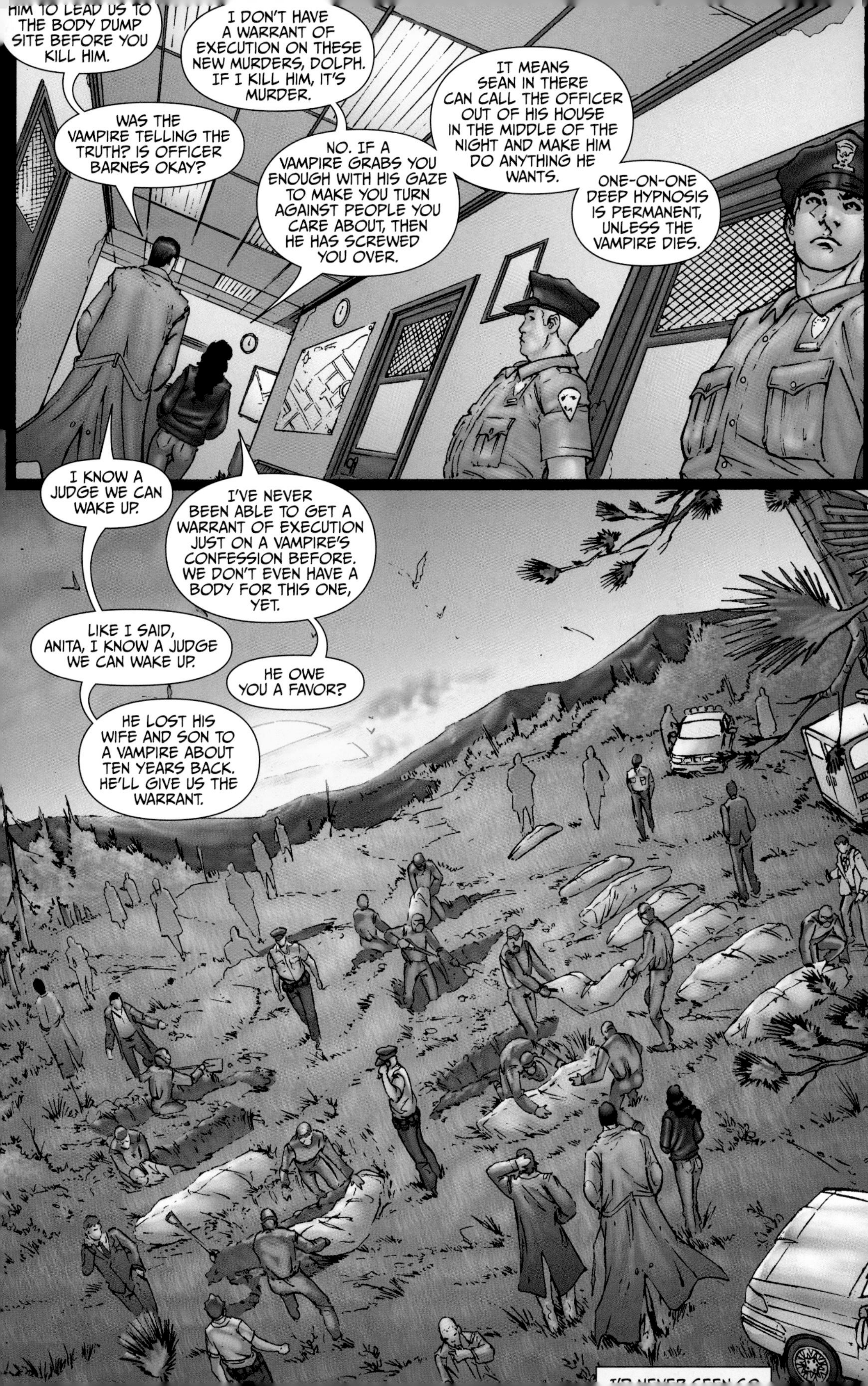

HIM TO LEAD US TO THE BODY DUMP SITE BEFORE YOU KILL HIM.
I DON'T HAVE A WARRANT OF EXECUTION ON THESE NEW MURDERS, DOLPH. IF I KILL HIM, IT'S MURDER.
WAS THE VAMPIRE TELLING THE TRUTH? IS OFFICER BARNES OKAY?
NO. IF A VAMPIRE GRABS YOU ENOUGH WITH HIS GAZE TO MAKE YOU TURN AGAINST PEOPLE YOU CARE ABOUT, THEN HE HAS SCREWED YOU OVER.
IT MEANS SEAN IN THERE CAN CALL THE OFFICER OUT OF HIS HOUSE IN THE MIDDLE OF THE NIGHT AND MAKE HIM DO ANYTHING HE WANTS.
ONE-ON-ONE DEEP HYPNOSIS IS PERMANENT, UNLESS THE VAMPIRE DIES.
I KNOW A JUDGE WE CAN WAKE UP.
I'VE NEVER BEEN ABLE TO GET A WARRANT OF EXECUTION JUST ON A VAMPIRE'S CONFESSION BEFORE. WE DON'T EVEN HAVE A BODY FOR THIS ONE, YET.
LIKE I SAID, ANITA, I KNOW A JUDGE WE CAN WAKE UP.
HE OWE YOU A FAVOR?
HE LOST HIS WIFE AND SON TO A VAMPIRE ABOUT TEN YEARS BACK. HE'LL GIVE US THE WARRANT.

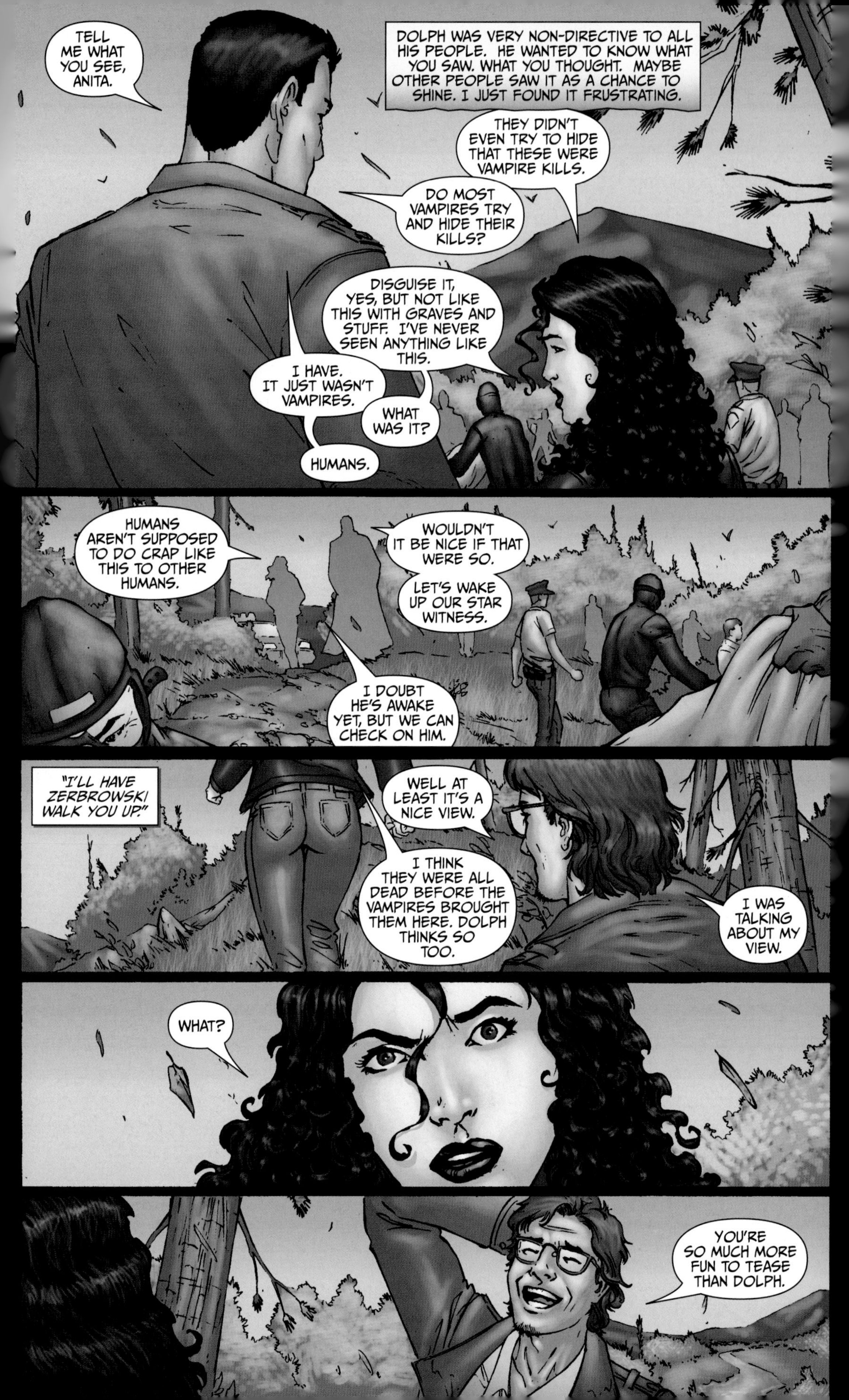
TELL ME WHAT YOU SEE, ANITA.
DOLPH WAS VERY NON-DIRECTIVE TO ALL HIS PEOPLE. HE WANTED TO KNOW WHAT YOU SAW. WHAT YOU THOUGHT. MAYBE OTHER PEOPLE SAW IT AS A CHANCE TO SHINE. I JUST FOUND IT FRUSTRATING.
THEY DIDN'T EVEN TRY TO HIDE THAT THESE WERE VAMPIRE KILLS.
DO MOST VAMPIRES TRY AND HIDE THEIR KILLS?
DISGUISE IT, YES, BUT NOT LIKE THIS WITH GRAVES AND STUFF. I'VE NEVER SEEN ANYTHING LIKE THIS.
I HAVE. IT JUST WASN'T VAMPIRES.
WHAT WAS IT?
HUMANS.
HUMANS AREN'T SUPPOSED TO DO CRAP LIKE THIS TO OTHER HUMANS.
WOULDN'T IT BE NICE IF THAT WERE SO.
LET'S WAKE UP OUR STAR WITNESS.
I DOUBT HE'S AWAKE YET, BUT WE CAN CHECK ON HIM.
"I'LL HAVE ZERBROWSKI WALK YOU UP."
WELL AT LEAST IT'S A NICE VIEW.
I THINK THEY WERE ALL DEAD BEFORE THE VAMPIRES BROUGHT THEM HERE. DOLPH THINKS SO TOO.
I WAS TALKING ABOUT MY VIEW.
WHAT?
YOU'RE SO MUCH MORE FUN TO TEASE THAN DOLPH.

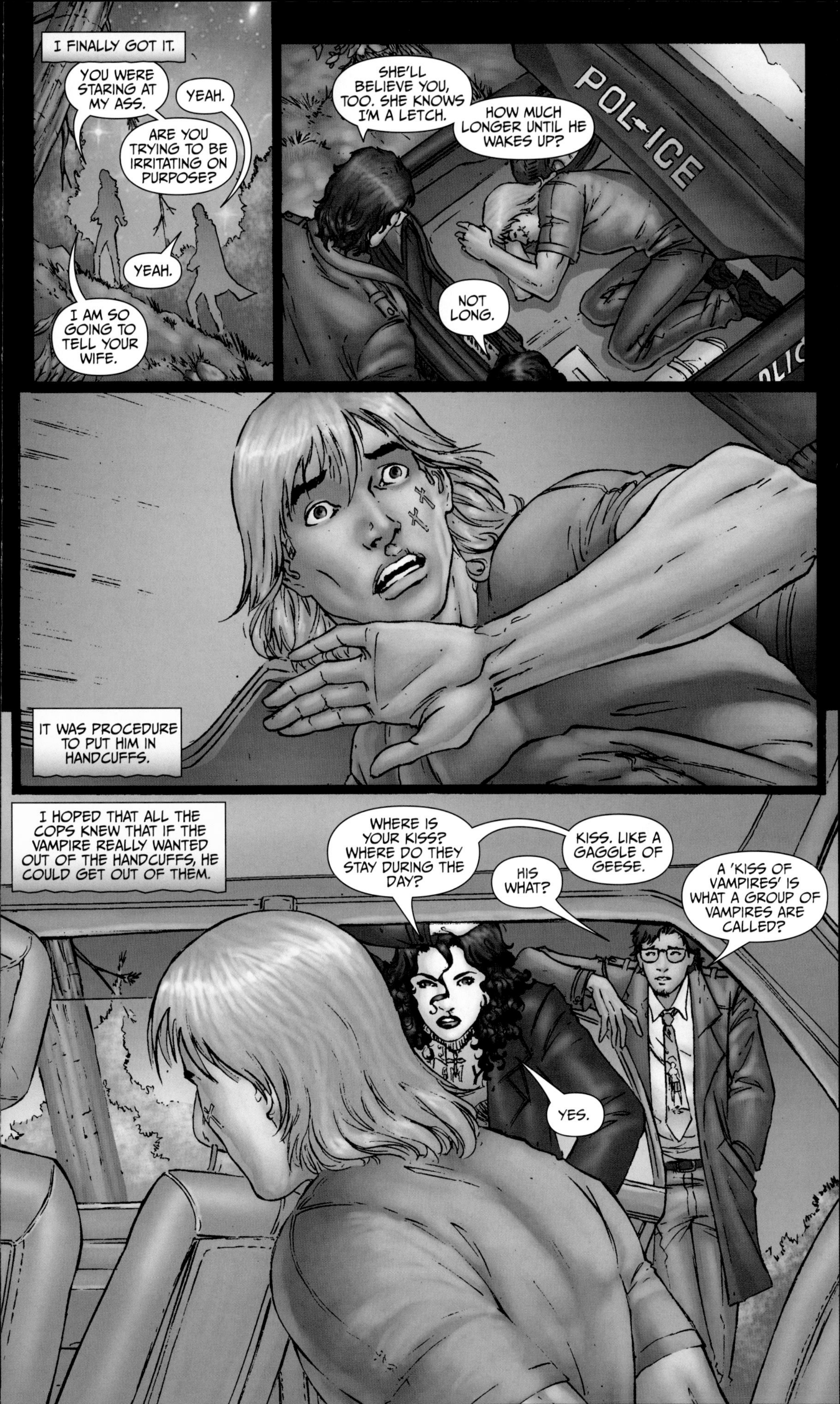
I FINALLY GOT IT.
YOU WERE STARING AT MY ASS.
YEAH.
ARE YOU TRYING TO BE IRRITATING ON PURPOSE?
YEAH.
I AM SO GOING TO TELL YOUR WIFE.
SHE'LL BELIEVE YOU, TOO. SHE KNOWS I'M A LETCH.
HOW MUCH LONGER UNTIL HE WAKES UP?
NOT LONG.
POL-ICE
IT WAS PROCEDURE TO PUT HIM IN HANDCUFFS.
I HOPED THAT ALL THE COPS KNEW THAT IF THE VAMPIRE REALLY WANTED OUT OF THE HANDCUFFS, HE COULD GET OUT OF THEM.
WHERE IS YOUR KISS? WHERE DO THEY STAY DURING THE DAY?
HIS WHAT?
KISS. LIKE A GAGGLE OF GEESE.
A 'KISS OF VAMPIRES' IS WHAT A GROUP OF VAMPIRES ARE CALLED?
YES.

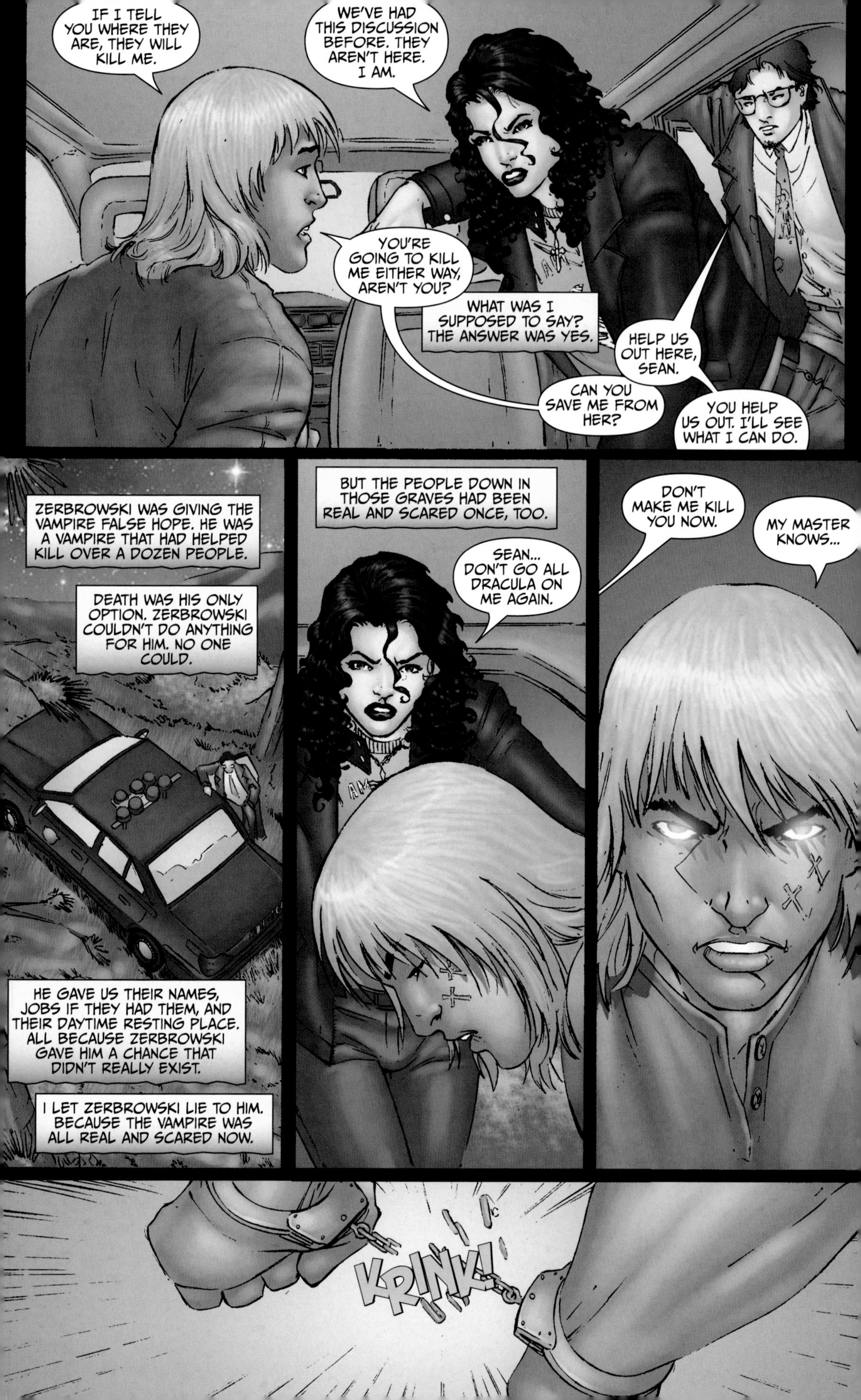
IF I TELL YOU WHERE THEY ARE, THEY WILL KILL ME.
WE'VE HAD THIS DISCUSSION BEFORE. THEY AREN'T HERE. I AM.
YOU'RE GOING TO KILL ME EITHER WAY, AREN'T YOU?
WHAT WAS I SUPPOSED TO SAY? THE ANSWER WAS YES.
HELP US OUT HERE, SEAN.
CAN YOU SAVE ME FROM HER?
YOU HELP US OUT. I'LL SEE WHAT I CAN DO.
ZERBROWSKI WAS GIVING THE VAMPIRE FALSE HOPE. HE WAS A VAMPIRE THAT HAD HELPED KILL OVER A DOZEN PEOPLE.
DEATH WAS HIS ONLY OPTION. ZERBROWSKI COULDN'T DO ANYTHING FOR HIM. NO ONE COULD.
HE GAVE US THEIR NAMES, JOBS IF THEY HAD THEM, AND THEIR DAYTIME RESTING PLACE. ALL BECAUSE ZERBROWSKI GAVE HIM A CHANCE THAT DIDN'T REALLY EXIST.
I LET ZERBROWSKI LIE TO HIM. BECAUSE THE VAMPIRE WAS ALL REAL AND SCARED NOW.
BUT THE PEOPLE DOWN IN THOSE GRAVES HAD BEEN REAL AND SCARED ONCE, TOO.
SEAN... DON'T GO ALL DRACULA ON ME AGAIN.
DON'T MAKE ME KILL YOU NOW.
MY MASTER KNOWS...
KRINK!

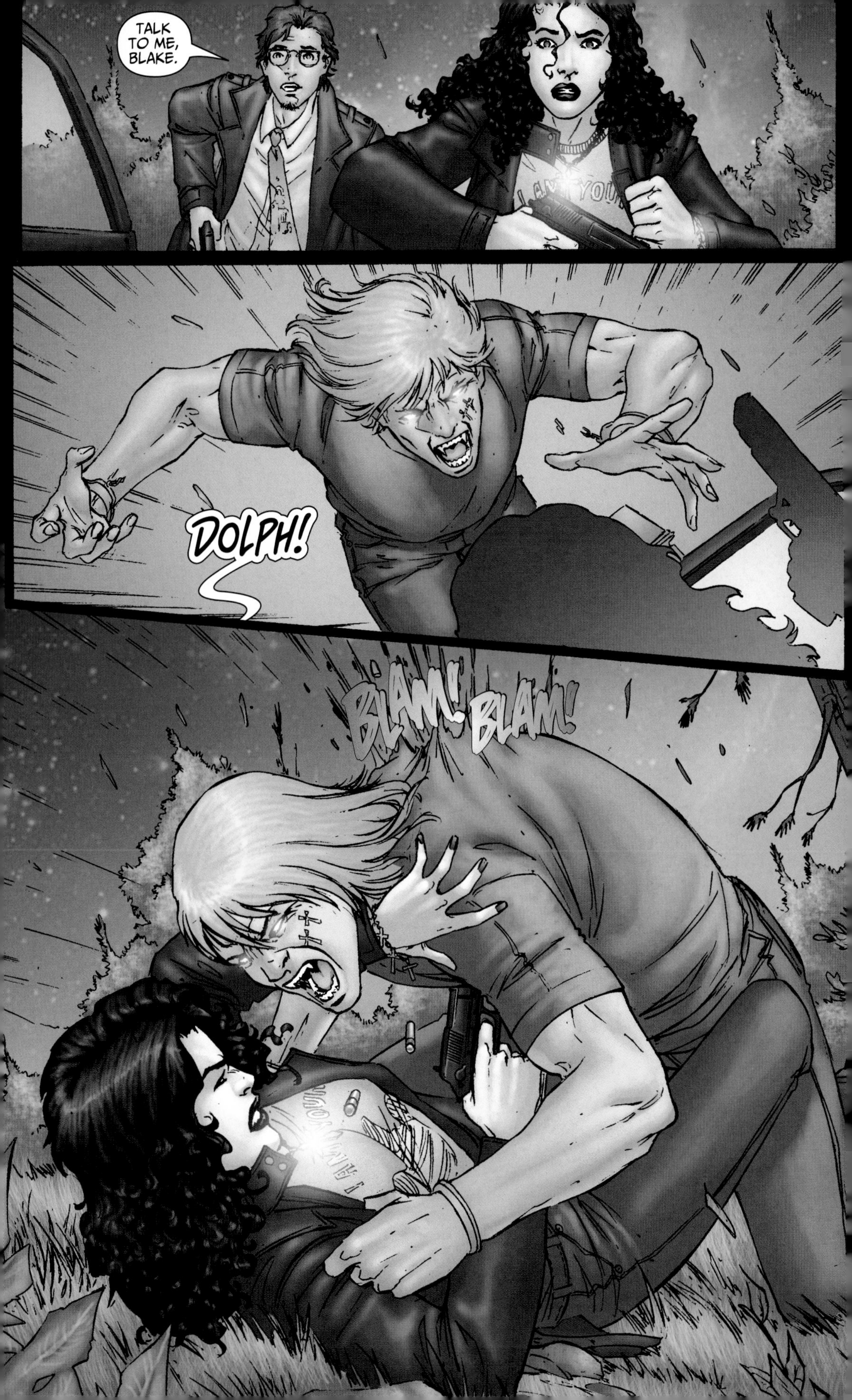
TALK TO ME, BLAKE.
DOLPH!
BLAM! BLAM!

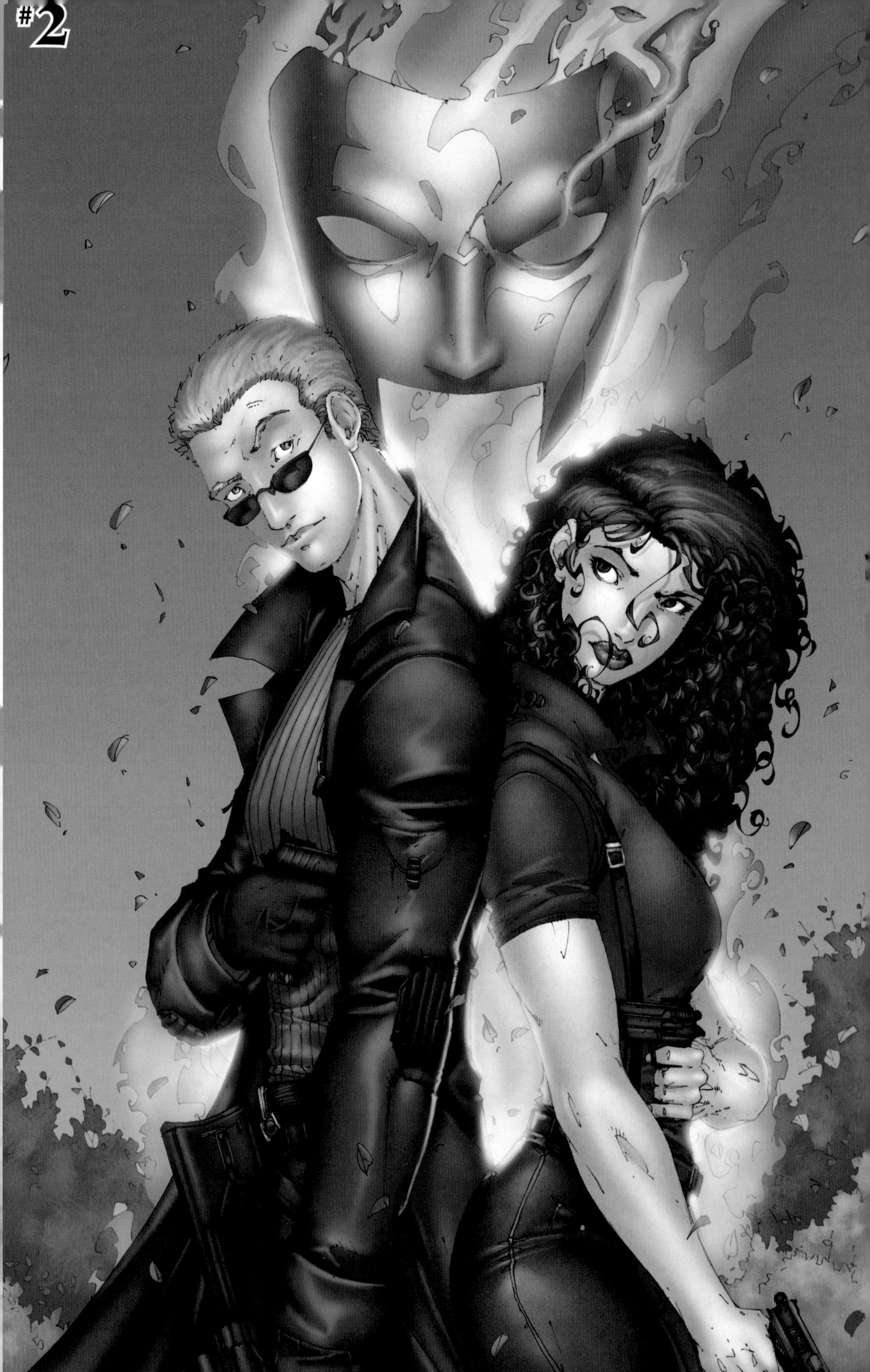
#2

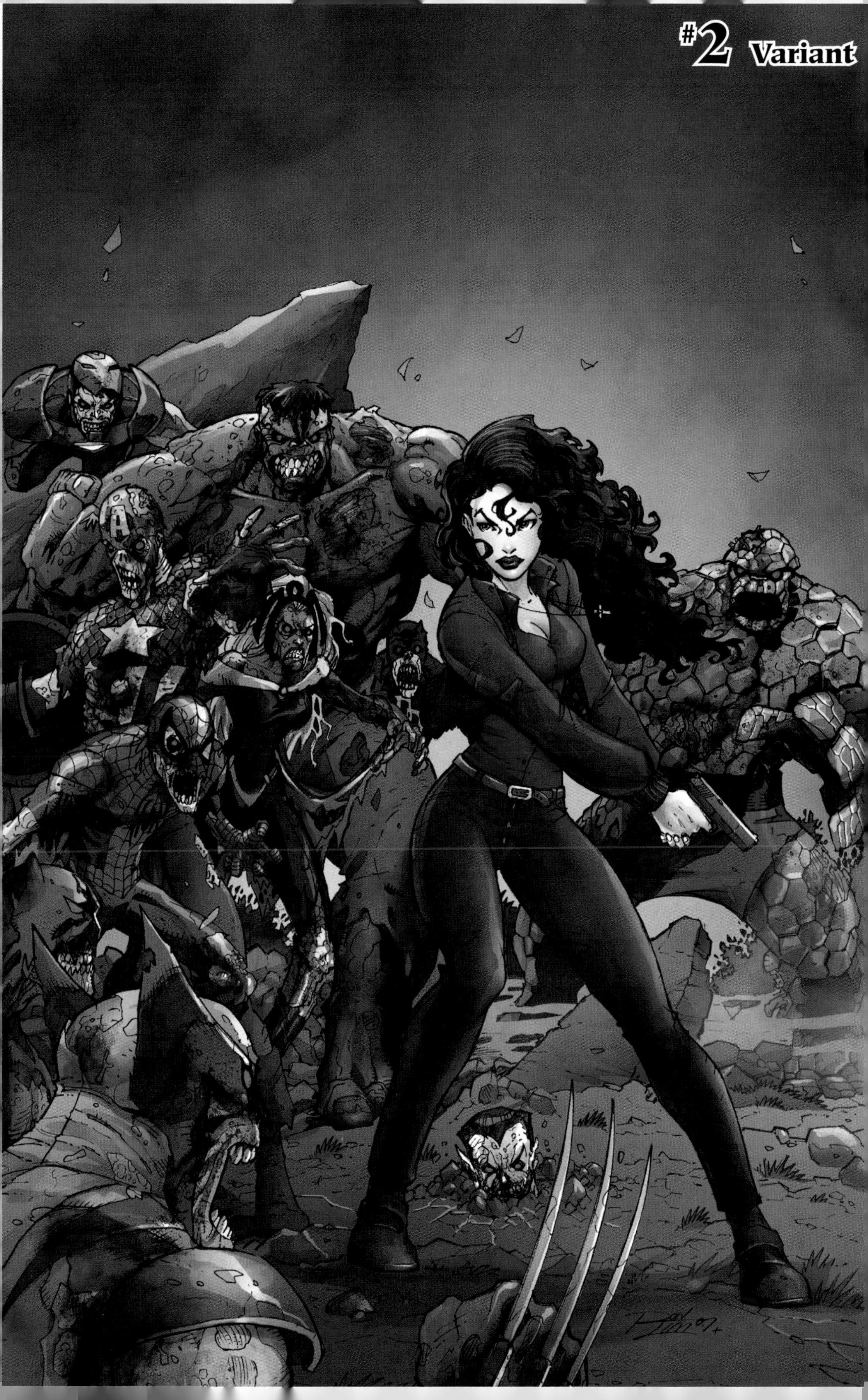

#2 Variant

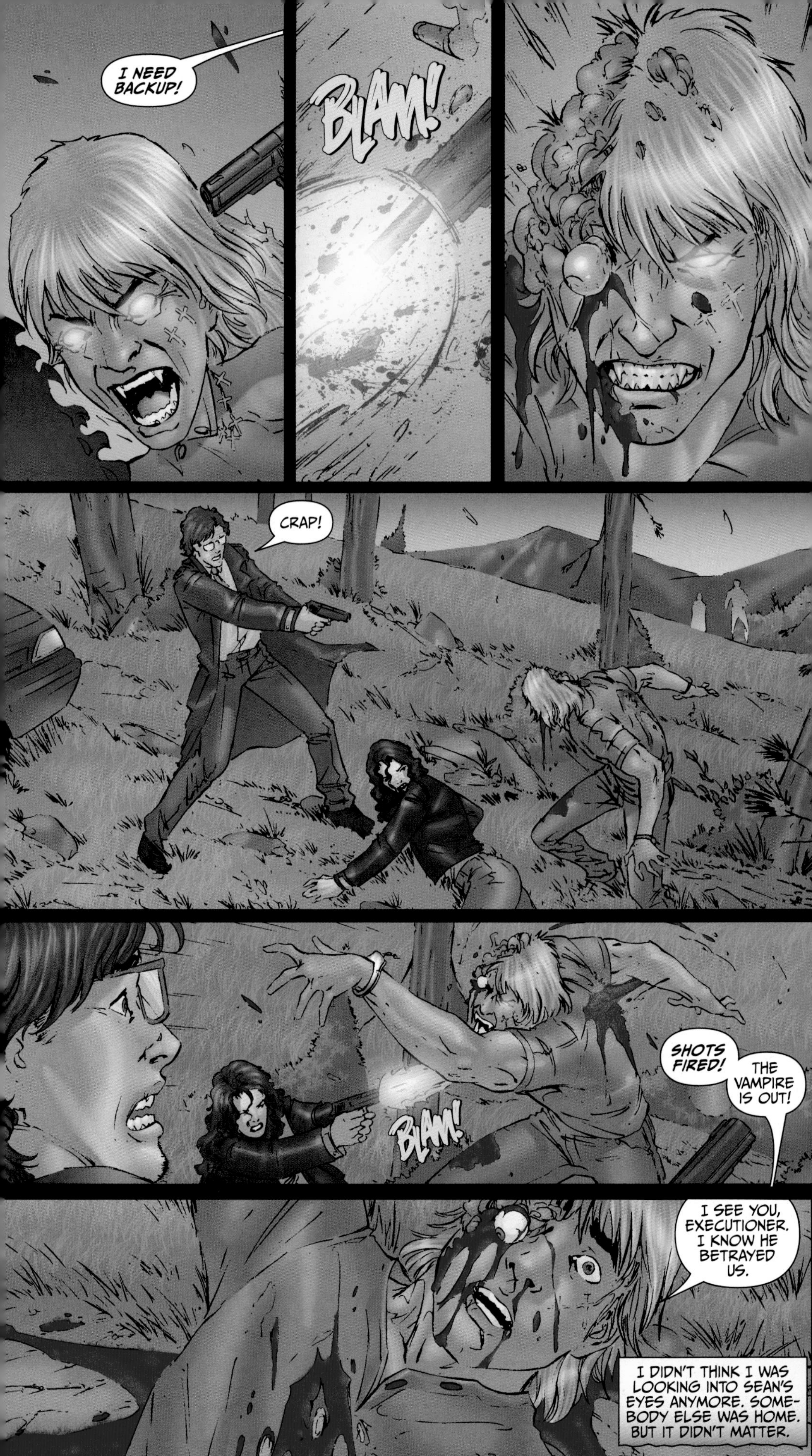
I NEED BACKUP!
BLAM!
CRAP!
BLAM!
SHOTS FIRED!
THE VAMPIRE IS OUT!
I SEE YOU, EXECUTIONER. I KNOW HE BETRAYED US.
I DIDN'T THINK I WAS LOOKING INTO SEAN'S EYES ANYMORE. SOMEBODY ELSE WAS HOME. BUT IT DIDN'T MATTER.

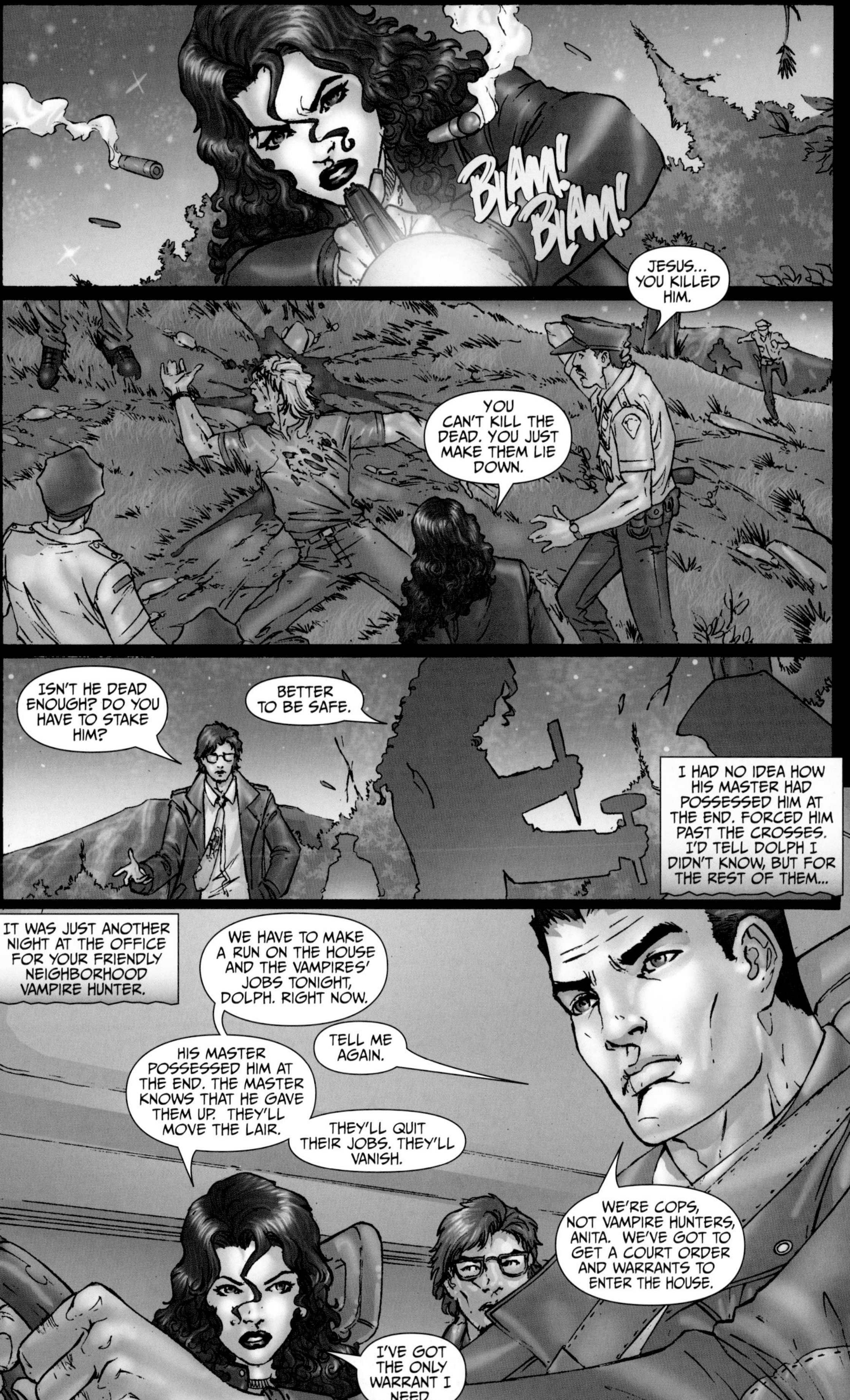
BLAM! BLAM!
JESUS... YOU KILLED HIM.
YOU CAN'T KILL THE DEAD. YOU JUST MAKE THEM LIE DOWN.
ISN'T HE DEAD ENOUGH? DO YOU HAVE TO STAKE HIM?
BETTER TO BE SAFE.
I HAD NO IDEA HOW HIS MASTER HAD POSSESSED HIM AT THE END. FORCED HIM PAST THE CROSSES. I'D TELL DOLPH I DIDN'T KNOW, BUT FOR THE REST OF THEM...
IT WAS JUST ANOTHER NIGHT AT THE OFFICE FOR YOUR FRIENDLY NEIGHBORHOOD VAMPIRE HUNTER.
WE HAVE TO MAKE A RUN ON THE HOUSE AND THE VAMPIRES' JOBS TONIGHT, DOLPH. RIGHT NOW.
TELL ME AGAIN.
HIS MASTER POSSESSED HIM AT THE END. THE MASTER KNOWS THAT HE GAVE THEM UP. THEY'LL MOVE THE LAIR.
THEY'LL QUIT THEIR JOBS. THEY'LL VANISH.
WE'RE COPS, NOT VAMPIRE HUNTERS, ANITA. WE'VE GOT TO GET A COURT ORDER AND WARRANTS TO ENTER THE HOUSE.
I'VE GOT THE ONLY WARRANT I NEED.

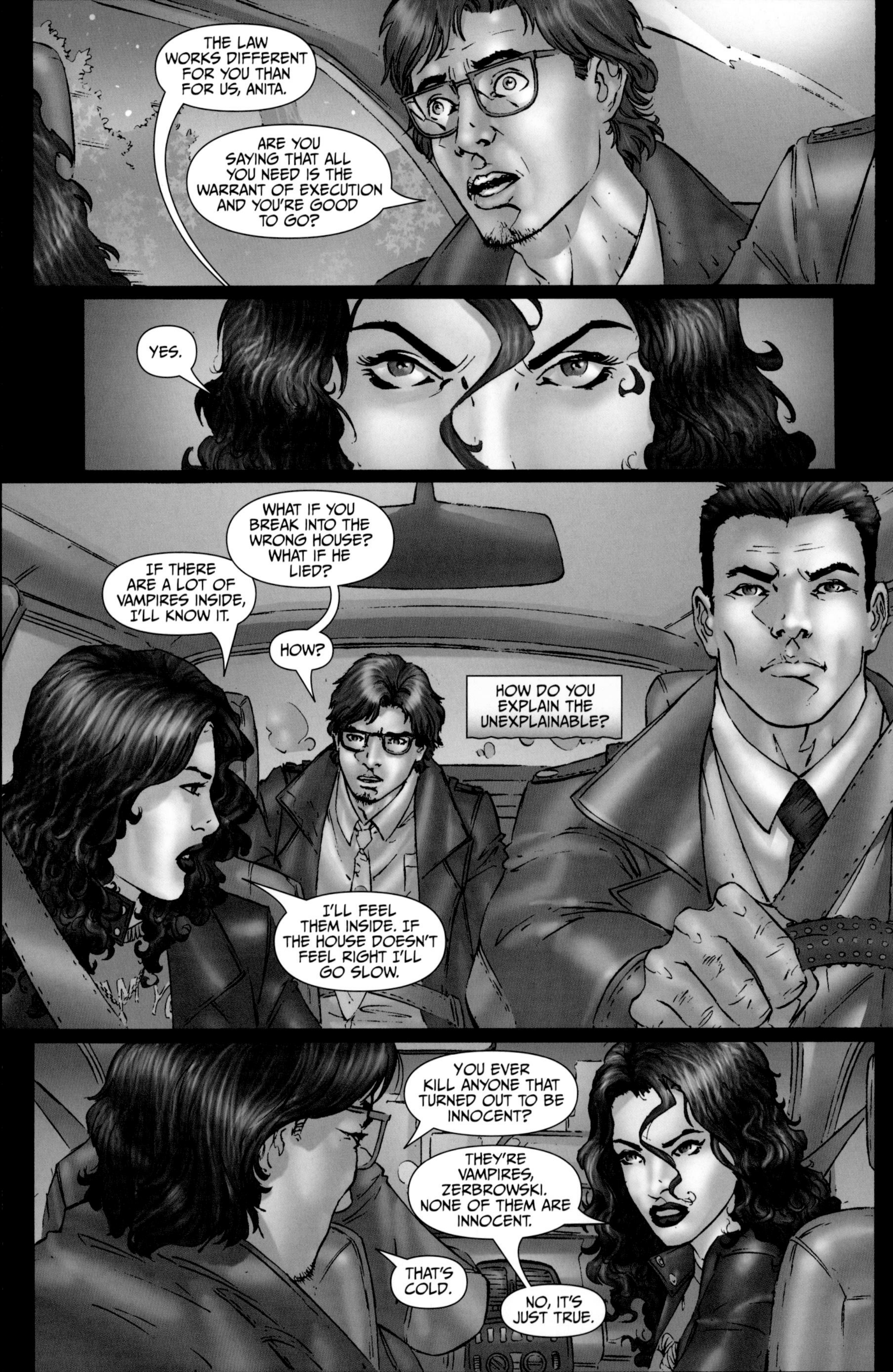
THE LAW WORKS DIFFERENT FOR YOU THAN FOR US, ANITA.
ARE YOU SAYING THAT ALL YOU NEED IS THE WARRANT OF EXECUTION AND YOU'RE GOOD TO GO?
YES.
IF THERE ARE A LOT OF VAMPIRES INSIDE, I'LL KNOW IT.
WHAT IF YOU BREAK INTO THE WRONG HOUSE? WHAT IF HE LIED?
HOW?
HOW DO YOU EXPLAIN THE UNEXPLAINABLE?
I'LL FEEL THEM INSIDE. IF THE HOUSE DOESN'T FEEL RIGHT I'LL GO SLOW.
YOU EVER KILL ANYONE THAT TURNED OUT TO BE INNOCENT?
THEY'RE VAMPIRES, ZERBROWSKI. NONE OF THEM ARE INNOCENT.
THAT'S COLD.
NO, IT'S JUST TRUE.

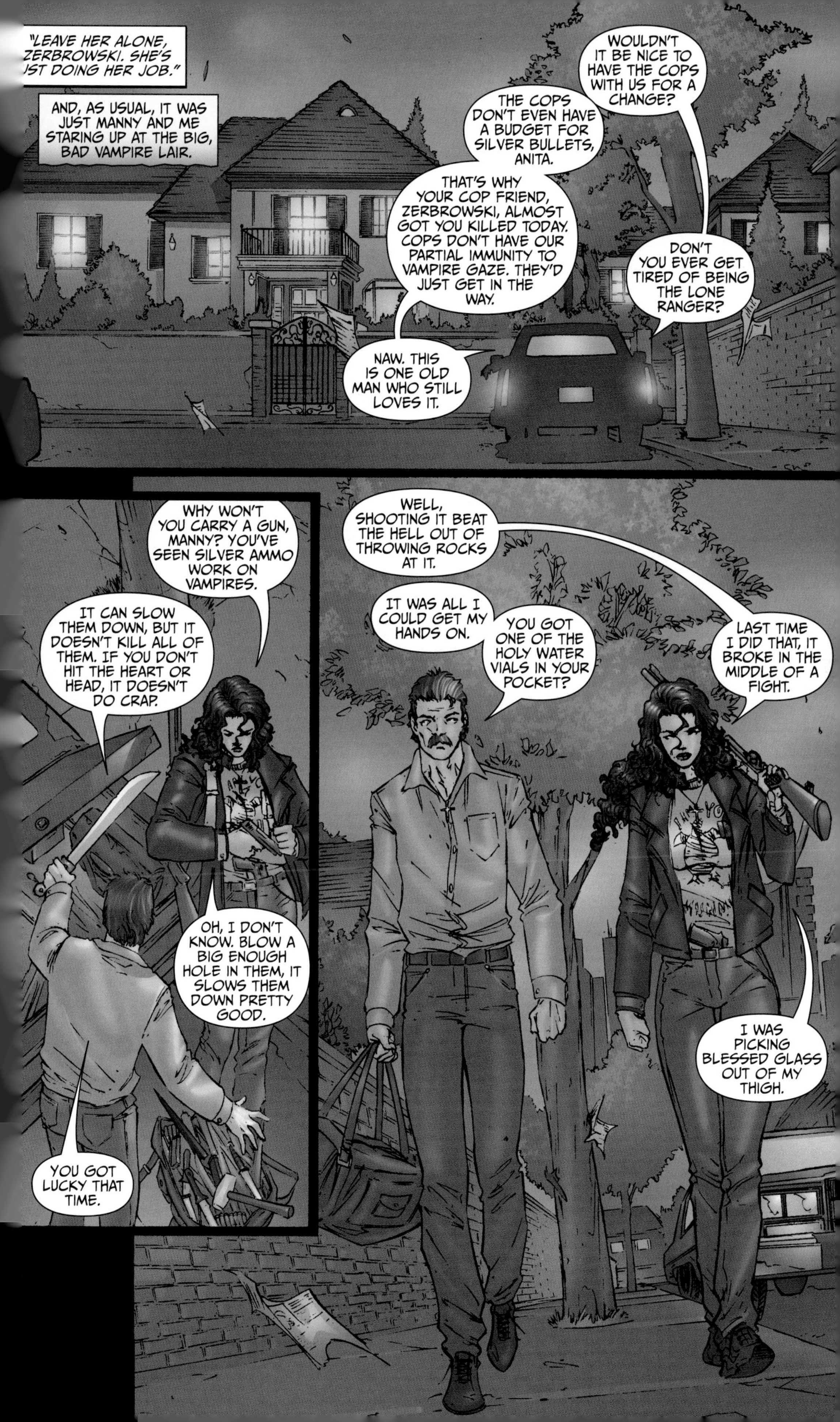
"LEAVE HER ALONE, ZERBROWSKI. SHE'S JUST DOING HER JOB."
AND, AS USUAL, IT WAS JUST MANNY AND ME STARING UP AT THE BIG, BAD VAMPIRE LAIR.
WOULDN'T IT BE NICE TO HAVE THE COPS WITH US FOR A CHANGE?
THE COPS DON'T EVEN HAVE A BUDGET FOR SILVER BULLETS, ANITA.
THAT'S WHY YOUR COP FRIEND, ZERBROWSKI, ALMOST GOT YOU KILLED TODAY. COPS DON'T HAVE OUR PARTIAL IMMUNITY TO VAMPIRE GAZE. THEY'D JUST GET IN THE WAY.
DON'T YOU EVER GET TIRED OF BEING THE LONE RANGER?
NAW. THIS IS ONE OLD MAN WHO STILL LOVES IT.
WHY WON'T YOU CARRY A GUN, MANNY? YOU'VE SEEN SILVER AMMO WORK ON VAMPIRES.
IT CAN SLOW THEM DOWN, BUT IT DOESN'T KILL ALL OF THEM. IF YOU DON'T HIT THE HEART OR HEAD, IT DOESN'T DO CRAP.
OH, I DON'T KNOW. BLOW A BIG ENOUGH HOLE IN THEM, IT SLOWS THEM DOWN PRETTY GOOD.
YOU GOT LUCKY THAT TIME.
WELL, SHOOTING IT BEAT THE HELL OUT OF THROWING ROCKS AT IT.
IT WAS ALL I COULD GET MY HANDS ON.
YOU GOT ONE OF THE HOLY WATER VIALS IN YOUR POCKET?
LAST TIME I DID THAT, IT BROKE IN THE MIDDLE OF A FIGHT.
I WAS PICKING BLESSED GLASS OUT OF MY THIGH.

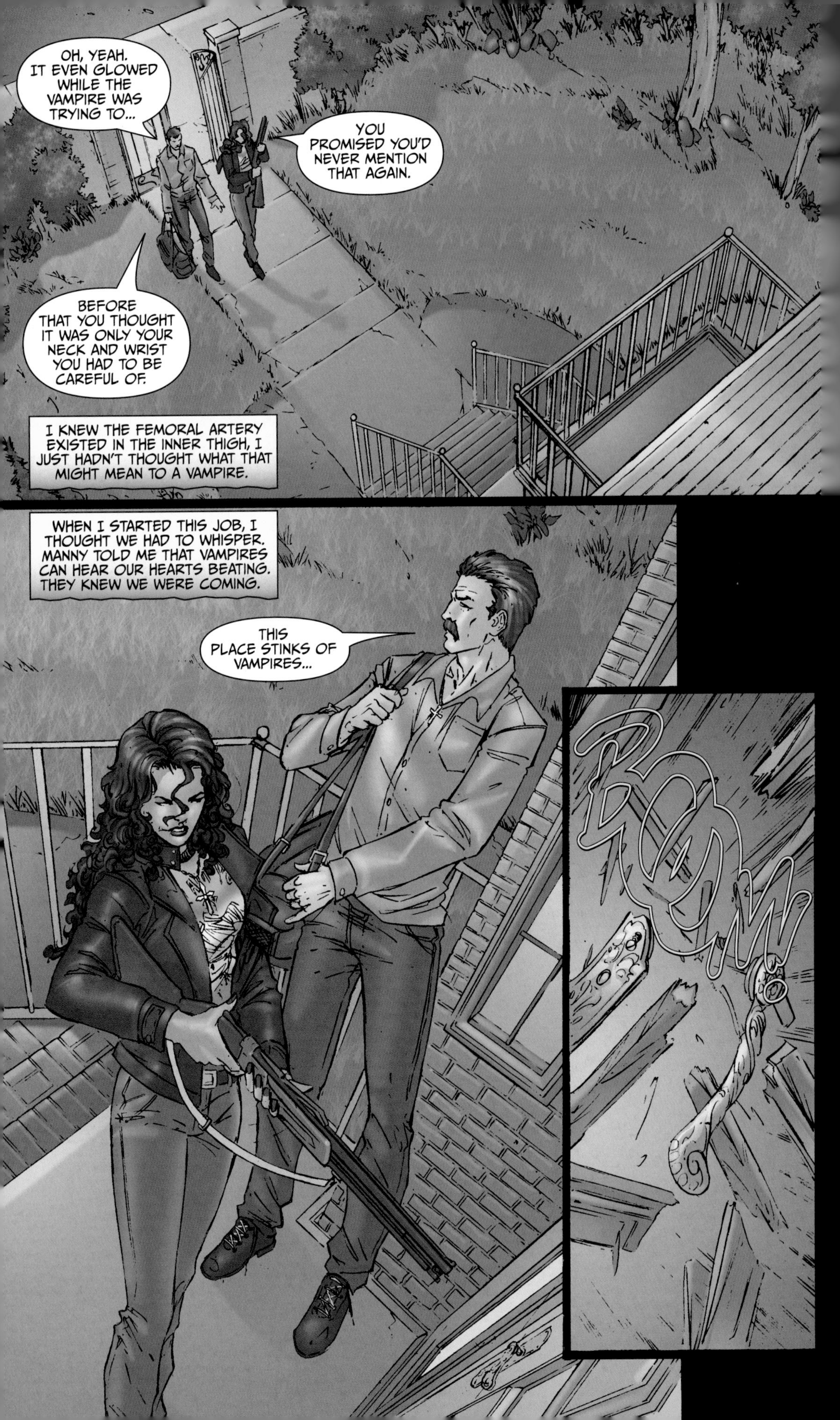
OH, YEAH. IT EVEN GLOWED WHILE THE VAMPIRE WAS TRYING TO...
YOU PROMISED YOU'D NEVER MENTION THAT AGAIN.
BEFORE THAT YOU THOUGHT IT WAS ONLY YOUR NECK AND WRIST YOU HAD TO BE CAREFUL OF.
I KNEW THE FEMORAL ARTERY EXISTED IN THE INNER THIGH, I JUST HADN'T THOUGHT WHAT THAT MIGHT MEAN TO A VAMPIRE.
WHEN I STARTED THIS JOB, I THOUGHT WE HAD TO WHISPER. MANNY TOLD ME THAT VAMPIRES CAN HEAR OUR HEARTS BEATING. THEY KNEW WE WERE COMING.
THIS PLACE STINKS OF VAMPIRES...
BOOM!

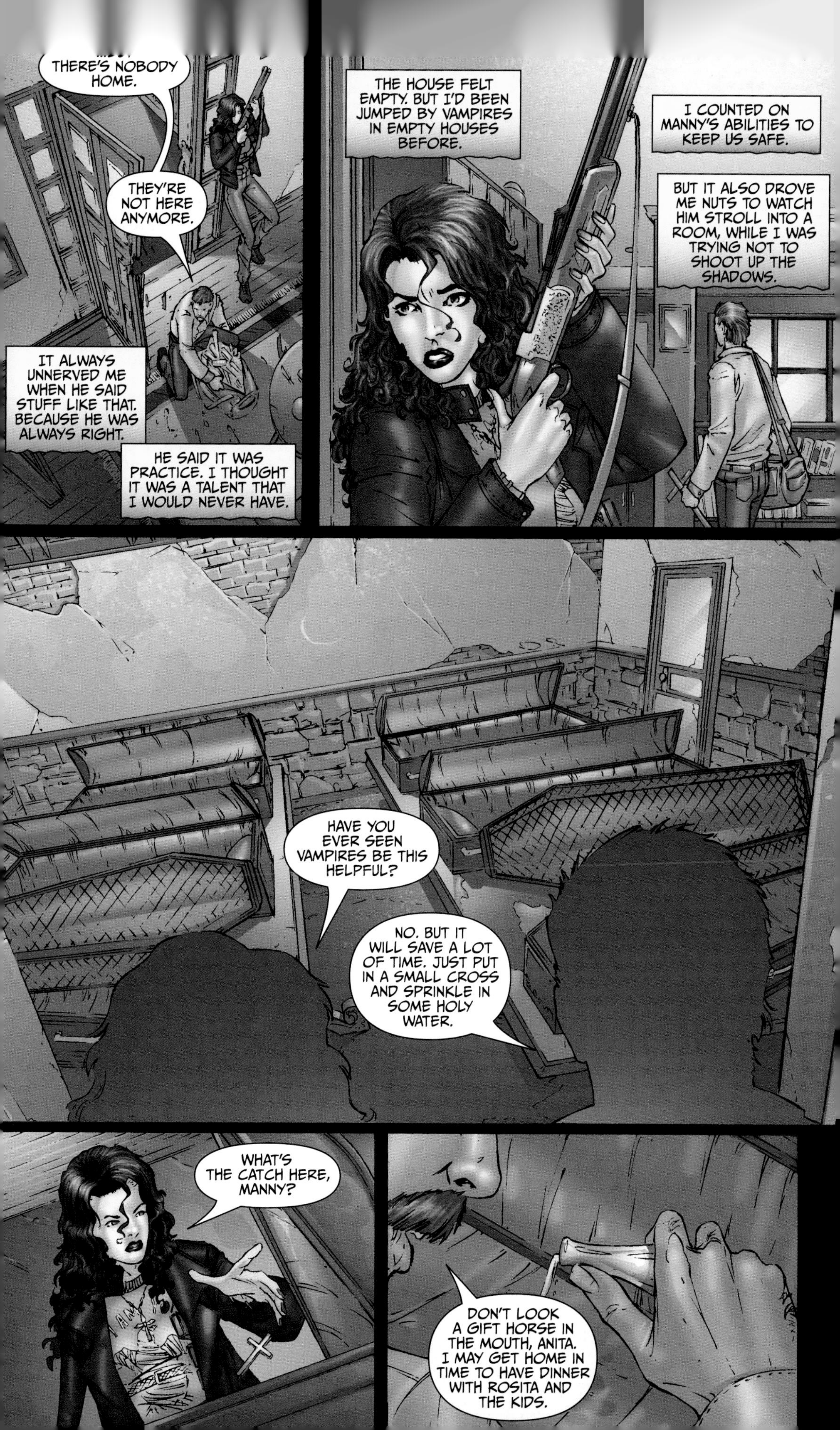
THERE'S NOBODY HOME.
THEY'RE NOT HERE ANYMORE.
IT ALWAYS UNNERVED ME WHEN HE SAID STUFF LIKE THAT. BECAUSE HE WAS ALWAYS RIGHT.
HE SAID IT WAS PRACTICE. I THOUGHT IT WAS A TALENT THAT I WOULD NEVER HAVE.
THE HOUSE FELT EMPTY. BUT I'D BEEN JUMPED BY VAMPIRES IN EMPTY HOUSES BEFORE.
I COUNTED ON MANNY'S ABILITIES TO KEEP US SAFE.
BUT IT ALSO DROVE ME NUTS TO WATCH HIM STROLL INTO A ROOM, WHILE I WAS TRYING NOT TO SHOOT UP THE SHADOWS.
HAVE YOU EVER SEEN VAMPIRES BE THIS HELPFUL?
NO. BUT IT WILL SAVE A LOT OF TIME. JUST PUT IN A SMALL CROSS AND SPRINKLE IN SOME HOLY WATER.
WHAT'S THE CATCH HERE, MANNY?
DON'T LOOK A GIFT HORSE IN THE MOUTH, ANITA. I MAY GET HOME IN TIME TO HAVE DINNER WITH ROSITA AND THE KIDS.

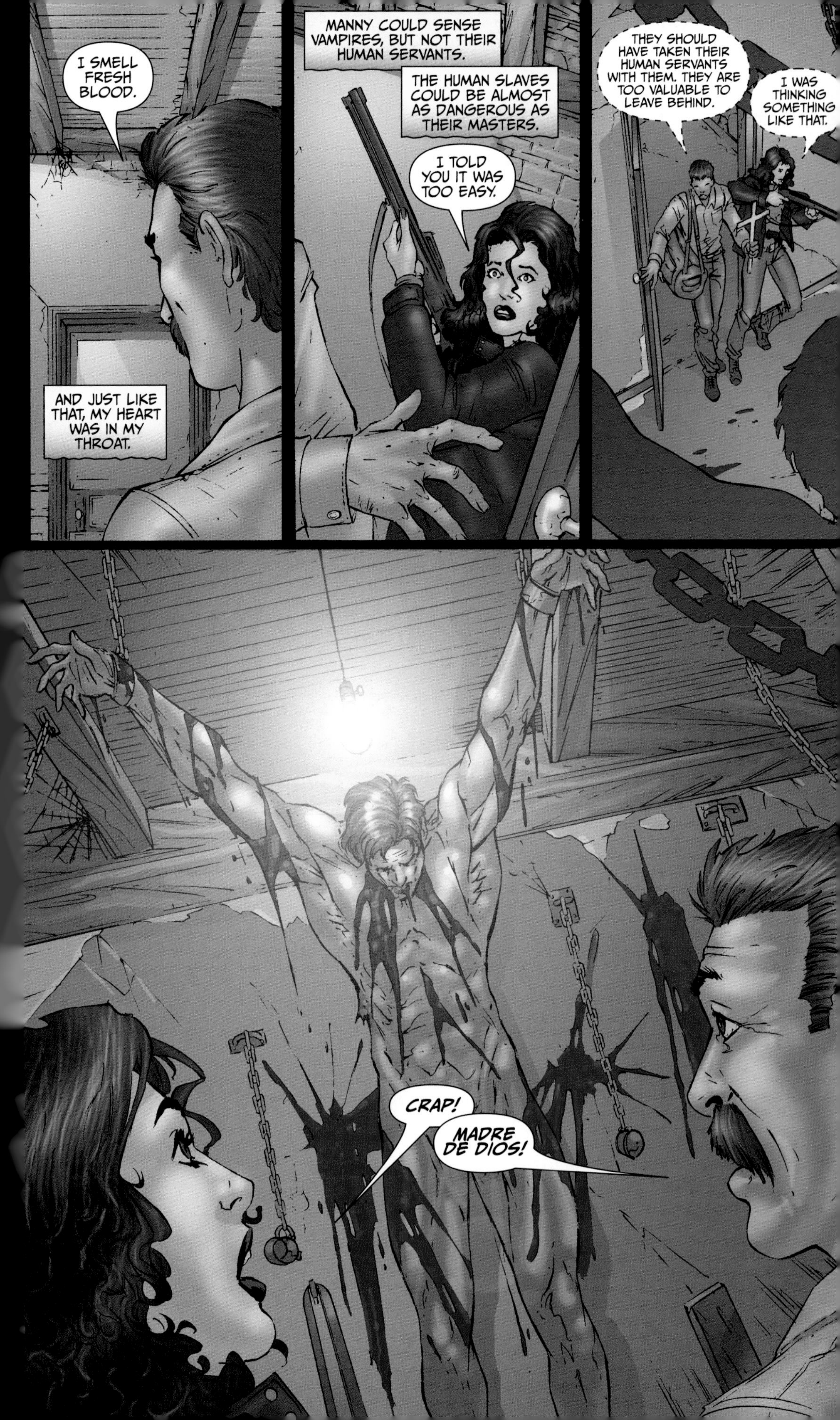
I SMELL FRESH BLOOD.
AND JUST LIKE THAT, MY HEART WAS IN MY THROAT.
MANNY COULD SENSE VAMPIRES, BUT NOT THEIR HUMAN SERVANTS.
THE HUMAN SLAVES COULD BE ALMOST AS DANGEROUS AS THEIR MASTERS.
I TOLD YOU IT WAS TOO EASY.
THEY SHOULD HAVE TAKEN THEIR HUMAN SERVANTS WITH THEM. THEY ARE TOO VALUABLE TO LEAVE BEHIND.
I WAS THINKING SOMETHING LIKE THAT.
CRAP!
MADRE DE DIOS!

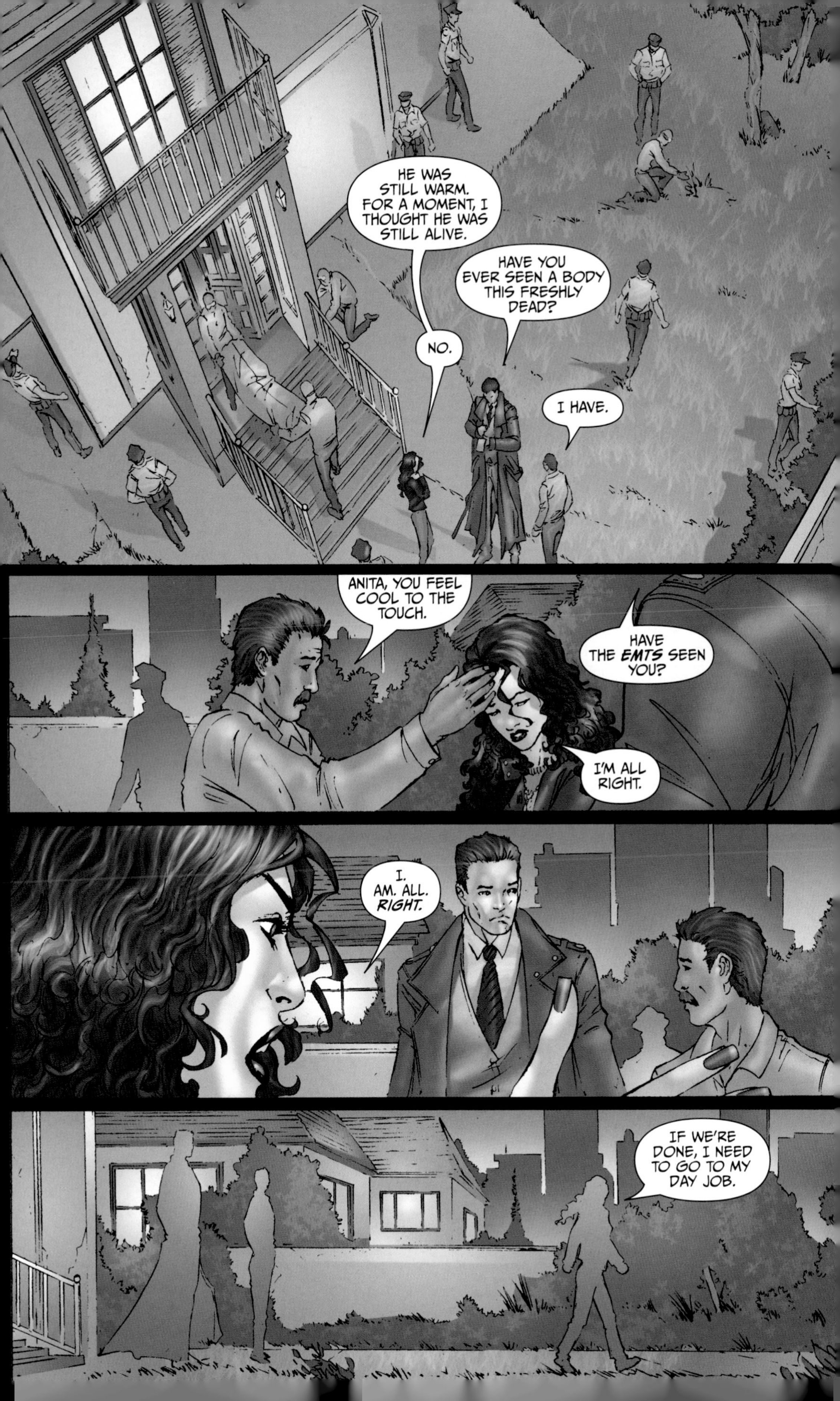
HE WAS STILL WARM. FOR A MOMENT, I THOUGHT HE WAS STILL ALIVE.
HAVE YOU EVER SEEN A BODY THIS FRESHLY DEAD?
NO.
I HAVE.
ANITA, YOU FEEL COOL TO THE TOUCH.
HAVE THE EMTS SEEN YOU?
I'M ALL RIGHT.
I. AM. ALL. RIGHT.
IF WE'RE DONE, I NEED TO GO TO MY DAY JOB.

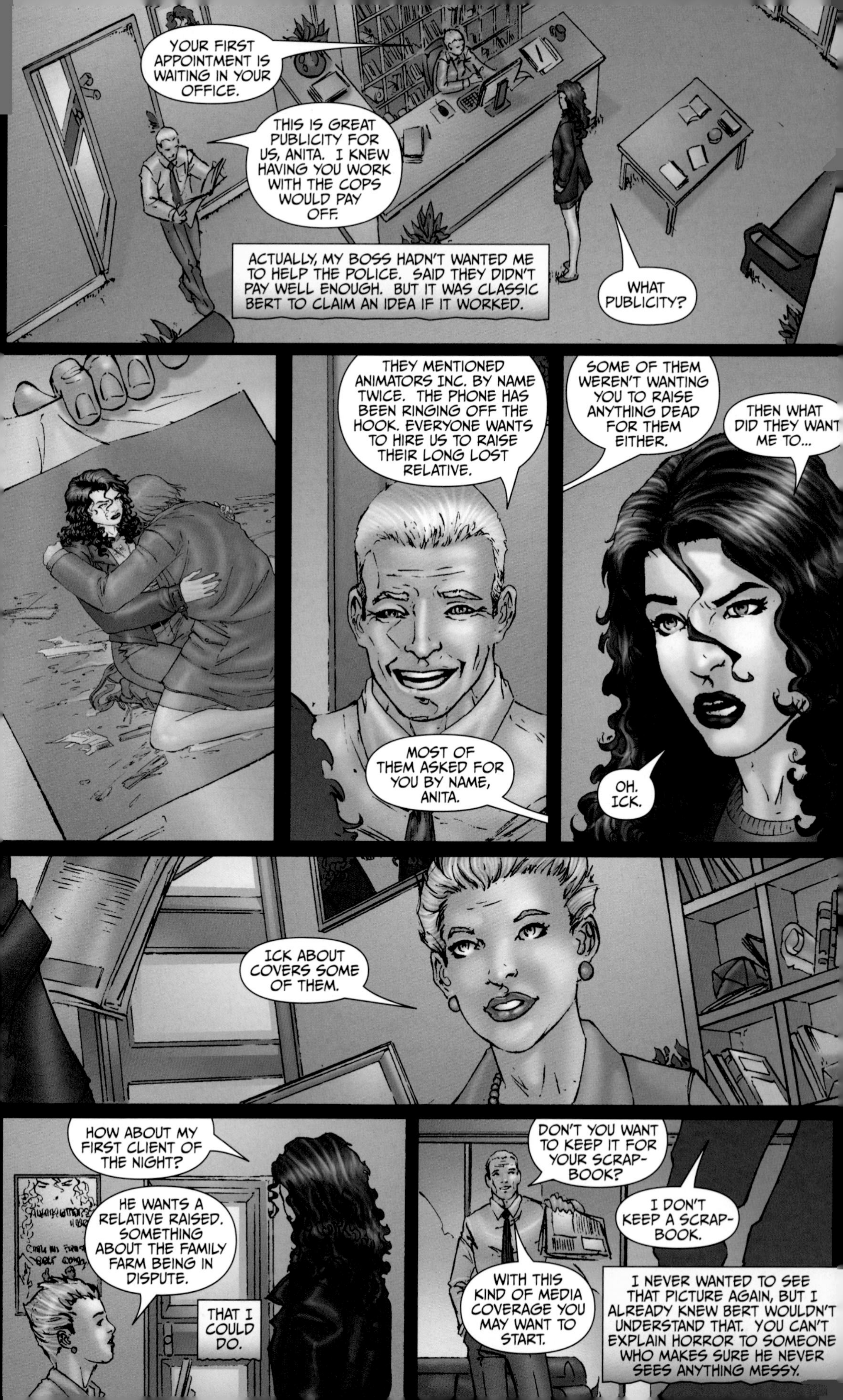
YOUR FIRST APPOINTMENT IS WAITING IN YOUR OFFICE.
THIS IS GREAT PUBLICITY FOR US, ANITA. I KNEW HAVING YOU WORK WITH THE COPS WOULD PAY OFF.
ACTUALLY, MY BOSS HADN'T WANTED ME TO HELP THE POLICE. SAID THEY DIDN'T PAY WELL ENOUGH. BUT IT WAS CLASSIC BERT TO CLAIM AN IDEA IF IT WORKED.
WHAT PUBLICITY?
THEY MENTIONED ANIMATORS INC. BY NAME TWICE. THE PHONE HAS BEEN RINGING OFF THE HOOK. EVERYONE WANTS TO HIRE US TO RAISE THEIR LONG LOST RELATIVE.
MOST OF THEM ASKED FOR YOU BY NAME, ANITA.
SOME OF THEM WEREN'T WANTING YOU TO RAISE ANYTHING DEAD FOR THEM EITHER.
THEN WHAT DID THEY WANT ME TO...
OH. ICK.
ICK ABOUT COVERS SOME OF THEM.
HOW ABOUT MY FIRST CLIENT OF THE NIGHT?
HE WANTS A RELATIVE RAISED. SOMETHING ABOUT THE FAMILY FARM BEING IN DISPUTE.
THAT I COULD DO.
DON'T YOU WANT TO KEEP IT FOR YOUR SCRAP-BOOK?
I DON'T KEEP A SCRAP-BOOK.
WITH THIS KIND OF MEDIA COVERAGE YOU MAY WANT TO START.
I NEVER WANTED TO SEE THAT PICTURE AGAIN, BUT I ALREADY KNEW BERT WOULDN'T UNDERSTAND THAT. YOU CAN'T EXPLAIN HORROR TO SOMEONE WHO MAKES SURE HE NEVER SEES ANYTHING MESSY.

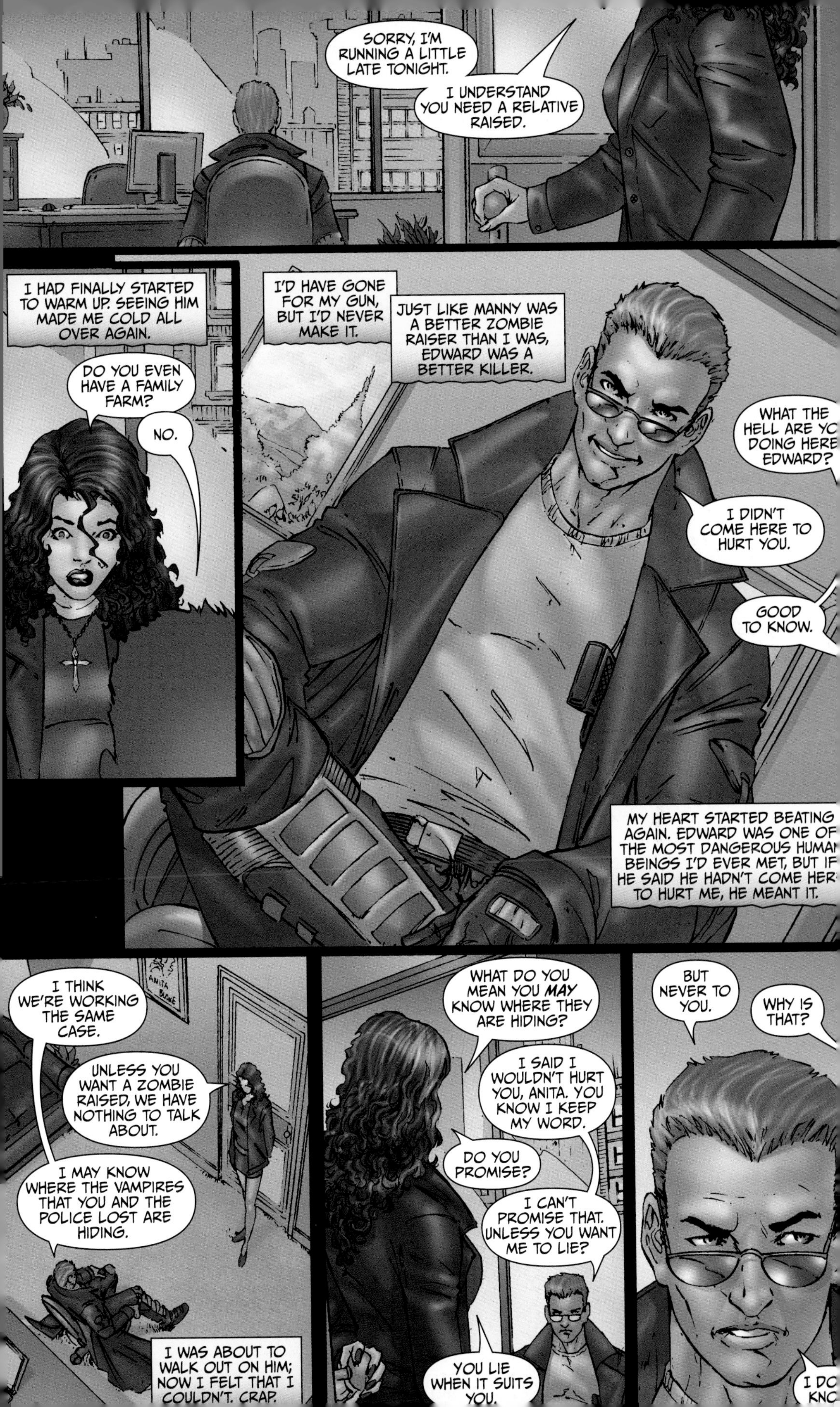

SORRY, I'M RUNNING A LITTLE LATE TONIGHT.
I UNDERSTAND YOU NEED A RELATIVE RAISED.
I HAD FINALLY STARTED TO WARM UP. SEEING HIM MADE ME COLD ALL OVER AGAIN.
I'D HAVE GONE FOR MY GUN, BUT I'D NEVER MAKE IT.
JUST LIKE MANNY WAS A BETTER ZOMBIE RAISER THAN I WAS, EDWARD WAS A BETTER KILLER.
DO YOU EVEN HAVE A FAMILY FARM?
NO.
WHAT THE HELL ARE YO DOING HERE EDWARD?
I DIDN'T COME HERE TO HURT YOU.
GOOD TO KNOW.
MY HEART STARTED BEATING AGAIN. EDWARD WAS ONE OF THE MOST DANGEROUS HUMA BEINGS I'D EVER MET, BUT IF HE SAID HE HADN'T COME HER TO HURT ME, HE MEANT IT.
I THINK WE'RE WORKING THE SAME CASE.
UNLESS YOU WANT A ZOMBIE RAISED, WE HAVE NOTHING TO TALK ABOUT.
I MAY KNOW WHERE THE VAMPIRES THAT YOU AND THE POLICE LOST ARE HIDING.
I WAS ABOUT TO WALK OUT ON HIM; NOW I FELT THAT I COULDN'T. CRAP.
WHAT DO YOU MEAN YOU *MAY* KNOW WHERE THEY ARE HIDING?
I SAID I WOULDN'T HURT YOU, ANITA. YOU KNOW I KEEP MY WORD.
DO YOU PROMISE?
I CAN'T PROMISE THAT. UNLESS YOU WANT ME TO LIE?
YOU LIE WHEN IT SUITS YOU.
BUT NEVER TO YOU.
WHY IS THAT?
I DO KNO

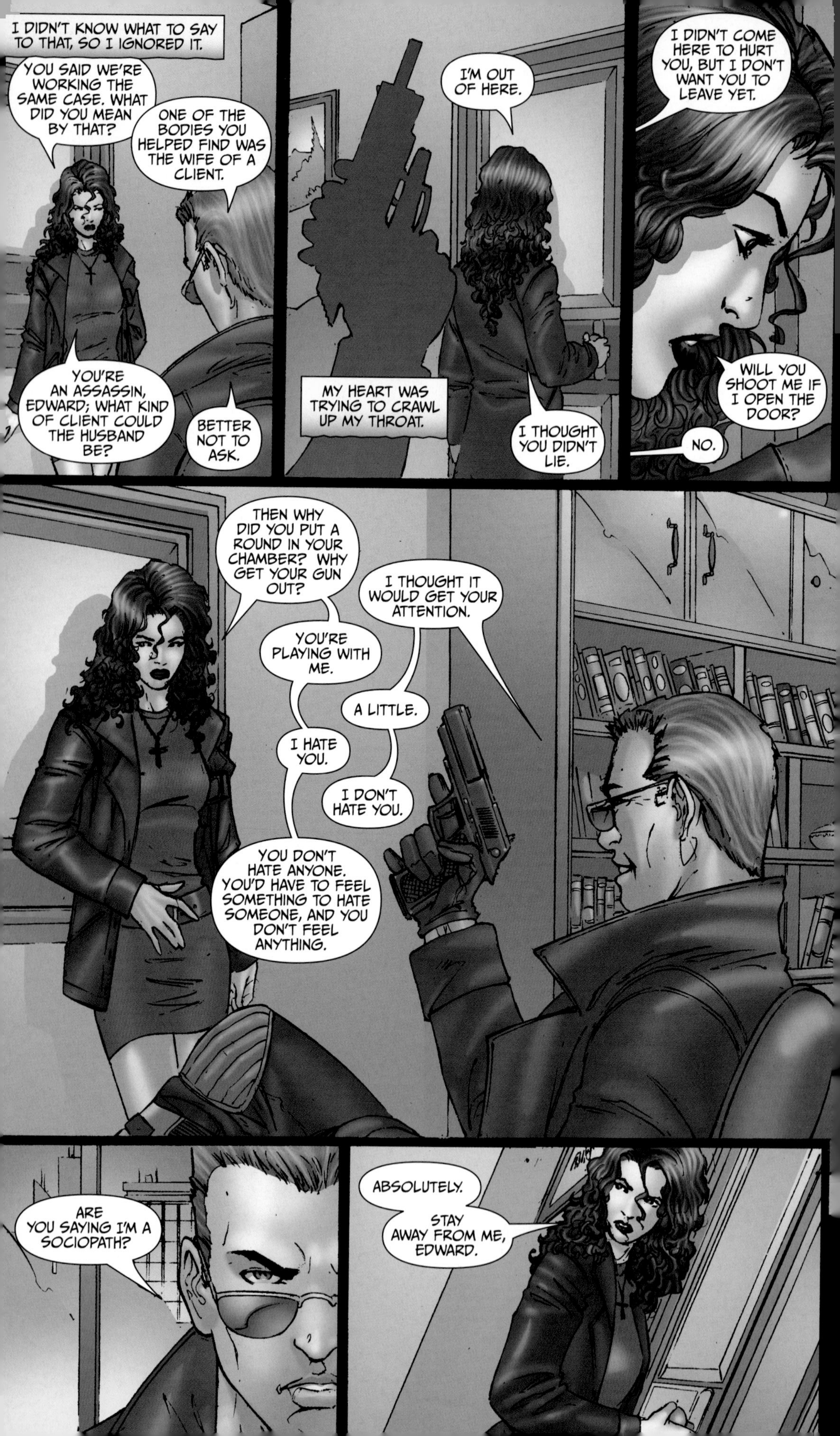
I DIDN'T KNOW WHAT TO SAY TO THAT, SO I IGNORED IT.
YOU SAID WE'RE WORKING THE SAME CASE. WHAT DID YOU MEAN BY THAT?
ONE OF THE BODIES YOU HELPED FIND WAS THE WIFE OF A CLIENT.
YOU'RE AN ASSASSIN, EDWARD; WHAT KIND OF CLIENT COULD THE HUSBAND BE?
BETTER NOT TO ASK.
I'M OUT OF HERE.
MY HEART WAS TRYING TO CRAWL UP MY THROAT.
I THOUGHT YOU DIDN'T LIE.
I DIDN'T COME HERE TO HURT YOU, BUT I DON'T WANT YOU TO LEAVE YET.
WILL YOU SHOOT ME IF I OPEN THE DOOR?
NO.
THEN WHY DID YOU PUT A ROUND IN YOUR CHAMBER? WHY GET YOUR GUN OUT?
I THOUGHT IT WOULD GET YOUR ATTENTION.
YOU'RE PLAYING WITH ME.
A LITTLE.
I HATE YOU.
I DON'T HATE YOU.
YOU DON'T HATE ANYONE. YOU'D HAVE TO FEEL SOMETHING TO HATE SOMEONE, AND YOU DON'T FEEL ANYTHING.
ARE YOU SAYING I'M A SOCIOPATH?
ABSOLUTELY.
STAY AWAY FROM ME, EDWARD.

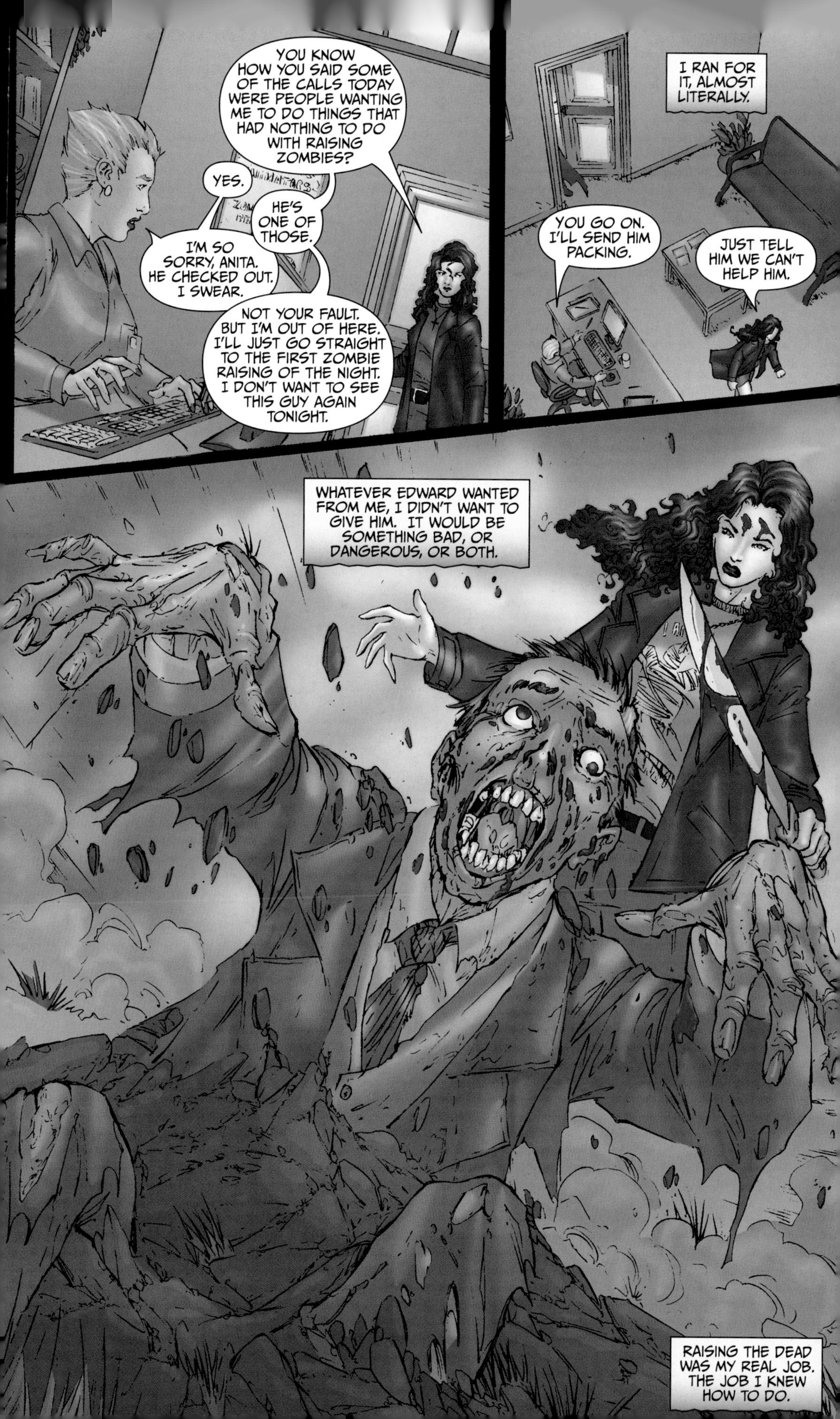

YOU KNOW HOW YOU SAID SOME OF THE CALLS TODAY WERE PEOPLE WANTING ME TO DO THINGS THAT HAD NOTHING TO DO WITH RAISING ZOMBIES?
YES.
HE'S ONE OF THOSE.
I'M SO SORRY, ANITA. HE CHECKED OUT. I SWEAR.
NOT YOUR FAULT. BUT I'M OUT OF HERE. I'LL JUST GO STRAIGHT TO THE FIRST ZOMBIE RAISING OF THE NIGHT. I DON'T WANT TO SEE THIS GUY AGAIN TONIGHT.
I RAN FOR IT, ALMOST LITERALLY.
YOU GO ON. I'LL SEND HIM PACKING.
JUST TELL HIM WE CAN'T HELP HIM.
WHATEVER EDWARD WANTED FROM ME, I DIDN'T WANT TO GIVE HIM. IT WOULD BE SOMETHING BAD, OR DANGEROUS, OR BOTH.
RAISING THE DEAD WAS MY REAL JOB. THE JOB I KNEW HOW TO DO.

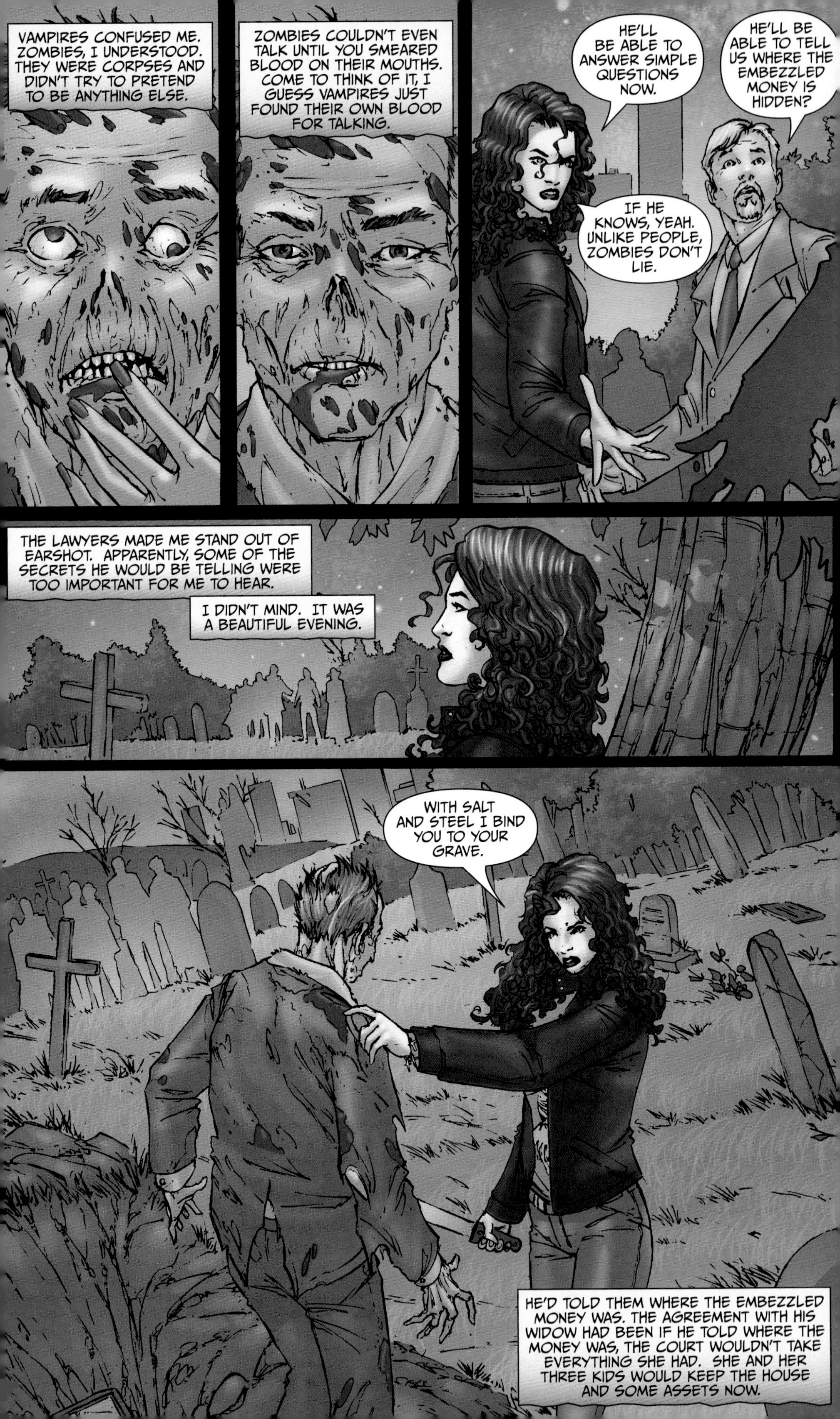
VAMPIRES CONFUSED ME. ZOMBIES, I UNDERSTOOD. THEY WERE CORPSES AND DIDN'T TRY TO PRETEND TO BE ANYTHING ELSE.
ZOMBIES COULDN'T EVEN TALK UNTIL YOU SMEARED BLOOD ON THEIR MOUTHS. COME TO THINK OF IT, I GUESS VAMPIRES JUST FOUND THEIR OWN BLOOD FOR TALKING.
HE'LL BE ABLE TO ANSWER SIMPLE QUESTIONS NOW.
HE'LL BE ABLE TO TELL US WHERE THE EMBEZZLED MONEY IS HIDDEN?
IF HE KNOWS, YEAH. UNLIKE PEOPLE, ZOMBIES DON'T LIE.
THE LAWYERS MADE ME STAND OUT OF EARSHOT. APPARENTLY, SOME OF THE SECRETS HE WOULD BE TELLING WERE TOO IMPORTANT FOR ME TO HEAR.
I DIDN'T MIND. IT WAS A BEAUTIFUL EVENING.
WITH SALT AND STEEL I BIND YOU TO YOUR GRAVE.
HE'D TOLD THEM WHERE THE EMBEZZLED MONEY WAS. THE AGREEMENT WITH HIS WIDOW HAD BEEN IF HE TOLD WHERE THE MONEY WAS, THE COURT WOULDN'T TAKE EVERYTHING SHE HAD. SHE AND HER THREE KIDS WOULD KEEP THE HOUSE AND SOME ASSETS NOW.

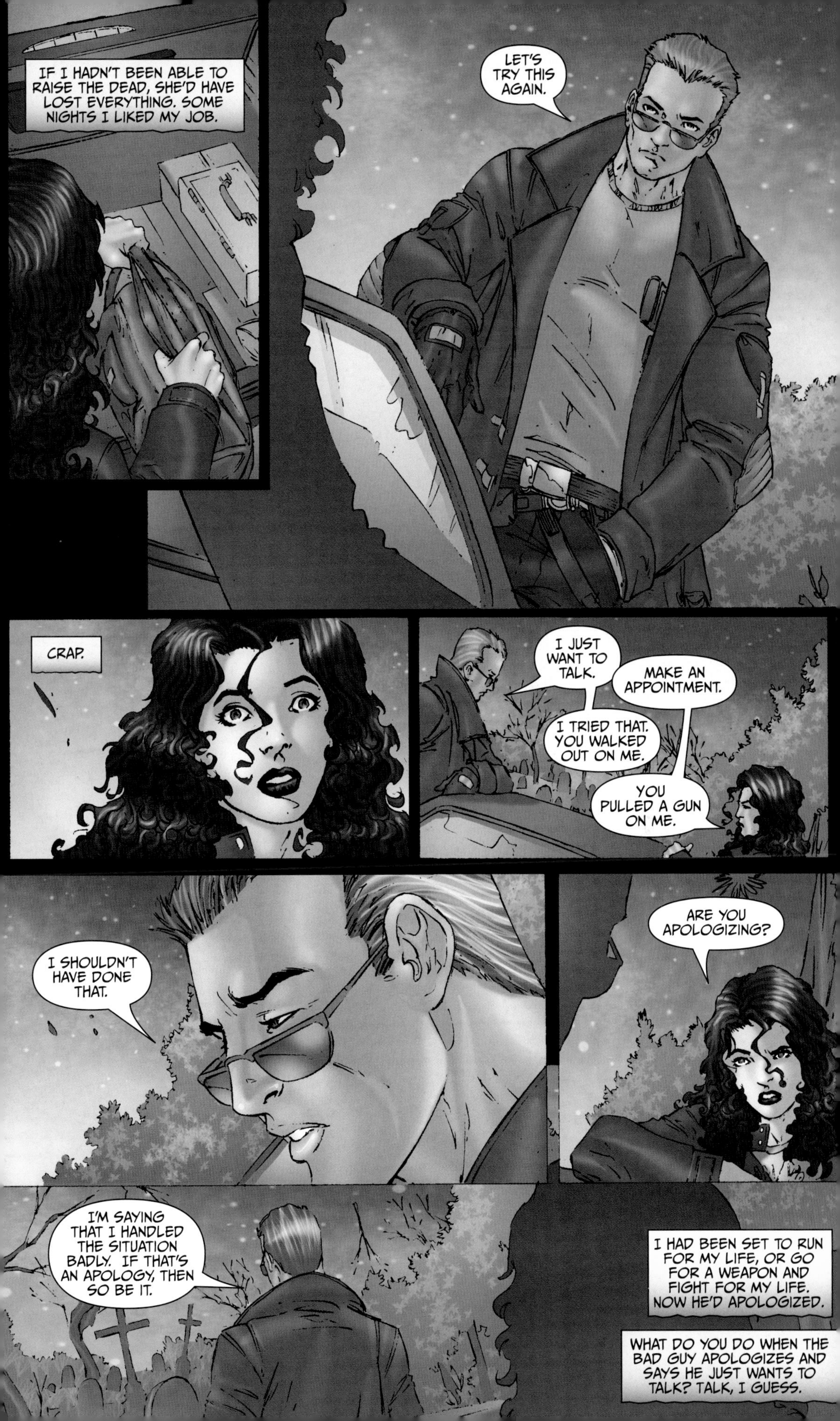
IF I HADN'T BEEN ABLE TO RAISE THE DEAD, SHE'D HAVE LOST EVERYTHING. SOME NIGHTS I LIKED MY JOB.
LET'S TRY THIS AGAIN.
CRAP.
I JUST WANT TO TALK.
MAKE AN APPOINTMENT.
I TRIED THAT. YOU WALKED OUT ON ME.
YOU PULLED A GUN ON ME.
I SHOULDN'T HAVE DONE THAT.
ARE YOU APOLOGIZING?
I'M SAYING THAT I HANDLED THE SITUATION BADLY. IF THAT'S AN APOLOGY, THEN SO BE IT.
I HAD BEEN SET TO RUN FOR MY LIFE, OR GO FOR A WEAPON AND FIGHT FOR MY LIFE. NOW HE'D APOLOGIZED.
WHAT DO YOU DO WHEN THE BAD GUY APOLOGIZES AND SAYS HE JUST WANTS TO TALK? TALK, I GUESS.

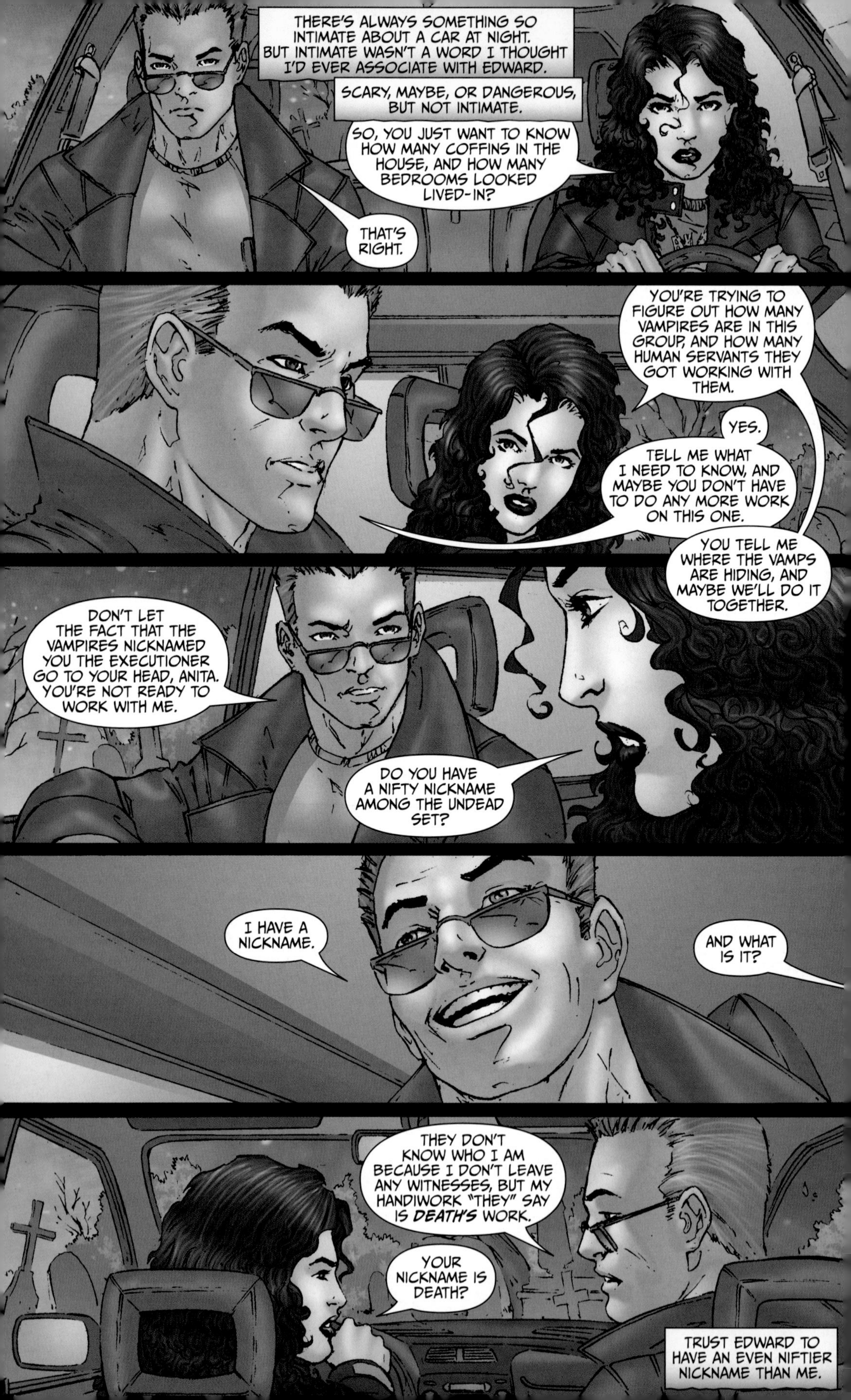
THERE'S ALWAYS SOMETHING SO INTIMATE ABOUT A CAR AT NIGHT. BUT INTIMATE WASN'T A WORD I THOUGHT I'D EVER ASSOCIATE WITH EDWARD.
SCARY, MAYBE, OR DANGEROUS, BUT NOT INTIMATE.
SO, YOU JUST WANT TO KNOW HOW MANY COFFINS IN THE HOUSE, AND HOW MANY BEDROOMS LOOKED LIVED-IN?
THAT'S RIGHT.
YOU'RE TRYING TO FIGURE OUT HOW MANY VAMPIRES ARE IN THIS GROUP, AND HOW MANY HUMAN SERVANTS THEY GOT WORKING WITH THEM.
YES.
TELL ME WHAT I NEED TO KNOW, AND MAYBE YOU DON'T HAVE TO DO ANY MORE WORK ON THIS ONE.
YOU TELL ME WHERE THE VAMPS ARE HIDING, AND MAYBE WE'LL DO IT TOGETHER.
DON'T LET THE FACT THAT THE VAMPIRES NICKNAMED YOU THE EXECUTIONER GO TO YOUR HEAD, ANITA. YOU'RE NOT READY TO WORK WITH ME.
DO YOU HAVE A NIFTY NICKNAME AMONG THE UNDEAD SET?
I HAVE A NICKNAME.
AND WHAT IS IT?
THEY DON'T KNOW WHO I AM BECAUSE I DON'T LEAVE ANY WITNESSES, BUT MY HANDIWORK "THEY" SAY IS *DEATH'S* WORK.
YOUR NICKNAME IS DEATH?
TRUST EDWARD TO HAVE AN EVEN NIFTIER NICKNAME THAN ME.

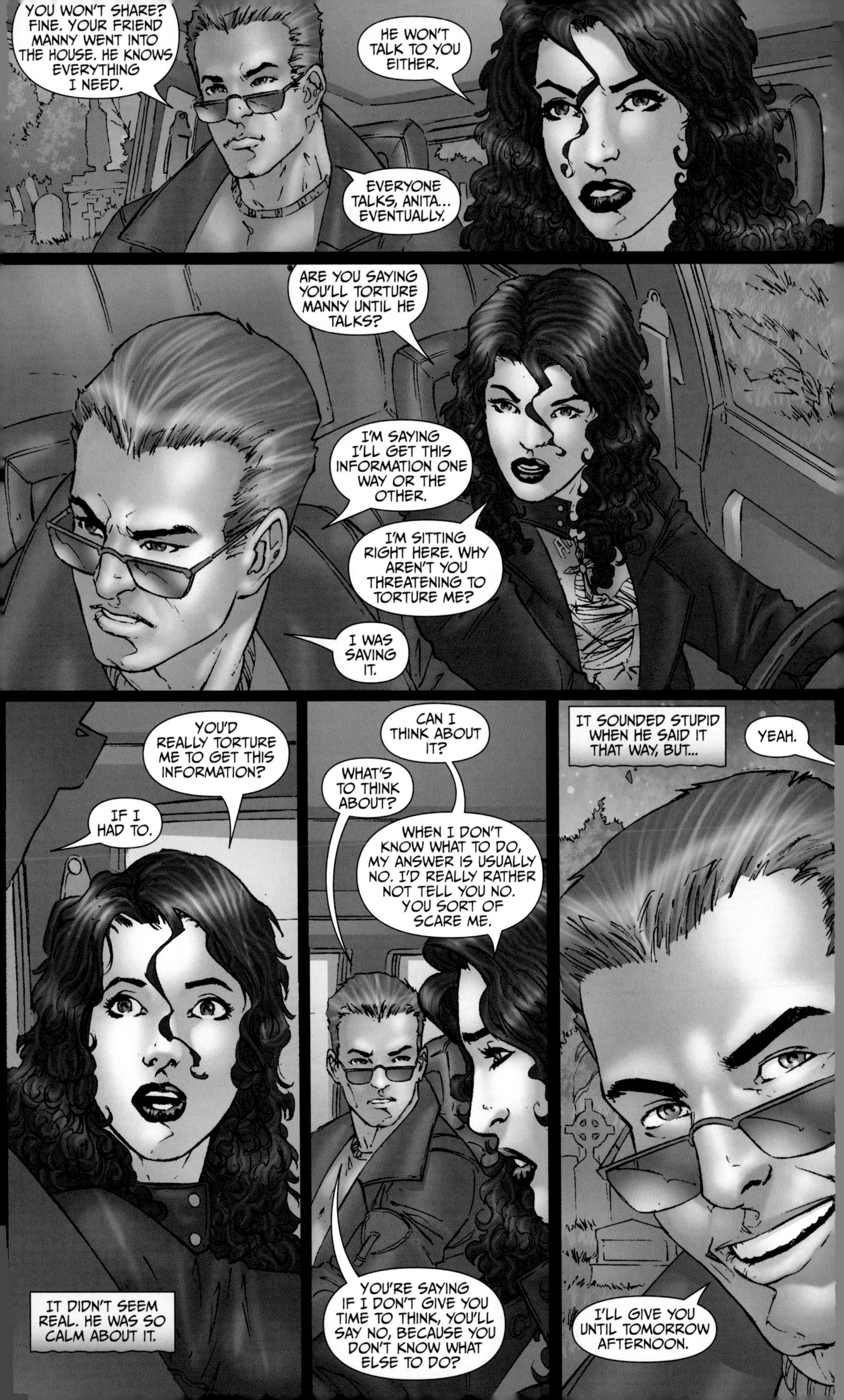
YOU WON'T SHARE? FINE. YOUR FRIEND MANNY WENT INTO THE HOUSE. HE KNOWS EVERYTHING I NEED.
HE WON'T TALK TO YOU EITHER.
EVERYONE TALKS, ANITA... EVENTUALLY.
ARE YOU SAYING YOU'LL TORTURE MANNY UNTIL HE TALKS?
I'M SAYING I'LL GET THIS INFORMATION ONE WAY OR THE OTHER.
I'M SITTING RIGHT HERE. WHY AREN'T YOU THREATENING TO TORTURE ME?
I WAS SAVING IT.
YOU'D REALLY TORTURE ME TO GET THIS INFORMATION?
IF I HAD TO.
IT DIDN'T SEEM REAL. HE WAS SO CALM ABOUT IT.
CAN I THINK ABOUT IT?
WHAT'S TO THINK ABOUT?
WHEN I DON'T KNOW WHAT TO DO, MY ANSWER IS USUALLY NO. I'D REALLY RATHER NOT TELL YOU NO. YOU SORT OF SCARE ME.
YOU'RE SAYING IF I DON'T GIVE YOU TIME TO THINK, YOU'LL SAY NO, BECAUSE YOU DON'T KNOW WHAT ELSE TO DO?
IT SOUNDED STUPID WHEN HE SAID IT THAT WAY, BUT...
YEAH.
I'LL GIVE YOU UNTIL TOMORROW AFTERNOON.

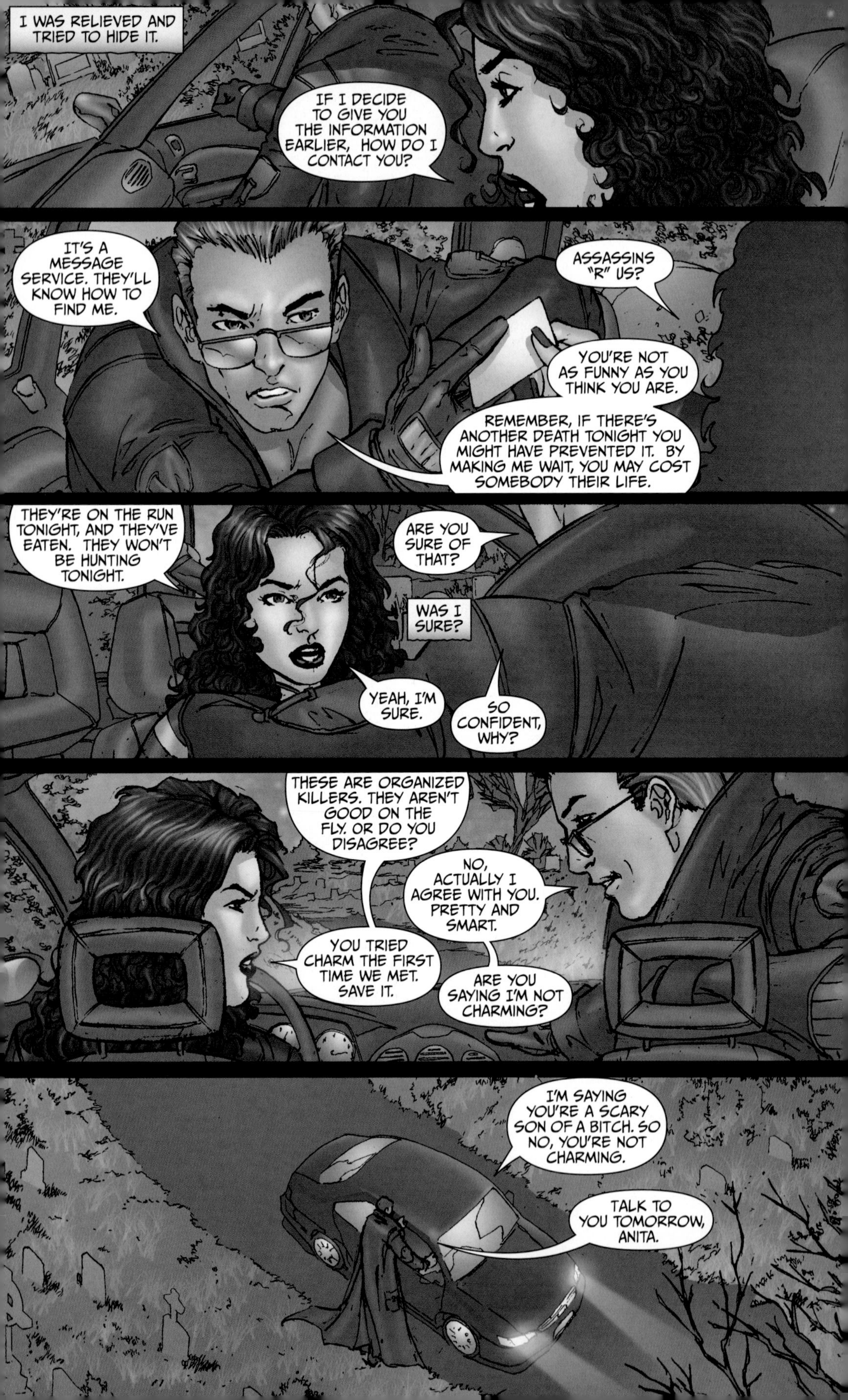
I WAS RELIEVED AND TRIED TO HIDE IT.
IF I DECIDE TO GIVE YOU THE INFORMATION EARLIER, HOW DO I CONTACT YOU?
IT'S A MESSAGE SERVICE. THEY'LL KNOW HOW TO FIND ME.
ASSASSINS "R" US?
YOU'RE NOT AS FUNNY AS YOU THINK YOU ARE.
REMEMBER, IF THERE'S ANOTHER DEATH TONIGHT YOU MIGHT HAVE PREVENTED IT. BY MAKING ME WAIT, YOU MAY COST SOMEBODY THEIR LIFE.
THEY'RE ON THE RUN TONIGHT, AND THEY'VE EATEN. THEY WON'T BE HUNTING TONIGHT.
ARE YOU SURE OF THAT?
WAS I SURE?
YEAH, I'M SURE.
SO CONFIDENT, WHY?
THESE ARE ORGANIZED KILLERS. THEY AREN'T GOOD ON THE FLY. OR DO YOU DISAGREE?
NO, ACTUALLY I AGREE WITH YOU. PRETTY AND SMART.
YOU TRIED CHARM THE FIRST TIME WE MET. SAVE IT.
ARE YOU SAYING I'M NOT CHARMING?
I'M SAYING YOU'RE A SCARY SON OF A BITCH. SO NO, YOU'RE NOT CHARMING.
TALK TO YOU TOMORROW, ANITA.

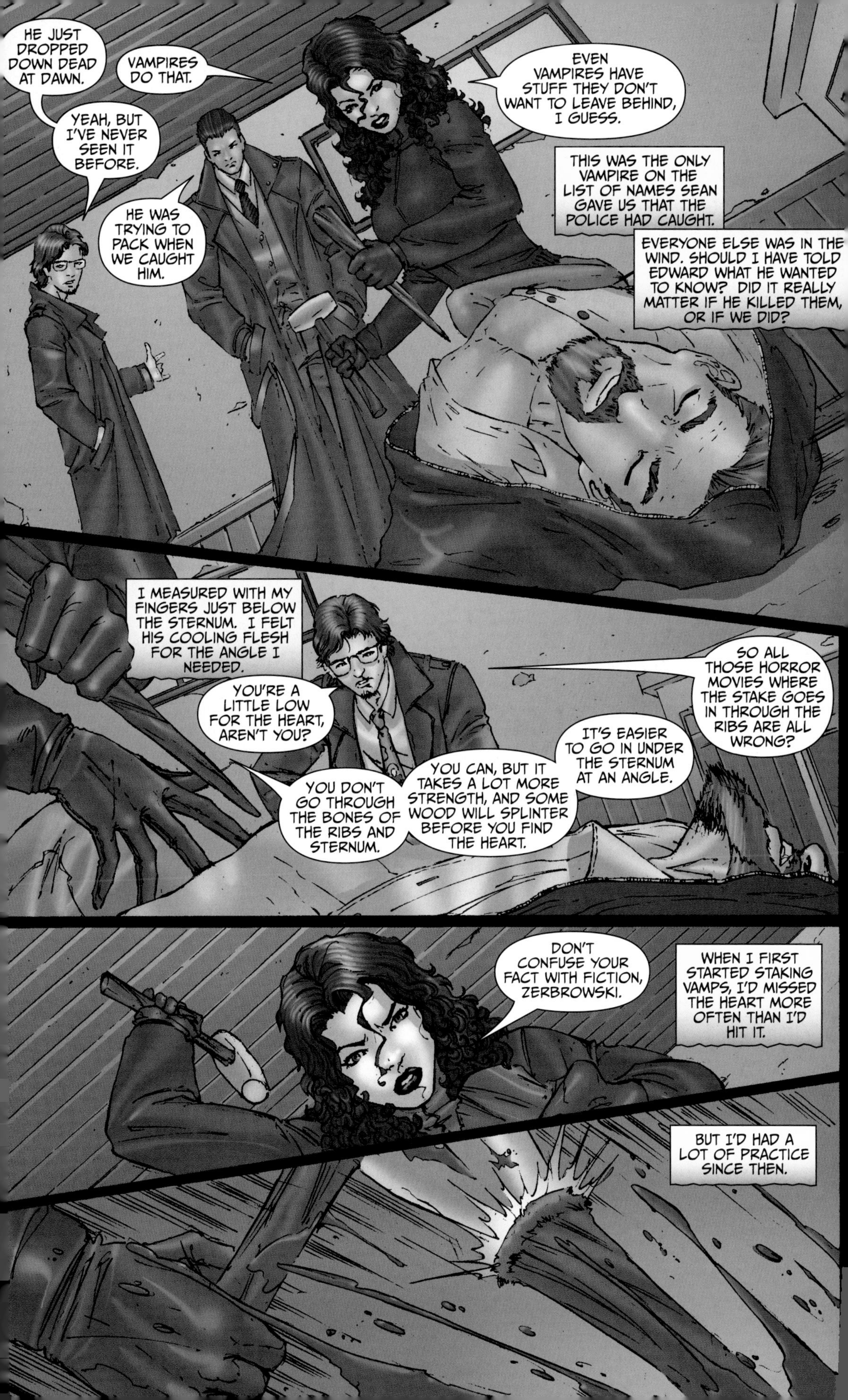
HE JUST DROPPED DOWN DEAD AT DAWN.
VAMPIRES DO THAT.
YEAH, BUT I'VE NEVER SEEN IT BEFORE.
EVEN VAMPIRES HAVE STUFF THEY DON'T WANT TO LEAVE BEHIND, I GUESS.
HE WAS TRYING TO PACK WHEN WE CAUGHT HIM.
THIS WAS THE ONLY VAMPIRE ON THE LIST OF NAMES SEAN GAVE US THAT THE POLICE HAD CAUGHT.
EVERYONE ELSE WAS IN THE WIND. SHOULD I HAVE TOLD EDWARD WHAT HE WANTED TO KNOW? DID IT REALLY MATTER IF HE KILLED THEM, OR IF WE DID?
I MEASURED WITH MY FINGERS JUST BELOW THE STERNUM. I FELT HIS COOLING FLESH FOR THE ANGLE I NEEDED.
YOU'RE A LITTLE LOW FOR THE HEART, AREN'T YOU?
YOU DON'T GO THROUGH THE BONES OF THE RIBS AND STERNUM.
YOU CAN, BUT IT TAKES A LOT MORE STRENGTH, AND SOME WOOD WILL SPLINTER BEFORE YOU FIND THE HEART.
IT'S EASIER TO GO IN UNDER THE STERNUM AT AN ANGLE.
SO ALL THOSE HORROR MOVIES WHERE THE STAKE GOES IN THROUGH THE RIBS ARE ALL WRONG?
DON'T CONFUSE YOUR FACT WITH FICTION, ZERBROWSKI.
WHEN I FIRST STARTED STAKING VAMPS, I'D MISSED THE HEART MORE OFTEN THAN I'D HIT IT.
BUT I'D HAD A LOT OF PRACTICE SINCE THEN.

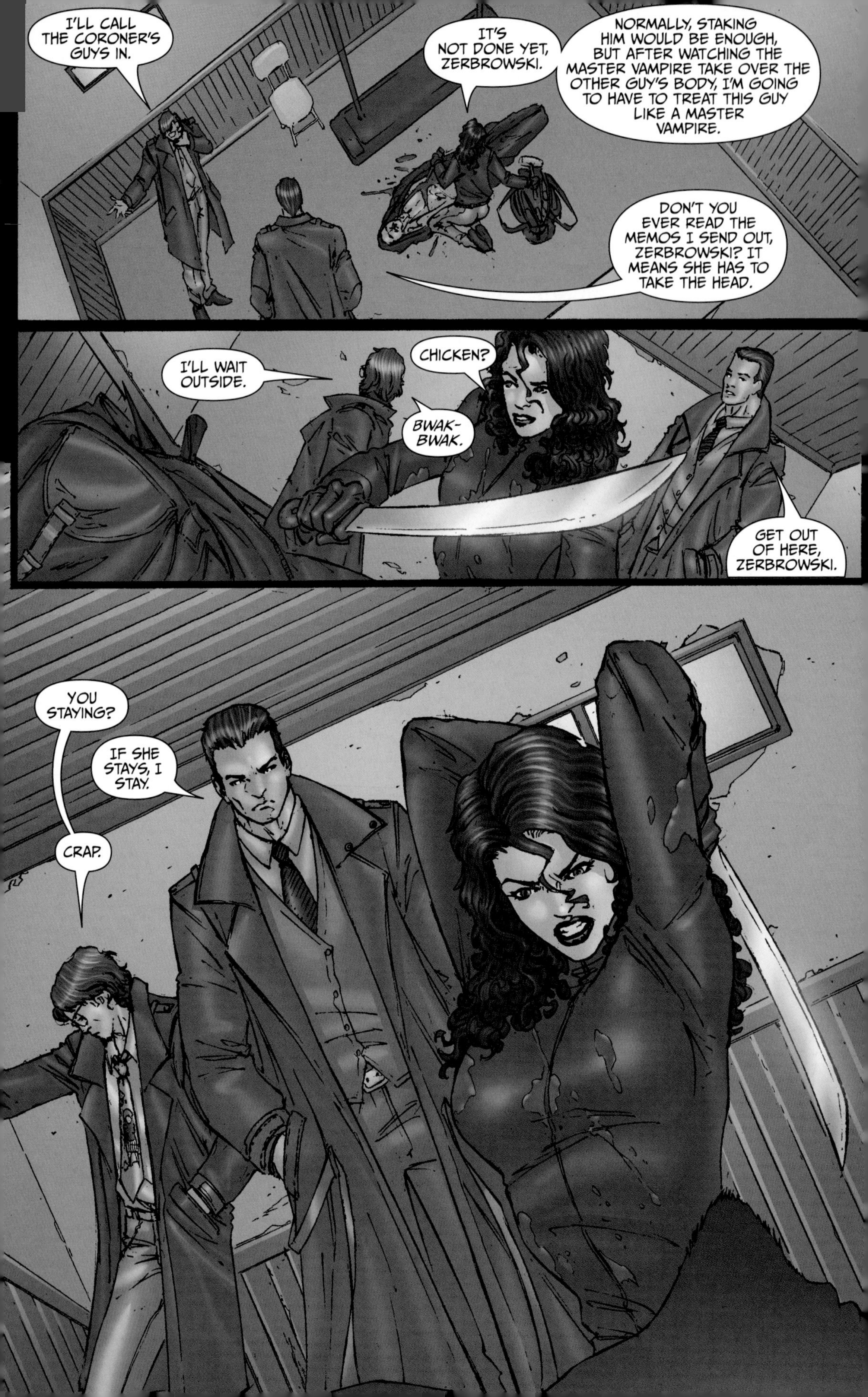
I'LL CALL THE CORONER'S GUYS IN.
IT'S NOT DONE YET, ZERBROWSKI.
NORMALLY, STAKING HIM WOULD BE ENOUGH, BUT AFTER WATCHING THE MASTER VAMPIRE TAKE OVER THE OTHER GUY'S BODY, I'M GOING TO HAVE TO TREAT THIS GUY LIKE A MASTER VAMPIRE.
DON'T YOU EVER READ THE MEMOS I SEND OUT, ZERBROWSKI? IT MEANS SHE HAS TO TAKE THE HEAD.
I'LL WAIT OUTSIDE.
CHICKEN?
BWAK-BWAK.
GET OUT OF HERE, ZERBROWSKI.
YOU STAYING?
IF SHE STAYS, I STAY.
CRAP.

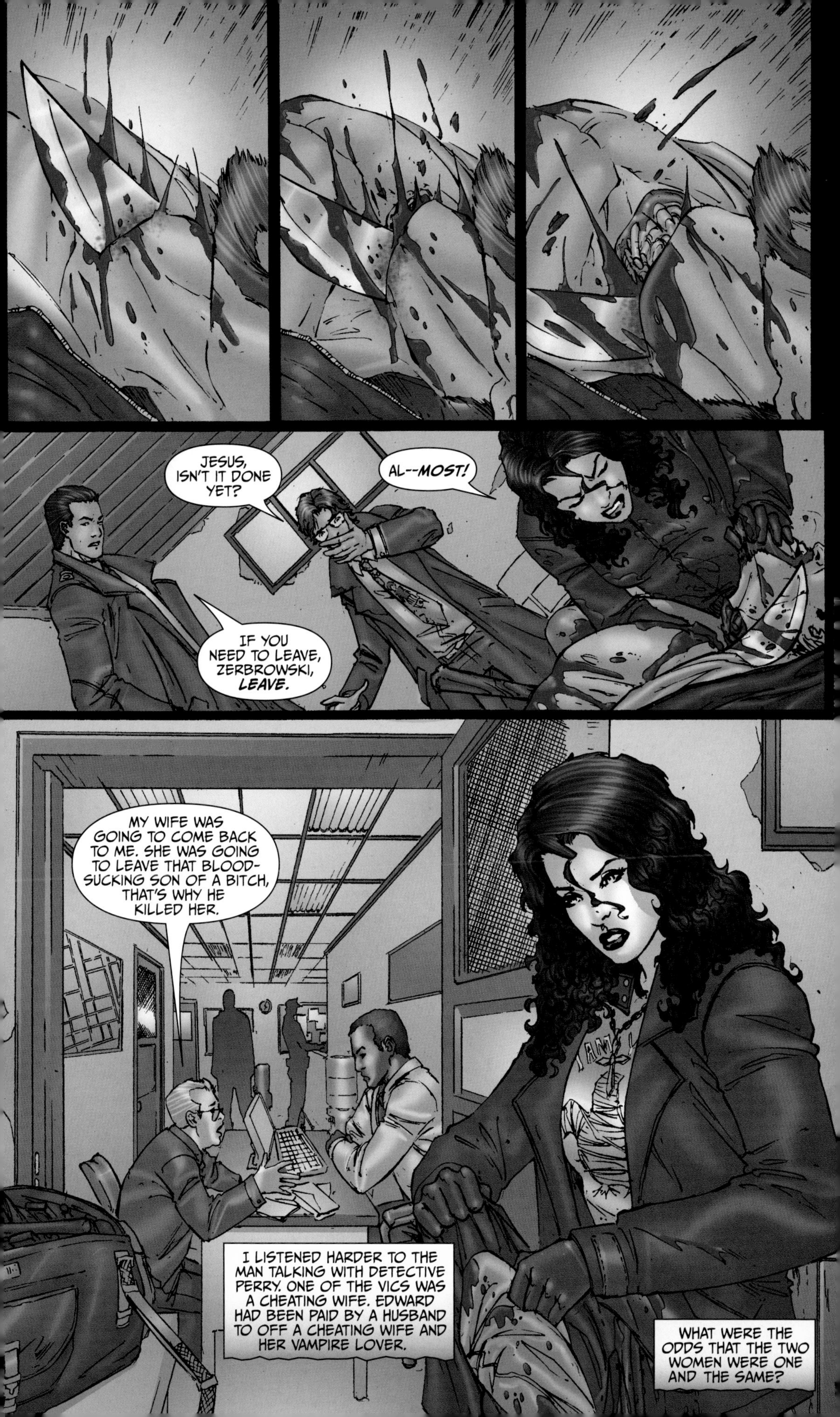
JESUS, ISN'T IT DONE YET?
AL--*MOST!*
IF YOU NEED TO LEAVE, ZERBROWSKI, ***LEAVE.***
MY WIFE WAS GOING TO COME BACK TO ME. SHE WAS GOING TO LEAVE THAT BLOOD-SUCKING SON OF A BITCH, THAT'S WHY HE KILLED HER.
I LISTENED HARDER TO THE MAN TALKING WITH DETECTIVE PERRY. ONE OF THE VICS WAS A CHEATING WIFE. EDWARD HAD BEEN PAID BY A HUSBAND TO OFF A CHEATING WIFE AND HER VAMPIRE LOVER.
WHAT WERE THE ODDS THAT THE TWO WOMEN WERE ONE AND THE SAME?

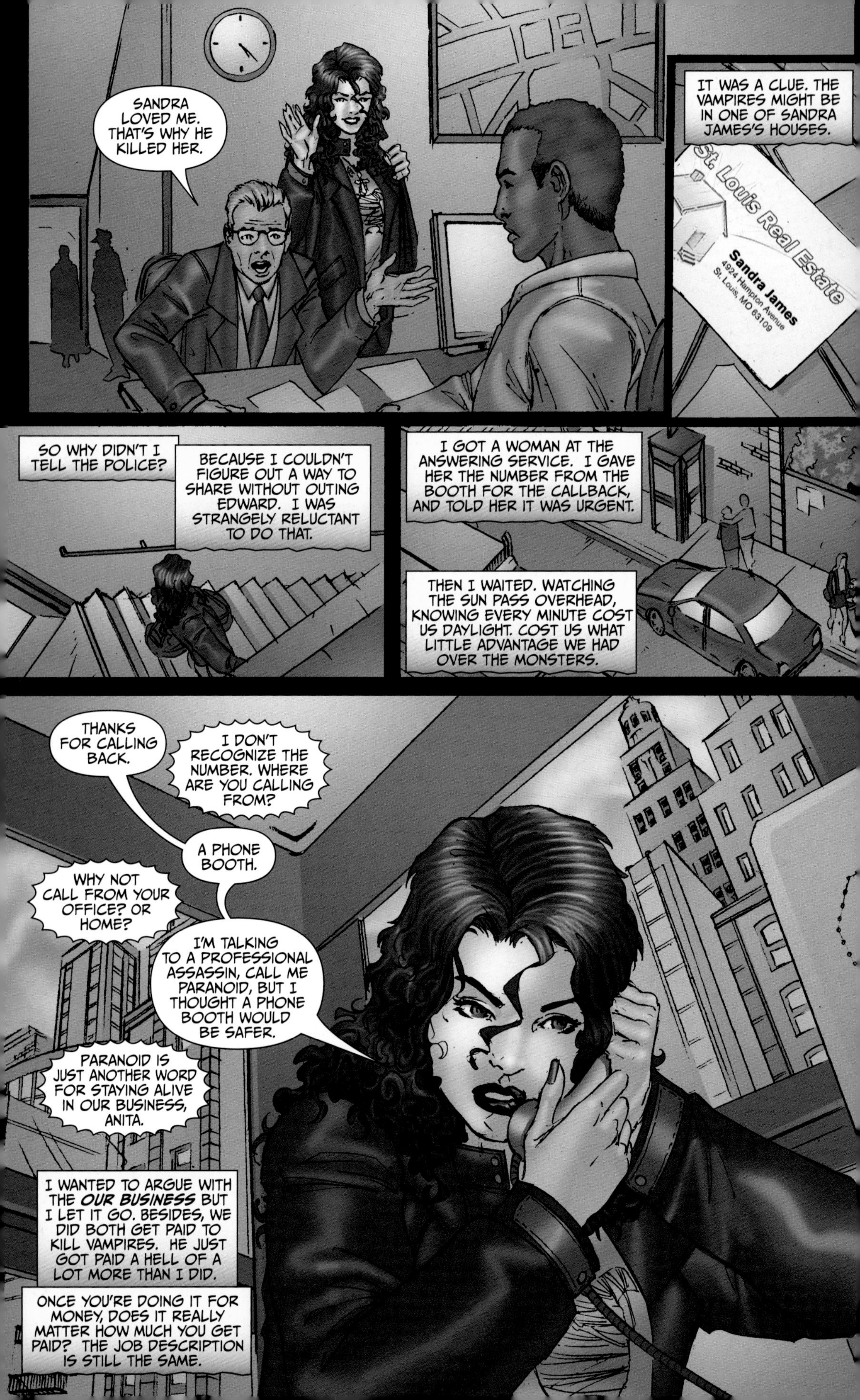
SANDRA LOVED ME. THAT'S WHY HE KILLED HER.
IT WAS A CLUE. THE VAMPIRES MIGHT BE IN ONE OF SANDRA JAMES'S HOUSES.
St. Louis Real Estate
Sandra James
4924 Hampton Avenue
St. Louis, MO 63109
SO WHY DIDN'T I TELL THE POLICE?
BECAUSE I COULDN'T FIGURE OUT A WAY TO SHARE WITHOUT OUTING EDWARD. I WAS STRANGELY RELUCTANT TO DO THAT.
I GOT A WOMAN AT THE ANSWERING SERVICE. I GAVE HER THE NUMBER FROM THE BOOTH FOR THE CALLBACK, AND TOLD HER IT WAS URGENT.
THEN I WAITED. WATCHING THE SUN PASS OVERHEAD, KNOWING EVERY MINUTE COST US DAYLIGHT. COST US WHAT LITTLE ADVANTAGE WE HAD OVER THE MONSTERS.
THANKS FOR CALLING BACK.
I DON'T RECOGNIZE THE NUMBER. WHERE ARE YOU CALLING FROM?
A PHONE BOOTH.
WHY NOT CALL FROM YOUR OFFICE? OR HOME?
I'M TALKING TO A PROFESSIONAL ASSASSIN, CALL ME PARANOID, BUT I THOUGHT A PHONE BOOTH WOULD BE SAFER.
PARANOID IS JUST ANOTHER WORD FOR STAYING ALIVE IN OUR BUSINESS, ANITA.
I WANTED TO ARGUE WITH THE *OUR BUSINESS* BUT I LET IT GO. BESIDES, WE DID BOTH GET PAID TO KILL VAMPIRES. HE JUST GOT PAID A HELL OF A LOT MORE THAN I DID.
ONCE YOU'RE DOING IT FOR MONEY, DOES IT REALLY MATTER HOW MUCH YOU GET PAID? THE JOB DESCRIPTION IS STILL THE SAME.

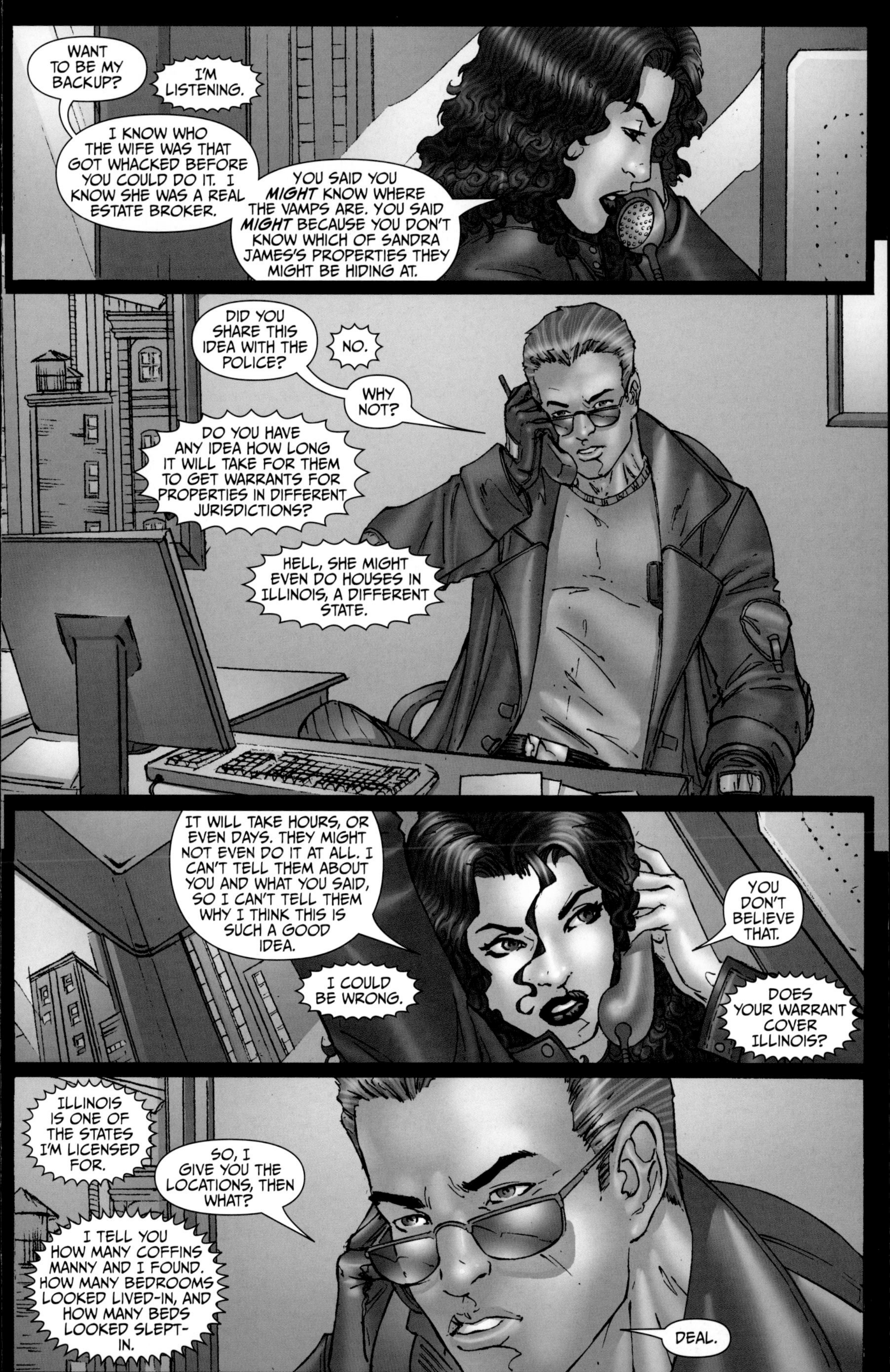
WANT TO BE MY BACKUP?
I'M LISTENING.
I KNOW WHO THE WIFE WAS THAT GOT WHACKED BEFORE YOU COULD DO IT. I KNOW SHE WAS A REAL ESTATE BROKER.
YOU SAID YOU *MIGHT* KNOW WHERE THE VAMPS ARE. YOU SAID *MIGHT* BECAUSE YOU DON'T KNOW WHICH OF SANDRA JAMES'S PROPERTIES THEY MIGHT BE HIDING AT.
DID YOU SHARE THIS IDEA WITH THE POLICE?
NO.
WHY NOT?
DO YOU HAVE ANY IDEA HOW LONG IT WILL TAKE FOR THEM TO GET WARRANTS FOR PROPERTIES IN DIFFERENT JURISDICTIONS?
HELL, SHE MIGHT EVEN DO HOUSES IN ILLINOIS, A DIFFERENT STATE.
IT WILL TAKE HOURS, OR EVEN DAYS. THEY MIGHT NOT EVEN DO IT AT ALL. I CAN'T TELL THEM ABOUT YOU AND WHAT YOU SAID, SO I CAN'T TELL THEM WHY I THINK THIS IS SUCH A GOOD IDEA.
YOU DON'T BELIEVE THAT.
I COULD BE WRONG.
DOES YOUR WARRANT COVER ILLINOIS?
ILLINOIS IS ONE OF THE STATES I'M LICENSED FOR.
SO, I GIVE YOU THE LOCATIONS, THEN WHAT?
I TELL YOU HOW MANY COFFINS MANNY AND I FOUND. HOW MANY BEDROOMS LOOKED LIVED-IN, AND HOW MANY BEDS LOOKED SLEPT-IN.
DEAL.

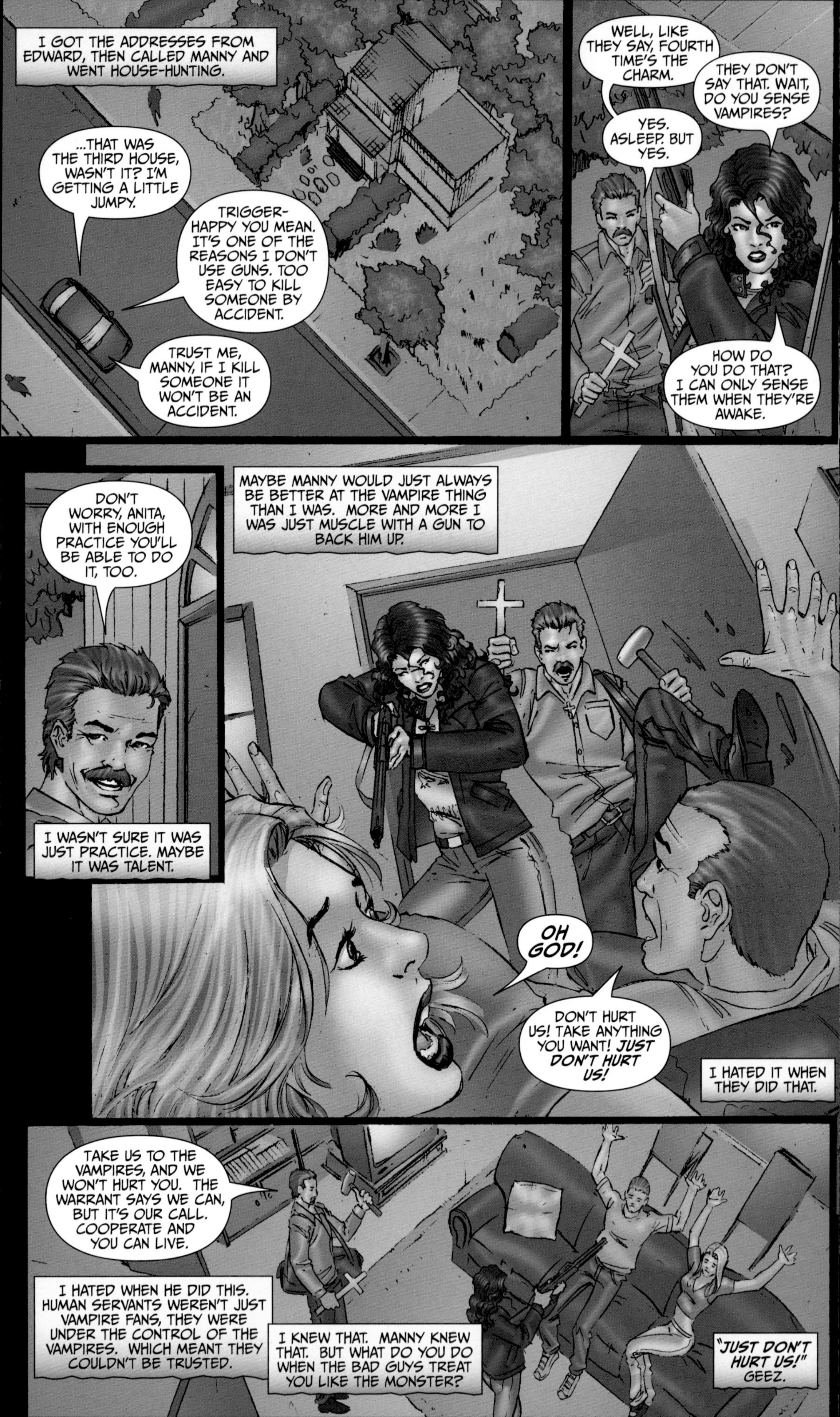

I GOT THE ADDRESSES FROM EDWARD, THEN CALLED MANNY AND WENT HOUSE-HUNTING.
...THAT WAS THE THIRD HOUSE, WASN'T IT? I'M GETTING A LITTLE JUMPY.
TRIGGER-HAPPY YOU MEAN. IT'S ONE OF THE REASONS I DON'T USE GUNS. TOO EASY TO KILL SOMEONE BY ACCIDENT.
TRUST ME, MANNY, IF I KILL SOMEONE IT WON'T BE AN ACCIDENT.
WELL, LIKE THEY SAY, FOURTH TIME'S THE CHARM.
THEY DON'T SAY THAT. WAIT, DO YOU SENSE VAMPIRES?
YES. ASLEEP. BUT YES.
HOW DO YOU DO THAT? I CAN ONLY SENSE THEM WHEN THEY'RE AWAKE.
DON'T WORRY, ANITA, WITH ENOUGH PRACTICE YOU'LL BE ABLE TO DO IT, TOO.
I WASN'T SURE IT WAS JUST PRACTICE. MAYBE IT WAS TALENT.
MAYBE MANNY WOULD JUST ALWAYS BE BETTER AT THE VAMPIRE THING THAN I WAS. MORE AND MORE I WAS JUST MUSCLE WITH A GUN TO BACK HIM UP.
OH GOD!
DON'T HURT US! TAKE ANYTHING YOU WANT! JUST DON'T HURT US!
I HATED IT WHEN THEY DID THAT.
TAKE US TO THE VAMPIRES, AND WE WON'T HURT YOU. THE WARRANT SAYS WE CAN, BUT IT'S OUR CALL. COOPERATE AND YOU CAN LIVE.
I HATED WHEN HE DID THIS. HUMAN SERVANTS WEREN'T JUST VAMPIRE FANS, THEY WERE UNDER THE CONTROL OF THE VAMPIRES. WHICH MEANT THEY COULDN'T BE TRUSTED.
I KNEW THAT. MANNY KNEW THAT. BUT WHAT DO YOU DO WHEN THE BAD GUYS TREAT YOU LIKE THE MONSTER?
"JUST DON'T HURT US!" GEEZ.

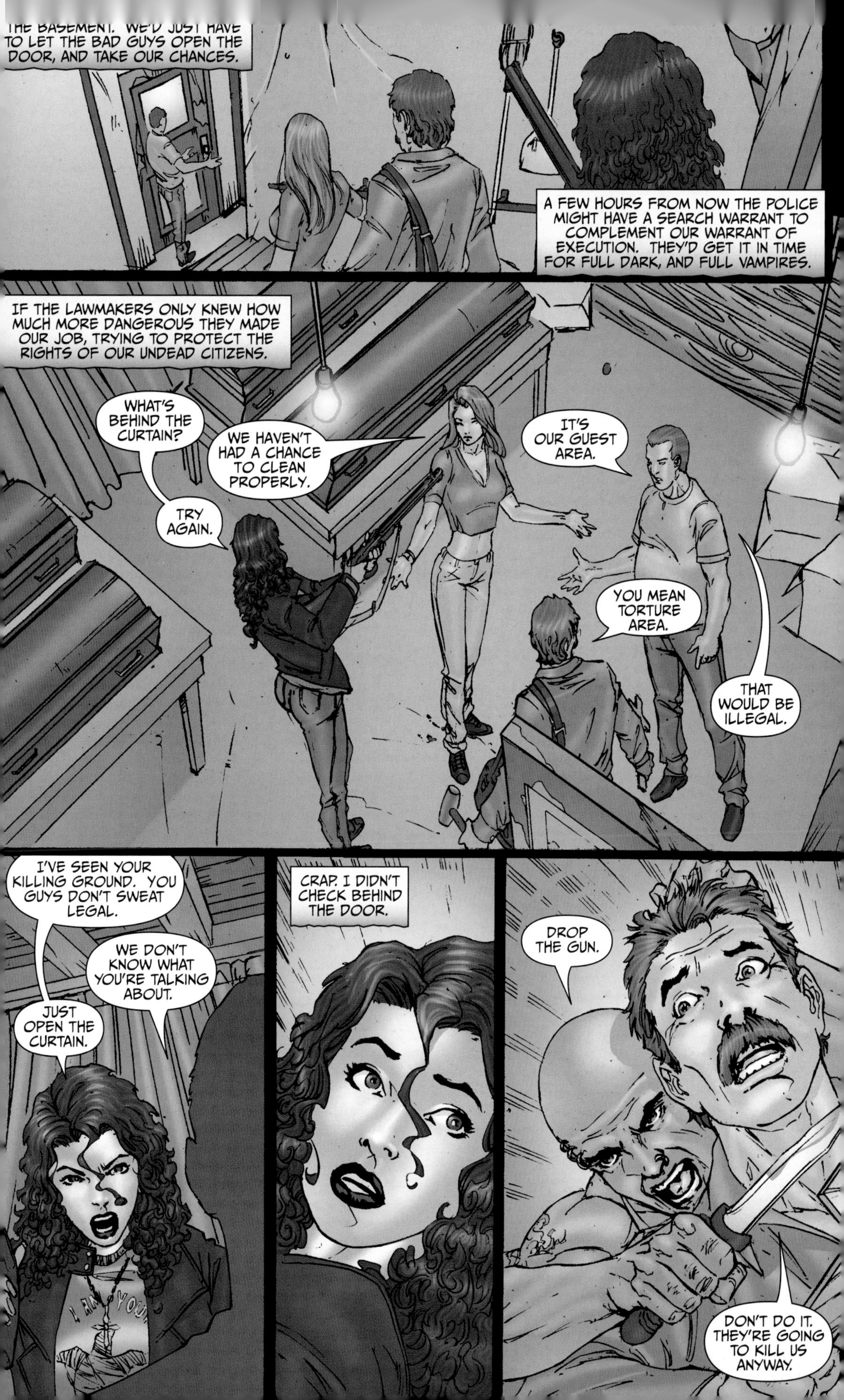
THE BASEMENT. WE'D JUST HAVE TO LET THE BAD GUYS OPEN THE DOOR, AND TAKE OUR CHANCES.
A FEW HOURS FROM NOW THE POLICE MIGHT HAVE A SEARCH WARRANT TO COMPLEMENT OUR WARRANT OF EXECUTION. THEY'D GET IT IN TIME FOR FULL DARK, AND FULL VAMPIRES.
IF THE LAWMAKERS ONLY KNEW HOW MUCH MORE DANGEROUS THEY MADE OUR JOB, TRYING TO PROTECT THE RIGHTS OF OUR UNDEAD CITIZENS.
WHAT'S BEHIND THE CURTAIN?
WE HAVEN'T HAD A CHANCE TO CLEAN PROPERLY.
TRY AGAIN.
IT'S OUR GUEST AREA.
YOU MEAN TORTURE AREA.
THAT WOULD BE ILLEGAL.
I'VE SEEN YOUR KILLING GROUND. YOU GUYS DON'T SWEAT LEGAL.
WE DON'T KNOW WHAT YOU'RE TALKING ABOUT.
JUST OPEN THE CURTAIN.
CRAP. I DIDN'T CHECK BEHIND THE DOOR.
DROP THE GUN.
DON'T DO IT. THEY'RE GOING TO KILL US ANYWAY.

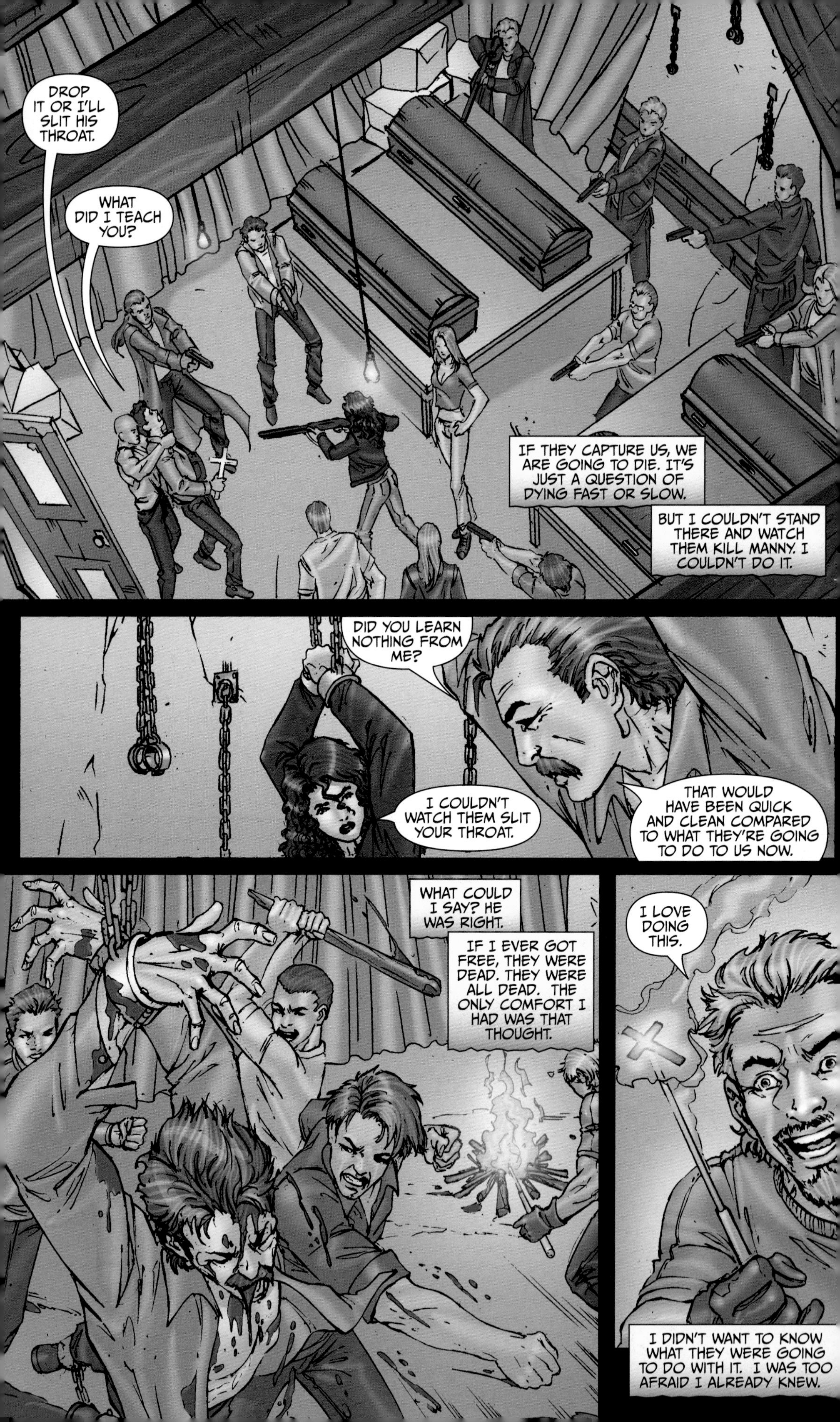
DROP IT OR I'LL SLIT HIS THROAT.
WHAT DID I TEACH YOU?
IF THEY CAPTURE US, WE ARE GOING TO DIE. IT'S JUST A QUESTION OF DYING FAST OR SLOW.
BUT I COULDN'T STAND THERE AND WATCH THEM KILL MANNY. I COULDN'T DO IT.
DID YOU LEARN NOTHING FROM ME?
I COULDN'T WATCH THEM SLIT YOUR THROAT.
THAT WOULD HAVE BEEN QUICK AND CLEAN COMPARED TO WHAT THEY'RE GOING TO DO TO US NOW.
WHAT COULD I SAY? HE WAS RIGHT.
IF I EVER GOT FREE, THEY WERE DEAD. THEY WERE ALL DEAD. THE ONLY COMFORT I HAD WAS THAT THOUGHT.
I LOVE DOING THIS.
I DIDN'T WANT TO KNOW WHAT THEY WERE GOING TO DO WITH IT. I WAS TOO AFRAID I ALREADY KNEW.

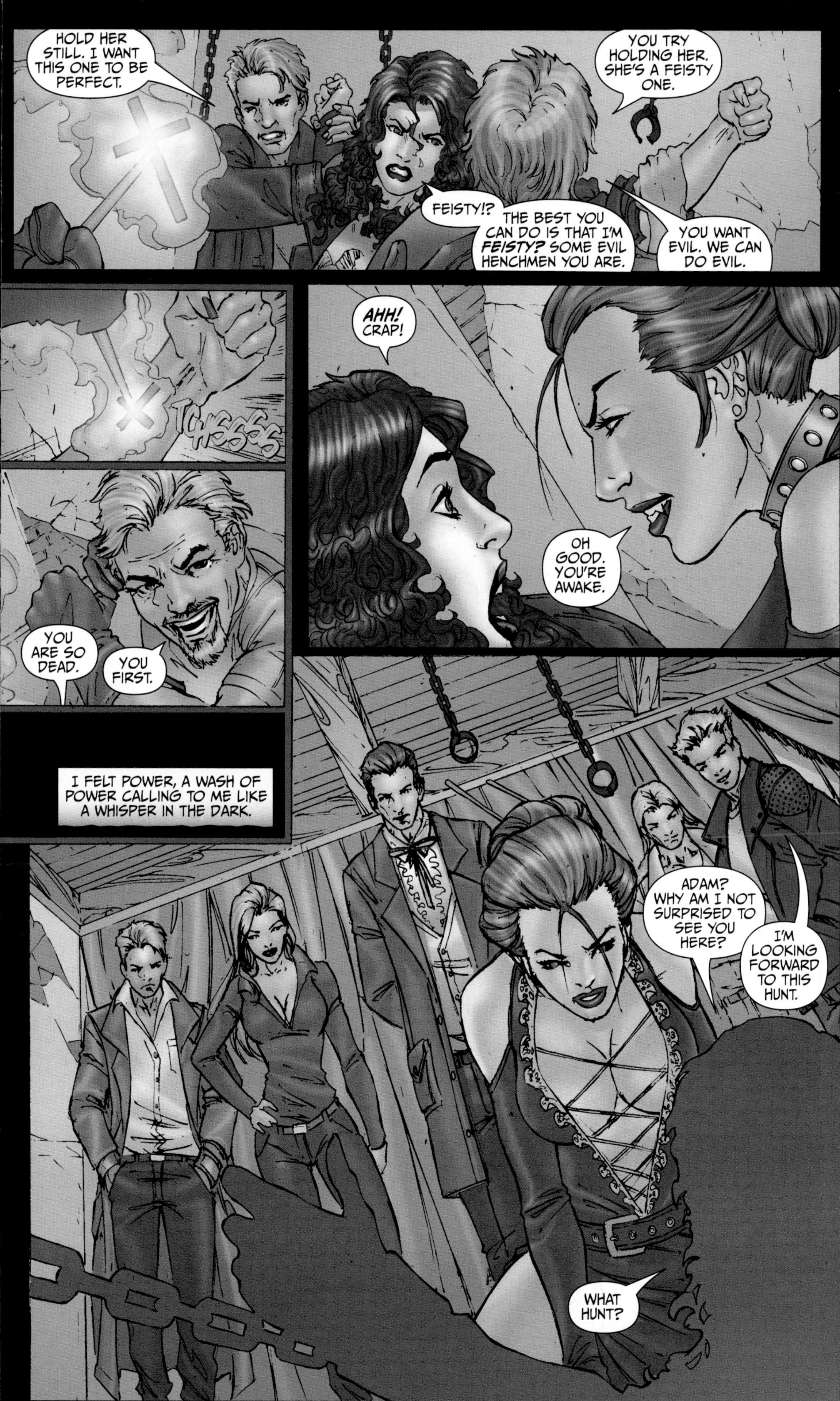
HOLD HER STILL. I WANT THIS ONE TO BE PERFECT.
YOU TRY HOLDING HER. SHE'S A FEISTY ONE.
FEISTY!?
THE BEST YOU CAN DO IS THAT I'M *FEISTY?* SOME EVIL HENCHMEN YOU ARE.
YOU WANT EVIL. WE CAN DO EVIL.
TCHSSSS
AHH! CRAP!
OH GOOD. YOU'RE AWAKE.
YOU ARE SO DEAD.
YOU FIRST.
I FELT POWER, A WASH OF POWER CALLING TO ME LIKE A WHISPER IN THE DARK.
ADAM? WHY AM I NOT SURPRISED TO SEE YOU HERE?
I'M LOOKING FORWARD TO THIS HUNT.
WHAT HUNT?

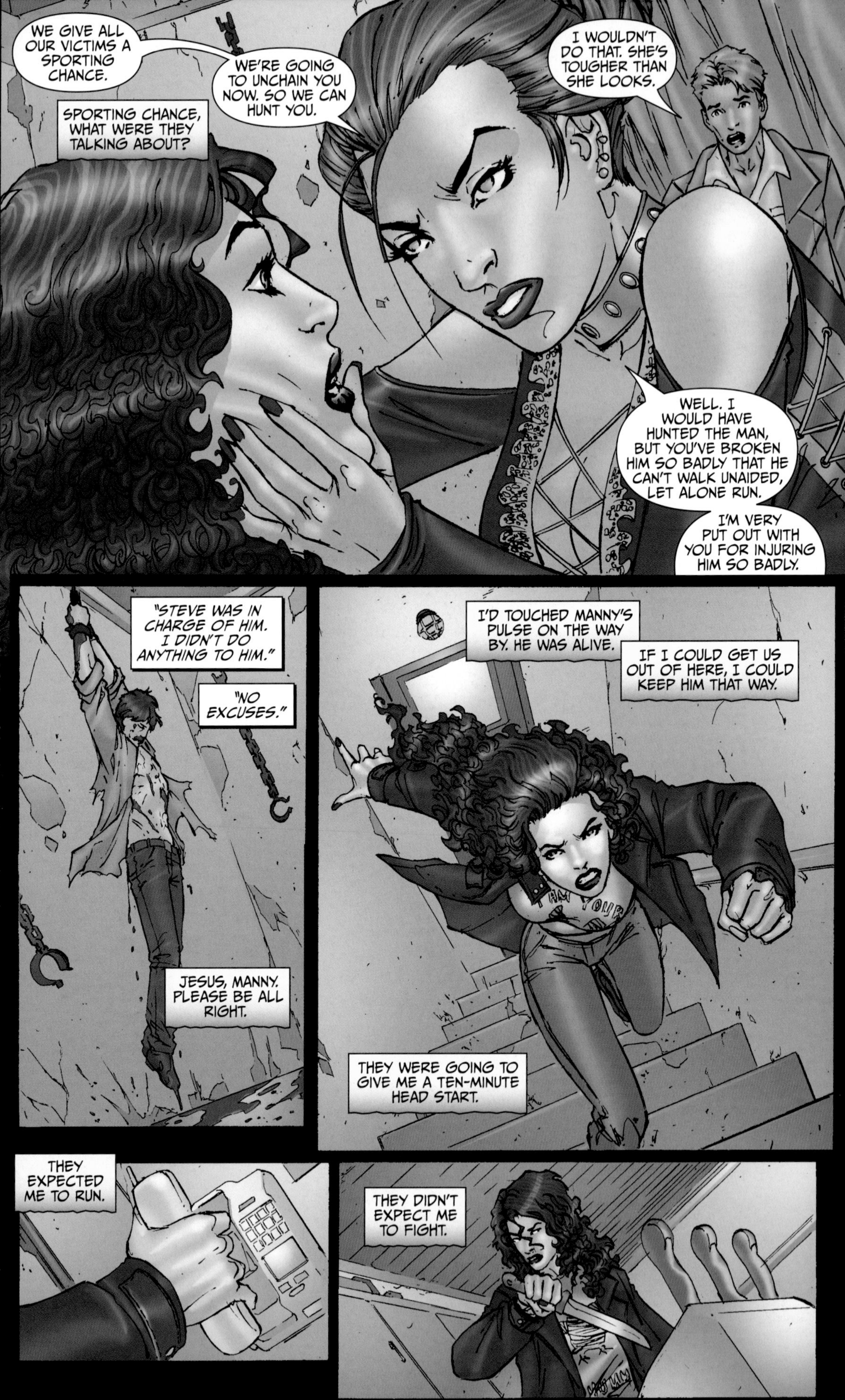
WE GIVE ALL OUR VICTIMS A SPORTING CHANCE.
WE'RE GOING TO UNCHAIN YOU NOW. SO WE CAN HUNT YOU.
I WOULDN'T DO THAT. SHE'S TOUGHER THAN SHE LOOKS.
SPORTING CHANCE, WHAT WERE THEY TALKING ABOUT?
WELL. I WOULD HAVE HUNTED THE MAN, BUT YOU'VE BROKEN HIM SO BADLY THAT HE CAN'T WALK UNAIDED, LET ALONE RUN.
I'M VERY PUT OUT WITH YOU FOR INJURING HIM SO BADLY.
"STEVE WAS IN CHARGE OF HIM. I DIDN'T DO ANYTHING TO HIM."
"NO EXCUSES."
JESUS, MANNY. PLEASE BE ALL RIGHT.
I'D TOUCHED MANNY'S PULSE ON THE WAY BY. HE WAS ALIVE.
IF I COULD GET US OUT OF HERE, I COULD KEEP HIM THAT WAY.
THEY WERE GOING TO GIVE ME A TEN-MINUTE HEAD START.
THEY EXPECTED ME TO RUN.
THEY DIDN'T EXPECT ME TO FIGHT.

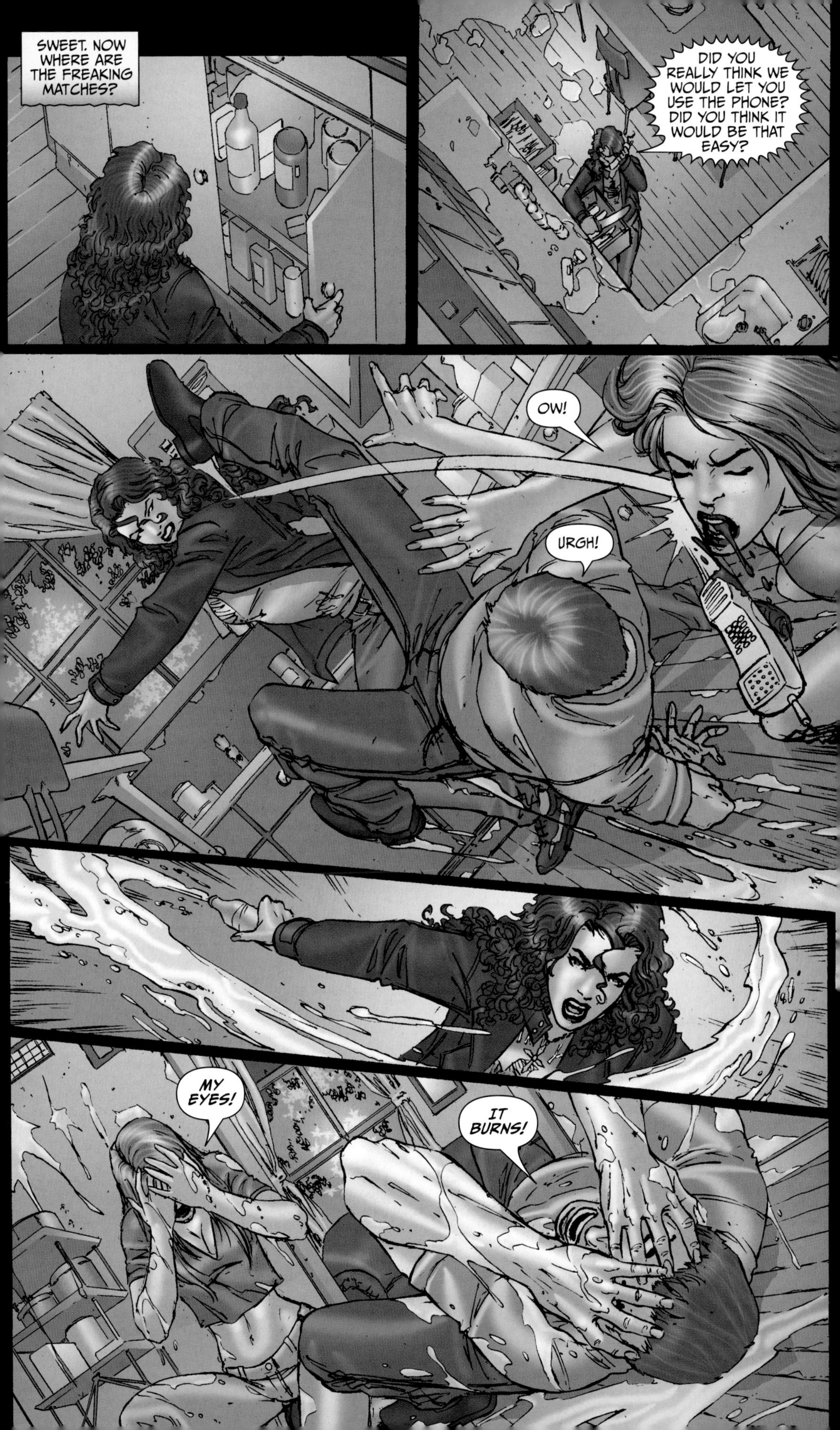

SWEET. NOW WHERE ARE THE FREAKING MATCHES?
DID YOU REALLY THINK WE WOULD LET YOU USE THE PHONE? DID YOU THINK IT WOULD BE THAT EASY?
OW!
URGH!
MY EYES!
IT BURNS!

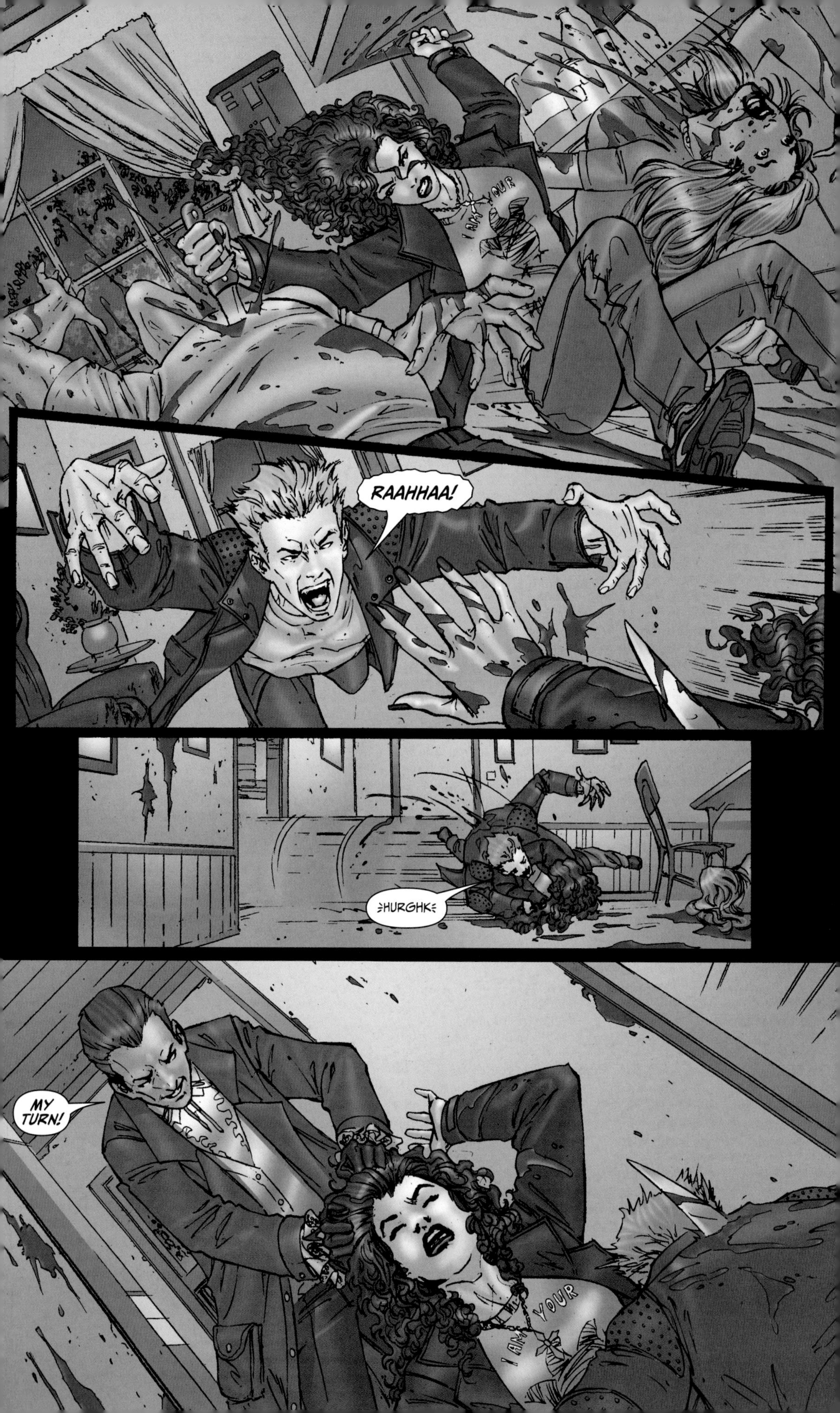
RAAHHAA!
HURGHK
MY TURN!

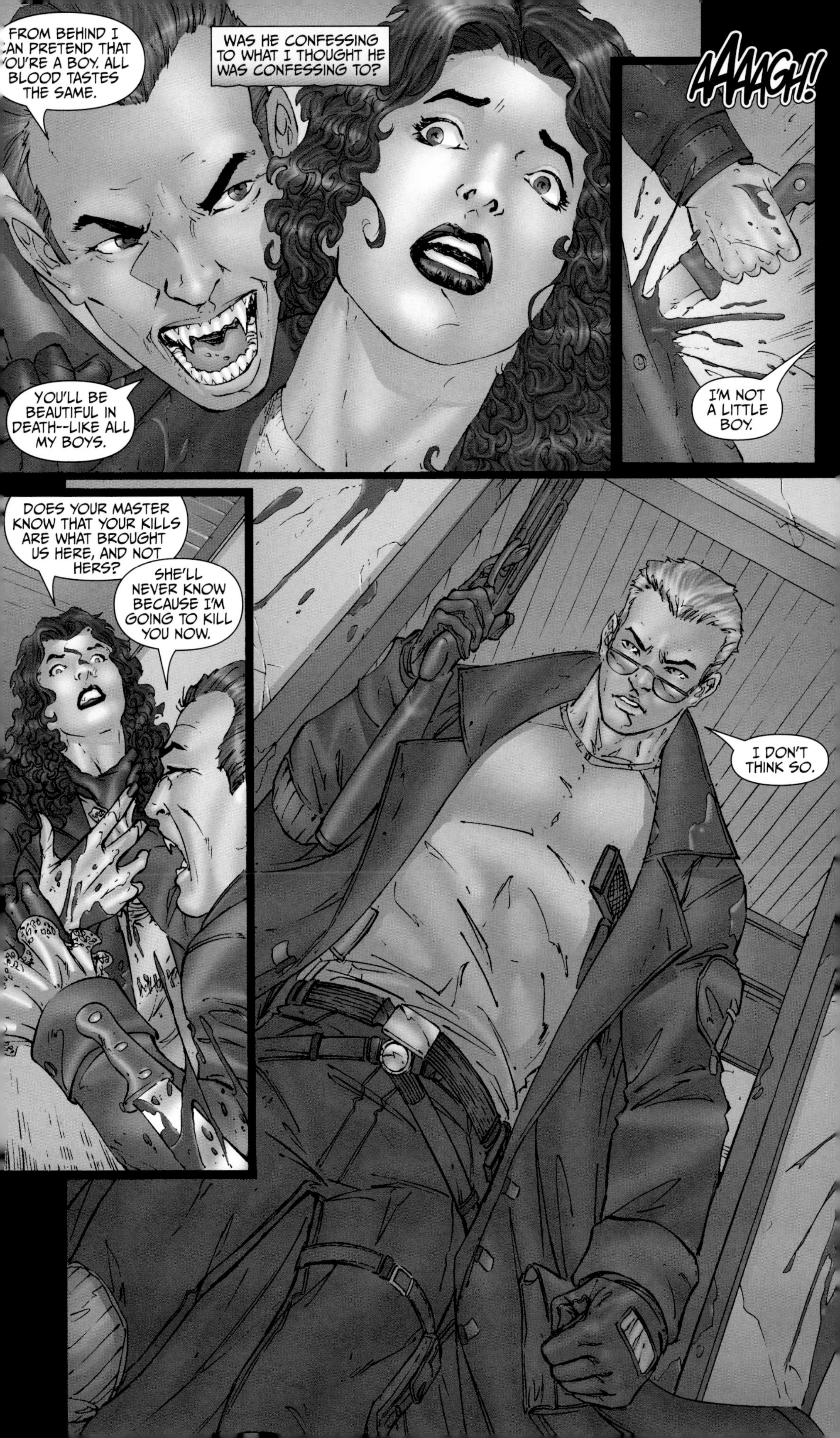
FROM BEHIND I CAN PRETEND THAT YOU'RE A BOY. ALL BLOOD TASTES THE SAME.
WAS HE CONFESSING TO WHAT I THOUGHT HE WAS CONFESSING TO?
YOU'LL BE BEAUTIFUL IN DEATH--LIKE ALL MY BOYS.
AAAAGH!
I'M NOT A LITTLE BOY.
DOES YOUR MASTER KNOW THAT YOUR KILLS ARE WHAT BROUGHT US HERE, AND NOT HERS?
SHE'LL NEVER KNOW BECAUSE I'M GOING TO KILL YOU NOW.
I DON'T THINK SO.

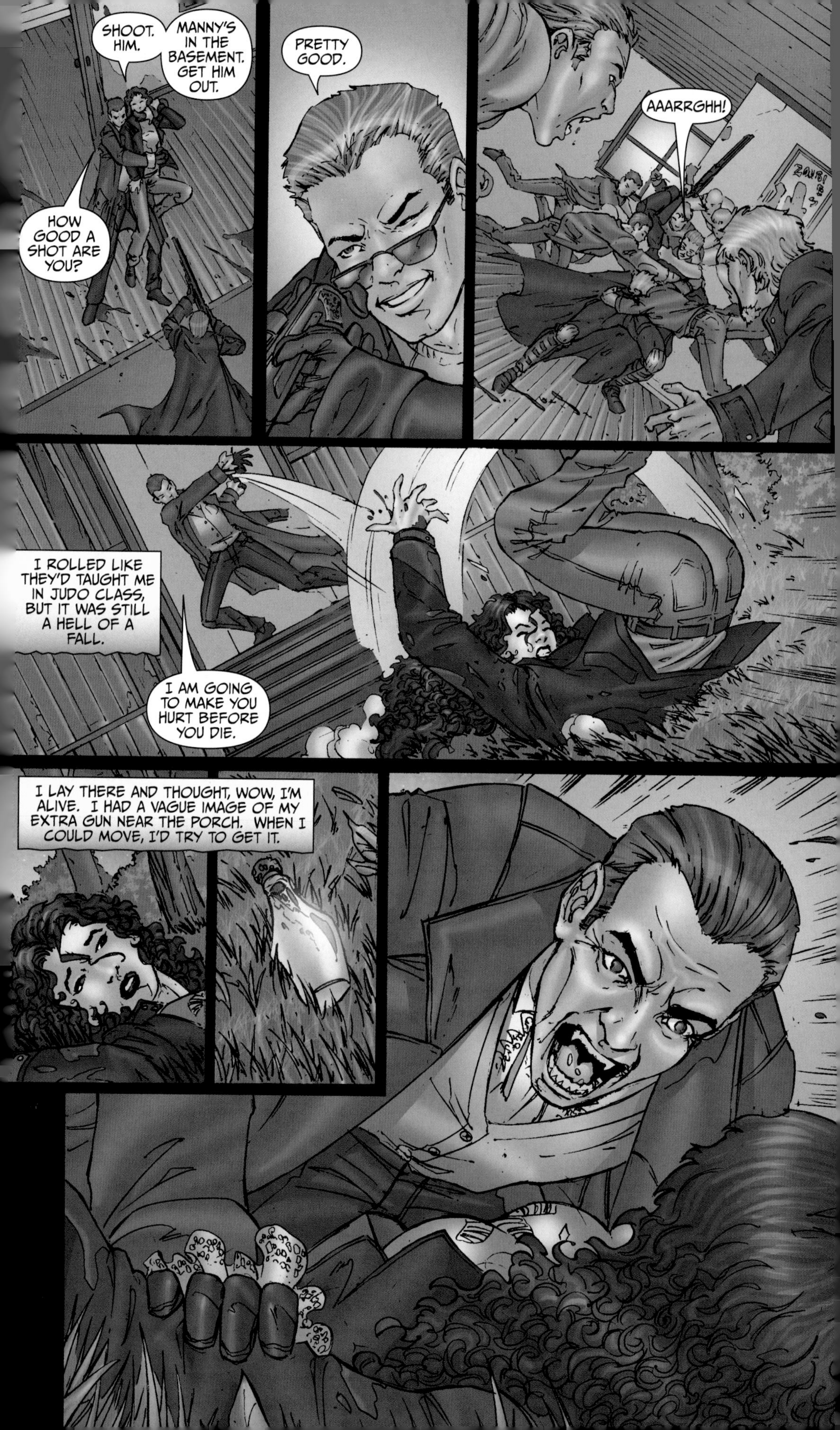
SHOOT. HIM.
MANNY'S IN THE BASEMENT. GET HIM OUT.
HOW GOOD A SHOT ARE YOU?
PRETTY GOOD.
AAARRGHH!
I ROLLED LIKE THEY'D TAUGHT ME IN JUDO CLASS, BUT IT WAS STILL A HELL OF A FALL.
I AM GOING TO MAKE YOU HURT BEFORE YOU DIE.
I LAY THERE AND THOUGHT, WOW, I'M ALIVE. I HAD A VAGUE IMAGE OF MY EXTRA GUN NEAR THE PORCH. WHEN I COULD MOVE, I'D TRY TO GET IT.

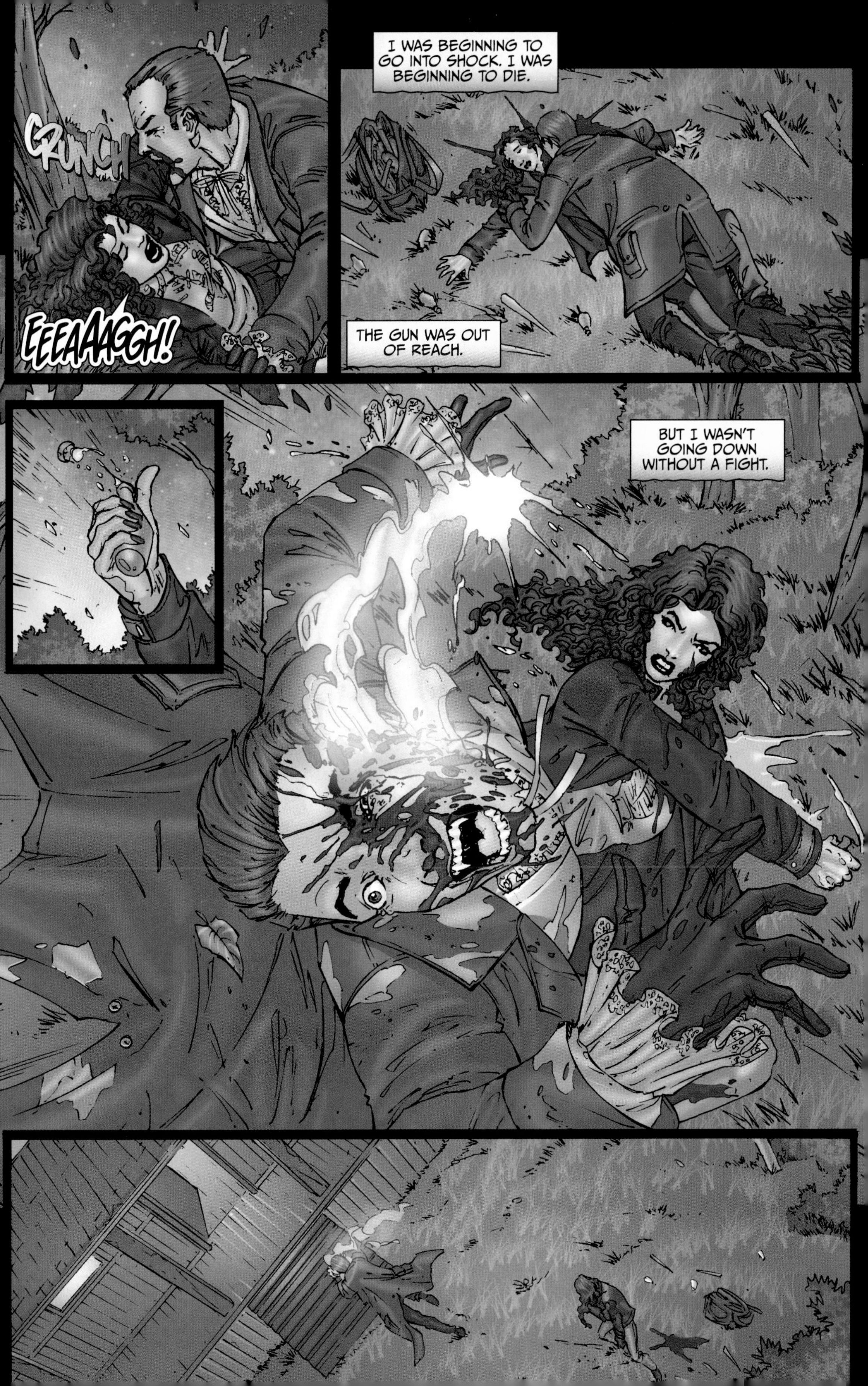
CRUNCH
EEEAAAGGH!
I WAS BEGINNING TO GO INTO SHOCK. I WAS BEGINNING TO DIE.
THE GUN WAS OUT OF REACH.
BUT I WASN'T GOING DOWN WITHOUT A FIGHT.

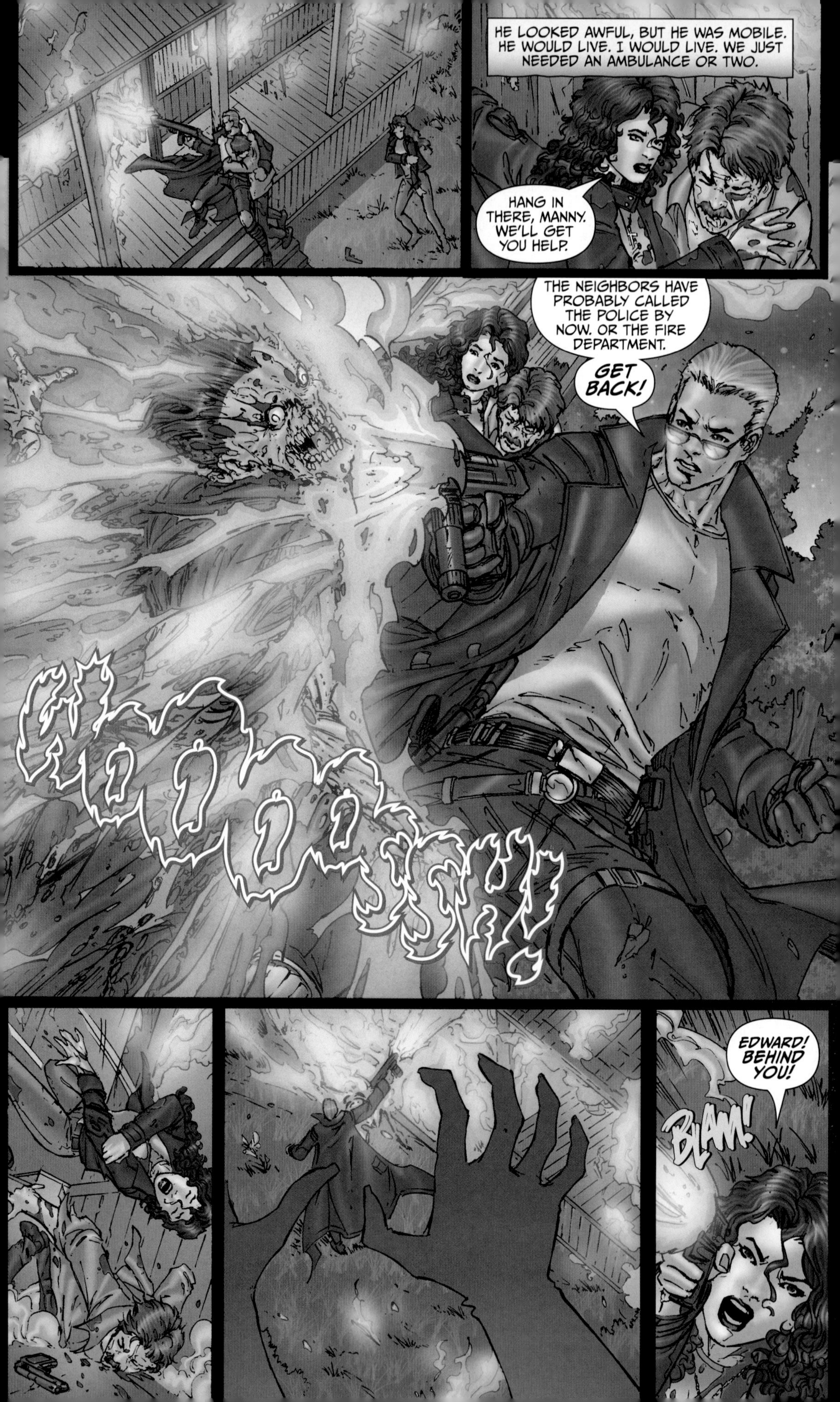
HE LOOKED AWFUL, BUT HE WAS MOBILE. HE WOULD LIVE. I WOULD LIVE. WE JUST NEEDED AN AMBULANCE OR TWO.
HANG IN THERE, MANNY. WE'LL GET YOU HELP.
THE NEIGHBORS HAVE PROBABLY CALLED THE POLICE BY NOW. OR THE FIRE DEPARTMENT.
GET BACK!
EDWARD! BEHIND YOU!
BLAM!

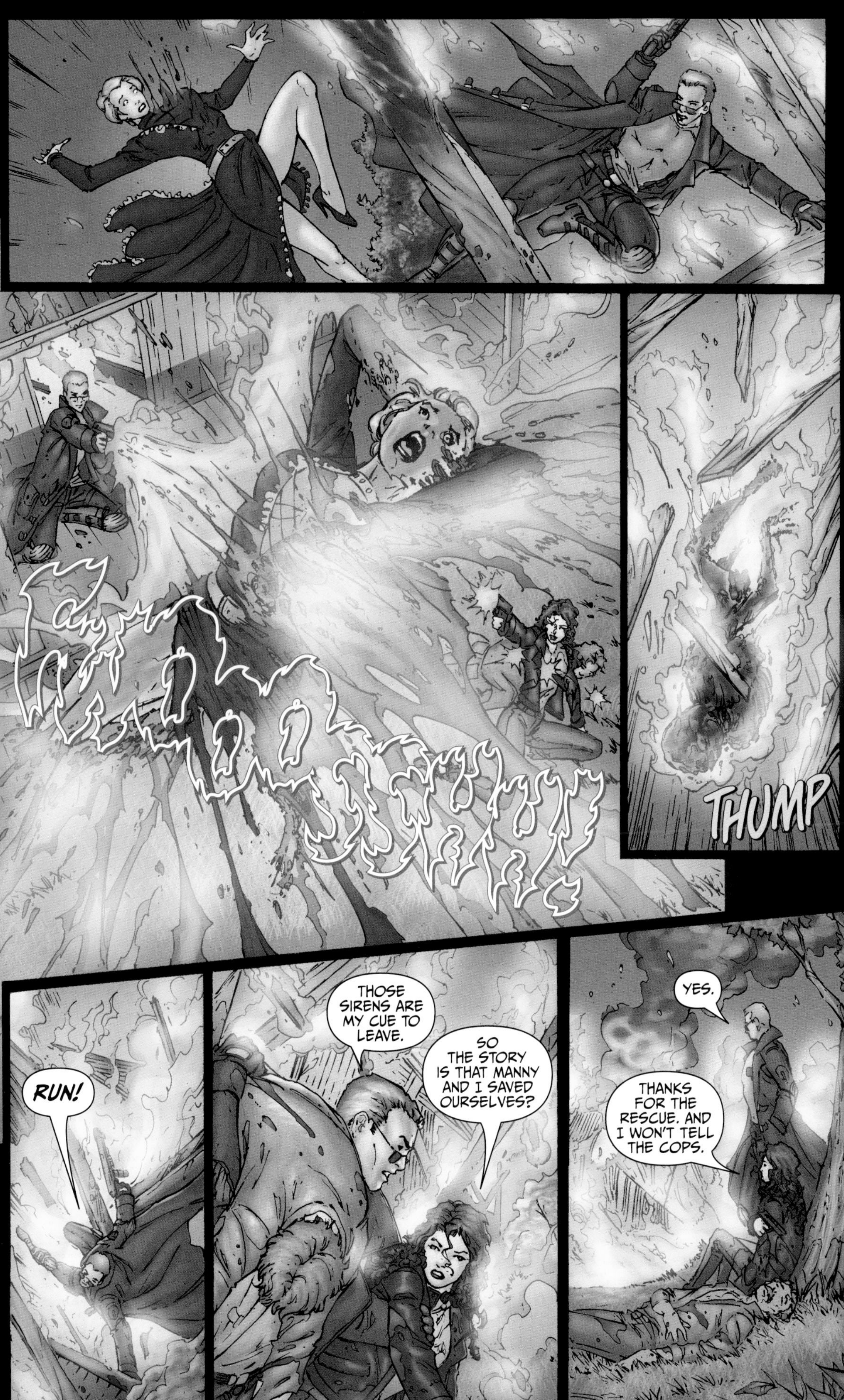
THUMP
RUN!
THOSE SIRENS ARE MY CUE TO LEAVE.
SO THE STORY IS THAT MANNY AND I SAVED OURSELVES?
YES.
THANKS FOR THE RESCUE. AND I WON'T TELL THE COPS.

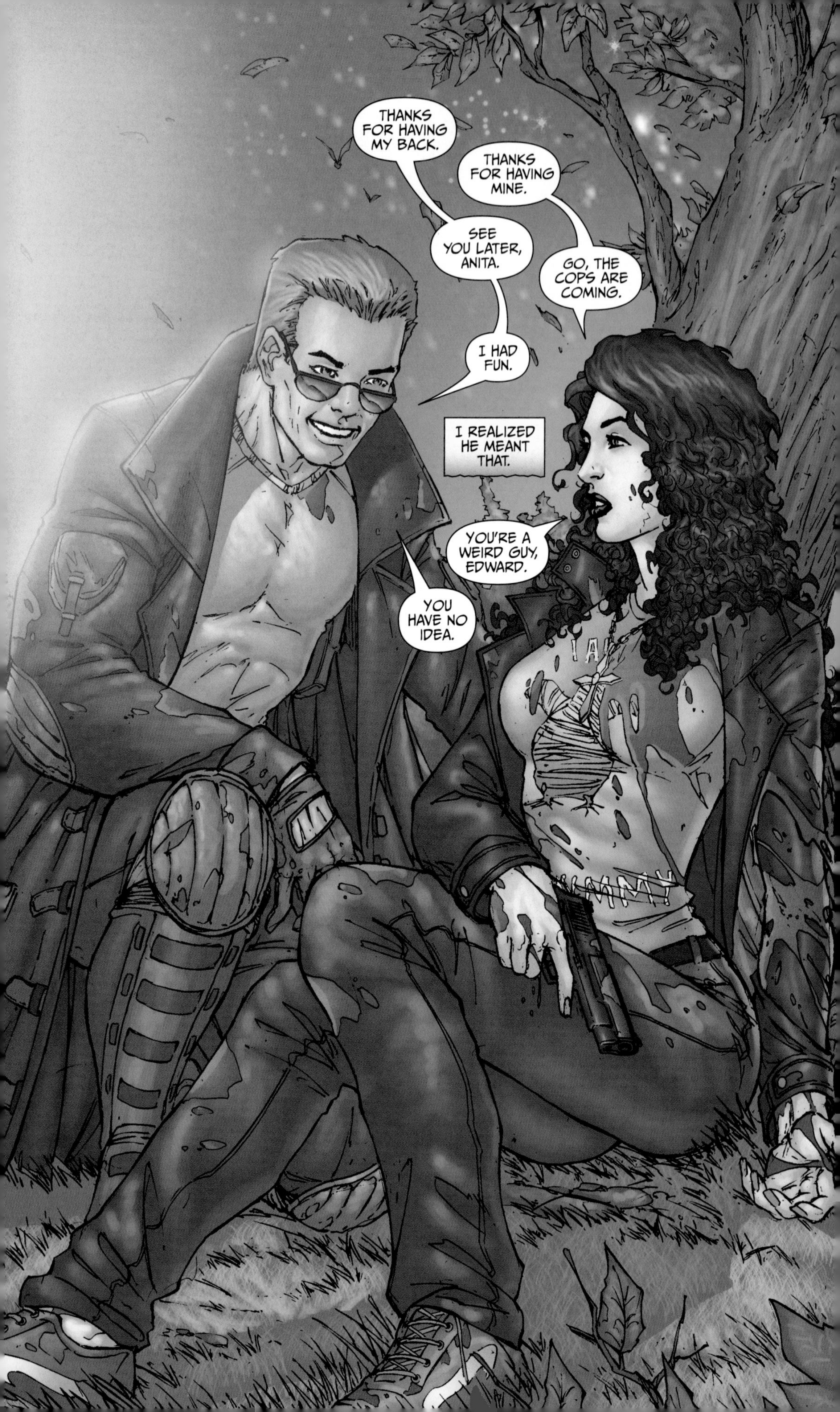
THANKS FOR HAVING MY BACK.
THANKS FOR HAVING MINE.
SEE YOU LATER, ANITA.
I HAD FUN.
GO, THE COPS ARE COMING.
I REALIZED HE MEANT THAT.
YOU'RE A WEIRD GUY, EDWARD.
YOU HAVE NO IDEA.

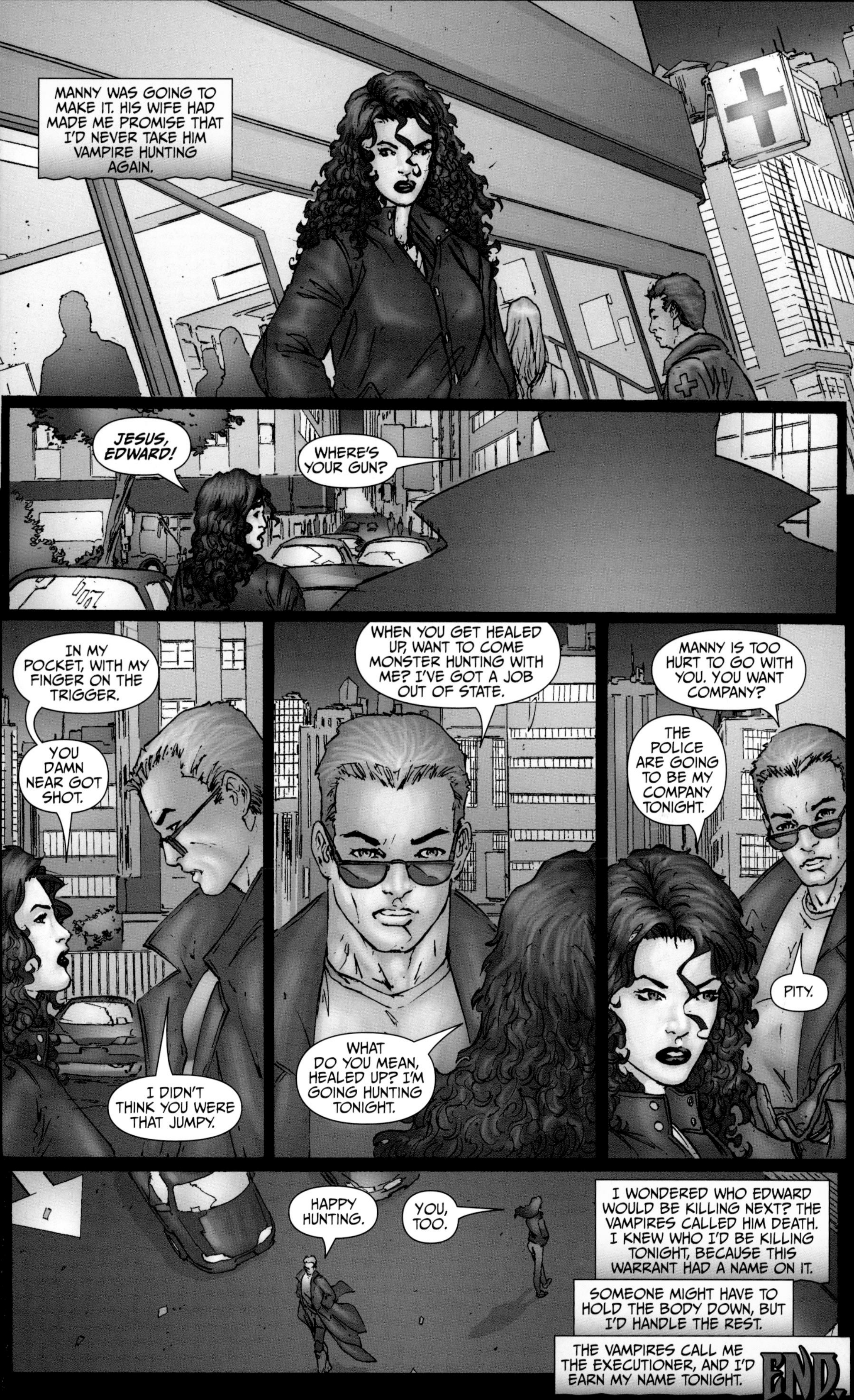
MANNY WAS GOING TO MAKE IT. HIS WIFE HAD MADE ME PROMISE THAT I'D NEVER TAKE HIM VAMPIRE HUNTING AGAIN.
JESUS, EDWARD!
WHERE'S YOUR GUN?
IN MY POCKET, WITH MY FINGER ON THE TRIGGER.
YOU DAMN NEAR GOT SHOT.
I DIDN'T THINK YOU WERE THAT JUMPY.
WHEN YOU GET HEALED UP, WANT TO COME MONSTER HUNTING WITH ME? I'VE GOT A JOB OUT OF STATE.
WHAT DO YOU MEAN, HEALED UP? I'M GOING HUNTING TONIGHT.
MANNY IS TOO HURT TO GO WITH YOU. YOU WANT COMPANY?
THE POLICE ARE GOING TO BE MY COMPANY TONIGHT.
PITY.
HAPPY HUNTING.
YOU, TOO.
I WONDERED WHO EDWARD WOULD BE KILLING NEXT? THE VAMPIRES CALLED HIM DEATH. I KNEW WHO I'D BE KILLING TONIGHT, BECAUSE THIS WARRANT HAD A NAME ON IT.
SOMEONE MIGHT HAVE TO HOLD THE BODY DOWN, BUT I'D HANDLE THE REST.
THE VAMPIRES CALL ME THE EXECUTIONER, AND I'D EARN MY NAME TONIGHT.
END.

A quick spoiler alert! For those who have *not* finished the novel, please be warned that this handbook does mention the ending to Guilty Pleasures.

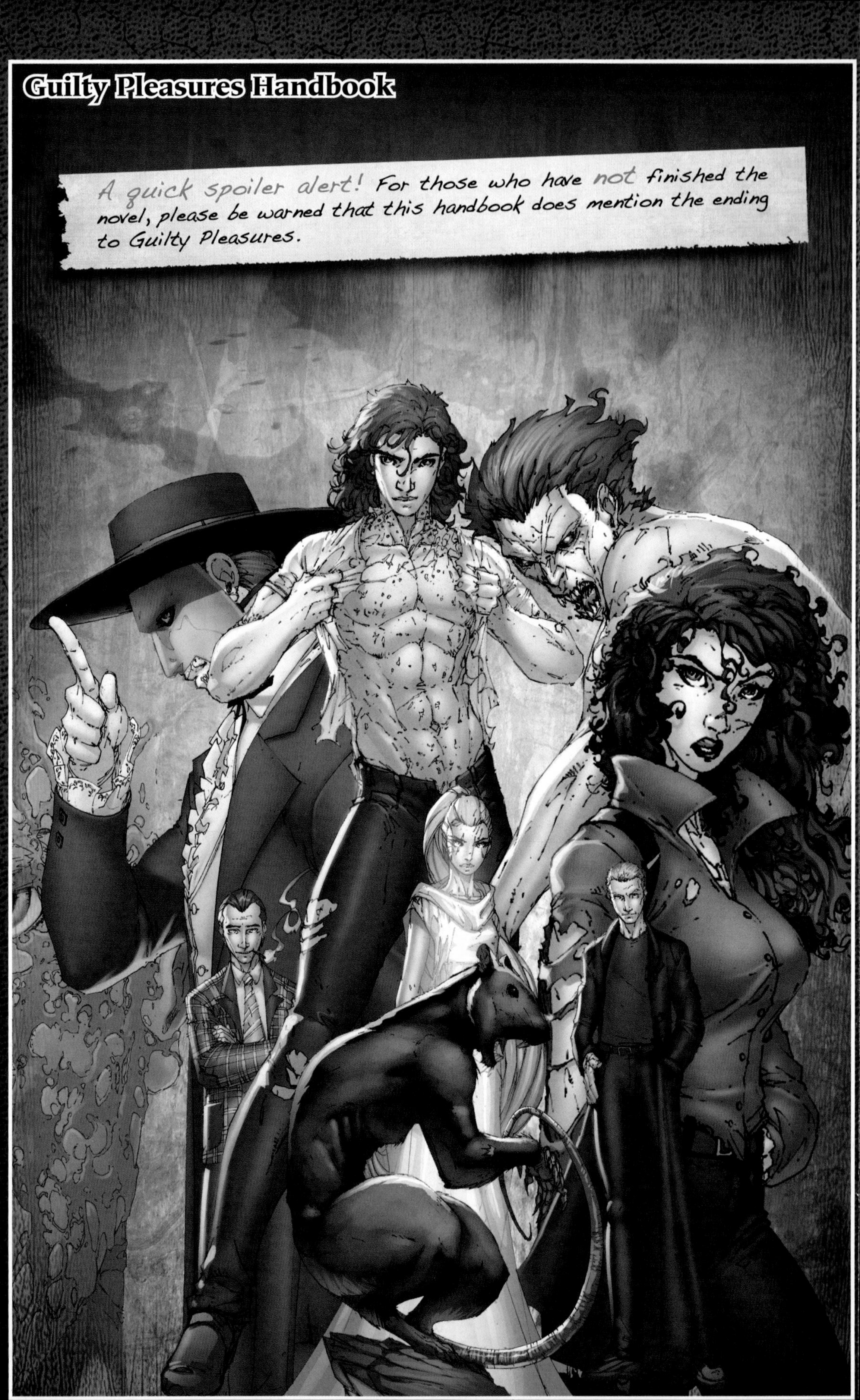

FIRST APPEARANCE: Guilty Pleasures (1993)

Anita Blake lives in a world parallel to our own, a world very much similar to the one outside your window, with one vital, major difference.

The supernatural is real, unquestionably so. Vampires, zombies, werewolves, and lycanthropes of every stripe not only stalk the world, but are part of everyday life, living openly and not so openly amongst the mass of greater humanity.

Lycanthropes of numerous species exist, including werewolves, wererats and wereleopards, spending their time in human form trying to hold down everyday jobs, and their time in furred form mingling with others of their own kind. Their lives are complicated by living stuck between two societies, neither of which they can deny. Despite it being a disease that, theoretically, anyone might be unfortunate enough to catch, many humans treat lycanthropes with prejudice, and often the lycanthropes have to hide their affliction to avoid persecution and keep their jobs. But even when they look human, lycanthropes are always aware of the beast within them, sharpening their senses and heightening their strength and reactions. Meanwhile lycanthrope society has its own rules and formalities, much closer to the animals they are related to than the human one they came from. No matter who they are as a human, if they are a lycanthrope, they must obey the orders of the highest ranking member of their particular species in their territory. And to make matters worse, some vampires have the power to control specific types of animals, including those werecreatures who share that genus.

There are animators and voodoo priests, people who can raise the dead as zombies. Though training is required to control their powers, they are born with an innate ability they cannot ignore, and like any human, animators come from many backgrounds. Some consider their powers a gift from God, though the Catholic Church disagrees, and has excommunicated any animators who consider themselves Catholic. Other animators think of their power as a curse, while yet others consider it simply an unusual talent. Since there is no law against raising the dead, some animators even do it professionally, allowing people a last chance to talk to loved ones or to settle disputed wills. Zombies meanwhile enjoy no rights; brought back from the grave but not to life, they exist so long as their master needs them. For a brief while after being raised they can recall who they formerly were, but this soon fades, which is probably for the best. Ghouls also stalk the cemeteries, undead carrion eaters who seem to crawl spontaneously from their graves. Little more than animals, they are thankfully cowardly, and most of the time are little threat to living humans even in packs.

Vampires have been around for thousands of years, if not longer. For most of that time, they preyed on humans and were, in turn, prey to vampire hunters. Immensely powerful and growing more so with each passing year, they were never easy targets, but two years ago they gained a new defense to stymie their pursuers – the law. The landmark Addison vs. Clark case redefined what was death and what was life, and recognized the civil rights of the undead. Now the U.S.A. is one of the few countries in the world where vampirism is acknowledged and legal, and the country is finding itself in the grips of an immigration tide the likes of which it has never seen before. Vampires have opened public businesses catering to the curious, bars, strip joints and even founded their own, pro-undead, religion. The lure of immortality, whatever the drawbacks, remains very appealing. Debates remain ongoing about the implications of Addison vs. Clark to inheritance laws, marriage vows, and whether the undead should be allowed to vote.

Both sides are struggling to adapt to this new status quo. Existing anti-vampire groups founded by survivors of vampire attacks have suddenly found themselves considered hate groups, and new organizations determined to either undo the law or eliminate vampires regardless have begun to spring up. Vampires, especially the older ones, are equally unsure, having built their own society and rules unknown to most humans; new recruits into the undead ranks often find it less idyllic than they imagined, as they learn they are subservient to vampires hundreds of years older than themselves. And after hundreds of years looking over your shoulder and not trusting most humans, many vampires find it difficult to believe after only two years that the law will truly protect them when others wish them ill.

In the bustling city of St. Louis, Missouri, the newly formed Regional Preternatural Investigations Team is charged with keeping the peace between these communities by investigating all crimes with a supernatural aspect, and apprehending or exterminating the guilty parties, assisted to the best of her abilities by Anita Blake: Animator, supernatural expert, and vampire slayer. The vampires know her as the Executioner…

VAMPIRE MURDERS

VICTIMS: Lucas, Maurice, Theresa, eight other unidentified vampires; while not counted as one of the official victims because he was human, the unidentified grounds keeper of Hillcrest Cemetery was also slain by Zachary's ghouls
SCENE OF CRIME: The District, St. Louis, Missouri.
GUILTY PARTIES: Zachary, ghoul pack
FIRST APPEARANCE: Guilty Pleasures (1993)

HISTORY: After the animator Zachary died, he was brought back to a semblance of life by a voodoo charm known as a gris-gris; it is likely that he had obtained this somewhere in anticipation of one day needing to rise from the dead, although it remains possible that another animator or a voodoo priest chose to resurrect Zachary without his foreknowledge. Regardless, Zachary arose from the grave shortly after his own funeral, discovering that alongside him many of the other corpses arose spontaneously as ghouls. He found to his surprise that the pack of some twenty ghouls instinctively understood and followed his orders, even overcoming their natural cowardice to take on potentially dangerous opponents.

To sustain the charm on the gris-gris which provided his unnatural life, Zachary had to regularly feed it vampire blood. Working for the master vampire of the city of St. Louis, Nikolaos, who was unaware that he was not alive, Zachary was able to use his insider knowledge to choose targets. For reasons undisclosed, he chose to pick his victims from those vampires who attended freak parties, sex gatherings where humans enamored of the undead would make themselves freely available for the vampires' every desire. Zachary would ambush lone vampires with his ghoul pack in different locations around the vampire neighborhood known as the District. Though ghouls possess superhuman strength and endurance, individually they could not match their vampire prey's own superhuman abilities; however, their strength of numbers saw them prevail each time, even when confronting master vampires, and they would rip out their target's heart and decapitate them, leaving Zachary free to take the blood he needed. Their first victim was Maurice, Rebecca Miles' lover, but several others followed, including two masters.

With the discovery of bodies, the police's Regional Preternatural Investigation Team (RPIT) began investigating, but they were hampered by the vampire community deliberately withholding information from them, not the least that there were six more victims than the police knew about. Zachary's ghouls also slew a human groundskeeper at Hillcrest Cemetery, presumably because he was in the wrong place at the wrong time and witnessed something Zachary did not want him to see. Meanwhile Nikolaos initiated her own hunt for the killer, unaware she harbored the culprit so close to herself. They found a witness to the second murder, the killing of a vampire named Lucas, and kidnapped him, but despite intense interrogation he failed to identify who or what had slain Lucas, probably because he recognized the killer as one of his interrogators. The witness hung himself rather than let the torture continue. At the suggestion of the vampire Jean-Claude, Nikolaos brought the animator Anita Blake in to hunt the killer, coercing her when she would not work for them willingly. Nikolaos also ordered Zachary to raise their witness as a zombie, so they could continue the questioning, but Zachary deliberately abused the zombie so that its mind broke, rendering it useless.

Because of this, Nikolaos set Zachary up to be killed, instructing him to raise a century-plus corpse as a test of his abilities, and instructing her minion Theresa to slay him if he failed. Zachary survived because Anita intervened, and combined her own powers with his to achieve the raising, but in so doing Anita also realized that Zachary was himself undead, although she did not immediately make the connection to his crimes. Because she had threatened him, Zachary chose Theresa as his next victim, and his ghouls made short work of her; but, fearing Anita was also getting too close, he decided to kill her too. He lured her and former hitman and vampire killer Edward to a cemetery, where he ambushed them with his ghoul pack, but they managed to escape. Now aware he was the killer, Anita informed the head of RPIT. Shortly afterwards Anita and Edward confronted Nikolaos, and to distract her, Anita informed Nikolaos of Zachary's misdeeds. Nikolaos ripped out his throat, but he survived because of the gris-gris charm, at least until a few minutes later, when Anita touched it with human blood, breaking its power and killing Zachary. Without his directions the ghoul pack presumably dispersed, and the vampire murders ended.

HISTORY: For most animators, the ability to raise the dead is either an embarrassing curse, a religious experience, or simply a curious talent. Four years ago, Bert Vaughn figured a way to turn it into a business, setting up Animators, Inc., where those with enough cash could pay to have the dead raised as zombies, usually as witnesses in legal cases, settling will disputes, but sometimes as a way of having a last word with a loved one who had passed away. A master showman, Bert soon grew the business, moving it from its initial spare room above a garage to bigger and better offices and hiring additional animators and secretarial staff. Though primarily aimed at raising the dead, the nature of the business attracted other clients who wished to utilize the animators' expert supernatural knowledge, especially after vampires won civil rights two years ago; never one to turn money away, Bert made sure there was a clause in his employees' contracts forcing them to meet with any client who paid a retainer. He also added Private Investigator Ronnie Sims on retainer to the company, available as and when a case might require her services.

Bert charges on a sliding scale, depending on the age of the corpse needing raising, starting from around $3,000 standard fee up to as much as $20,000 for raising someone more than 100 years dead, a feat few animators are capable of. Business remains good despite these charges, and three months ago the company moved to its current offices, sharing the building with psychologists, plastic surgeons, lawyers, a marriage counselor, and a real estate company. Sadly, Bert's sartorial sense does not match his business one, and his office color scheme leaves much to be desired. Wanting a homey feel for the reception room, Bert chose pale green walls with oriental designs, a thick green carpet, and copious plants dotted around, including a couple of trees whose tops nearly touch the ceiling; Animator Anita Blake thinks it resembles a cross between a mortuary and a plant shop. The three offices are colored in pastel blues, intended by Bert to soothe clients, but instead making them feel cold.

Bert chose the smallest office for himself, with the other four animators timesharing the remaining two; due to the unsociable hours animating demands, it is rare for everyone to be in at the same time. The company's most capable animator is 24 year-old Anita Blake; as well as being able to raise century-plus zombies, she is also on retainer to the police as a supernatural expert and the State of Missouri, as well as two other state's licensed vampire executioner. Considering her the most appealing and least threatening looking employee, Bert has focused most of the company's publicity pushes on Anita, having her do radio interviews and magazine articles. Anita's mentor, who taught her both to raise zombies and slay vampires, is Manny; now 54, he was a traditionalist when it came to slaying, preferring stakes over guns, but after spending four months in the hospital following a vampire hunt two years ago, he has been convinced by his wife Rosita to retire from slaying for the sake of her and the children, and now sticks exclusively to animating. Bert has also hired the pro-vampire Jamison Clarke, and Charles, a competent but squeamish corpse raiser with a four year old child.

The company employs two secretaries: Mary, the day secretary, a grandmother in her fifties who keeps her short hair immobile through excessive hairspray, and Craig, the night secretary.

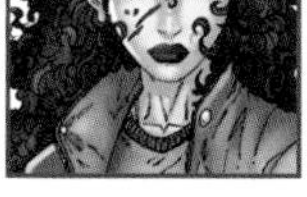

ANITA BLAKE

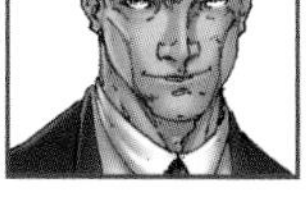

BERT VAUGHN

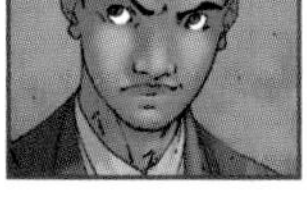

JAMISON CLARKE

ANITA ON ANIMATORS, INC.: "We animators had the talent, but Bert knew how to make it pay."

FOUNDER AND CEO: Bert Vaughn
ANIMATORS: Anita Blake, Jamison Clarke, Charles (last name unrevealed), Manny Rodriguez; Craig, Mary (secretaries, last names unrevealed)
FORMER MEMBERS: None known
BASE OF OPERATIONS: Animators, Inc. offices, St. Louis, Missouri

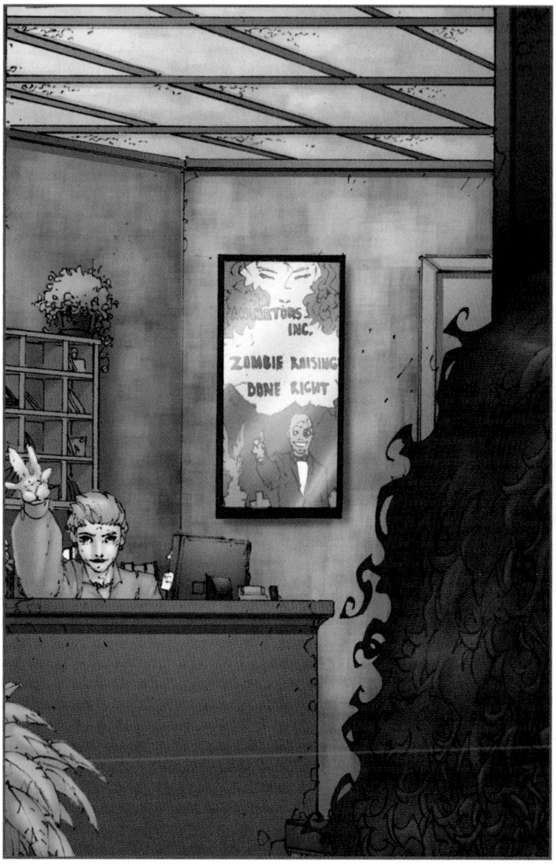
INC.
ZOMBIE RAISING
DONE RIGHT

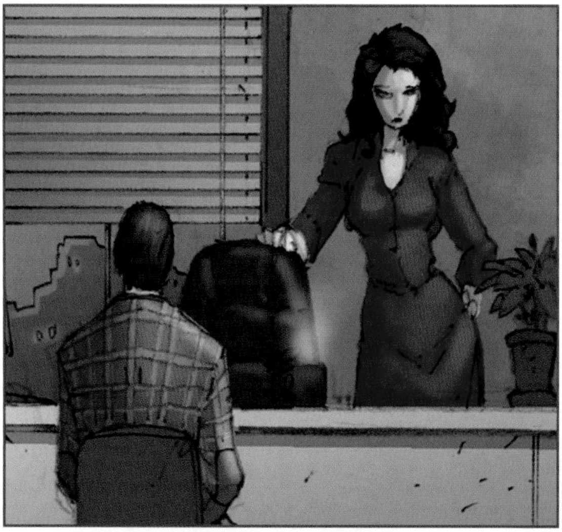

AUBREY

ANITA ON AUBREY: "The mind behind the voice was like nothing I had ever felt. It was ancient, terribly ancient"

REAL NAME: Aubrey (full name unrevealed)
ALIASES: None
ANITA'S NICKNAMES: Long-fang
CLASSIFICATION: Vampire
OCCUPATION: Dancer, Guilty Pleasures
PLACE OF BIRTH: Unrevealed
CITIZENSHIP: Unrevealed
BASE OF OPERATIONS: Circus of the Damned, St. Louis
KNOWN RELATIVES: None
ALLIES: Nikolaos, Theresa, Burchard, Winter, Valentine
GROUP AFFILIATION: Nikolaos' Kiss
ENEMIES: Anita Blake, Edward
EDUCATION: Unrevealed
FIRST APPEARANCE: Guilty Pleasures (1993)

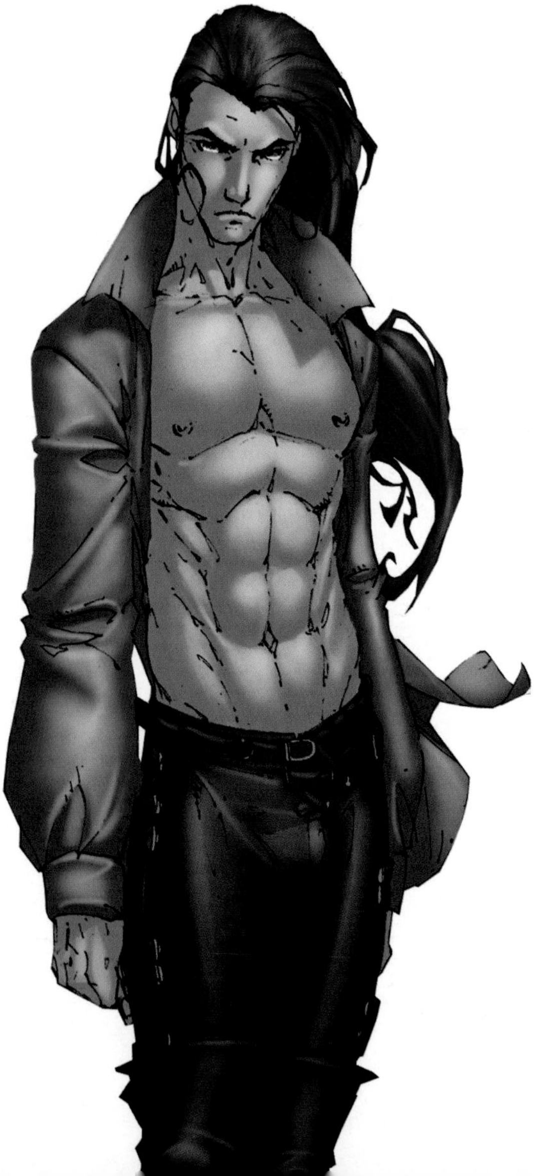

HISTORY: As with most elder vampires, much of Aubrey's past remains a mystery. He is a little over 500 years old, having originally died some time in the 14th century, and given his appearance and the era mostly likely hailed from somewhere in Europe, possibly France given that he appeared to find hearing French a calming influence in later years. By the modern day he had crossed the Atlantic and settled in St. Louis, where the child vampire Nikolaos held sway. It is likewise unrevealed how he became a vampire and who turned him, though Nikolaos might well have been responsible, given her dominance over him in the modern day; if she was not then he eventually fell under her influence. She ruled with an iron fist and mercurial temper, and when Aubrey displeased her in some unspecified manner, he suffered her preferred punishment for recalcitrant vampires, imprisonment in a cross-sealed coffin to starve without the human option of dying until she deigned to release him. Let out after three months, Aubrey emerged insane, his humanity eroded to a thin veneer which could shatter at the slightest provocation to unleash a bestial fury.

When several of St. Louis' vampires were mysteriously murdered, Nikolaos was persuaded by Jean-Claude, one of the city's more powerful master vampires, to employ Anita Blake, human animator and liaison to the police's supernatural task force, to find the killer's identity. After Anita refused an initial offer of employment, Nikolaos ordered Aubrey and Jean-Claude to blackmail Anita into taking the case. Using a human lackey, Monica Vespucci, Anita was lured to Jean-Claude's vampire strip club, Guilty Pleasures, on the pretext of attending her friend Catherine Maison's bachelorette party. While Anita was briefly called away on police business, Aubrey took the opportunity to bring Catherine on stage and entrance her; Anita returned to find her friend completely within his power. Not content with now being able to summon and control Catherine whenever he wished, Aubrey attempted to likewise dominate Anita, calling her to the stage after he had dismissed Catherine back to her seat in the audience. Aware of the implications of allowing Aubrey to control her, with considerable effort Anita resisted, but after Aubrey promised not to try to force his will on her, she reluctantly joined him voluntarily on stage. Almost immediately, Aubrey broke his word, again seeking to force her to approach him; this awoke her underlying animator powers, allowing her to again resist, and even look directly into his mesmerizing eyes. Intrigued, Aubrey moved closer, managing the lesser feat of holding her paralyzed, and then attempted to bite her; terror allowed Anita to once more shatter his control over her, and she pushed him away. Losing his temper at this repeated defiance, Aubrey attacked Anita, throwing her around the stage and barely noticing when she drew a silver knife and pierced the skin near his heart. Jean-Claude intervened and calmed Aubrey before either combatant could inflict serious damage to the other.

After convincing the audience that the fight had been part of the act, the group retired backstage to Jean-Claude's office. Though Aubrey wanted Catherine present, at Anita's insistence she was sent home unbitten, though not before Aubrey wiped her memories of the night's events and made it clear to Anita that Catherine's life was forfeit if Anita did not cooperate. Anita noted in turn that she was aware Aubrey's hold over Catherine could now only be ended by the death of one of them, an implicit threat Aubrey casually dismissed. He was less amused when she demanded a guarantee of Catherine's safety from Aubrey's master, initially insisting that no one controlled him. Reminded by Jean-Claude that Nikolaos wanted Anita unharmed, Aubrey reluctantly contained his desire to beat humility into the defiant animator, his self-control further tested by Anita's continual insults en route to seeing Nikolaos. However when Anita saw through a ruse to pass Theresa off as the city's master and demanded the vampires stop playing stupid games, Aubrey's restraint snapped, and without warning he delivered a backhanded blow which nearly killed Anita. Though she survived thanks largely to Jean-Claude's swift intervention, Nikolaos was furious with Aubrey, and consigned him to a coffin prison for his transgression.

Nikolaos freed Aubrey, having him assist in kidnapping the stripper Phillip from Guilty Pleasures. Having wrongly become convinced Phillip was the recalcitrant Anita's lover, and knowing he was under the insubordinate Jean-Claude's aegis (who was himself now confined to a coffin for defying her), Nikolaos wanted to reaffirm her dominance over both by showing they could not protect Phillip from her wrath. In front of Anita, Nikolaos ordered Aubrey and Valentine to slay Phillip; though she tried to intervene, Anita was too slow to prevent Aubrey ripping Phillip's throat out. Witnessing her horrified reaction, Aubrey taunted Anita with the threat of going after Catherine too; provoking him with insults, Anita lured Aubrey close, then rammed a concealed silver blade between his ribs and into his heart, but was unable to make sure she had slain him before Nikolaos overpowered her. Because of his considerable age, Aubrey revived once the dagger was removed, but a couple of days later Anita returned in the daytime with the assassin Edward to finish the job. Finding Aubrey asleep in his coffin beneath the Circus of the Damned, Edward injected Aubrey with silver nitrate. Too powerful for this to kill him, Aubrey awoke and seized his assailant by the throat, slowly choking Edward and casually ignoring Anita when she shot him between the eyes with a silver bullet. Switching weapons, Anita blew Aubrey's head to smithereens with a close-range shotgun blast; even this seemed insufficient to finish Aubrey off, and he continued to strangle Edward until Anita fired the shotgun a second time, this time destroying his heart and much of his chest, finally permanently slaying him.

HEIGHT: Unspecified
WEIGHT: Unspecified
EYES: Brown
HAIR: Brown or Auburn
AGE: Between 500 and 550 years old

DESCRIPTION: Aubrey initially appeared to have silken hair, ivory colored skin and solid, bottomless, brown eyes, though his extreme beauty was almost certainly hypnotically enhanced. When angered, he would become bestial, hissing, snarling and growling, his long fangs extending below his lips, from which he would ferally lick blood.

DEMEANOR: Following his original confinement, which was for three months, Aubrey was mentally unstable and retained only a mask of humanity; the slightest defiance could shatter this and unleash a berserk rage which even other vampires feared. While in this state, he was largely oblivious to minor injuries, cutting his own lips with his extended fangs and spitting at the mouth. Unpredictable, he sometimes found things inappropriately amusing, demonstrating a rich laugh which would fade into hysterical hissing and faint giggles. Proud, he disliked being reminded that he was not his own master and could be easily provoked by insults.

NOTABLE SKILLS: Aubrey moved with the fluid grace of an elder vampire, centuries of experience making his every movement practiced and precise; similarly when he was not moving, he exhibited the perfect stillness of the long dead, allowing him to nearly blend into the background even without employing his hypnotic powers. Despite his age, he seemingly lacked combat training, relying instead on his vampiric abilities.

NOTABLE ABILITIES: Aubrey possessed superhuman strength to an unspecified degree; given that even new vampires are able to lift small cars with ease, it seems likely that Aubrey would be at least this strong, and certainly a backhanded slap was sufficient to inflict potentially fatal injuries on Anita Blake. He could move almost too fast for the human eye to follow. Though he would become inert in daytime, he was old enough to be able to awaken if attacked in this state. Like most vampires, though resistant to conventional weapons he was vulnerable to crosses, sunlight, wooden stakes through the heart, and damage inflicted by

silver weapons; however his great age allowed him to revive from having his heart pierced by a silver blade once the weapon was removed, and an injection of silver nitrate into his veins merely served to annoy him. Aubrey was likewise unbothered by small caliber silver bullets, even when shot between the eyes, and despite being decapitated, Aubrey's body was able to persist in strangling Edward until his heart was also destroyed; whether he could have eventually recovered from the beheading if this last wound had not been inflicted or his body simply retained a brief façade of life is uncertain.

An older vampire, Aubrey had developed hypnotic abilities to the level where he casually enhanced his appearance to onlookers, and masked his movements to generate the illusion of being able to teleport. He could mentally dominate most humans with ease, calling them to him or freezing them on the spot they stood, and if he placed them in a deep trance even once, he would be able to summon and control them thereafter until either Aubrey or his victim died; his voice was apparently less textured than Jean-Claude's, but made up for this with the sheer power provided by his ancient mind, and he could wipe selected memories from those he controlled. His senses were accentuated, granting superior night vision and allowing him to smell a human's emotional state.

ANITA BLAKE

ANITA ON ANITA: "I am The Executioner, and I don't date vampires. I kill them."

REAL NAME: Anita Blake
ALIASES: The Executioner
ANITA'S NICKNAMES: Ms. Cynical
JEAN-CLAUDE'S NICKNAMES: Ma petite
CLASSIFICATION: Human
OCCUPATION: Animator, civilian liaison to RPIT, vampire executioner
CITIZENSHIP: U.S.A.
PLACE OF BIRTH: Unrevealed
BASE OF OPERATIONS: St. Louis, Missouri
KNOWN RELATIVES: Judith (stepmother), Josh (stepbrother), unidentified father
ALLIES: Edward, Jean-Claude, Manny, Phillip, Ronnie Sims
GROUP AFFILIATION: RPIT, Animator's Inc.
ENEMIES: Aubrey, Burchard, Nikolaos, Theresa, Valentine, Zachary
EDUCATION: College Graduate, BS Preternatural Biology
FIRST APPEARANCE: Guilty Pleasures (1993)

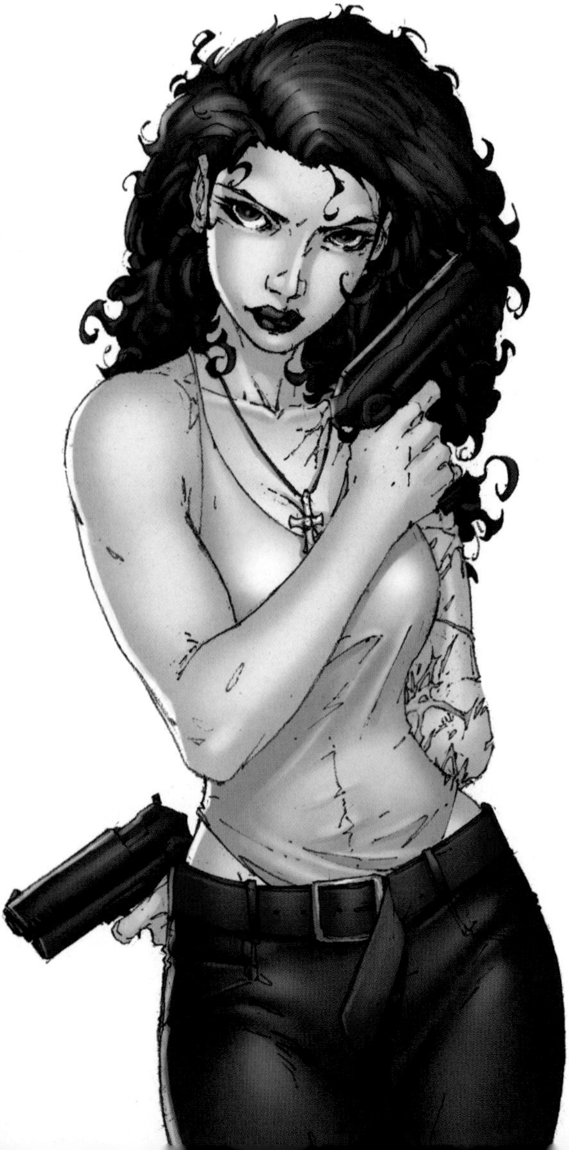

HISTORY: Anita Blake was born with the rare ability to raise zombies, a talent that has shaped her life. At some point she met the animator Manny, who trained her in the art of corpse raising; he also taught her to slay vampires, much to the distress of most of her family. Anita and Manny both joined Animators, Inc., a company which raised the dead, mostly to settle will disputes or allow loved ones a final chance to speak to the departed. Staunchly religious, when the Pope excommunicated all animators until they agreed to stop raising the dead, Anita became Episcopalian; she remains a regular churchgoer.

Anita's killings eventually saw vampires nickname her "The Executioner." Three years ago Anita took down a vampire pack which was slaughtering the Chin family; having used up all her bullets, Anita found the only survivor, Beverly, as one of the vampires was about to kill her. Anita threw a silver knife into the vampire's shoulder, but only managed to annoy her target, who turned on her. The vampire had Anita pinned to the ground and was preparing to bite her when Beverly struck it repeatedly about the head with a silver candlestick, continuing hysterically until the vampire's entire skull was smashed in. Three years ago Anita also met Veronica "Ronnie" Sims, a private detective who went on retainer to Animators, Inc., and who became one of Anita's closest friends; apart from being one of the few people to get Anita's sense of humor, Ronnie was also one of the few friends whom Anita felt both truly understood the risks Anita's life involved, and who could look after themselves if they got caught up in that life. Ronnie became Anita's exercise buddy, and they visited one another in hospital when their respective lives resulted in serious injuries.

Anita also met another person she could trust to handle himself in a fight. Edward was a hitman who had switched to killing supernatural creatures because regular humans weren't challenging enough. Though they helped one another on occasion, Anita was under no illusion that Edward would have any problems torturing or killing her if it suited his purposes. Two years ago, after the Addison vs. Clark court ruling granted vampires civil rights, making it illegal to slay a vampire without a warrant, Anita and Manny were sent after a pack of six vampires who between them had slain 23 people; Edward accompanied them on the kill. During the assault Manny was severely injured and nearly died, while Anita, separated from the others, ran into the worst of the group, the vampire Valentine, accredited with killing 10 children. Valentine overpowered Anita, tearing up her left arm and breaking it as she tried to fend him off, then ripping open and snapping her collarbone as he fed from her. Grasping around desperately with her uninjured arm for something to fend him off with, Anita found a vial of holy water, which she threw in his face; he fled as his flesh boiled away, and Anita believed him dead, since Edward set the building alight with the flamethrower he had brought. Physical therapy gave Anita back the use of her arm; Manny spent four months in hospital, and at the insistence of his wife Rosita, retired from vampire slaying thereafter. Anita gradually accumulated several other scars, including one on the back when a vampire's human servant stabbed Anita with her own stake, and a cross-shaped one on her left forearm, when a vampire's human servant thought it would be amusing to brand her; in both cases, Anita slew the individuals who injured her. She also suffered a knee injury, which continued to give her problems running up inclines even after it had healed.

The authorities formed a new task force to deal with supernatural crimes, the Regional Preternatural Investigation Team (RPIT), and Anita was put on retainer as their civilian expert on the supernatural; Sergeant Rudolph "Dolph" Storr, head of the squad, soon learned to value her input. Presumably around this time she developed her relationship with Dead Dave, a former cop turned vampire, who provided her insider knowledge on cases pertaining to the vampire community, and Irving Griswold, a werewolf reporter at the St. Louis Post-Dispatch, who shared information with her in return for exclusives. During one case in the vampire-run District, she met Jean-Claude, owner of the Guilty

Pleasures vampire strip club and one of the city's master vampires. He found himself intrigued by her ability to partially resist his mental powers and enamored of her beauty.

Recently, out of professional courtesy, Anita joined other animators in attending the funeral of the animator Zachary, although she hadn't known him when he was alive. Unknown to her at the time, he was restored to a semblance of life again by a voodoo gris-gris charm. Needing to feed it to sustain the magic, he led a pack of ghouls in murdering several vampires; Anita assisted RPIT in investigating these, but, partially because the vampire community withheld information, they failed to make any real progress. However the city's master vampire, Nikolaos, was eager to solve the killings herself, unaware the culprit was in her own employ. At Jean-Claude's suggestion, they decided to hire Anita direct, sending Willie McCoy, the only vampire Anita had known when he was a human. However Anita refused to work for vampires; refusing to take no for an answer, Nikolaos ordered Jean-Claude and her minion Aubrey to coerce Anita's cooperation. They lured her to Guilty Pleasures under the pretext of attending her close friend Catherine Maison's bachelorette party; Anita was called away by RPIT to examine a murdered caretaker, concluding he had been killed by ghouls. She returned to Guilty Pleasures, and returned to find that Aubrey had placed Catherine into a deep trance, allowing him to summon her whenever he wanted. Although Aubrey failed to do the same to Anita, the threat of violence against her friend was enough to make Anita agree to hunt for the vampire killer. However, Anita demanded an audience with Aubrey's master, Nikolaos, to get a guarantee that Aubrey would not harm Catherine afterwards. Initially the vampires tried to pass another of Nikolaos' minions, Theresa, as Aubrey's master, but when Anita instantly saw through their ploy, an enraged Aubrey struck her. To save the badly injured Anita's life, Jean-Claude gave her the first mark, the initial step to making her his human servant, which granted her enhanced recuperative powers.

The rapidly healing Anita was then placed in Nikolaos' dungeon, beneath the Circus of the Damned, where wererats under Nikolaos' control tried to break her spirit. Instead Anita fought them off until the rat king Rafael, who did not want his people working for Nikolaos, intervened on her behalf. After the wererats departed, Anita was taken before Nikolaos, who tried to break her will; Anita resisted, but realized just how dangerous and powerful the city's master was. Nikolaos informed Anita that they had a witness to the second murder, but that he had hung himself before providing anything useful; however Zachary had raised the witness as a zombie so they could continue the questioning. Anita watched as Zachary broke the zombie's mind, unaware that he was doing so deliberately to prevent anyone present from learning he was the killer they sought. Nikolaos lost her temper, and Zachary and Anita were forced to flee for their lives while Jean-Claude battled her; losing, and aware that Nikolaos would lock him inside a cross-wrapped coffin to starve, Jean-Claude secretly reached out with his mind and marked Anita for a second time, allowing him to feed through her and communicate to Anita through her dreams. As Anita exited the Circus, she was intercepted by Valentine, still alive but badly scarred from their prior encounter; he promised to kill her once Nikolaos lifted her prohibition against harming Anita.

Anita's life was further complicated when Edward informed her that he had been hired to kill the city's master, and that he knew Anita had met with his target; Anita feigned ignorance. Though Edward clearly knew she was lying, he agreed to give her a few days to "find" the information, after which he would come back to extract it, by force if necessary. The next day, Anita told Ronnie of some of her predicament, and asked her friend to check into anti-vampire hate groups in case they might be involved in the killings, while she pursued other leads. Visiting work to collect files, she was met by Phillip, a stripper who worked for Jean-Claude, who first claimed to be looking for his missing employer, and then offered his help getting her access to people who would not normally talk to the Executioner. Though suspecting he was under orders

to watch her for someone, probably Nikolaos, Anita agreed, using him to talk to Rebecca Miles, girlfriend of the first victim. Miles let slip that her boyfriend had attended freak parties, sex gatherings where vampire junkies could meet vampires. Phillip confirmed that some of the other victims had done so too, and Anita asked him to get her into one. That night Phillip took Anita to the next freak party; finding the interactions too intense, Anita went outside for some air, only to discover Zachary attempting to raise a century-dead corpse in the adjacent cemetery, with Theresa monitoring him, under orders from Nikolaos to slay him if he failed. Thinking she was helping a fellow human, Anita forced Theresa to let her assist Zachary, but while raising the zombie Anita remembered attending Zachary's funeral, and spotted the gris-gris; despite discovering his secret, Anita failed to make the connection to the murders. Leaving the cemetery, Anita ran into Nikolaos, who had been covertly watching. Nikolaos realized angrily that Jean-Claude had given Anita the second mark, but was distracted from harming her when Phillip arrived, having come from the party looking for Anita. Phillip pleaded with Nikolaos, reminding her he had agreed to spy on Anita in return for a promise that she would not be hurt. Nikolaos began to punish Phillip for his defiance, but was interrupted when the nearby party was attacked by members of the Church of Eternal Life; Nikolaos fled.

The next day Anita was called early in the morning to a new vampire murder, and learned that Theresa was the latest victim. Afterwards, having heard from Ronnie that she had found someone inside Humans Against Vampires (HAV) willing to talk to them, Anita visited Ronnie's office to meet the contact, and learned it was Beverly Chin; because of her debt to Anita, Beverly agreed to spy on HAV for them. The attack on the party the night before suggested another possible lead, and Ronnie and Anita visited the Church of Eternal Life, making an appointment to see its founder Malcolm that evening. However as they left the Church, an assassin tried but failed to kill Anita. She returned to the Church that evening for her meeting with Malcolm, and surreptitiously learned he had probably met with Edward shortly before the murders began, causing Anita to worry that Edward was the killer. However more pressing matters came up, when she learned that Nikolaos had kidnapped Phillip and wanted her to come to the Circus immediately. There Nikolaos expressed her displeasure at Phillip's defiance the night before, and at Jean-Claude's marking of Anita; though she believed Anita's claims that she had not known what Jean-Claude had done, Nikolaos ordered Phillip's death to prove to Jean-Claude's followers that their master could not protect them. Anita was unable to stop Aubrey ripping Phillip's throat out, though she did manage to stab him in the heart with a silver blade before Nikolaos overpowered her and bit her.

Anita awoke in Guilty Pleasures, dropped there by Nikolaos to continue her hunt for the vampire killer. Having resolved to slay Nikolaos, when Edward caught up with Anita outside the club, Anita told him she would give him Nikolaos in return for being in on the kill. Edward cleansed Anita's bite wound with holy water, and Anita contacted Irving Griswold to set up a meeting with Rafael. However, Zachary, worried Anita was getting too close, lured Edward and Anita to a cemetery, and ambushed them with his ghoul pack; Anita finally realized Zachary was the vampire killer, and he admitted to having sent the gunman to the Church, before setting his ghouls on them, but the pair narrowly escaped.

Rafael agreed to lead Anita and Edward through the underground tunnels into the Circus to catch Nikolaos and her followers unawares. They successfully slew Valentine and Aubrey before Nikolaos, her human servant Burchard, and Zachary caught them; Nikolaos had been awake in the daytime amusing herself by having Zachary raise Phillip as a zombie. Nikolaos forced Anita to battle Burchard, but during the fight Anita revealed Zachary's crimes. Nikolaos ripped Zachary's throat out, and while she was distracted, Anita managed to slay Burchard. Nikolaos attacked Anita, but Edward shot the vampire, who turned her attention on him instead; before she could slay Edward, Anita snatched up Burchard's sword and ended Nikolaos' unlife. The major threat eliminated, Anita turned her attention to Zachary, being kept alive despite his wounds by the gris-gris; deducing that human blood would destroy the charm, Anita used her own wounds to finish him off. Afterwards, Anita freed Jean-Claude from his coffin, and sadly laid Phillip back to rest.

HEIGHT: 5'3" approximately
WEIGHT: 106 lbs.
EYES: Dark brown
HAIR: Black
AGE: 24

DESCRIPTION: Anita has dark brown eyes, nearly black, with black, curly, shoulder-length hair and pale skin, her appearance showing a mixture of her combined Latin and German heritage. Anita is slender but curvy, short but muscular. She generally prefers to wear long sleeved blouses to better conceal her weapons and scars.

DISTINGUISHING FEATURES: Anita has a cross-shaped burn scar on her inner left forearm and right above it on the bend of the same arm a mound of scar tissue, extensive bite scarring on the left side of her collar bone and a stake scar on her back.

DEMEANOR: Anita is sarcastic and flippant, believes in facing her fears head on rather than letting them rule her, and doesn't make idle threats. Prior to gaining immunity from Jean-Claude's marks, Anita prided herself on her natural ability to partially resist vampire mind tricks. She strongly dislikes blackberries, mushrooms, green peppers, injections, and diet drinks, though nowhere near as much as she dislikes vampires; on the other hand, she tolerates brussel sprouts and high-heeled shoes as necessary evils, and actively likes penguins, collecting stuffed toy ones. She believes in doing virtually anything for a friend, and considers a human betraying another human to the monsters as one of the worst possible crimes. To sleep, she listens to classical music such as Chopin or Mozart.

NOTABLE SKILLS: Anita is an excellent shot and capable knife fighter and hand-to-hand combatant. She jogs regularly as part of her fitness regime, so that she can run hard when she needs to, and is able to bench press 100 lbs. She is knowledgeable about various supernatural creatures, able to identify many by the wounds they leave in victims.

EQUIPMENT: Anita almost always wears a silver crucifix around her neck, and carries a Browning Hi-Power 9mm loaded with silver bullets in her shoulder holster, which also holds up to 26 rounds of extra ammunition. She often carries a more concealable Firestar 9mm in a concealed inside-the-pants holster. She has an array of silver knives, with arm, thigh, wrist and ankle holsters giving a choice of where to conceal them. Her vampire hunting kit includes stakes and a hammer, and she has also used syringes full of silver nitrate and a sawn-off shotgun with silver payload, both provided by Edward. She sometimes also wears a small charm bracelet with three small crosses on a silver chain. Anita has a police-issue ID which grants her access to crime scenes.

Her zombie raising equipment includes live chickens or goats for sacrifice, a machete for killing them, and homemade ointment which includes graveyard and certain herbs, used as part of the ceremony.

NOTABLE ABILITIES: Anita has the inherent ability, focused through training and ritual, to raise the corpses of the dead as zombies. She is powerful enough to raise even century-old corpses whose bodies have turned to dust and bone fragments, her powers reforming the body from these remains. Once raised, the zombie is usually under her control, until she returns it to the ground. She has good night vision.

Presumably as an extension of her animator power, Anita had a level of resistance to vampire mind tricks even before she was marked by Jean-Claude. She is also able to recognize vampires and lycanthropes trying to pass for human, and has an innate talent for estimating the age and power level of most vampires. After receiving Jean-Claude's marks, she has accelerated healing and near total immunity to vampire mind powers.

HISTORY: Burchard was a human servant of the master vampire Nikolaos. He received his fourth mark nearly six centuries ago, and enjoyed an elongated lifespan as a result. His history prior to working for Nikolaos is unrevealed, but given his claimed 603 years of age, he would have been born around 1390, and if the faint British accent he displayed in the modern day was an accurate indication of his origins, he would have been born during the reign of King Richard II, and been the right age to fight in France under Henry V, perhaps even at Agincourt. After encountering Nikolaos and receiving the marks, Burchard faithfully served Nikolaos over the centuries as a fighter, with few guessing how old he was. In recent times, Burchard resided beneath the Circus of the Damned, Nikolaos' base of operations in St. Louis. Burchard attended to Nikolaos as she enlisted vampire hunter Anita Blake to investigate the recent rash of murders among the most powerful vampires in St. Louis.

When Nikolaos realized that Anita had received her first mark from the vampire Jean-Claude, she and Burchard interrogated Anita, surprised to discover that Anita was ignorant of the effects of becoming a human servant. They revealed the mark's meanings to Anita, and Nikolaos had Burchard feed on her to demonstrate how he had become virtually immortal. Nikolaos had Burchard restrain Anita while they tortured and ultimately murdered her friend, Phillip

Anita resolved to destroy Nikolaos, and gained access to the Circus of the Damned with fellow vampire hunter, Edward, let in by Rafael and his wererats, who knew the routes through underground tunnels which led into the Nikolaos' dwelling. Anita and Edward slew the vampires Aubrey and Valentine before Burchard, Zachary and Nikolaos discovered them. Burchard removed their weapons, and they began to punish Anita by revealing how they had killed Phillip and raised him as a zombie. Nikolaos instructed Anita to face Burchard in a knife fight in order to save Edward's life, and ordered Burchard to injure her as a lesson, but let her live so that she would still serve them. Anita was outclassed by Burchard's superior skill, but in the midst of the fight she revealed that Zachary was the killer Nikolaos sought. Zachary panicked and fired a shot, making Burchard duck. Anita then drove a knife into Burchard's back, and stabbed him again in his throat; as his lifeblood spurted out, Anita delivered a final third thrust, and Burchard collapsed, presumably dead. Anita subsequently slew Nikolaos with Burchard's sword, erasing any chance that Burchard might have survived his injuries.

HEIGHT: Unspecified, notably taller than Anita, as his reach is twice hers.
WEIGHT: Unrevealed
EYES: Brown
HAIR: Bald, very little hair on head
AGE: 603 (unspecified as to how much of this was before becoming a servant, when he still aged)

DESCRIPTION: Burchard had a thin, narrow face, with dark eyes made more noticeable by his nearly hairless head. He spoke with a deep, cultured, vaguely British-accented, voice.

DEMEANOR: Six hundred years serving Nikolaos had solidified Burchard's military demeanor; he would automatically stand rigidly to attention most of the time, and appeared unsurprised by most events he witnessed, presumably feeling he had seen it all before. He was quietly confident in fights, and seemed only concerned with his master's welfare. If he ever disagreed with Nikolaos or opposed her will, he had long since accepted the futility of standing up to her, and viewed the attempts of others to do so as a teacher viewed an errant and stupid child.

BURCHARD ON HIMSELF: "I have been given the fourth mark and will live as long as my mistress needs me."

REAL NAME: Burchard (full name unrevealed)
ALIASES: None
ANITA'S NICKNAMES: None
CLASSIFICATION: Vampire's servant
OCCUPATION: Human servant of Nikolaos, possibly former soldier
CITIZENSHIP: Unrevealed, possibly British
BASE OF OPERATIONS: Circus of the Damned, St. Louis, Missouri
KNOWN RELATIVES: None
ALLIES: Nikolaos, Winter, Aubrey, Theresa, Valentine, unidentified black vampire
GROUP AFFILIATION: Nikolaos' Kiss
ENEMIES: Anita Blake, Edward
EDUCATION: Unrevealed
FIRST APPEARANCE: Guilty Pleasures (1993)

NOTABLE SKILLS: A soldier with nearly 600 years experience, Burchard was highly skilled in multiple weapon types. As well as guns, he was exceptionally adept with knife fighting, and seemingly a master swordsman. Experience had taught him to anticipate most opponents' moves, and he was also knowledgeable in the art of concealing weapons about one's person.

EQUIPMENT: Burchard often carried a variety of weapons, including semiautomatic guns, knives, and swords.

NOTABLE ABILITIES: Burchard had a number of superhuman powers as a result of having been given the fourth mark. His endurance and recuperative powers were far in excess of the human norm, he could receive instructions from his master telepathically or in his dreams across unspecified distances and could provide her energy, no matter what distance or impediments were between them, allowing her to siphon energy from him; he would replenish his own energy in such a case by eating and drinking extra. Most remarkably, Burchard did not age because he has fed off of Nikolaos's blood, cementing his bond to her; the feeding experience was clearly akin to sex for both parties. It is possible the marks granted other, as yet unseen, abilities.

CHURCH OF ETERNAL LIFE

ANITA ON THE CHURCH OF ETERNAL LIFE: "Everyone fears death… But at the Church of Eternal Life, they promise just what the name says. And they can prove it."
CURRENT MEMBERS: Bruce, Malcolm, many unidentified others
BASE OF OPERATIONS: Page Avenue, St. Louis, Missouri
FIRST APPEARANCE: Guilty Pleasures (1993)

HISTORY: The Church of Eternal Life is a recent institution founded by vampires, which seeks to convert willing humans to their goals and lifestyle. The church has manufactured its own religion and beliefs based upon the nature of vampirism, and the allure that some humans have for vampiric life. Humans are attracted to the church by its promise of immortality for the congregation, a claim which many religions make, but which the vampires can visibly deliver upon. As a result, the Church of Eternal Life is a flourishing organization in cities where congregations have taken root.

Membership within the church includes vampires themselves and humans who hope to one day become vampires. Membership is restricted to those 18 and older. Members of the congregation evangelize during the daytime, visiting the homes of humans to recruit new members. Services are held in the evening when the vampiric members of the congregation are able to attend. The services are similar to those of many faiths, including a sermon and an arrangement of worship songs based on the tunes of hymnals from the Christian faith (such as "Bringing in the Sheaves"). In the fellowship time following services, coffee and blood are provided to the congregation. The church's architecture naturally contains no religious imagery that would be harmful to vampires, but does feature abstract stained glass windows such as would be found in a Christian church. Vampires who are not members of the church look down upon the church organizers, and hostilities have broken out between members and non-members of the church. However, the church's most vocal opposition comes from Humans Against Vampires and the Catholic Church.

In St. Louis, the church is led by Malcolm, one of the city's most powerful master vampires, founder of the Church of Eternal Life. Their main building is just off Page Avenue, deliberately far from the main vampire District of the city, a generic looking church deliberately lacking the religious iconography of regular churchs. Above the double doors at the building's entrance is a sign, "Enter Friend and Be at Peace." Some of the St. Louis church congregation have turned to violence, attacking "freak parties" armed with clubs and persecuting those attending, but Malcolm is quick to publicly disavow the church's support of any violent activities. However he exercises deliberately lax discipline over his flock on this area, suggesting a tacit approval. The only identified human member of Malcolm's congregation is Bruce, a secretary in the church, who arranges Malcolm's appointments during the daytime. Supporters of the church include Jamison Clarke of Animators, Inc., who at one point advised his client Mrs. Franks when her teenage son sought to join the church. Anita Blake caught wind of this, and offered the services of her friend Raymond Fields, an expert on vampire cults, hoping that the Franks would seek a second opinion.

When Anita was investigating the murders of several prominent vampires in the St. Louis area, she included members of the Church of Eternal Life as suspect, believing that the killer was targeting vampires who participated in "freak parties." Anita's suspicions were strengthened when she learned Malcolm had apparently met with Edward, an assassin specializing in supernatural targets, and seemed confirmed when Anita was attacked by a human servant outside the church's facilities. However, the servant had been dispatched by the true killer Zachary, hoping to throw Anita off his trail. Anita later had an interview with Malcolm and attempted to connive a confession from him, but as Malcolm had nothing to do with the murders, this failed. Noting that Anita had been marked by Jean-Claude, he offered the church's services to her, should she have need of them in the future.

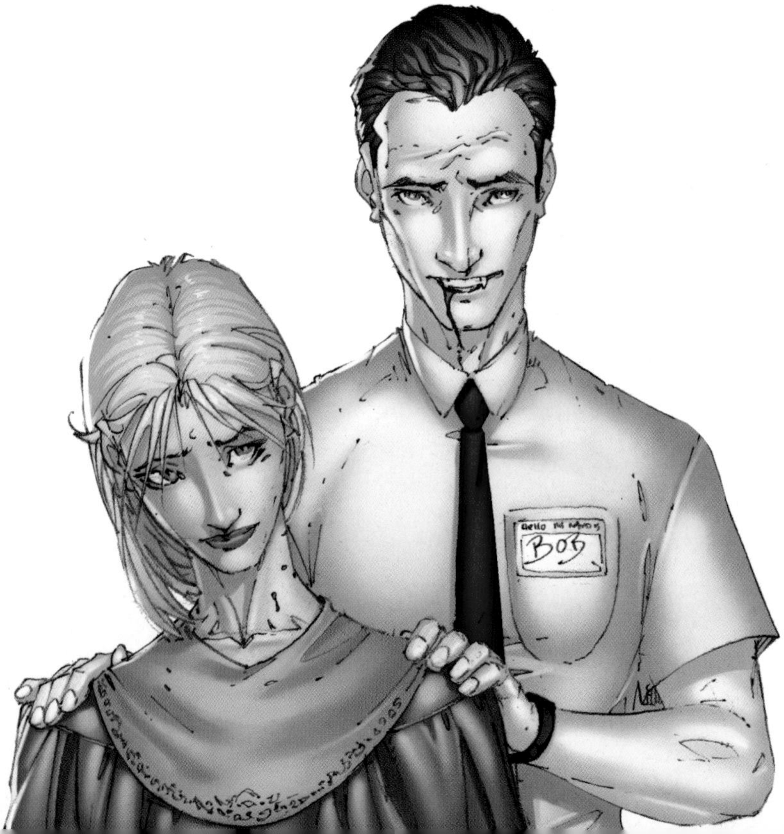
BOB

DEAD DAVE'S

HISTORY: The bar Dead Dave's was opened a couple of years ago by a former police officer named Dave, who was kicked off the St. Louis police force when he became a vampire under unrevealed circumstances. As manager of the bar Dave and his staff picked up much of the gossip about the local vampires and their groupies, including their daytime resting places. Though willing to share much of his information with the police, Dave resented the prejudice of his former comrades, so he eventually formed an informal arrangement with Anita Blake, an animator who worked part-time as a supernatural expert for the police. This way Dave could help out on the occasional case without either Dave or the police actually talking to each other; because Dave would never admit he was helping the police, Anita would always make a show of paying a nominal amount for the information, but Dave's insider knowledge of the District was often invaluable to the force in solving cases involving the undead. With dark glass windows and quiet during the daytime, the bar is also Dave's home. While he is resting during the day, his employee Luther runs things and deals with any business problems that come up during that time.

Recently, while Blake was investigating a series of vampire murders for St. Louis's master vampire, she came to Dead Dave's to find information on Phillip, a human dancer at the strip club Guilty Pleasures. She met with Luther, who told her what he had heard about Phillip. He informed her of the boasts of pedophile vampire Valentine, who claimed he was the first vamp to have ever done Phillip, and that the boy had loved it so much that he had become a vampire junkie and turned freak to get his fixes. When Blake asked about the daytime resting place of Valentine so she could kill him off before he could finish his vendetta against her, Luther tentatively refused, fearing that the other vampires living in the District would burn the bar down if they learned he had given such information to humans, but told Blake he would ask Dave, and that if he agreed to it Luther would tell Blake what she wished to know. Blake eventually learned the location from another source, sparing Dave and Luther the possible stigma of giving out such sensitive information.

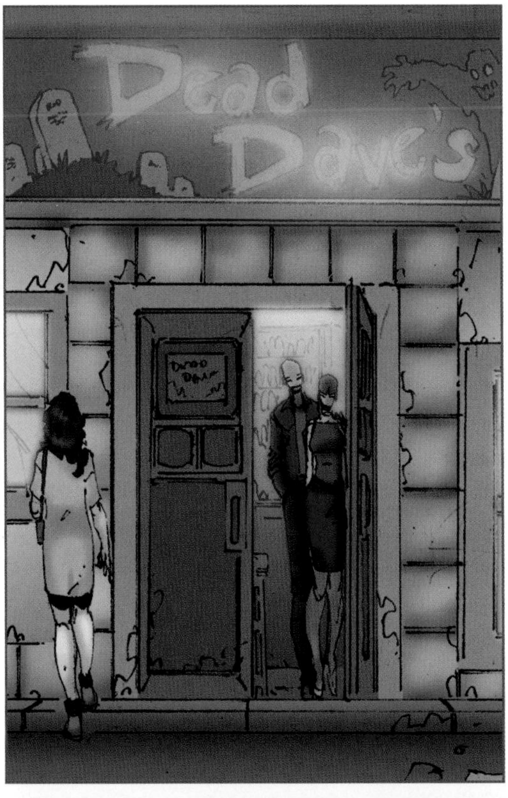
Dead Dave's

ANITA ON DEAD DAVE'S: "The proprietor was an ex-cop who had been kicked off the force for being dead. Picky, picky."
CURRENT MEMBERS: Dave (owner/night manager), Luther (bartender/day manager)
BASE OF OPERATIONS: The District, St. Louis, Missouri
FIRST APPEARANCE: Guilty Pleasures (1993)

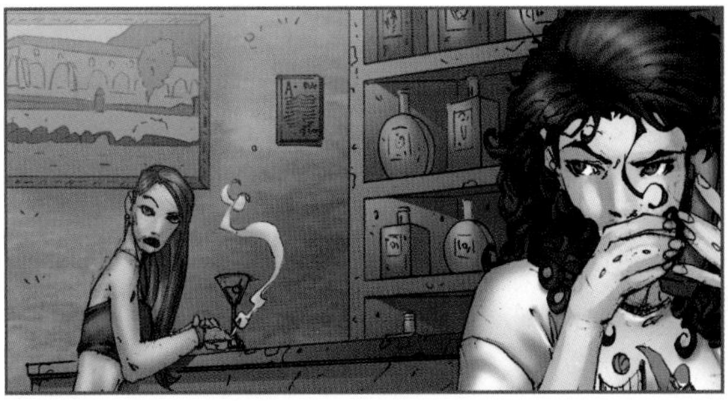

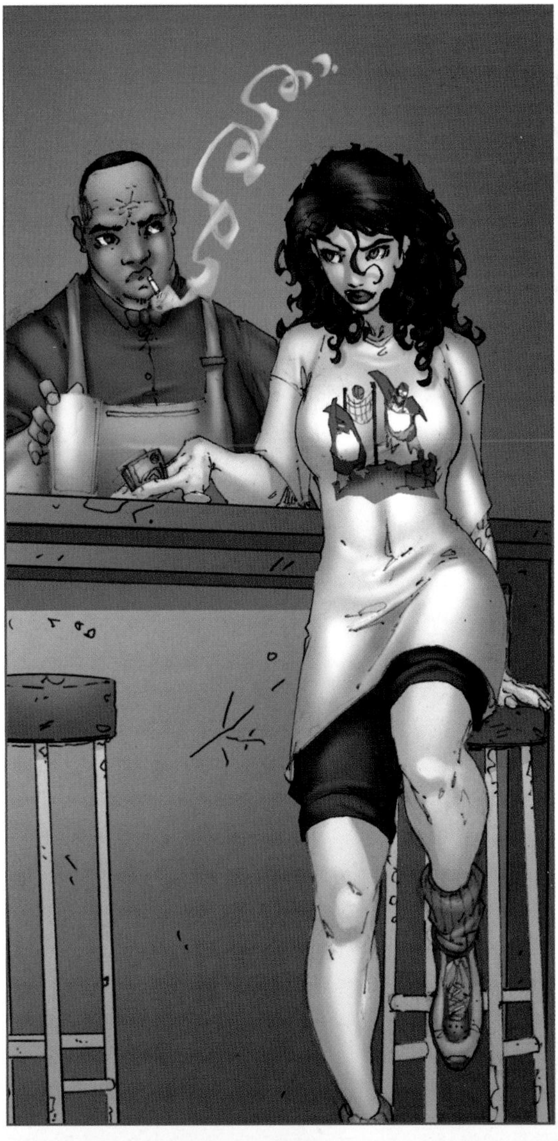

EDWARD

ANITA ON EDWARD: "He was not an imposing man, not frightening, if you didn't know him. But if I was The Executioner, he was Death itself."

REAL NAME: Unrevealed
ALIASES: Teddy; Ned
ANITA'S NICKNAMES: Edward the Chameleon, Death
CLASSIFICATION: Human
OCCUPATION: Paranormal Bounty Hunter, Assassin
CITIZENSHIP: U.S.A.
BASE OF OPERATIONS: Unrevealed
KNOWN RELATIVES: None
ALLIES: Anita Blake
GROUP AFFILIATION: None
ENEMIES: Aubrey, Burchard, Valentine, Zachary
EDUCATION: Unrevealed
FIRST APPEARANCE: Guilty Pleasures (1993)

HISTORY: Edward is a paranormal bounty hunter. His past a mystery, it is rumored that he was once a hit-man, but that he found the job insufficiently engaging, and turned his hand to more interesting prey. He now specializes in tracking and killing vampires, lycanthropes and other monsters, the more powerful the better. He finds them far more challenging to kill than humans and regards tracking and trying to kill a thousand year old master vampire as an interesting challenge.

He is the perfect killer, with little conscience, and really enjoys his work. A master fighter, he is an expert with many weapons, including guns and knives. His preferred weapon appears to be the Uzi, but he also favors a knife. He has developed many unusual ways of killing vampires, including the use of a flame thrower and a silver nitrate lethal injection.

Morally ambiguous, Edward will not hesitate to torture or kill people, including those who he knows well, in order to get the job done, and has little regard for innocent bystanders. Unsurprisingly he does not like dealing with the police. He normally uses his charm and good looks to extract information leading him to his targets, often working his way into freak parties, attended by vampire groupies, who can provide insider information to the local vampire scene of whichever city he is in. Once an attack begins, Edward slips into "perfect-killer" mode, during which time he appears to be completely emotionless.

It is unclear how Edward and vampire hunter Anita Blake first met, but despite their differing moralities, or perhaps because of them, the two hit it off. Anita is probably the closest thing to a friend Edward has, and he feels she is the least helpless person he knows. In turn, Anita finds she cannot help but like Edward, despite the blood on his hands, perhaps in part because he makes no attempt to hide what he really is from her, and because he is the one person she never needs to feel she is endangering with her presence. Anita regards him as one of the most dangerous and deadliest killers she knows and is genuinely afraid of him, despite their friendship. Edward has worked with Anita on multiple previous occasions and they form a good team. Two years previously, he helped Anita and her fellow animator Manny track down Valentine's group of vampires, cornering them in their house, Edward went in armed with a flamethrower, unconcerned with collateral damage, and together they killed five vampires and two human servants, before Edward burned the house down. It was presumably Edward who got Anita to hospital afterwards, as she had most of her collarbone ripped apart during the assault by Valentine. He was very surprised to later learn that Valentine survived the attack.

Edward recently turned up in St. Louis around the same time the undead animator Zachary began killing vampires, having been hired to slay the city's master vampire. It is unclear who hired him, but it may have been Malcolm, vampire leader of the Church of Eternal Life, himself a master vampire and thus perhaps wanting to eliminate a dangerous rival in a deniable way. Certainly, evidence suggests Edward met with Malcolm shortly before the vampire killings began, so if Malcolm was not his employer, then Edward may have been trying to confirm if Malcolm was his target, as Edward was uncertain as to the master's identity. Hearing a rumor that Anita had met with the master, Edward broke into her apartment, catching her off guard when she came home and asking her to supply him the location of the master's lair. Anita lied to him, denying she knew, but because of their past, Edward decided to give her a few days grace to change her mind, suggesting he would pop back in a few days if his other sources failed to uncover it, to see if she had happened to learn it in the meantime. He also agreed to supply her with a shotgun, casually breaking into her apartment a day later to deliver it, along with a note telling her she had twenty-four hours more to supply him with the information he wanted. Knowing the vampires would slay her and possibly her friend Catherine Maison if they found out she had provided him with the information, Anita was afraid that she would have to fight him as a result and had no doubt that Edward would torture or kill her.

Following other leads, Edward used the vampire junkie Darlene to get invited to a local freak party under the guise of Teddy, only to run into Anita again, following leads on the vampire murders. Aware that the killer she sought was using the freak parties to choose his victims, Anita began to suspect Edward was her culprit, and that impression enhanced when she learned of his earlier meeting with Malcolm. The next night Edward broke into Anita's apartment to wait for her; however, anticipating this, Anita did not return home. When she called to check her answering machine, Edward overheard the messages too, and learned that Anita's ally Phillip had been kidnapped by Nikolaos, the city's master, and was being tortured to force Anita to meet with her. Before Anita hung up, Edward picked up the phone and offered to help, but fearing for Phillip's life, she declined.

The next morning, Edward caught up with Anita as she walked out of the vampire strip bar Guilty Pleasures, where Nikolaos' minions had left her after Nikolaos had finished with Anita. Because Nikolaos had slain Phillip, Anita agreed to provide Edward with the location of Nikolaos' lair, on the understanding that she intended to come too and settle her own score with the master. Using holy water, Edward assisted Anita in cleansing a bite Nikolaos' had inflicted on her, burning out the infection which might otherwise allow Nikolaos to control Anita. Sticking with Anita, Edward accompanied her when she was called to a graveyard meeting, supposedly with a Thomas Jensen to lay his zombie daughter to rest; this proved to be a trap, and both of them were attacked by ghouls under the control of Zachary, who had been fearful Anita was getting too close to his secret. Despite being caught with insufficient firepower to take down the ghoul horde, Edward and Anita managed to escape, using fuel in a nearby caretaker's hut to burn their way to freedom.

Edward and Anita met with the rat king Rafael, and arranged for his wererats to lead them through underground caverns and tunnels in the back way into Nikolaos' lair under the Circus of the Damned. They found Nikolaos' vampire coterie sleeping in their coffins, and began slaying them using Edward's lethal silver nitrate injections, but when Edward opened the coffin of the five hundred year old Aubrey, the vampire awoke despite it being daylight outside. Aubrey grabbed Edward by the throat and was throttling him, until Anita slew him, blasting his head off and blowing his chest away with two shotgun blasts. Unfortunately they discovered the thousand year old Nikolaos was not in her coffin, and were caught off-guard by her return to the coffin room. Held at gunpoint by her servant Burchard and by Zachary, Edward and Anita were stripped of their weapons, and Nikolaos used Edward as a hostage to force Anita to fight Burchard, Anita distracted Nikolaos by revealing she knew the murderer's identity, and Zachary panicked, shooting at Anita. Nikolaos let Edward go to rip out Zachary's throat, then lunged for Anita, who had managed to slay the distracted Burchard. Before she could reach her target, Nikolaos was shot by Edward, who had snatched up Zachary's gun. Barely bothered by the wound, Nikolaos turned on him and bit him. Anita saved his life by killing Nikolaos with Burchard's sword, and after her death Edward was given immediate medical treatment by the wererat Lillian, emerging from the conflict with only a dislocated shoulder, a vampire bite and two broken bones.

HEIGHT: 5'8"
WEIGHT: Unrevealed; slender
EYES: Blue
HAIR: Blond
AGE: Unrevealed

DESCRIPTION: Edward comes across as a deliberately unimposing man, with a slender build and short blond hair. He has perfected a harmless, good ol' boy grin which puts people off their guard and shows a lot of boyish charm; it is uncertain whether these are genuine or a carefully constructed mask. When working he can become extremely intense, and is capable of adapting his appearance and personality to blend in wherever he goes.

DEMEANOR: Edward has no conscience, and kills without hesitation. If Edward felt it were absolutely necessary for his survival, he would not hesitate to kill Anita. However he is also a valuable ally, and willing to go out of his way to help her when their goals are not in conflict. He enjoys a challenge, viewing the killing of vampires, lycanthropes and other monsters as his personal entertainment. When faced with the possibility of being killed by a ghoul horde, Edward made it clear he would kill himself first, rather than let the monsters have the satisfaction.

NOTABLE SKILLS: Edward is a deadly fighter, and expert with multiple varieties of weapons, from knives and small caliber firearms, through rifles and up to flamethrowers. He is also a skilled lock pick, and has contacts who can get him illegal weapons at short notice. He has the chameleon like ability to blend into situations and adopt many disguises.

EQUIPMENT: Edward commonly carries multiple firearms and knives concealed about his person, and more if he expects to fight. He routinely carries high-caliber silver rounds for use against vampires and lycanthropes, and has been known to use both shotguns and flamethrowers on occasion. He carries vials of silver nitrate, which can be injected into sleeping vampires to kill them swiftly and noiselessly.

FREAK PARTIES

ANITA ON FREAK PARTIES: "A man stood in the center of the room, a drink in his hand. He looked like he had just come from Leather 'R' Us."

MEMBERS: Crystal, Darlene, Harvey, Lucas, Madge, Maurice, Rebecca Miles, Phillip, Rochelle
BASE OF OPERATIONS: Mobile; moves to new location with each party.
FIRST APPEARANCE: Guilty Pleasures (1993)

HISTORY: In vampire slang, freaks are humans who like vampires, or are attracted to them; given that many vampires use mind powers to entice victims and make feeding pleasurable, it is unsurprising that some people become swiftly addicted after a vampire has fed off them. Freak parties are illicit gatherings of freaks, where they can share their unusual sexual predilections with others of similar taste, and having passing encounters with vampires — at the parties freaks can have vampires almost any way they want, and the vampires can have them. The only dress code is to wear something that shows off their scars, and while there are rules to the parties to protect people while they are in the main room, once someone agrees to go to a bedroom with another attendee restrictions are lifted and other partygoers cannot intervene. Given the risqué nature of the activities, the parties move locations regularly and are a closed community, with new participants only joining on the recommendation of existing party goers. The night seems to begin with the human participants meeting for casual sexual encounters first, an entrée before the main course begins when the vampires involved arrive. Groups such as the Church of Eternal Life object strenuously to freak parties, and have been known to violently disrupt them when they learn of one, attacking the freaks attending. Others, such as the hitman Edward, use the parties as sources of information, attending them to pick up insider gossip about local vampires he has been hired to kill.

Unfortunately for the freak community of St. Louis, the undead animator Zachary found yet another use for the parties, as a source of potential victims. Requiring vampire blood to sustain the charm which granted his unnatural life, Zachary chose his targets from amongst those vampires on the freak party circuit. His first victim was Maurice, who used to pass round his "property," Rebecca Miles, at the parties for other vampires to sample. Nine other victims followed, including two master vampires. Despite this, no one in the freak community drew the connection, but eventually animator Anita Blake, hired to identify the killer, did. Assisted by Phillip, a vampire junkie and former circuit regular, Anita attended the next party, run by the couple Madge and Harvey at their home on Zumbehl Road in Saint Charles county.

Anita found the party disquieting for a number of reasons, not least because of the overt sexual interest several of the partygoers directed to either her or Phillip, but found little information which would help her case. The arrival of Edward, under the alias Teddy, and the open resentment of Edward's "cover date" Darlene, who was jealous because of Anita's supposed involvement with Phillip caused Anita further discomfort. Realizing that Phillip was also finding being there difficult, due to his own addiction and history with many fellow partygoers, Anita offered to leave, but Phillip noticed Harvey spying on them, and to prevent him getting suspicious, Phillip bit Anita on the neck. Anita angrily went outside to get some space, and subsequently witnessed the party being brought to an abrupt close by the arrival of members of the Church of Eternal Life.

Freak party regulars include Maurice, Rebecca, Phillip and Darlene, as well as Rochelle, a black woman whose relatively new scars suggest she is a recent convert, and the extremely insecure and emotionally vulnerable Crystal, a blond, obese older woman with an obsessive interest in Phillip.

GHOULS

TRAITS: Ghouls are undead creatures who feed on the flesh of living, dead, or undead creatures. Pack animals, they will not normally travel any great distance between cemeteries and usually do not attack living beings unless the potential prey is wounded or defenseless, but in large numbers ghouls can be bolder and more likely to swarm a live target. Ghouls are easily frightened by crowds and are afraid of fire. Their intelligence is only slightly above that of an animal, they do not wear clothing, and they are not capable of human speech, communicating with one another through high-pitched squeals. Ghouls can be injured through conventional means, but cannot be permanently slain unless decapitated, burned alive, or delivered a similar destructive blow. Unlike zombies, Ghouls' bodies are not in a state of decomposition. Their physical strength is greater than that of a normal human, allowing them to rip a human body limb from limb. Their skin is paler than it would have been in life, looking like it has been dipped in silver-grey paint; their teeth and fingernails grow, the latter becoming long black talons, and their eyes glow a crimson red. Ghouls are not active during daylight hours, but begin activity earlier in the evening than vampires. When eating, they will disembowel their food, cracking open the prey's rib cage to eat the internal organs.

LENGTH: Various
WEIGHT: Various
EYES: Crimson
SKIN: Silver-grey

HISTORY: The exact origins of ghouls are not known. They are believed to arise from cemeteries where the blessings over the soil have been eroded due to age or a number of satanic or evil rites which have been performed, removing the holy protection over the dead. Some believe that evil people who die are brought back as ghouls, or that people who have been bitten by a supernatural creature such as a vampire or lycanthrope will transform into a ghoul. What is certain is that ghouls are the remains of deceased people which rise from cemeteries. In some cases, the entire population of a cemetery has risen as ghouls. Ghouls usually frequent the cemetery from which they rose.

In one case, when the undead animator Zachary rose from his grave the other bodies in his graveyard rose with him as ghouls. These ghouls, numbering at least twenty, exhibited loyalty to Zachary, and could be made to obey simple commands from him. Under Zachary's direction, his ghouls would even attack armed humans, and they did not threaten Zachary himself. Zachary believed that ghouls came from cemeteries where animators and zombies had been raised. Further, he suspected that ghouls rose from cemeteries where zombies had been raised, and that the more zombies which had been raised, the more ghouls would be created. Zachary could not share his theories with other animators because of his need to conceal his own undead status.

Zachary made frequent use of his ghouls in the St. Louis area, leading them away from their native cemetery into other areas, at one point having them kill a human caretaker who presumably discovered them. Needing vampire blood to sustain the charm which granted him continued life, Zachary used his ghouls to overpower his victims, ripping them limb from limb. Aware of Anita Blake's investigation of the murders and hoping to kill her, Zachary lured her out to a cemetery, fooling her into believing that she was there to meet one of her clients to return a zombie to the ground. Zachary and his ghouls surrounded Anita and her companion, the vampire hunter Edward. When Edward threatened Zachary he used some of the ghouls to guard him while he sent the others to kill Anita and Edward. Unable to reach their car, Edward and Anita fled into the temporary shelter of a groundskeeper's shack, where they were able to start a fire using gasoline stored within, driving the ghouls away. Anita subsequently killed Zachary; the fate of his ghouls is not known.

ANITA ON GHOULS: "Ghouls are like pack animals, wolves maybe, but a lot more dangerous."
KNOWN MEMBERS: None named
BASE OF OPERATIONS: Various, known to frequent cemeteries
FIRST APPEARANCE: Guilty Pleasures (1993)

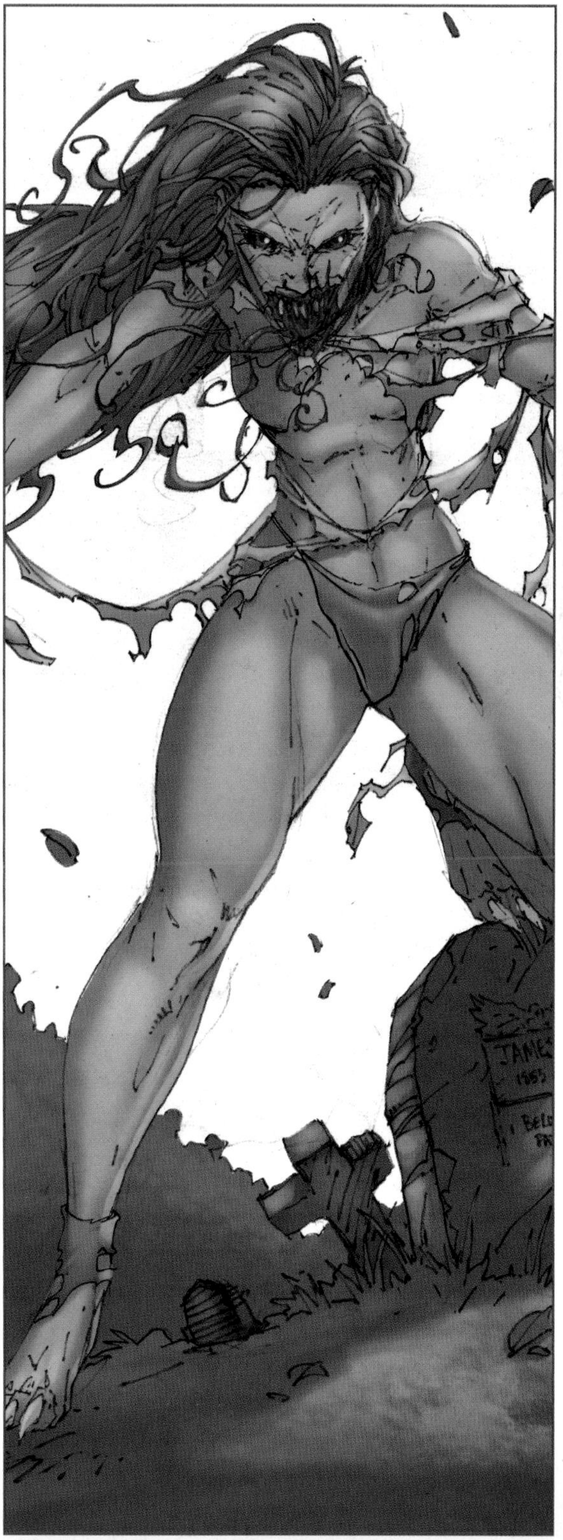

GUILTY PLEASURES

ANITA ON GUILTY PLEASURES: "There was a large sign on the door. 'No crosses, crucifixes or other holy items allowed inside.'"
CURRENT MEMBERS: Jean-Claude (owner), Buzz (bouncer), Robert, Phillip (dancers), other unidentified employees
BASE OF OPERATIONS: The District, St. Louis, MO
FIRST APPEARANCE: Guilty Pleasures (1993)

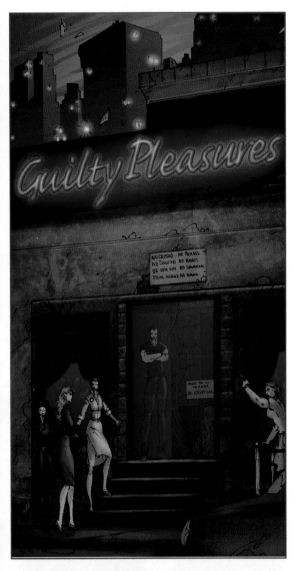

HISTORY: The club Guilty Pleasures is billed as the world's only vampire strip club, where human patrons can watch vampires in safety. While some acts involve a vampire vicariously allowing the human audience to experience the fantasy of being seduced by a vampire and feeding its needs (using a willing human dancer as an audience stand-in), other acts involve standard dancing moves and nothing more. Located just a couple of blocks from the I-70 East, it is one of the hottest clubs in the St. Louis neighborhood called the District, so busy that normally it does not permit table reservations. Vampire Jean-Claude owns the club, and MC's the acts presented on the club's stage. The club has a holy item check person, since the presence of such articles can cause serious harm to vampires. The club also employs vampire waiters to give the human customers a "safe" fright while serving them food.

Police business brought the Regional Preternatural Investigation Team's civilian supernatural expert Anita Blake to Guilty Pleasures, where she caught the attention of Jean-Claude. As a result, when a murderer capable of killing master-level vampires slew several of St. Louis' undead, Jean-Claude suggested Blake to the master of the St. Louis vampires, Nikolaos, as the person to find the killer. Blake refused to help, so Nikolaos arranged a scheme to blackmail Blake into working for them. The vampires, through groupie Monica Vespucci, arranged to have Blake and her close friend Catherine Maison attend one of the shows at Guilty Pleasures. During the opening act, Jean-Claude made an attempt to ensnare Blake with his powers, but a timely call from the local police department broke the spell before Jean-Claude succeeded, forcing the head vampires to go to their back-up plan. While Blake helped investigate a brutal murder at a local cemetery, Nikolaos' vampire servant Aubrey pretended to be one of the club's acts, luring Maison on stage, and succeeded in putting her into a deep trance state, guaranteeing she would forever be his to call and control, or at least till one of them died. When Blake returned to the club and realized what had happened, Aubrey tried to do the same thing to her, but Blake was barely able to use her own supernatural powers to stop him, and the enraged Aubrey attacked her. Stopping the fight before it went too far, Jean-Claude convinced Blake to pretend to be vampire herself long enough to fool the audience into believing what they had witnessed was of part of the show instead of an actual attack. Once backstage, Blake reluctantly agreed to help find the killer so long as Aubrey stayed away from Catherine.

A few days later, Nikolaos had her minions kidnap the human dancer Phillip from the club in an attempt to demonstrate to the other vampires that Jean-Claude did not have the power to stop her, and to punish both Phillip and Blake for their earlier defiance of her will. After torturing Blake over the marks Jean-Claude had given her to keep both of them alive, Nikolaos had Phillip killed and an unconscious Blake returned to Robert, Jean-Claude's second at the club, as a warning to those who followed Jean-Claude that Nikolaos was more powerful that Jean-Claude, who she was holding prisoner in her base of operations. After Blake killed Nikolaos and freed Jean-Claude from her punishment room, Jean-Claude returned to the club and resumed his management duties there.

JEAN-CLAUDE

HISTORY: The vampire Jean-Claude admits to being 205 years old, but otherwise much of his past remains shrouded in mystery. He speaks with a French accent, and if this is not an affectation, combined with his age it suggests he would have been born during the so-called Age of Reason.

Of his pre-vampiric life, the only detail he has let slip is that blackberries were a favorite food, one that he has missed the taste of in the centuries since he died, as vampires do not eat food. At some point since becoming a vampire Jean-Claude was attacked by someone wielding a blessed cross, leaving a scar on his chest where it touched him; Jean-Claude says he killed the person who did that.

Jean-Claude traveled to the United States and set up home in St. Louis. Two years ago, the Addison vs. Clark case saw the undead gain civil rights, preventing anyone from murdering them simply because they were vampires and allowing them to own property; unlike some older vampires who were wary of the change and humanity, Jean-Claude embraced it, perhaps founding and certainly owning Guilty Pleasures, allegedly the only vampire strip bar in the world. By now a master vampire, he gathered around himself several loyal followers, including the hundred year old Robert and the neophyte vampire Buzz; however, either for reasons of humility or secrecy, he told his followers not to openly call him "master." Estimated to be the fifth most powerful master vampire in the city, he accepted the rule but not the dominance of the most powerful, Nikolaos; unfortunately Nikolaos was not the type to accept any dissension and Jean-Claude presumably realized it was only a matter of time before they clashed over something, if they had not done so already.

When the city formed the new Regional Preternatural Investigation Team to police supernatural crime, it wasn't long before their work brought them to the vampire-run District and Guilty Pleasures. Meeting their civilian expert on the supernatural, Jean-Claude was intrigued; Anita Blake was an animator, someone with the innate ability to turn corpses into zombies, and a vampire slayer, now licensed to execute criminal vampires in the wake of Addison vs. Clarke. As well as being beautiful, Anita was exceptionally strong willed, and with her own magical powers to back her up, she was capable of resisting, to some extent, the mental powers of even a master vampire. She also had a cross-shaped scar, similar to his own, on her left arm, where an attacking vampire lackey had branded her, a symmetry Jean-Claude found amusing. Jean-Claude found himself attracted to Anita, hitting on her and unashamedly trying to bespell her each time they met, well aware she knew he was doing so, treating it almost as a contest. Despite her deep-routed dislike of vampires and their mind control, Anita took his games with comparatively good grace, perhaps because she never expected him to win. At some point it seems likely that Jean-Claude decided that Anita would make a powerful ally in the inevitable struggle to come against Nikolaos, though he knew better than to openly suggest this.

When someone successfully murdered ten of the city's vampires, including two masters more powerful than Jean-Claude, and neither the police nor the vampires could catch the killer, Jean-Claude suggested to Nikolaos that they recruit Anita to find the culprit. They sent the new vampire Willie McCoy to hire Anita, but she refused to work for vampires; not willing to take no for an answer, Nikolaos ordered Anita be forced to work for them. Nikolaos forbade Jean-Claude to feed; knowing that Nikolaos liked to punish those who angered or failed her by locking them inside cross-chained coffins to starve until their wills broke, Jean-Claude anticipated that this was a likely outcome if Anita was not recruited. Aware that one of his followers, a regular patron of Guilty Pleasures, Monica Vespucci, worked alongside Anita's friend Catherine Maison, Jean-Claude had Monica lure Anita to the club on the pretext of attending Catherine's bachelorette party. While Anita was temporarily called away on police business, one of Nikolaos' minions, Aubrey, placed Catherine into a deep trance, ensuring she would be his to call until one or the

ANITA ON JEAN-CLAUDE: "Every time we met, he did his best to bespell me, and I did my best to ignore him. I had won up until now."

REAL NAME: Jean-Claude
ALIASES: None
ANITA'S NICKNAMES: None
CLASSIFICATION: Master Vampire
OCCUPATION: Club Owner, Guilty Pleasures Night Club; Master of the City of St. Louis.
CITIZENSHIP: Unrevealed; may be French
PLACE OF BIRTH: Unrevealed; possibly France
BASE OF OPERATIONS: Guilty Pleasures, St. Louis, Missouri
KNOWN RELATIVES: none
ALLIES: Anita Blake, Buzz, Phillip, Robert, Willie McCoy, Monica Vespucci
GROUP AFFILIATION: Nikolaos' Kiss
ENEMIES: Nikolaos
EDUCATION: Unrevealed
FIRST APPEARANCE: Guilty Pleasures (1993)

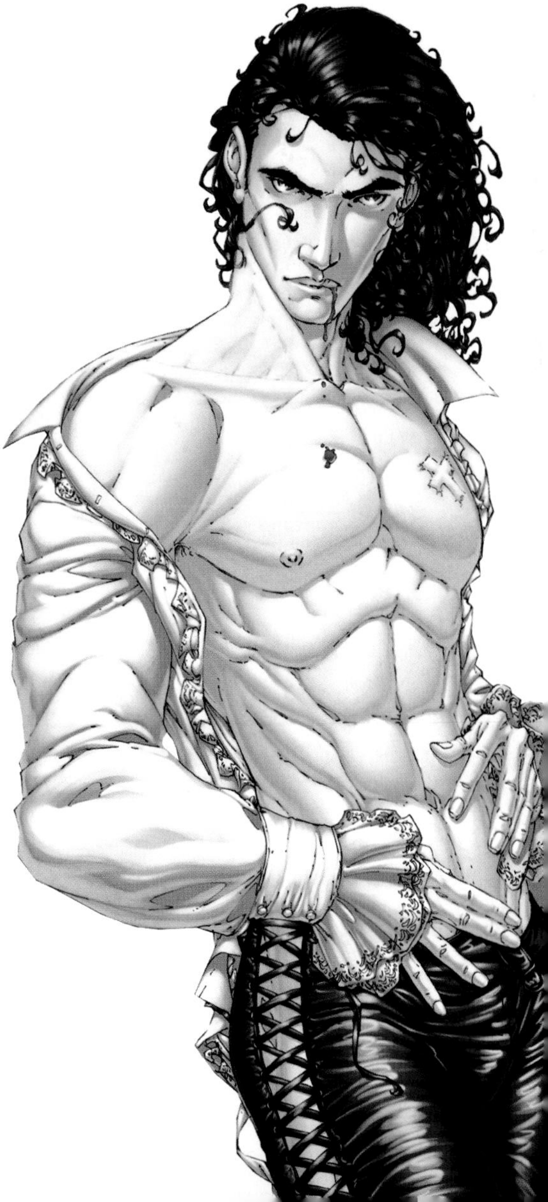

other of them died; when Anita returned, Aubrey tried but failed to do the same to Anita, then attacked her in a rage. Jean-Claude stopped the fight, but used the threat to Catherine to force Anita to agree to take the case. However, aware that Jean-Claude was not Aubrey's master, she demanded a meeting with Nikolaos to elicit a guarantee that Aubrey would not harm her friend. Jean-Claude escorted Anita to the meeting; to prevent the regular police patrols from becoming suspicious of them, he insisted on them holding hands as if they were a couple, and when a police cruiser passed nearby, Jean-Claude stole a kiss to complete the illusion. To his own surprise, Jean-Claude found himself literally shaken by the kiss, a combination of his hunger and a deeper attraction to Anita than he had realized.

Though Jean-Claude told them it would not work, at first the vampires tried to fool Anita by passing off Theresa, another of Nikolaos' followers, as the city's master; sure enough, Anita immediately recognized Theresa was not powerful enough to be Aubrey's master. However when Anita demanded they stop playing games, Aubrey lost his temper, badly injuring her with a casual blow. To save her life, and in preparation to allow himself to withstand Nikolaos' wrath, Jean-Claude used the pretext of making sure Anita would be healthy enough to carry out her mission to give her the First Mark, sharing his own life force with her, the initial step in turning Anita into his human servant. This also increased her resistance to vampiric mind-control, giving Anita a better chance of getting through her meeting with the true Nikolaos without falling under her influence. Though Anita did finally agree to investigate the murders, the audience with Nikolaos did not go well, and she had to flee when another of Nikolaos' minions, Zachary, finally snapped his master's short temper. Knowing he was already intended to be punished for having given Anita the first mark, Jean-Claude interposed himself between Nikolaos and the fleeing Anita, openly challenging Nikolaos' power. Swiftly losing, Jean-Claude reached out with his power, and covertly gave Anita the Second Mark, two tongues of blue flame merging his life force with Anita. Though Anita was not aware of what he had done, this was the second stage in binding her as his human servant, allowing him to enter her dreams and to sustain himself through her.

Not wishing to make Jean-Claude a martyr to his followers, Nikolaos let him live, as expected, by placing him in a coffin secured by chains and a cross to starve. To Nikolaos' annoyance, as the days passed Jean-Claude showed no signs of weakening, as he secretly fed off Anita's own life force, a process Anita experienced as a marked increase in appetite. Meanwhile Jean-Claude appeared in Anita's dreams, trying to communicate with her through imagery. In the first dream, the same night he was locked away, he appeared to her trapped in a blood-filled coffin, from which he arose saying that he had no choice before biting her, symbolically feeding from her. The next night, after Nikolaos had discovered Anita was now almost totally resistant to her illusory powers and begun to suspect what Jean-Claude had done, he appeared in Anita's dreams eating blackberries; when Anita noted that vampires did not eat solid food, he agreed and pushed the bowl towards her, then warned Anita that Nikolaos would kill them both and that they needed to strike first. The final dream came after Nikolaos had bitten Anita, putting her own mark in competition to Jean-Claude's; Anita dreamt of Jean-Claude trying to force her to drink his blood the way a fully marked servant would do, only for Nikolaos to intrude. Anita woke up screaming.

Soon after Anita slew Nikolaos and freed Jean-Claude from his coffin. He congratulated her on eliminating Nikolaos; she hit him in the gut with the butt of her shotgun. He apologized, but informed her he could not take back the marks, though he did agree to stay out of her dreams. Now the new master of the city, Jean-Claude continues to pursue Anita, who continues to resist her obvious attraction to him.

HEIGHT: Unrevealed; tall.

WEIGHT: Unrevealed
EYES: Midnight Blue
HAIR: Black
AGE: Admits to being 205

DESCRIPTION: Perhaps because the patrons of Guilty Pleasures expect it, Jean-Claude tends to dress the way vampires are stereotypically expected to, wearing antique shirts with large amounts of lace and long cuffs, left open just enough to give glimpses of his bare chest. He is tall, with black shoulder length softly curling hair, and midnight blue eyes. He has long-fingered hands, and his voice is rich, melodious and textured.

When he calls on his full power, his humanity folds away; his skin becomes white, his eye sockets fill with blue fire, and his hair floats around his death-pale face.

DISTINGUISHING FEATURES: He has a cross-shaped scar burned into his chest.

DEMEANOR: Jean-Claude is unfailingly gentlemanly and flirtatious. Even when admonishing one of his minions, he seems to remain calm and unthreatening, although their scared reaction hints that he can be far more terrifying when he wants.

NOTABLE ABILITIES: Jean-Claude has superhuman strength and the ability to survive most injuries, due to his vampiric nature and powers of self-healing. His mental powers are well-developed, allowing him to casually enhance how most people see him, or, combined with his superhuman speed, to seemingly appear and disappear at will; attractive and alluring, he is one of the most powerful vampires in the city, and can affect entire audiences at the same time. If someone looks directly into his eyes, he can instantly entrance them to do virtually anything he wants. He can mark a human, gradually making them his personal servant; the first mark grants the subject the ability to look directly into a vampire's eyes without being bespelled, and accelerates the person's healing. The second mark makes them immune to all but the most powerful vampire's mental powers, allows the subject's master to feed from their lifeforce and communicate through dreams. The third allows direct telepathic communication, and the fourth makes them unswervingly loyal and able to live unaging due to having fed off their master's blood, cementing thier bond to him. Like all vampires, Jean-Claude is vulnerable to crosses and holy water. He requires regular feeding to survive, usually, but can also survive on the life force of his human servant, Anita.

MALCOLM

HISTORY: Malcolm is a master vampire, one of the most powerful and oldest-surviving vampires in the St. Louis area. Allegedly as his bid for seeking integration within human society, Malcolm founded the Church of Eternal Life, a religious cult which recruits humans who seek to become vampires themselves. Although the majority of his congregation is comprised of vampires, Malcolm insists he does not exploit his powers over them, instead claiming to permit them their free will. He also claims to not condone violent activity, although several of his congregation have been known to assault people who attend "freak parties." Malcolm insists that these are an aberrant minority, but also declines to punish those involved, suggesting they have his tacit approval. Like most vampires, Malcolm casts an illusion of himself that causes him to appear more handsome than he actually is. His altered appearance is more befitting of his position as a church leader, and assists him in swaying the minds of others without using actual mental influence upon them. In his early encounters with the animator Anita Blake, Malcolm was successful in presenting his illusionary self to her.

Two nights before a series of vampires in St. Louis were killed by an unknown person, Malcolm met with Ted, presumably an alias of Edward, an assassin specializing in supernatural targets. Since Edward subsequently admitted to friends that he had been hired to kill the city's master vampire, it seems likely that either Edward was confirming that Malcolm was not his target, or more probably that Malcolm was the one who hired him. Nikolaos, the city's master vampire, subsequently employed Anita Blake to determine who the murderer was. Following a false lead, she investigated the Church of Eternal Life, suspecting that the killer was targeting vampires who participated in "freak parties," just as some of Malcolm's congregation had been known to do. Anita came to the church with her friend Veronica Sims and set up the appointment through Malcolm's human secretary, Bruce. While there, a man under Nikolaos' thrall attemped to assassinate Anita on the orders of Zachary, the real vampire murderer. Anita was able to kill him instead and now suspected he was a servant of Malcolm because of where the assassination attempt occurred.

Anita returned that evening to question Malcolm, and discovered that because she had been marked by the master vampire Jean-Claude, she could now see through Malcolm's illusion and recognize his true appearance. Anita did her best to wring a confession of guilt out of Malcolm, but failed, though Malcolm's reaction to being accused of hiring an assassin clearly hit a nerve, and the revelation that she had been attacked on the steps of his church clearly angered Malcolm. Recognizing that Anita had been marked by another vampire, Malcolm offered the church's services to her, should she have need of them in the future.

HEIGHT: Unrevealed, tall
WEIGHT: Unrevealed, thin
EYES: Blue
HAIR: Yellow
AGE: Approximately 300

DESCRIPTION: Malcolm is tall and almost painfully thin, with large, bony hands and an angular face. His hair, presumably blond in life, has faded over hundreds of years in darkness to goldfinch yellow. However even without trying his presence is palpable, his vampiric mind spills over and can be felt as a prickling on the skin. His voice is deep and soothing.

DEMEANOR: As the head of an inclusive church, Malcolm makes a point of coming across as friendly and approachable, with practiced smiles which do not display his fangs. However, he is as manipulative as his fellow master vampires, though perhaps with nobler motives, and his good humored front can evaporate instantly if someone gets too close to uncovering something he wants hidden, such as his apparent contact with the assassin Edward.

NOTABLE ABILITIES: Malcolm is among the most powerful vampires in the St. Louis area. Although he possesses all the abilities of a master vampire, he does not exploit his power over the minds of his followers. He casts an illusion of himself over weaker minds so that he appears stronger and more handsome than he actually is. Like all vampires, he has superhuman strength, resistance to injury, and regenerative abilities, but requires regular ingestion of blood in order to remain at his peak. He can move with incredible speed, crossing a room almost faster than the human eye can detect. He is also vulnerable to religious iconography and holy water, and must remain in a coma-like state during daylight hours

ANITA ON MALCOLM: "Malcolm's presence filled the small room like invisible water, chilling and pricking along my skin, knee-deep and rising."

REAL NAME: Malcolm (last name unrevealed)
ALIASES: None
ANITA'S NICKNAMES: Billy Graham of Vampires
CLASSIFICATION: Master Vampire
OCCUPATION: Leader of the Church of Eternal Life
CITIZENSHIP: USA
PLACE OF BIRTH: Unrevealed
BASE OF OPERATIONS: Church Of Eternal Life St. Louis, MO
KNOWN RELATIVES: None
ALLIES: None
GROUP AFFILIATION: Church of Eternal Life
ENEMIES: Nikolaos, H.A.V.
EDUCATION: Unrevealed
FIRST APPEARANCE: Guilty Pleasures (1993)

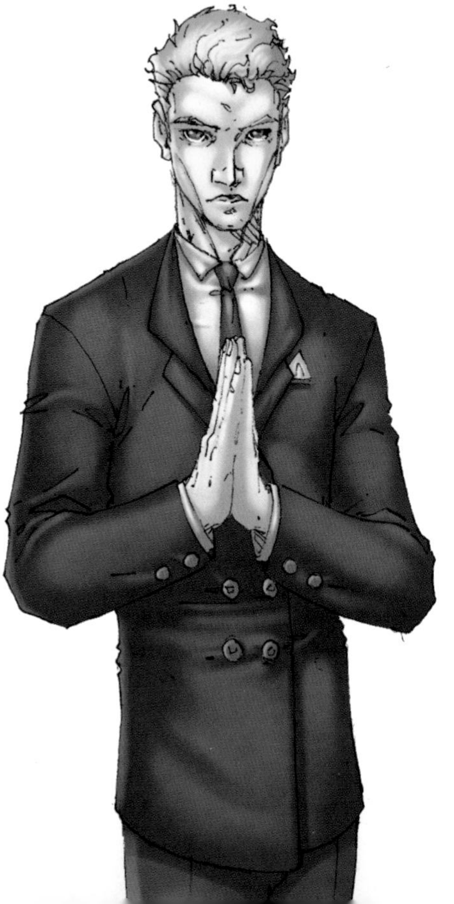

WILLIE MCCOY

ANITA ON WILLIE MCCOY: "Willie McCoy had been a jerk before he died. His being dead didn't change that."

REAL NAME: Willie McCoy
ALIASES: None known
ANITA'S NICKNAMES: None
CLASSIFICATION: Vampire
OCCUPATION: Informant and petty criminal; former servant to Nikolaos.
CITIZENSHIP: U.S.A.
BASE OF OPERATIONS: St. Louis
KNOWN RELATIVES: None
ALLIES: Anita Blake
GROUP AFFILIATION: Nikolaos' kiss
ENEMIES: Nikolaos
EDUCATION: Unrevealed
FIRST APPEARANCE: Guilty Pleasures (1993)

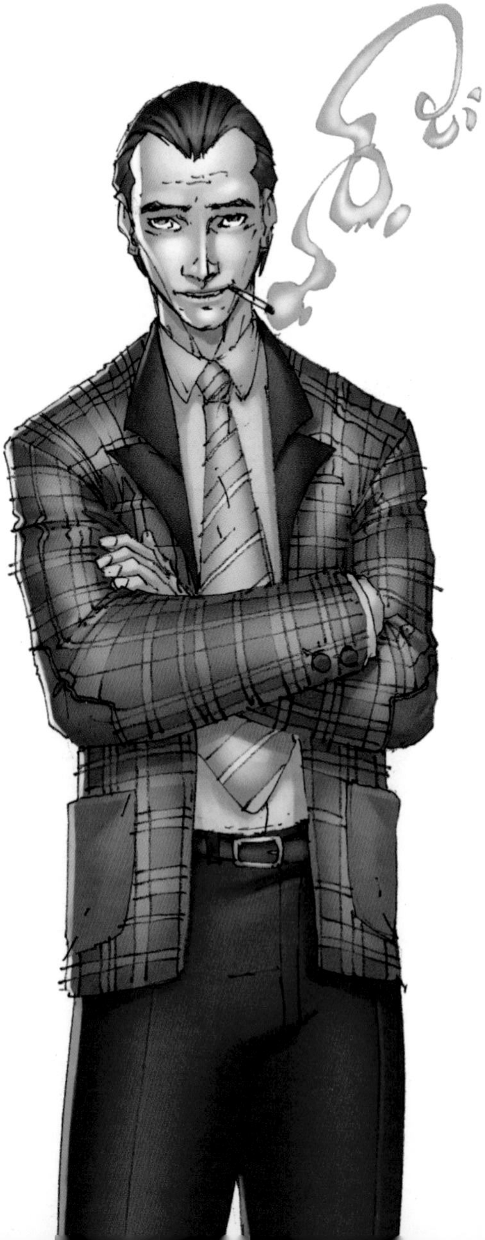

HISTORY: Willie McCoy is a former street informant and petty criminal recently turned vampire. In his previous existence, he sold information and ran errands for criminal gangs. Anita had used him as an informant on occasion. How he turned is unrevealed, but it seems to have been voluntary and he is the first person Anita has known as both a human and a vampire. As a newly turned vampire, he is subservient to master vampires, including both Jean-Claude and Nikolaos.

When Nikolaos wanted to hire Anita to investigate vampires being slain by an apparent serial killer, she sent Willie to Animators, Inc., presumably because he already knew her. When Anita refused, Willie warned her that his bosses would not take no for an answer; Anita took this as a threat, but Willie seemingly meant it sincerely as a warning. Nikolaos punished Willie for failing to hire Anita, imprisoning him in a cross- and chain-bound coffin to starve for a couple of days. He was later released, now terrified of Nikolaos' wrath, and accompanied Nikolaos as her servant to a cemetery in the Saint Charles neighborhood, where Nikolaos confronted Anita outside the Freak Party. Willie seemed genuinely concerned for Anita, and tried to help her by warning her not to antagonize Nikolaos, but his entreaties to Anita only served to anger Nikolaos. When Anita's companion, Phillip, tried to intervene, Willie stopped him on Nikolaos' order, but when the Church of Eternal Life attacked the Freak Party, Nikolaos fled, leaving Willie behind. Willie assisted Anita getting the injured Phillip to Anita's car, and drove them to safety. Nikolaos subsequently kidnapped and tortured Phillip; learning this, Willie called Anita to warn her, leaving a message on Anita's answering machine. However he was caught doing this and once again punished by Nikolaos, who re-imprisoned him in the coffin. After her defeat of Nikolaos, Anita opened his coffin, but left him in peace to go about his business.

Despite having been a bit of jerk and low-life as a human, Willie would appear to have gained some moral fiber as a vampire, helping Anita out on many occasions despite putting himself at risk, and Anita has been forced to admit that while he may have been a bad person as a human, he was an excellent person as a vampire.

HEIGHT: A little over 5'3"
WEIGHT: Unrevealed, thin
EYES: Brown
HAIR: Black
AGE: Unrevealed, only became a vampire in last couple of years

DESCRIPTION: Willie is a thin man, with short slicked-back black hair and a series of nervous twitches. His face is thin and triangular. He also has terrible fashion-sense, with a tendency for badly coordinated polyester and plaid clothing in loud colors. However, he recently acquired a gold tiepin. A new vampire, he flashes his fangs a lot, partly deliberately, partly because he has yet to learn how not to.

DEMEANOR: Willie retains much of the nervousness he displayed while living, especially now that he is subservient to the violent tempers of elder vampires, but he also relishes the reaction most humans have to his vampire status, in part for the novelty of it, and in part because he is unused to anyone fearing him. A jerk in life, he gradually shows signs of ironically becoming a better person now that he is undead.

NOTABLE SKILLS: None. He has demonstrated a distinct lack of fighting skill.

NOTABLE ABILITIES: Willie has superhuman strength and the ability to move quicker than most humans can perceive, though as he is a recently turned vampire, these powers are far less than other vampires. His senses are inhumanly acute, and he can smell fear on humans. He has yet to learn how to use mind powers to appear to vanish, nor can he control people with his voice. He is also vulnerable to crosses and holy water, and requires regular feeding to survive.

HISTORY: Nikolaos was only a young child when she became a vampire under undisclosed circumstances some thousand or more years ago. When she had been a vampire for around four hundred years, presumably by this time a master vampire, she chose a man called Burchard, possibly an English soldier, to become her human servant, granting him extended life in return for his fealty. At some point they emigrated to the United States of America, eventually settling in St. Louis; the most powerful vampire in the city, she became its master, ruling the city's undead with an iron hand, and laying claim to its wererat population as well, since rats were her animal to call. It's unclear whether this happened before the passage of the laws which granted vampires civil rights two years ago, or if her arrival was more recent, although the defiant stance of the wererat leader Rafael to her attempts to control his people suggest one of them was a newcomer to St. Louis, since Nikolaos viciously punished or slew those who disobeyed her, feeling fear was the way to maintain control. She would regularly trap vampires who had angered or failed her in chained coffins with crosses to keep them in, to starve until their minds or spirits broke; in one case, Aubrey's, Nikolaos kept him confined for three months and he emerged insane. It may well have been on Nikolaos' orders that all the members of a New York-based vampire gang which attempted to gain a foothold in St. Louis were chopped to pieces and publicly left out as an example to others. However, the greatest potential threat to her rule came from the city's other master vampires, including Jean-Claude, owner of Guilty Pleasures, and Malcolm, head of the Church of Eternal Life, both of whom had their own followers and might one day move against her.

Recently someone, most likely Malcolm, hired the hitman Edward to slay Nikolaos; unbeknownst to Nikolaos, he started hunting for her daytime resting place. Around the same time one of Nikolaos' own minions, Zachary, began to murder vampires using a pack of ghouls under his control; having previously died, Zachary had been brought back to a semblance of life using a voodoo charm known as a gris-gris, but to sustain the enchantment he needed to regularly feed it vampire blood. Unaware of who was behind the killings, Nikolaos grew concerned as ten vampires fell to the killer, including two of the city's most powerful masters. They caught a human witness to the second murder, and Nikolaos interrogated him, but he hung himself in terror before providing any useful information. Unwilling to trust the police to bring a vampire killer to justice, Nikolaos listened to Jean-Claude's suggestion that they hire animator Anita Blake for the job; new vampire Willie McCoy was given the task of hiring Blake, and when he failed, Nikolaos put Willie into one of her cross-chained coffins. Nikolaos then had Aubrey and Jean-Claude blackmail Anita by threatening one of her friends; Anita agreed to help, but demanded an audience with Nikolaos to elicit a guarantee that her friend would remain unharmed. Before reaching Nikolaos, Aubrey attacked Anita, and to save her life Jean-Claude gave her the first mark, accelerating her healing; Nikolaos locked Aubrey away again for disobeying her order that Anita was not to be injured, lest that make her unable to do the task before her, and angered at Jean Claude for granting Anita partial immunity to her mental powers, she also imprisoned him in the same fashion.

Wanting to scare Anita before their meeting, Nikolaos had her placed in the dungeons under the Circus of the Damned, Nikolaos' home, and ordered the wererats to terrorize the animator; however this ploy failed, in part due to Anita's resolve in a crisis, and in part due to the intervention of Rafael, who ordered the wererats away. Nikolaos granted Anita an audience, initially growing angry with Anita's flippant defiance, but soon calming after she proved to Anita that she could rip the animator's mind apart if she chose to do so. Nikolaos had instructed Zachary to raise their dead witness as a zombie, so they could continue to question him, and let Anita watch the interrogation; however Zachary, fearful of what it might reveal, deliberately broke the zombie's fragile mind. Enraged, Nikolaos ordered Zachary and Anita to depart before she killed them; as her anger grew out of control, Jean-Claude used his own power to push Anita out

NIKOLAOS: "If you fail me again, large or small, I will tear your throat out, and my children will bathe in a shower of your blood."

REAL NAME: Unrevealed; may be Nikolaos
ALIASES: None
ANITA'S NICKNAMES: None
CLASSIFICATION: Master Vampire
OCCUPATION: The Master Vampire of the City of St. Louis.
CITIZENSHIP: Unrevealed
PLACE OF BIRTH: Unrevealed
BASE OF OPERATIONS: Circus of the Damned, St. Louis, Missouri
KNOWN RELATIVES: None
ALLIES: Aubrey, Burchard, Theresa, Winter, Valentine, unidentified black vampire
GROUP AFFILIATION: None
ENEMIES: Anita Blake, Edward, Jean-Claude, Malcolm
EDUCATION: Unrevealed
FIRST APPEARANCE: Guilty Pleasures (1993)

of the room and turned to face Nikolaos' wrath. Despite his best efforts, Nikolaos swiftly overpowered him and added him to her coffin-bound collection. She ordered one of Jean-Claude's followers, the human stripper Phillip, to accompany Anita on her daytime investigations, and seduce her to give Nikolaos' further leverage; after meeting and coming to like Anita, Phillip agreed to continue only after Nikolaos promised not to harm Anita.

That night, suspecting Zachary had lost his edge, Nikolaos ordered him to raise a hundred year dead corpse as a test of his power, instructing her minion Theresa to slay him should he fail. Nikolaos observed from a distance as Zachary initially failed, but then was spared by the unexpected arrival of Anita, who combined powers with him to raise the zombie. Nikolaos confronted Anita, angry that she had removed her excuse to have Zachary killed, but realized that Anita now seemed able to see her scar, and began to suspect that Jean-Claude had given Anita the second mark. Nikolaos was further annoyed when Phillip tried to intervene, reminding Nikolaos of her promise. Before Nikolaos could do Phillip permanent harm, she was forced to flee by the arrival of members of the Church of Eternal Life. Convinced he had become Anita's lover, Nikolaos had her minions kidnap Phillip from Guilty Pleasures the next evening, torturing him and using him to draw Anita to her lair. Even though Nikolaos realized Anita had not known about the second mark, Nikolaos had Aubrey murder Phillip as a warning to Jean-Claude's followers that their master could not protect them, and then bit Anita, the first step in gaining complete power over her. She then had Anita dumped back at Guilty Pleasures to continue hunting the vampire killer. Two days later Anita returned before nightfall, led through the underground tunnels into the Circus by Rafael's people and accompanied by Edward. They slew Nikolaos' vampire minions, but were caught by Nikolaos, who had been out of her coffin having Zachary raise Phillip for her own amusement. Nikolaos held Edward hostage to force Anita to fight Burchard, but during their battle, Anita distracted her by telling her Zachary was the killer they sought. Nikolaos pounced on Zachary, ripping his throat out, then turned to learn that Anita had managed to slay Burchard; berserk, Nikolaos lunged for Anita, but as she did so, Edward shot her. Nikolaos turned her attention to him, and was about to kill him when Anita used Burchard's sword to nearly decapitate her, then rammed it through Nikolaos' chest, pinning her to the wall and finally ending her millennia long existence.

HEIGHT: 4'7" approximately
WEIGHT: Unrevealed
EYES: Blue-grey
HAIR: White-blond
AGE: Over 1000

DESCRIPTION: Nikolaos was in her early teens when she died, in the early stages of puberty, and retains the look of a little girl. She is under five foot tall, has small, partially-formed breasts, her face is rounded and pleasant, her hair is a shiningly white-blond, and her eyes are blue-grey; she dresses in girly dresses, speaks with a girly singsong voice and her laugh is high-pitched and charming. She has a small scar near her upper lip from before she became a vampire; normally she conceals this with her mind powers. Her breath smells of peppermints, although the observant can notice an underlying smell of fresh blood and recent murder. She puts on a well-rehearsed air of youthful innocence and sweetness, even having her hand-carved throne just high enough so that she can sit with her legs swinging slightly off the ground. Like all older vampires, she can become completely motionless. When angered, her façade drops away instantly, losing the childish mannerisms, and her voice becomes harsh and adult. Unleashing the full force of her power, her eyes become like blue glass glowing with an inner fire, her bones and veins stand out against paper-white skin, and her hair dances about her skeletal head.

DISTINGUISHING FEATURES: Child, small scar above lip

DEMEANOR: Nikolaos often portrays herself like an innocent child, giggling and high voiced, but can instantly become ancient, adult and humorless. Her moods are mercurial, and she can switch instantly back and forth several times in a conversation, depending on if she feels things are going the way she wants. She brooks no defiance, expecting to always be obeyed without question, and likes those around her to fear her, as she feels that gives her power over them. She dislikes it when people penetrate her false persona.

NOTABLE ABILITIES: A master vampire, Nikolaos' powers have grown considerably with age. She routinely uses her powerful mental abilities to make others see her as perfect in her beauty, hiding small imperfections such as her scar. She moves with the skill and grace from centuries of practice, switching from complete stillness to blurring speed; combined with her mind powers, she can seem to appear and disappear at will. Her power is so great that she can strip apart with ease the mind of someone as powerful as Anita Blake, tearing it like sharp knives in the brain and peeling it away to utterly destroy it if she wants. Even after Anita received the second vampire mark, supposedly granting immunity to vampiric mind tricks, Nikolaos could tweak her perceptions, though she had to work to do so. She can telekinetically generate powerful, storm force winds, and levitate, something not even other master vampires have been seen to do. All her senses are enhanced to an unknown degree. She is incredibly strong, with a grip like steel, and able to send grown humans flying with the slightest touch.

Nikolaos can summon and control rats; even wererats are not immune, although their human minds allows them a degree of resistance if they are not too close to her. While still vulnerable to holy icons, silver and sunlight, Nikolaos seems to have developed some resistance over the centuries, and no longer needs to sleep during the day; she can also take some sustenance from fear in lieu of blood. She can mark humans, turning them into her servant; it is unclear if she can do this to more than one human at a time, although her threats to Anita suggest it may be possible. She can feed off her servant Burchard's life energy to sustain herself, communicate with him telepathically, and has kept him alive and unaging for over 600 years by feeding him once with her own blood.

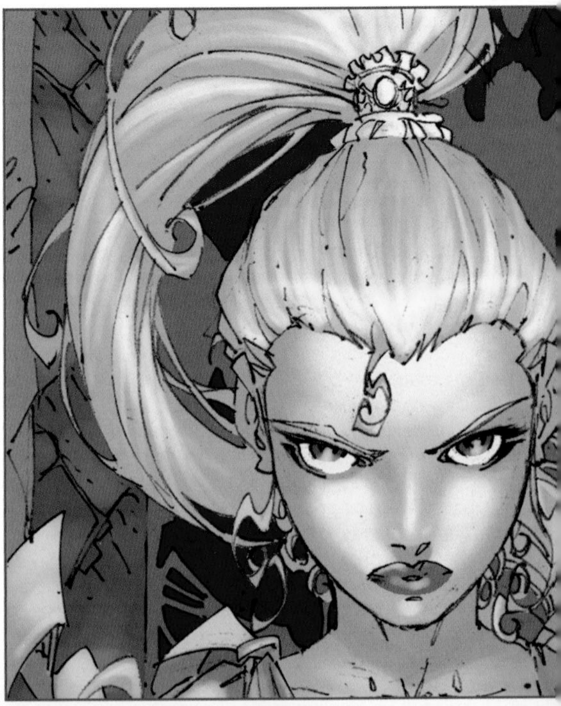

HISTORY: Phillip is one of the human dancers at the vampire strip club Guilty Pleasures. When he was still a young boy, the pedophile vampire Valentine attacked Phillip, leaving him with lifelong scars on his left collarbone and elsewhere. When he was much older Phillip became a vampire junkie, regularly attending freak parties, where those humans who wished to be "had" by a vampire, or to "have" a vampire any way they wanted, met up with obliging vampires. Phillip also gained a job at the club during this time, where he fulfilled the fantasy of many of the club patrons, first by stripping on stage, then by allowing a vampire stripper to feed on him and telepathically broadcast the emotions involved to the watching patrons. Eventually, uncomfortable with the unwanted attentions of some of his fellow party-goers such as Crystal and worried that he might end up a broken wreck like some of the other regulars, Phillip decided to stop attending the parties.

A few months later, the St. Louis vampires decided to blackmail animator Anita Blake into helping them solve a series of vampire murders, luring her down to Guilty Pleasures. The night they did so, Phillip was one of the dancers on stage, and Blake witnessed him perform, paired as the willing "meal" of the vampire dancer Robert. The next day Phillip was ordered by head vampire Nikolaos to keep watch over Blake and possibly seduce her to keep her on the case. Phillip showed up at Animators, Inc., where Blake worked, on the pretext of asking about the whereabouts of missing club owner Jean-Claude; Anita's colleague Jamison Clarke jumped to the conclusion that Phillip was Anita's lover, and to spare herself further embarrassment, Anita rushed Phillip out of the office. Over lunch Anita informed Phillip that Nikolaos had chosen to punish Jean-Claude for defying her, and Phillip offered to help Anita solve the case, helping her get those close to the dead vampires to open up in a way they wouldn't for the police. They went to the apartment of Rebecca Miles, girlfriend of the first slain vampire, Maurice, where Phillip convinced Miles to cooperate with Blake despite Miles's fear for the life of her current vampire boyfriend Jack. Miles told Blake she and Maurice had been at a freak party the night he was killed, but could tell her nothing more. On Anita's behalf, Phillip checked on the other victims and confirmed they were all regulars on the freak party circuit. He reluctantly agreed to find a party for Blake and use his own reputation on the party scene to get them both invited, not mentioning to her his own issues with attending. He then had her leave him at the club, and unknown to Blake reported back to Nikolaos. Having begun to like Blake, he sought and was given her reassurance that Blake would not be hurt.

That night Phillip took Blake to a freak party in a St. Louis suburb, using the cover story that he and Blake were lovers, and that she was a survivor of a real vampire attack who had been talked into attending her first such party. He introduced Blake to many of the party circuit's regulars, several of whom tried to seduce him with varying degrees of success. Phillip finally retreated to the bathroom with Blake, where he 'marked' Blake with a bite on the neck to convince a spying fellow partygoer of their charade, and to distract Blake from asking about which vampire was giving him orders. Annoyed at him for this, Blake went outside the house to get some space, and discovered a zombie-raising in progress in the nearby cemetery. Phillip followed and caught up with Blake after she had successfully helped fellow animator Zachary raise a century-old zombie for the amusement of Nikolaos's vampire group. He tried to keep Nikolaos from hurting Blake like she had promised, but Nikolaos easily stopped him, injuring him for his standing up to her. The arrival of human and vampire members of the Church of Eternal Life, who disapproved of the freak parties and intended to put a somewhat violent end to the depraved gathering at the house, interrupted them before Nikolas could do too much damage to Phillip. Nikolaos fled the area before the Church members found them, while Blake and Phillip managed to escape in their car. Safely away from the house, Phillip was proud but shaken by the fact that he had stood up to the head vampire, and was gratified Blake thought him brave as well, though she made it plain he was to never do anything so stupid again. Phillip admitted Nikolaos had been ordering

ANITA ON PHILLIP: "The smile he flashed me was full of potential, a little evil, a lot of sex."

REAL NAME: Phillip (last name unrevealed)
ALIASES: None
ANITA'S NICKNAMES: Phillip of the many scars
CLASSIFICATION: Human
OCCUPATION: Dancer, vampire junkie
CITIZENSHIP: U.S.A.
BASE OF OPERATIONS: Guilty Pleasures, St. Louis, Missouri
KNOWN RELATIVES: None
ALLIES: Anita Blake, Jean-Claude, Robert
GROUP AFFILIATION: None
ENEMIES: Aubrey, Nikolaos, Valentine, Zachary
EDUCATION: Unrevealed
FIRST APPEARANCE: Guilty Pleasures (1993)

him the past couple of days, before Blake left him at the club.

Later that night Nikolaos, believing Phillip had been seduced by Blake rather than the other way around, and angry at Blake over her perceived lie about how she could see through certain vampire tricks (at the time Blake was unaware Jean-Claude had given her the second vampire "mark" to aid in keeping him fed in his prison), had Phillip kidnapped from the club. He was taken to the dungeon under Nikolaos' base, the indoor amusement park Circus of the Damned, to be tortured as punishment for his standing up to her earlier, and to punish Blake as well. The vampire Willie McCoy, out of a sense of friendship to Blake, alerted her to the kidnapping, and then Nikolaos called Blake to order her presence. Blake arrived at the Circus to find Nikolaos and two of her vampire minions, Aubrey and Valentine, feeding off a chained Phillip. After agreeing to a "talk" with Nikolaos about Jean-Claude's recent actions, Blake was granted a few minutes time alone with Phillip, who tried to reassure him that she'd get them both out of the place alive. Unfortunately, Nikolaos later decided to prove to Jean-Claude's followers that he did not have the power to oppose her by killing someone Jean-Claude had given his protection to, and sent Aubrey and Valentine to kill Phillip. Blake desperately rushed to Phillip's rescue, but arrived too late to prevent Aubrey from tearing out his throat.

Two nights later, Nikolaos decided to amuse herself by having Zachary raise Phillip and watch as the zombie tried to kill Aubrey before Aubrey rekilled him. To give the dead Phillip a slightly better chance in the fight she had him brought to Aubrey before sunset when he was asleep in his coffin but still able to move if disturbed. However, Nikolaos found her plans for the night interrupted when she learned Blake and her human ally, the hitman Edward, had secretly entered her base and had killed the other vampires who slept there, including Aubrey. After Nikolaos had Zachary and her human servant Burchard take them prisoner, she taunted Blake with the idea of having Phillip put through his paces, then had everybody brought down to the dungeon. There Phillip's memory of his last living minutes began to return, and he fled keening to a corner, unable to handle the recollection. After Blake and Edward killed the other three and freed Jean-Claude from his prison, Blake took Phillip back to the shallow grave he had been raised from, and comforted him as much as she could before he asked Blake to return him to the grave, which she sadly did. Phillip's body was later reburied at a local cemetery, where Blake visited it every time she had a zombie-raising job to do there.

HEIGHT: Unrevealed
WEIGHT: Unrevealed
EYES: Brown
HAIR: Brown
AGE: Unrevealed; presumably in his 20s

DESCRIPTION: Phillip was well built, and though not a muscleman, kept his body toned, with flat, rippling chest muscles. He was well tanned, except on his extensive scars. He had a sculpted jawline and had perfected a dazzling, melt-in-your-mouth sexy smile. He tended to choose skin-tight clothing to display his body to its best advantage, wearing more revealing apparel when in the company of those who would not find his scars off-putting.

DISTINGUISHING FEATURES: Phillip has extensive scars across much of his body. The main one is on his collarbone, which shows signs of Valentine ripping apart the skin and bone there. He has scars on the bend of each arm, and his neck is covered with neat little bite marks, so many that it resembles a drug addict's arm. His chest is covered in scar tissue, both pink, new scars and older, white ones.

DEMEANOR: Phillip likes to project a confidently sexual attitude, flirting with any female he meets. However, under this remains the frightened child first attacked by Valentine. He is loyal to those he cares about, even finding the courage to face down Nikolaos, whom he is (rightfully) terrified of. Phillip found sexual pleasure in being bitten, and liked to mark his human dalliances by biting them.

NOTABLE SKILLS: Phillip was a talented dancer who kept himself in excellent physical shape. Despite his athletic physique, he was a poor fighter.

REGIONAL PRETERNATURAL INVESTIGATION TEAM

HISTORY: Though vampires gained civil rights two years ago as a result of the groundbreaking Addison vs. Clark ruling, the St. Louis Police Department's Regional Preternatural Investigation Team (RPIT, usually pronounced "Rip It") has only recently been formed, largely as a half-hearted effort to placate the liberals and the press. Its remit is to investigate all supernatural crime, whether it be committed against humans or against the supernatural beings themselves, including vampires, lycanthropes, zombies, ghouls, and more. Derogatorily known as "the Spook Squad," it is not considered a positive career move to join it, and it is comprised mostly of police officers who have aggravated their superiors in some way or another. Despite this, and in large part due to the no-nonsense leadership of methodical veteran officer Dolph Storr, RPIT tries to do the best job it can. Aware that they are often dealing with things which normal people have little knowledge of, RPIT has secured the services of animator and vampire slayer Anita Blake, who serves as a civilian expert on the supernatural, whose assistance has been invaluable in identifying creatures which might have inflicted specific wounds on attack victims, and explaining the differences between different species of supernatural creatures. Dolph at least values her contributions highly, and seems to consider her a member of the unit in all but name.

Other unit members include Zerbrowski and Detective Clive Perry. Zerbrowski likes to loudly flirt with Anita, displaying a locker room sense of humor; attempts to embarrass the quick witted and acerbic Blake in this manner always backfire against Zerbrowski, but both parties take the humor in good nature, and Zerbrowski persists, clearly enjoying the banter. Perry is the squad's most recent recruit, a tall, slender, soft spoken black man. Unfailingly pleasant, it is a mystery to the others what he might have done to upset anyone enough to have been assigned to RPIT.

RPIT often finds official business bringing them down to the Riverfront, known as the city's main vampire-owned area and known as the District to its inhabitants. The taskforces' recent cases have included the series of vampire murders eventually traced back to the undead animator Zachary and his ghouls. Despite RPIT's best efforts, they had little success in solving the case themselves, due in no small part to the fact that the vampire community, along with the humans who worked and lived in the District not only distrusted the new human laws, but their enforcers as well. So, they withheld pertinent information and covered up vital evidence, including the fact that there had actually been six additional vampire murders which were never reported to law enforcement of any kind. RPIT persisted working on the case regardless, as well as investigating the death of the Hillcrest Cemetery caretaker at the claws of what appeared to be a ghoul pack. Eventually it transpired both cases were related, as Zachary's ghouls had been the culprits at Hillcrest too. The city's vampire master Nikolaos forced Anita into investigating the murders without the taskforces' back-up, and she eventually uncovered Zachary's involvement, passing this information on to Dolph prior to killing both Nikolaos and Zachary. Given that her slaying of Nikolaos was not legally sanctioned, Anita may well have neglected to mention that action to Dolph; it is unknown if she informed him of Zachary's demise, allowing him to close RPIT's file on that case.

ANITA ON RPIT: "I could never imagine Perry doing something rude enough to piss someone off, but you didn't get assigned to the squad without a reason."

CURRENT MEMBERS: Sergeant Dolph Storr, Clive Perry, Zerbrowski; Anita Blake is attached to them as a civilian advisor
BASE OF OPERATIONS: St. Louis, Missouri
FIRST APPEARANCE: Guilty Pleasures (1993)

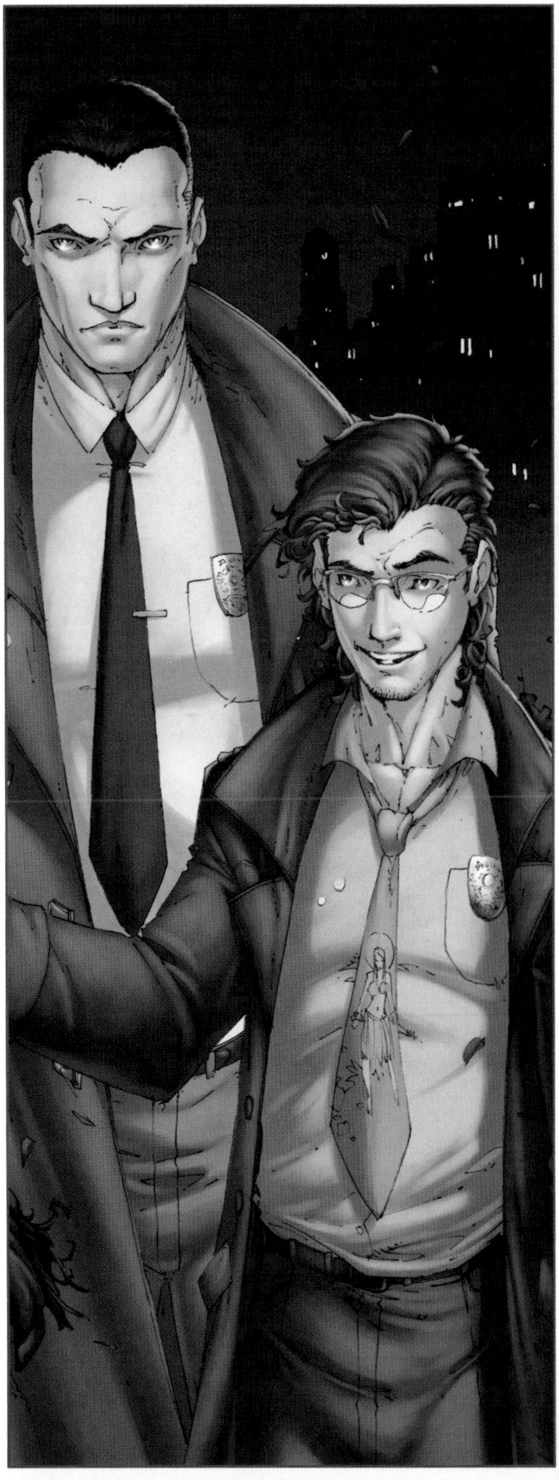

ROBERT

ANITA ON ROBERT: "The vampire wasn't as old as Jean-Claude, nor as good. I sat there feeling the press and flow of over a hundred years of power, and it wasn't enough."

REAL NAME: Robert (last name unrevealed)
ALIASES: None known
ANITA'S NICKNAMES: None
CLASSIFICATION: Vampire
OCCUPATION: Dancer, Guilty Pleasures
CITIZENSHIP: U.S.A.
BASE OF OPERATIONS: Unrevealed
KNOWN RELATIVES: None
ALLIES: Jean-Claude, Phillip
GROUP AFFILIATION: Nikolaos' Kiss
ENEMIES: Aubrey, Nikolaos, Valentine
EDUCATION: Unrevealed
FIRST APPEARANCE: Guilty Pleasures (1993)

HISTORY: Robert is a roughly one hundred-year-old vampire who works at the vampire strip club Guilty Pleasures. He sometimes runs the club when owner Jean-Claude is absent on other duties. He is also one of the strippers at the club, using his hypnotism powers on the audience to 'suddenly' appear on stage and feed off a fellow human stripper, mindlinking with the audience to allow them to feel what the dancers involved felt, then kissing those in the audience who wish it.

On the night animator Anita Blake attended the club as part of a bachelorette party with vampire wannabe Monica Vespucci and bride-to-be Catherine Maison, Robert was one of the strippers working the crowd, feeding off fellow dancer Phillip. Helping Jean-Claude attempt to put Blake under his power, Robert made a grab for Blake from the stage, but Blake was able to move out of his reach in time, something few humans could do. Robert was visibly shaken by Anita's ability to resist his mesmeric powers.

A few days later a group of vampires under the command of the city's ruling vampire Nikolaos invaded the club and kidnapped Phillip despite Robert's best efforts to hold them off. After Nikolaos killed Phillip, she delivered an unconscious Blake to Robert as a warning to those who followed Jean-Claude that he did not have the power to stop her. Robert took Blake to the main office where she eventually woke up. He tried to help Blake recover from her ordeal, but she was still too angry at him for not being able to protect Phillip, and she ordered him to leave her. He did so, but not before leaving her a note telling her where her weapons were at in the club.

HEIGHT: Unrevealed; tall
WEIGHT: Unreveald
EYES: Blue
HAIR: Blond
AGE: Approximately 100

DESCRIPTION: Robert is tall, with a handsome, square-jawed face and long blond hair. Like most vampires, he routinely uses his mesmeric abilities to enhance his appearance, with an inhumanly beautiful face and a palpable sense of masculinity. Acting the vicious vampire attacker on stage, he moves with a deliberate sense of violence, and makes himself bestial when he reveals his fangs.

DEMEANOR: Largely unrevealed. His stage act puts across a violent and dangerous appearance, but that seems largely for show. He is loyal to Jean-Claude, viewing the elder vampire as his master and treating Anita Blake with respect as his master's human servant.

NOTABLE SKILLS: Skilled dancer.

NOTABLE ABILITIES: Robert can cloud the minds of normal humans with his telepathy, making himself inhumanly beautiful at will. He can also mask his movements, preventing others from seeing his movements until he wishes them to notice him; however his powers are noticeably less developed than his master, Jean-Claude, and failed to fool animator Anita Blake even before she was gifted with immunity to mesmerism by Jean-Claude's marking of her. The upper limits of his strength are unknown, though he can bench-press at least the weight of an average car. Like all vampires, he requires regular blood to sustain himself, and during the day returns to a corpselike sleep. He is vulnerable to silver, sunlight, and holy icons.

RONNIE SIMS

HISTORY: Private eye Veronica "Ronnie" Sims is Anita Blake's best friend, and the only one Anita feels is capable of handling herself in a fight (colleagues like Dolph and slightly untrustworthy acquaintances like Edward notwithstanding). They first met three years ago, presumably around the same time that Ronnie was first put on retainer for Animators, Inc., the company Anita works for. The pair hit it off, sharing similarly deprecatory humor, becoming exercise buddies and, when necessary, visiting one another in hospital. Anita felt that unlike her own family, Ronnie could understand the work she did killing vampires, because of the violence Ronnie's own job sometimes entailed; Ronnie is smart enough to know how dangerous it can sometimes be to be around Anita, and usually makes sure she is armed when helping Anita with a case. Though she works for Animators, Inc., Ronnie can also be hired directly, working from her south-west corner office in a high building from which you can see the vampire-owned District.

The day after Anita was threatened into taking up an investigation of the recent vampire killings by the city's head vampire, Ronnie visited her apartment. Swiftly realizing something was wrong, Ronnie was one of the few people Anita confided in as to her predicament, and offered her assistance. Anita asked Ronnie to look into the possible involvement of anti-vampire hate groups, which Anita could not hope to approach because of her own supernatural powers. Ronnie soon discovered rumors of a death squad within Humans Against Vampires (HAV), but Anita asked her to dig deeper, afraid that passing on this rumor to the vampires would merely cause them to massacre potentially innocent people. Ronnie managed to find a HAV member, Beverly Chin, willing to talk to them, and arranged a meeting between Beverly and Anita, after which Beverly agreed to delve further on their behalf. Ronnie subsequently accompanied Anita on a visit to the vampire-run Church of Eternal Life, another possible suspect group for involvement in the killings. Ronnie played the part of an intimidating bodyguard to help Anita scare the church secretary Bruce into arranging an appointment with Malcolm, the church head. On the way out of the church, Ronnie spotted a gunman in time to tackle Anita out of the way of his first shot; the gunman entered the building after them, and when Anita denied being his target, he turned to shoot Ronnie. Anita shot him dead, her bullets striking the would-be assassin mere seconds before Ronnie's did the same. Though Anita was unwilling to drag Ronnie deeper into the case following this incident, she did entrust her with knowledge of a safety deposit box containing a letter with all her findings to that point, in case her meeting with Malcolm went badly.

HEIGHT: 5'9"
WEIGHT: Unrevealed
EYES: Grey
HAIR: Blond page boy
AGE: Mid 20's

DESCRIPTION: Ronnie is physically fit, standing several inches taller than her friend.

DEMEANOR: Ronnie remains calm in a crisis, and takes most things in her stride. She has a similar sense of humor to Anita, and happily teases her friend; she knows Anita well enough to spot when she is not being wholly honest, but knows her well enough not to push. Like Anita, Ronnie enjoys the look of pain on Bert Vaughn's face (Owner of Animator's Inc) when he has to pay their fees. However, after shooting the gunman, Ronnie was visibly shaken, not wishing to be reminded that she had killed a man.

NOTABLE SKILLS: Ronnie is an exceptional private detective, is in excellent physical condition and is a lethal shot with a firearm.

EQUIPMENT: Ronnie often carries firearms.

ANITA ON RONNIE SIMS: "Ronnie is a private detective. We take turns visiting one another in hospital."

REAL NAME: Veronica Sims
ALIASES: None
ANITA'S NICKNAMES: Ronnie
CLASSIFICATION: Human
OCCUPATION: Private detective
CITIZENSHIP: U.S.A.
PLACE OF BIRTH: Unrevealed
BASE OF OPERATIONS: Ronnie has a Private Detective agency that overlooks the Vampire District in St. Louis. Mo.
KNOWN RELATIVES: Unidentified father
ALLIES: Anita Blake
GROUP AFFILIATION: On retainer to Animators, Inc.
ENEMIES: Unidentified assassin
EDUCATION: Unrevealed
FIRST APPEARANCE: Guilty Pleasures (1993)

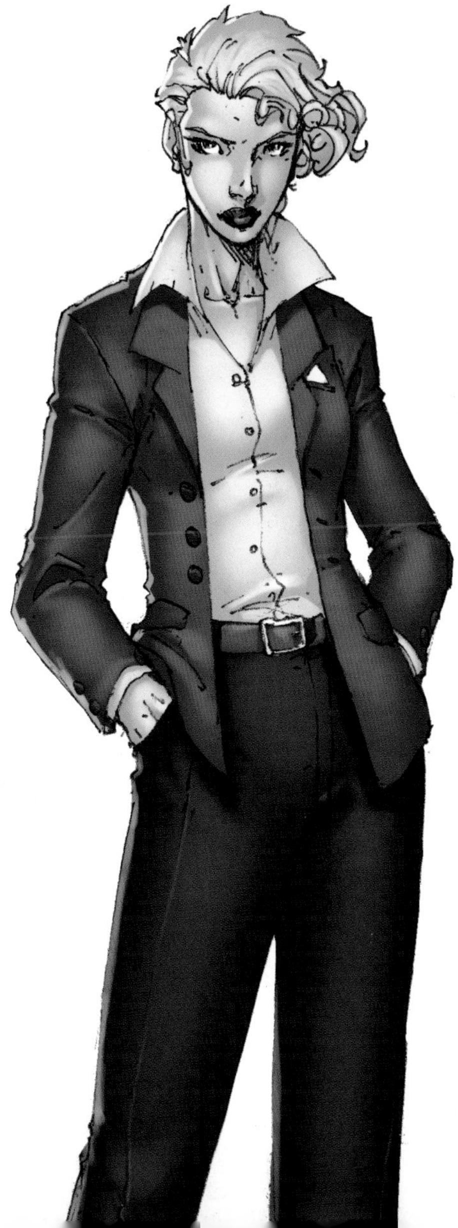

THERESA

ANITA ON THERESA: "The female vampire reclined on the bed. She looked like a vampire should. Long, straight black hair fell around her shoulders. Her dress was full-skirted and black."

REAL NAME: Theresa, (last name unrevealed)
ALIASES: Nikolaos
ANITA'S NICKNAMES: Theresa Mistress of the Dark
CLASSIFICATION: Master Vampire
OCCUPATION: Stalking horse – A vampire who poses for another vampire to hide their identify for some reason.
CITIZENSHIP: Unrevealed
BASE OF OPERATIONS: Circus Of The Damned
PLACE OF BIRTH: Unrevealed
KNOWN RELATIVES: Unrevealed
ALLIES: Aubrey, Burchard, Nikolaos, Valentine, unidentified black vampire
GROUP AFFILIATION: Nikolaos' Kiss
ENEMIES: Anita Blake, Zachary
EDUCATION: Unrevealed
FIRST APPEARANCE: Guilty Pleasures (1993)

HISTORY: Theresa is a roughly one-hundred to one-hundred-fifty-year-old vampire, who was born somewhere outside the U.S., and one of the servants of the master vampire Nikolaos. When vampires Jean-Claude and Aubrey used animator Anita Blake's friend Catherine Maison to blackmail Blake into helping the St. Louis vampire community catch a murderer that was killing vampires, Blake demanded to see Aubrey's master to assure Maison's continued survival. The vampires decided to test Blake by taking her to a non-descript cheap hotel and telling her Theresa was Nikolaos, but Blake swiftly saw through their deception, noting that Theresa felt less powerful than Aubrey, and thus could not be Nikolaos. When Blake demanded an end to the vampires' games Aubrey backhanded her into unconsciousness. Theresa and Jean-Claude moved the unconscious Blake to a dungeon under the undead amusement park/warehouse Circus of the Damned, where Theresa watched in amused amazement as Jean-Claude gave the just-awakened Blake a portion of his power to aid in her recovery; Theresa informed a stunned Blake that she had just been 'marked' as Jean-Claude's human servant. Theresa then left to update Nikolaos on Blake's condition, with Jean-Claude soon following, leaving Blake to the mercy of a group of wererats that had been summoned by Nikolaos. A short time later Theresa returned to the dungeon to find that the wererats had left despite orders to stay until dismissed; she correctly presumed this was due to the intervention of the rat king Rafael. Disgusted, Theresa brought Blake to Nikolaos, observing as Blake angered Nikolaos and was punished for her defiance, then watched Nikolaos' animator Zachary bring forth a zombiefied witness to one of the vampire murders, only to learn the zombie's mind had been broken by Zachary's careless handling of it. She then stood by while Nikolaos angrily ordered the two humans from her presence and imprisoned rival Jean-Claude in her punishment room for his part in the night's failures.

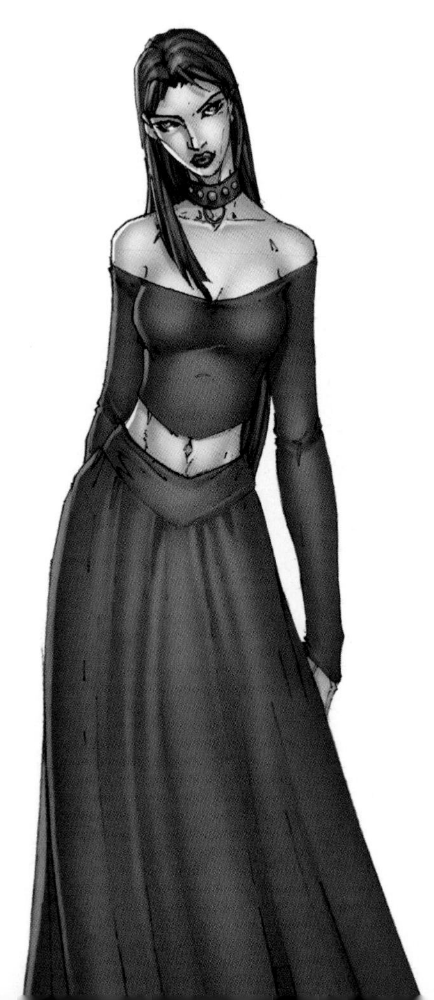

The next night Nikolaos instructed Zachary to raise a hundred-year-old corpse, Estelle Hewitt, ordering Theresa to lead her fellow vampires in slaying Zachary if he failed. As Nikolaos had suspected, Zachary found the zombie was too old for him to be able to raise, and Theresa and the other vampires present would have tried to slay him then, but Blake, who had been attending a freak party nearby, intervened. To Theresa's annoyance, Blake offered to help Zachary raise the zombie using herself as a focus for their combined powers. Theresa at first refused, but granted her request after being reminded that Nikolaos had insisted Blake not be harmed. Blake and Zachary succeeded in raising the zombie, using Blake's own blood as the sacrifice, and Theresa joined the other vampires in abusing the zombie before Nikolaos ordered it returned to its grave. Later that night a vengeful Zachary, the person behind the recent vampire slayings, confronted Theresa a block from the Circus of the Damned, and his undead ghoul pack killed her, ripping her head from her body, so that Zachary could use her blood to feed the gris-gris charm that had raised him from the grave and kept him alive and well.

HEIGHT: Unrevealed
WEIGHT: Unrevealed
EYES: Black
HAIR: Black
AGE: Between 100 and 150

DESCRIPTION: Theresa dressed in what could be described as stereotypical vampire clothing, wearing all black outfits with black leather high-sided and high-heeled boots. She had an unidentified accent, pronouncing her r's thickly.

DEMEANOR: Theresa was arrogant and sadistic, enjoying taunting Zachary when he was under sentence of death and mistreating the zombie Estelle Hewitt.

NOTABLE ABILITIES: Theresa could cloud human minds with a form of telepathy. She could move at super-human speeds for short distances, making it appear to ordinary humans like she could vanish at will. She was super-strong, able to bench-press weight equivalent to that of a small car, though the upper limits to that strength was unrevealed. Like all vampires she required to drink blood to sustain herself, and was vulnerable to sunlight, silver and holy icons.

HISTORY: A little over a hundred years undead, the vampire Valentine's origins might be hinted at by his Southern accent and preference for dressing in sharp clothes in the style of a Mississippi riverboat gambler. He was a particularly depraved vampire who became notorious in the St. Louis area for his brutality, boasting that he had bitten the dancer Phillip when he was a youth, and that the trauma of the assault was what had driven Phillip to become a junkie for vampire bites. Valentine's activities led to a high bodycount, and in recent years he fell in with a group of five other vampires who between them slew at least twenty-three people, ten of whom were accredited to Valentine. The courts licensed vampire hunter Anita Blake to exterminate them, and she attacked their home with her ally, Edward, an assassin who specialized in slaying supernatural beings. During the clash, Valentine assaulted Anita and bit her in the collarbone. As he lapped at her blood and licked the hole he had made in her neck, grating his teeth on her bones, she narrowly saved herself by striking him in the face with a vial of holy water, leaving him horribly scarred. The house Valentine was in was finally burned down by Edward using a flamethrower, and the two hunters believed that Valentine was destroyed.

However, Valentine survived, and took to wearing masks of gold or silver to conceal his scars. He fell under the protection of St. Louis' most powerful master vampire, Nikolaos. Two years after Valentine's scarring, Nikolaos brought in Anita to solve the rash of vampire murders in St. Louis. Valentine ran into Anita as she departed from meeting Nikolaos at the Circus of the Damned. Valentine reminded her of the wounds she had inflicted upon him, and checked her for the scars he had given her to prove that she was the one who had scarred him. He made it clear that he intended to have revenge upon her. Nikolaos' servants Winter and Zachary helped ward Valentine off and remind him that Nikolaos needed Anita for the investigation. Valentine told Anita that when Nikolaos removed her protection, he would kill her. Anita began to prepare by seeking the location of Valentine's daytime resting place.

Valentine and fellow vampire Aubrey helped torture Phillip on behalf of Nikolaos, hoping that they could force Anita's continued assistance. After they slew Phillip, Anita assaulted Aubrey and Valentine, attempting to kill them, but Nikolaos brought her down and sent her away. However, Anita schemed to destroy Nikolaos, and invaded the Circus of the Damned with Edward. Finding Valentine in his coffin, Edward provided two syringes of silver nitrate that were injected into his blood, seemingly killing him. Anita later blasted him in the chest with a shotgun just to make certain.

HEIGHT: Unrevealed; tall   **WEIGHT:** Unrevealed; slender
EYES: Brown   **HAIR:** Auburn
AGE: Over 100

DESCRIPTION: Valentine preferred to dress in rich colored clothes with lace trimming, and straight-brimmed hats. The left side of his face was scarred and pitted, melted away, with his eye surrounded by pinkish-white scar tissue, and he wore masks of gold or silver to conceal the damage, covering everything but his mouth and chin.

DISTINGUISHING FEATURES: Badly scarred face, usually concealed by distinctive gold or silver masks.

DEMEANOR: Valentine was a sadistic killer who enjoyed inflicting pain on his victims. He seemed to prefer lapping up his victims' blood like a cat lapping milk, rather than sucking on the wound. He has an unhealthy obsession with young boys. Often noting how much "fresher" their blood tastes.

NOTABLE ABILITIES: Valentine was a ruthless vampire who enjoyed exploiting his powers. He did not demonstrate any mental abilities, but presumably possessed at least low-level mesmerism. He possessed superhuman strength and senses, resistance to injury, and regenerative

ANITA ON VALENTINE: "He had haunted my nightmares for years, nearly killed me."

REAL NAME: Valentine (full name unrevealed)
ALIASES: None
ANITA'S NICKNAMES: None
CLASSIFICATION: Vampire
OCCUPATION: Servant of Nikolaos, killer; possibly former gambler
CITIZENSHIP: U.S.A. (presumed)
BASE OF OPERATIONS: Circus of the Damned, St. Louis, Missouri
PLACE OF BIRTH: Unrevealed
KNOWN RELATIVES: None
ALLIES: Aubrey, Nikolaos
GROUP AFFILIATION: Unidentified group slain by Anita and Edward, Nikolaos' Kiss
ENEMIES: Anita Blake, Edward
EDUCATION: Unrevealed
FIRST APPEARANCE: Guilty Pleasures (1993)

abilities, but his face was permanently scarred by holy water. He required regular ingestion of blood in order to remain at his physical peak. He was also vulnerable to religious iconography, silver, and holy water, and had to remain in a coma-like state during daylight hours.

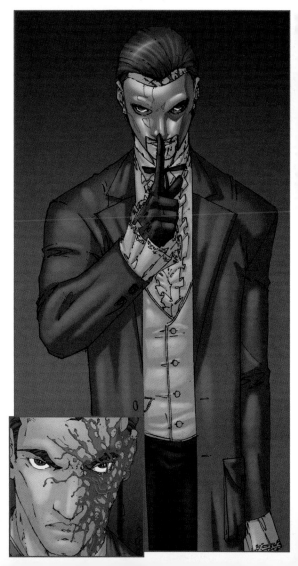

VAMPIRES

KNOWN MEMBERS: Aubrey (destroyed), Buzz, Dead Dave, Jack, Jean-Claude, Lucas (destroyed), Malcolm, Maurice (destroyed), Willie McCoy, Nikolaos (destroyed), Robert, Theresa (destroyed), Valentine (destroyed), others
BASE OF OPERATIONS: Active worldwide
FIRST APPEARANCE: Guilty Pleasures (1993)

TRAITS: Vampires are created from human beings. It takes three bites on three subsequent nights to become a vampire. Draining of blood is part of the process, though not all of it, as not everyone bitten becomes a vampire, and the full requirements to go from being mortal to vampire are unconfirmed. One legend suggests that the would-be vampire has to also drink some vampire's blood, which may have some veracity given that many vampire junkies seem to like biting as much as being bitten. Once a vampire, the person is no longer able to eat normal food, instead sustaining themselves by drinking human blood; as drinking animal blood will cause the vampire to contract a wasting disease that will eventually kill him, and certainly most vampires prefer human donors, willing or otherwise, piercing the skin using fangs or claw-like fingernails. A vampire does not age nor decay, and though they can starve, they cannot starve to death. Their strength becomes superhuman; able to lift cars with ease, they move with incredible celerity, their senses are enhanced dramatically, to the point where they can tell a human's emotional state from their scent or hear whispered comments from some distance away, and they become extremely difficult to harm. Wounds from most objects, even bullets, heal in seconds without causing the vampire any seeming discomfort; however they cannot easily heal wounds caused by silver or holy water (both of which will leave scars), can be repelled or even burned on contact by crosses wielded by people with faith, dislike garlic, and burn in sunlight. They are also vulnerable to fire, or wounds to the heart caused by wooden or silver weapons. As the assassin Edward has proven, injections of silver nitrate are lethal to younger vampires, although they become more resistant as they grow older; a 100 year old vampire required two injections to die, while one of 500 seemed merely annoyed by the injection. During daylight younger vampires enter a corpse-like sleep; at their most vulnerable, they usually hide their daylight resting places. Older vampires gradually become able to stir during daytime if disturbed, and eventually a vampire may gain the power to be awake at least part of the day. Younger vampires tend to show off their fangs when speaking or smiling, whilst older ones can be recognized by the incredible smoothness of their movement, results of centuries of practice, counterpointed by their complete stillness when not in action.

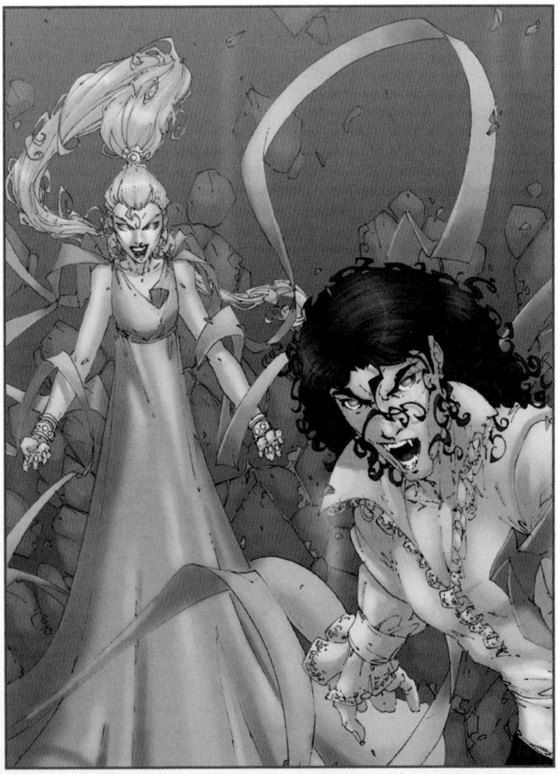

A vampire's greatest weapon is its mind. As they get older, vampires learn to dominate the minds of mortals, initially learning small perceptual tricks such as blanking out their movements so it looks like they can appear or disappear at will, or hiding their own blemishes and imperfections. There may be a limit to this beautifying trick, as at least two older vampires, Valentine and Jean-Claude, have visible scars, though it is possible they leave them visible out of choice. At least some vampires can control certain species of animal, even commanding sentient were-creatures of that breed. Vampires can hypnotize humans, most easily if they look into the vampire's eyes, but also as the vampire gains power, through their voice or even direct mental contact. The oldest known vampire thus far, Nikolaos, could levitate and manipulate storm force winds. When an older vampire calls on their full power, their mask of humanity falls away, with their eyes glowing and their face and body becoming skeletal.

Some vampires can turn humans into servants, though this may be limited to masters and there may be a restriction as to how many servants a single vampire has. By psychically "marking" their chosen servant, they gain an increasingly close bond; the first mark grants the servant some of their master's strength, giving them accelerated healing, plus some resistance to vampiric mind powers. The second mark allows the master vampire to take energy from the human servant and to communiicate with them through thier dreams. The third allows for direct telepathic communication, while the fourth makes the servant immortal, so long as having drunk of their master's blood. It is unknown if further marks can be given, or what powers they might grant.

LENGTH: Varies
WEIGHT: Varies
EYES: Varies, older vampires eyes can seem to glow when using mind powers
SKIN: Varies

HISTORY: The origins of the vampire race are unknown, although they have existed for as long as humanity has existed. Though increasingly powerful the older they get, human hunters and internecine struggles seem to have kept their numbers down, and there seem to be few vampires more than 100 years old. Each city or region inhabited by vampires is ruled by the most powerful master vampire present, usually but not always the oldest. It is unclear what requirements exist to become a master; while age is part of it, it is not the sole requisite, as in St. Louis the 500 year-old Aubrey was not a master while the 205 year-old Jean-Claude was. It may be linked to a vampire's followers, or perhaps that vampires under the direct control of a master never fully develop their own powers, however old they are. Two years ago the United States granted vampires civil rights, allowing them to operate openly and leading to a flock of immigrants from less welcoming countries. Vampires may now only be legally slain by licensed law enforcement individuals with a warrant, or in self-defense. Vampire businesses have sprung up in larger cities, often based around tourism for the curious human. The U.S.'s busiest city for such vampire-watching is New York, with St. Louis a close second. It has a large vampire population, and, prior to the recent vampire murders, had at least five master vampires in residence; now there are two known masters, Malcolm, head of the Church of Eternal Life, and Jean-Claude, owner of Guilty Pleasures and master of the city.

BERT VAUGHN

HISTORY: Bert Vaughn was born with the ability to make money. While most animators were struggling to cope with their powers, Bert transformed what many thought of as a curse into a profitable business, founding Animators, Inc. The business grew swiftly, growing from being just Bert in a spare room above a garage to swanky offices with four of his animators, including Anita Blake, within four years, largely due to Bert's efforts as a showman, moneymaker, scallywag and borderline cheat. Bert would do anything for cash, so long as it wasn't quite illegal, and feels his staff should think likewise. Two of his animators, Anita and Manny, served as vampire killers, prior to the undead gaining civil rights, and with Bert happily pocketing his share of the police retainer, Anita continues in the same capacity as a vampire executioner licensed in three states; meanwhile Bert takes on clients who want advice about joining the Church of Eternal Life and becoming vampires, carefully steering those clients to a member of the Animators, Inc. team who isn't Anita, such as Jamison Clarke.

When the vampire Willie McCoy approached Animators, Inc. hoping to hire Anita to investigate the recent serial vampire killings, Bert attempted in vain to persuade Willie to hire Clarke instead, correctly believing Anita would turn down the work, and thus the fee. After Anita unexpectedly took the case, she confided in Bert that she had been coerced to do so through threats directed at her friends; initially claiming he would never knowingly endanger her, when Anita called him on this, Bert cheerfully admitted he was lying, but that he would have charged more. However when Anita warned him that she would quit and take her clients with her if he ever forced her to meet with a vampire client again without first running it past her, Bert became colder, but eventually backed down gracefully when he realized she meant it.

Bert subsequently passed on a message to Anita that Thomas Jensen, was willing to let Anita return his zombie daughter to the grave, unwittingly luring her into an ambush arranged by the zombie Zachary.

HEIGHT: 6'4"
WEIGHT: Unrevealed; broad
EYES: Pale gray
HAIR: White
AGE: 40's

DESCRIPTION: Bert is a large man with an athlete's frame, now softening around his middle. He has an outdoors tan, which contrasts sharply with his close-cut white hair and almost colorless gray eyes.

DEMEANOR: Bert is always calculating the odds, looking for angles to make money. Usually smiling insincerely, the only time he displays genuine pleasure is when he is making money; he is unapologetic to those who know him well enough to see through his masks, and gives the impression he would do anything for the right price, so long as he feels he can get away with it. Conversely, losing money for any reason is the one thing guaranteed to upset or anger him.

NOTABLE SKILLS: Bert possesses considerable business acumen, and is a skilled showman, excellent at publicizing his business. However he is a poor judge of people, largely due to his inability to empathize.

NOTABLE ABILITIES: Bert is an excellent business manager and has the ability and showmanship to make Animator's Inc. a profitable business for all involved.

ANITA ON BERT VAUGHN: "There was something a little frightening about a man who knew he was not a nice person and didn't give a damn."

REAL NAME: Bert Vaughn
ALIASES: None
ANITA'S NICKNAMES: Mr. Sincerity, Mr. Charm
CLASSIFICATION: Human
OCCUPATION: Business manager
CITIZENSHIP: U.S.A.
PLACE OF BIRTH: Unrevealed
BASE OF OPERATIONS: Animators, Inc. offices, St. Louis, Missouri
KNOWN RELATIVES: None
ALLIES: None
GROUP AFFILIATION: Animator's Inc.
ENEMIES: None
EDUCATION: Unrevealed
FIRST APPEARANCE: Guilty Pleasures (1993)

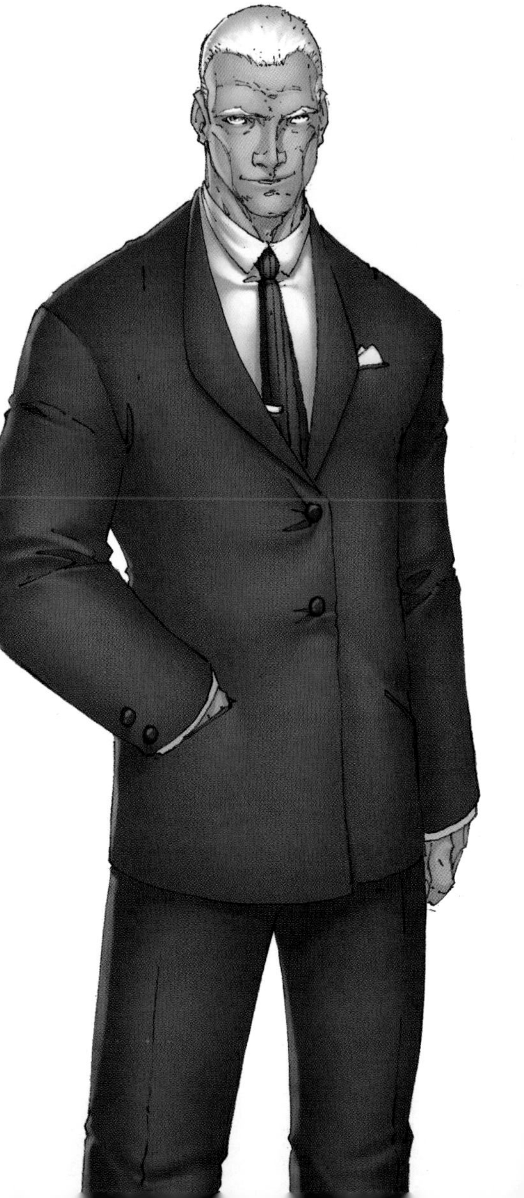

WERERATS

ANITA ON WERERATS: "Cries, moans, the popping of bones, a curious sliding sound like a knife drawing out of flesh. The wererats were changing from human to animal. It sounded like it hurt – a lot."

KNOWN MEMBERS: Louis, Lillian, Rafael, several unnamed others
BASE OF OPERATIONS: Unrevealed.
FIRST APPEARANCE: Guilty Pleasures (1993)

TRAITS: Wererats are one of a number of breeds of lycanthropes, humans inflicted with a supernatural virus which allows them to take on the power and appearance of a specific species of animal, in this case, rats. The virus can be caught by being scratched by a lycanthrope, and possibly through bites too; the process is unpredictable, and a victim of a lycanthrope attack might survive a serious wound uninfected, or be turned by even the slightest scratch. Inoculations similar to those for rabies exist for lycanthropy, and can be effective if given quickly enough following initial infection; however the inoculation can also cause the infection, so using them is a calculated risk. An infected individual will transform for the first time at the next full moon, after that it appears that though full moons trigger an involuntary change, lycanthropes can choose to switch forms willingly the rest of the time. The transformation is extremely painful, as bones and flesh reshape, and wererats at least seem to prefer changing in privacy, out of sight of human eyes.

Wererats have both forms available to them; they retain their full intellect in both. Those powerful enough have a third, hybrid man-beast form. Their original human forms appear normal to a casual observer, but display a feeling of contained energy to those who know what to look for.

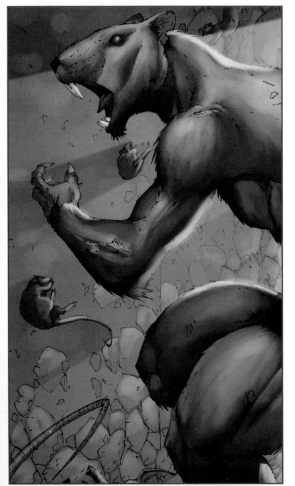

Even in this form, they have enhanced senses, able to tell by smell the mood of nearby humans; what other abilities carry over to human form is uncertain. Their hybrid form, availble only to the strongest of them, may be that of a humanoid rat, covered in fur the color of their human hair, with long curved tails that lash around when they are angry. They walk on the balls of their elongated feet, with both hands and feet ending in sharp claws. Their heads become narrow and ratlike, with black-button eyes, wire-like whiskers, long pink tongues and several inch long, blade-like incisors; combined with a mouth not suited to human speech, these teeth make speaking difficult for most wererats. In this form many wererats prefer wearing loose cut-off jeans or maternity dresses to conceal their still noticeably human sexual organs; however some wererats seem to embrace their animal side and go naked, flaunting themselves. They can communicate with one another through squeaking, and possess heightened hearing, agility and endurance; they are significantly stronger and faster than normal humans, and move with a scrambling, sliding grace, contorting through small spaces without noticeably slowing. While regular weapons can cause them injury, they will heal from most wounds given time, but are vulnerable to silver. They can command regular rats with gestures. Their second form is that of a full rat, but a giant one, about the size of a German Shepherd dog.

LENGTH: Varies
WEIGHT: Varies
EYES: Varies; commonly black in rat form
SKIN: Varies

HISTORY: In recent times the wererats of St. Louis have seen a power struggle over who controls their rodere. Their chosen leader is Rafael, the rat king, who seems to hold his throne by strength of arm; however, the master vampire Nikolaos was able to call and control rats, and saw the wererats as an extension of her domain. Rafael feels the wererats are people as well as rats, and so have a choice, and had ordered his roderie not to answer Nikolaos' summons. Presumably either Nikolaos or Rafael had only come to power recently, as Nikolaos brooked no defiance, and was unlikely to have tolerated Rafael's stance for long.

One unidentified blond wererat, who may have had leadership ambitions of his own, made it clear he believed that Rafael's days were numbered if he did not obey their "master," and when Nikolaos wanted to terrorize the captive animator Anita Blake, the blond wererat led three of his fellows, along with thousands of regular rats, through tunnels into Nikolaos' dungeons beneath her base in the Circus of the Damned. They attacked Anita, threatening to rape her, but used to humans being incapacitated by terror, were unprepared for her combat skills. She narrowly held them off and embarrassed the blond in front of his followers, until the confrontation was ended by the arrival of Rafael. He dismissed the other wererats and overpowered the blond, making it clear that further defiance would end in death.

Later, when Anita needed a covert route back into the Circus, she approached Rafael and the rats for help, telling him she planned to slay Nikolaos. While he hoped she would succeed, Rafael made it clear that his rats could not assist her in the actual fight, as none of them would be able to resist Nikolaos' control so close to her. However he agreed to lead her and her ally Edward through the tunnels; luckily Anita succeeded in her mission, ending the power of Nikolaos over Rafael's people.

Apart from Rafael and the blond wererat, only two other wererats have been identified so far, both close allies of Rafael. One is Louie, a square faced man with dark brown eyes, a slender body and small build but muscular arms. He appears affable, chatty, and knowledgeable about caves. The other is Lillian, a doctor, whose rat form's fur is virtually gray, and who treated Edward and Anita's wounds after their battle with Nikolaos and her minions.

WINTER

HISTORY: Winter was a minion of the master vampire Nikolaos based at the Circus of the Damned. Given his muscular physique and apparel, it seems likely that he may also have worked as a strongman within the carnival when not working on behalf of Nikolaos. Though a willing and unswerving lackey of the vampires, he lacked any sign of vampire bites, suggesting he might have been under consideration to become a human servant, similar to Nikolaos' unaging manservant Burchard, whom Winter sometimes worked with as an assistant, or perhaps apprentice.

Shortly after a string of vampires were murdered in St. Louis, Nikolaos coerced the vampire executioner Anita Blake into investigating the killings. At their first meeting, Anita provoked Nikolaos into a rage with her sarcasm and defiance, and while the vampire Jean-Claude tried to hold Nikolaos back, Anita fled her wrath alongside the animator Zachary, another of Nikolaos' servants. On the stairs leading up from Nikolaos' lair to the Circus of the Damned, they ran into Winter; informed by Zachary of Anita's identity, Winter treated with dubious amusement the revelation that the petite woman, a good foot shorter than him, was the "Executioner" feared by so many of the city's undead. Having been instructed by an unknown party to check on Nikolaos' well-being, Winter realized it would not be wise to interrupt her confrontation with Jean-Claude, and instead he escorted Anita and Zachary back to the surface. However, at the stairs' exit, they were stopped by Valentine, one of Nikolaos' vampire servants who had an old grudge against Anita. Aware his master wanted Anita unharmed to hunt the killer, Winter placed himself between her and Valentine, much to the vampire's amusement. Reminded of Nikolaos' orders, Valentine made it clear he did not intend to harm Anita that night, but threatened to kill Winter if Anita did not show him the scars he had given her in their last encounter; Anita acquiesced, and Valentine let her depart. Winter stayed behind, seemingly to guard Anita's back.

A few days later Nikolaos had one of Jean-Claude's people, Phillip, kidnapped, threatening him as a way of punishing Anita's continued defiance. Told to come to the Circus, Anita was met by Winter and Burchard; the elder man instructed Winter to check Anita for concealed weapons and remove them before they entered Nikolaos' presence. Winter did so, but missed a knife in an ankle sheath. Accompanying them down into Nikolaos' dungeon, Winter restrained Anita while Nikolaos bit Phillip in front of them, and then joined them in Nikolaos' throne room where Nikolaos explained to Anita what was expected of her in the future. Though Anita was cooperating, Nikolaos ordered Phillip's death anyway, as a message to Jean-Claude's other followers; anticipating Anita would try to intervene, Winter restrained her again, but she pretended to faint, and when he let her go, she snatched the blade from her ankle, rammed it into Winter's groin, then pulled the blade out and fled to assist Phillip, leaving Winter to bleed to death.

HEIGHT: At least 6'3"
WEIGHT: Unrevealed; muscular build
EYES: Blue
HAIR: White
AGE: Unrevealed, presumably 20s

DESCRIPTION: Winter was tall and exceptionally muscular, with enormous biceps, bulging neck muscles and no excess fat whatsoever. He had no hint of a tan, cotton-white hair shaved close to his head and icy blue eyes, giving the overall impression of being virtually colorless. He wore minimal and tight clothing, designed to display his physique to its maximum potential.

DISTINGUISHING FEATURES: Extremely muscular.

DEMEANOR: Winter was clearly proud of his strength, his bodybuilder physique requiring a lot of work to maintain, his clothing chosen to show that off as much as possible, and clearly enjoying the impressed reactions of those he met. He also seemed to enjoy letting others presume he was a vampire, deliberately smiling without showing his teeth; this may also explain his lack of tan, a necessary part of the deception. A willing servant of Nikolaos, he was smart enough to be afraid of dealing with her anger, but seemed unafraid of the danger of fighting other vampires, knowing that he had no choice but to protect Anita, as he would be punished if he allowed her to be harmed.

NOTABLE SKILLS: Exceptionally strong, Winter claims he can bench press 400 lbs. However, it seems he relied overly on his strength, as his lack of fighting experience and overconfidence against the much smaller Anita Blake eventually proved fatal.

ANITA ON WINTER: "He was the first bodybuilder I'd seen who didn't have a tan. All that rippling muscle was done in white, like Moby Dick."

REAL NAME: Unrevealed; possibly Winter
ALIASES: None
ANITA'S NICKNAMES: Mr. Macho, Mr. Muscles
CLASSIFICATION: Human
OCCUPATION: Servant of Nikolaos, possible carnival strongman
CITIZENSHIP: U.S.A.
PLACE OF BIRTH: Unrevealed
BASE OF OPERATIONS: Circus of the Damned, St. Louis, Missouri
KNOWN RELATIVES: None
ALLIES: Aubrey, Burchard, Nikolaos, Zachary
GROUP AFFILIATION: Nikolaos' Kiss
ENEMIES: Anita Blake
EDUCATION: Unrevealed
FIRST APPEARANCE: Guilty Pleasures (1993)

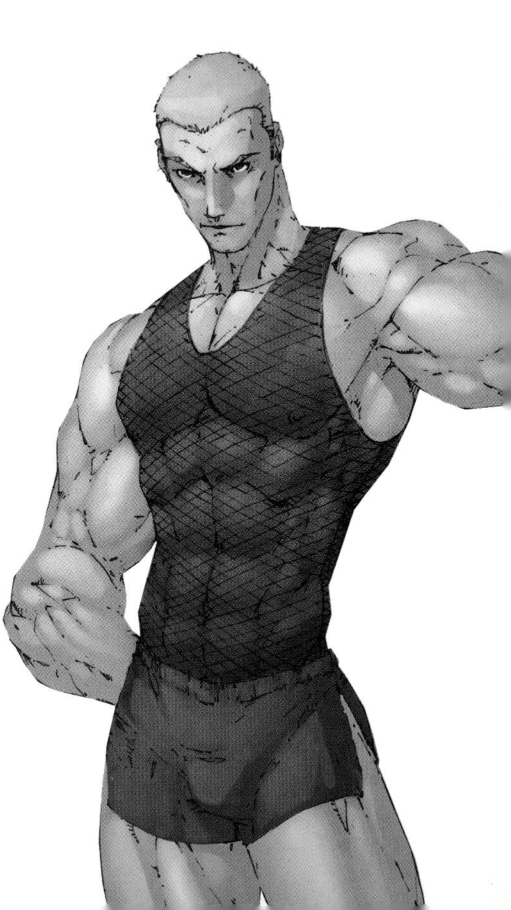

ZACHARY

ANITA ON ZACHARY: "I now knew where I had seen him before. I had been at his funeral."

REAL NAME: Zachary (last name unrevealed)
ALIASES: None
ANITA'S NICKNAMES: None
CLASSIFICATION: Unrevealed type of undead
OCCUPATION: Animator, serial killer, underling
CITIZENSHIP: U.S.A.
BASE OF OPERATIONS: Circus of the Damned
PLACE OF BIRTH: Unrevealed
KNOWN RELATIVES: None
ALLIES: His ghouls, formerly Aubrey, Burchard, Nikolaos, Winter
GROUP AFFILIATION: Nikolaos' Kiss
ENEMIES: Anita Blake, Nikolaos, Theresa, Edward
EDUCATION: Unrevealed
FIRST APPEARANCE: Guilty Pleasures (1993)

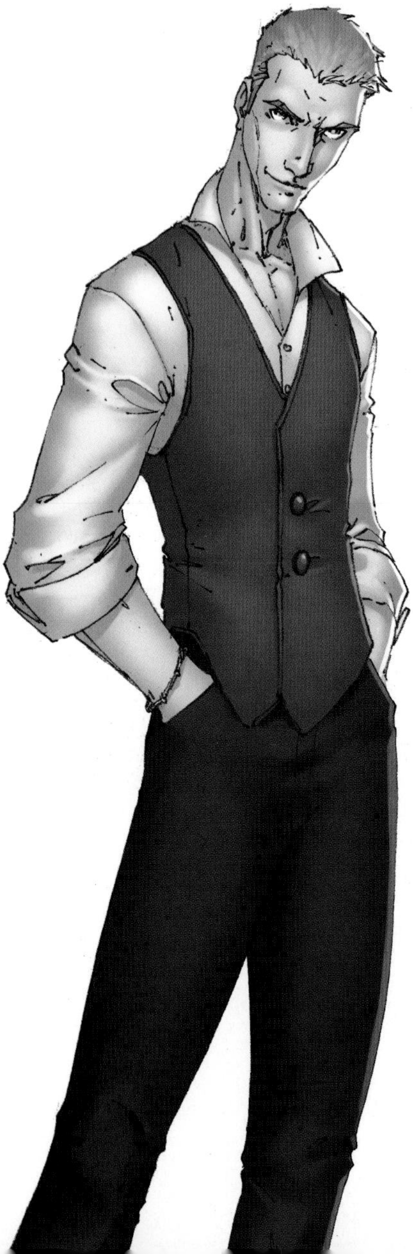

HISTORY: Zachary was once an animator, but died under unrevealed circumstances. Due to their small community, his funeral was attended by fellow animators out of professional courtesy, including Anita Blake, even though she had barely a passing knowledge of who he was. Under unrevealed circumstances, perhaps because he had prepared for the eventuality of his own demise, Zachary was raised from the dead in a state similar to that of a zombie, but possessed complete independence, maintaining his existence using a voodoo charm known as a gris-gris, which had to be supplied with the blood of vampires to sustain its enchantment. At the same time that Zachary was awakened, the entire cemetery's supply of corpses were raised with him as ghouls, and these ghouls became obedient to Zachary's will. Zachary theorized that ghouls were created from cemeteries where animators had been raised, but he could not explore this theory further, since discussing it with another animator would also mean he needed to reveal his true nature to them.

Zachary was in the employ of Nikolaos, the most powerful master vampire of St. Louis; it is unclear if he worked for her before his death, or had only taken up his post afterwards. Nikolaos mistakenly believed him to still be a human, and continued to use him as an animator. His privileged position gave Zachary insider knowledge on the identities and residences of St. Louis' most powerful vampires, which Zachary exploited to feed his gris-gris. Using his ghouls, Zachary began a string of murders within St. Louis' vampire population. Before long he had slain ten vampires for his gris-gris, only four of which the police were aware of. His victims included two of the most powerful master vampires in St. Louis. He also sent his ghouls out on raids, killing the caretaker of a cemetery on one evening.

However, Zachary had been observed on one of his murders by a human. Nikolaos had the human captured and interrogated, but the witness was so frightened that when he was left alone, he hung himself, using his belt as a noose. Nikolaos directed Zachary to raise the witness as a zombie so that they could continue their questioning. Zachary did so, but when he was put in charge of the interrogation he used the opportunity to break the witness' mind, rendering him useless. At the same time, Nikolaos had manipulated Anita Blake into investigating the vampire murders, and she was present as Zachary brought the zombie to Nikolaos. Anita did not recognize Zachary, but quickly surmised that the zombie had been broken, and was now useless; Nikolaos was enraged by Zachary's "mistake" and he and Anita were forced to flee her presence. As Anita was sent to begin her investigation, Zachary was assigned to be her daytime contact to Nikolaos, and provided her with a matchbook containing his phone number.

Nikolaos began to suspect that Zachary was an incompetent animator and requested that Zachary raise Estelle Hewitt, a woman who died in 1866, to prove his worth, well aware that most animators could not raise a corpse more than a century dead. Nikolaos intended for him to fail so that she would have an excuse to have him killed, sending Theresa and a small coterie of other vampires with orders to execute Zachary when he could not perform the task. As predicted, Zachary's ritual failed, and Theresa was already beginning to torment Zachary when Anita Blake chanced upon the scene. Her arrival granted Zachary a stay of execution; believing she was helping a fellow human and aware that reforming a corpse from dust to raise it was beyond most animators' reach, Anita bargained with Theresa to assist Zachary, reminding Theresa that while Nikolaos might want Zachary punished, she did not want Anita hurt. Anita intended to combine power with Zachary, using herself as a focus, and sacrificing their own blood to reactivate the blood circle he had created by sacrificing a goat, providing Zachary with the means to fulfill his mission. Though Zachary's dead blood was actually of no use, unaware of this Anita's own blood and power proved sufficient, and they raised Estelle. However as Estelle dug her way out of the grave, Anita finally remembered where she had seen Zachary before. Spotting the gris-gris and recognizing its significance, though not what kind of blood it fed upon, Anita made it quietly clear she knew his true status; when she made to touch the gris-gris, Zachary stopped her, knowing that human blood would break the spell and kill him. He quickly assured the angry Anita that the people he was feeding to the gris-gris were ones who would not be missed, but surrounded by hostile vampires, Anita was unable to quiz him further, and failed to make the connection to the vampire slayings. Later that evening, Zachary made Theresa the latest victim for his gris-gris, taking revenge on her for threatening him.

Although Anita had yet to surmise the complete truth about him, Zachary decided that he could not allow her to continue. He contacted one of Nikolaos' human servants and directed him to assassinate Anita, claiming it was an order from Nikolaos herself. The assassin made his attempt while Anita and her friend Veronica Sims were visiting the Church of Eternal Life, incorrectly believing that the murders were linked to the church. Anita killed the assassin and suspected that the church had sent him after her, still unaware of Zachary's machinations.

In order to lead Anita into a trap, Zachary arranged a false meeting with animator cause célèbre, Thomas Jensen. Jensen had raised his daughter Iris as a zombie in the hopes of obtaining her forgiveness for sexually abusing her, but Iris would not forgive him. Anita was lured into Zachary's trap believing that Jensen was finally ready to allow Iris to return to the ground. Anita and Edward, a fellow vampire hunter, came to the cemetery expecting to meet the Jensens, but were instead confronted by Zachary and at least twenty of his ghouls. Anita finally realized that he must be the vampire murderer, and he admitted it to them. Finding that Edward was armed, Zachary had some of the ghouls encircle him for protection, and dispatched the others to kill the duo while he fled. However Anita happened to have the matchbook he had given her earlier on her person, and she used supplies from the cemetery's gardening shack to start a fire and escape. Anita made arrangements with the police to give a statement so that if she failed to destroy Nikolaos and her followers Zachary would be brought to justice.

Nikolaos, still unaware of Zachary's duplicity, arranged for him to raise Phillip as a zombie, for her amusement. With the aid of the wererats, Anita and Edward gained access to the Circus of the Damned and began to kill each of Nikolaos' vampires while they slept. However, Zachary and Burchard interrupted them in their work and took them prisoner, then revealed Phillip's resurrection as a zombie to her. Nikolaos ultimately chose to have Anita fight Burchard for her life, but during the clash Anita revealed that Zachary was the vampire murderer. Nikolaos flew into a rage and tore out Zachary's throat. This gave Anita the opportunity she needed to destroy Burchard, and then Nikolaos herself. Recalling how he had stopped her touching his gris-gris with her own blood back during the raising of Estelle, Anita destroyed his gris-gris before he could heal from his injuries, killing him for good. Anita subsequently returned Phillip to his grave. The fate of Zachary's ghouls is not known.

HEIGHT: Unrevealed
WEIGHT: Unrevealed; thin
EYES: Pale green
HAIR: Sandy blond
AGE: Unrevealed

DESCRIPTION: Zachary had a thin, angular face with high cheekbones, neither good looking nor ugly.

DEMEANOR: Zachary's sole goal was to stay alive. Initially he demonstrated a level of cocky showmanship, displaying his zombie witness with a flourish, but when faced with death, he crumbled, begging for his life. When he felt he had the upper hand, he was ruthless and took pleasure in killing those he felt had endangered his secret.

NOTABLE SKILLS: Skilled animator, presumably aware of at least a little voodoo lore.

EQUIPMENT: Zachary wore a voodoo gris-gris, a rope band with beads and feathers woven into it. Fed by regular doses of vampire blood, it sustained his undead life, and prevented even the most lethal wounds from killing him, letting them heal within minutes. His animator equipment included a long hunting knife with one jagged edge, and a pint jar full of off-white faintly luminous homemade ointment with glowing green flecks of graveyard mold in it. Zachary also sometimes carried guns.

NOTABLE ABILITIES: In life, Zachary was a powerful animator with exceptional skill at awakening zombies and returning them to the ground. After his resurrection, his abilities as an animator were reduced by his own undead state, though they were still powerful compared to most animators. He was also in command of a pack of at least twenty ghouls who could be made to follow simple orders and defend him.

ZOMBIES

ANITA ON ZOMBIES: "He could pass for human better than any vampire in the room, but he was more a corpse than any of them."

KNOWN MEMBERS: Albert Grundick (presumed laid to rest), unidentified witness to Lucas' murder, Estelle Hewitt (laid to rest), Phillip (laid to rest), Iris Jensen
BASE OF OPERATIONS: Varies
FIRST APPEARANCE: Guilty Pleasures (1993)

TRAITS: Zombies are corpses raised from the dead with a semblance of human life and, initially, human memories, either by trained animators, humans with an innate affinity for raising the dead, or voodoo priests. Depending on the cause of death, some zombies created from the recently dead can pass for living, at least briefly, to those not used to dealing with the dead. Older corpses start more decayed, though a sufficiently powerful animator can make corpses reform from dust and fragments of bone, though the resulting zombie will have bones visible beneath the grayish waxen skin, and the eyes may have dried out to resemble shriveled grapes.

To raise a zombie, an animator employs a blood ritual, which begins with the sacrificial death of small animal, usually a chicken for the recently dead or a goat for those interred longer. The animator uses the animals blood to create a protective circle around the grave, then remaining within

the circle, the animator rubs the blood upon their face, hands, and chest, as well as on the grave and/or headstone. An ointment containing flecks of graveyard mold and other, undisclosed ingredients is then applied over the blood. The animator performs a chant and calls the subject by name, infusing their will, their power into the dead body causing it to rise as a zombie. The animator must quickly offer the zombie a taste of live blood to facilitate the restoration of its human memories, usually from the recently killed sacrificial animal, although in some instances the animator may use their own blood to complete the ceremony. All zombies take a while after being awoken to gather their thoughts and recover their memories of life, with the more recently deceased recalling quicker than those long departed. A sufficiently powerful animator can, if they want, stop the zombie from remembering its own death, at least for a time. Zombies can be returned to the grave by a second ritual, and since most zombies are only briefly brought back, this is usually done by the same animator who raised it.

Not truly alive, all zombies have, for a brief period, is the memory of what they were, but with the passage of time they will deteriorate, both physically and mentally. The mental deterioration can be slowed by treating them well, with their minds lasting for about a week in some instances; conversely, zombies retain some basic emotions, including fear, and ill treatment will accelerate the process, and in extreme cases can break a zombie's mind in minutes. The physical decomposition can be slowed by feeding them raw meat, and there is one recorded case of a zombie still looking human after three years, sustained by meat such as lamb. There are three recorded cases of zombies going mad and, on their own volition, attacking people, craving flesh.

Because they initially retain memories, zombies can be questioned about events they witnessed prior to dying, and they are incapable of lying unless, presumably, instructed to do so by the animator controlling them. However, complex questions confuse them, and they respond better to simple, yes/no queries, making them poor witnesses, as they have to be led through their testimony. Because they can utilize full human endurance without fear of exhaustion or physical damage, zombies are capable of superhuman feats of strength. They obey the orders of their animator without fail, although eventual loss of mental faculties requires the use of more specific orders as necessary.

There is a theory that if the subject of a raising ceremony is the corpse of an animator, the power unleashed may animate other corpses as ghouls, carrion eaters with animal-level intelligence who live in packs and rarely venture from cemeteries; however, the full nature of ghoul creation remains largely a mystery. Another, connected theory suggests that the more zombies are raised in a given cemetery, the more ghouls will spontaneously arise.

LENGTH: Varies   **WEIGHT:** Varies
EYES: Varies   **SKIN:** Varies

HISTORY: The practice of zombie-raising, when legally done, is most commonly practiced to resolve inheritance matters following intestate deaths, such as in the case of Albert Grundick, who left behind two conflicting wills and was raised to ask which was the correct one, thus avoiding years of court wrangling. In other instances it may be done to allow surviving family to seek emotional closure, although this can cause its own problems; Iris Jensen was raised to allow her abusive father to beg her forgiveness, but when she wouldn't grant it, he refused to allow her to be returned to the grave, keeping her around with both mind and body decaying for over seven years. Zombies may also be raised to provide witness to events such as murders, but their lack of understanding limits their value in such cases. Unfortunately unscrupulous animators have also been known to raise zombies for others' amusement, such as when Estelle Hewitt was raised simply to allow vampires to torment her.

BRUCE

REAL NAME: Bruce (last name unrevealed)
ALIASES: None
ANITA'S NICKNAMES: None
CLASSIFICATION: Human
OCCUPATION: Secretary
CITIZENSHIP: U.S.A.
PLACE OF BIRTH: Unrevealed
BASE OF OPERATIONS: Church of Eternal Life, off Page Avenue, St. Louis
KNOWN RELATIVES: None
ALLIES: None
GROUP AFFILIATION: Church of Eternal Life
ENEMIES: None
EDUCATION: Unrevealed
FIRST APPEARANCE: Guilty Pleasures (1993)

HISTORY: Bruce works at the Church of Eternal Life as Malcolm's secretary, fielding requests to see him and keeping track of Malcolm's appointments. More than simply an employee, he clearly fully embraces the Church's doctrine, as evidenced by his openly displayed bite marks. While practiced and smooth at dealing with most of his daily encounters, he is unused to dealing with violence, presumably why he was not involved in arranging the assassin Edward's appointment to see Malcolm.

During the St. Louis vampire murders, Anita Blake suspected that followers of the Church might be involved in the slayings, and with her friend Ronnie Sims she visited the Church to speak to Malcolm. Initially presuming they were standard visitors considering joining the congregation, Bruce was thrown when Anita told him of her actual reason for visiting, especially as she exaggerated her hypothesis to claim she had proof of the Church's involvement in the murders. Caught off-guard, the normally unflappable Bruce penciled in a meeting for Anita for the evening, when Malcolm would be awake. He had just begun to regain his composure, but it was again shattered when he witnessed Anita and Ronnie kill a would-be assassin who targeted them as they were leaving the Church. His genuinely terrified reaction and insistence that the Church didn't condone violence convinced Anita that Bruce, at least, was not involved in her case. Clearly shaken, Bruce left a somewhat incoherent message informing Malcolm of his appointment with Anita, and failed to mention the attack on her.

HEIGHT: Unrevealed
WEIGHT: Unrevealed; slender
EYES: Brown
HAIR: Brown
AGE: Early 20s

DESCRIPTION: Bruce presents a deliberately well-groomed but easy-going front. Slender and youthful, he keeps his hair short and neatly cut, and accentuates his already attractive brown eyes with a pair of wire-framed glasses. His manner is practiced and friendly, from a welcoming smile to a carefully measured handshake, encouraging visitors to the Church to feel at ease. The only thing which conflicts with this otherwise impeccable presentation are healing bite marks on his throat, but given his affiliations and the rest of his presentation, leaving the marks highly visible is deliberate. However even these bites are neater and less off-putting to those who see them than the usual scars left on vampires' regular victims.

BUZZ

REAL NAME: Buzz (last name unrevealed)
ALIASES: None known
ANITA'S NICKNAMES: None
CLASSIFICATION: Vampire
OCCUPATION: Bouncer, Guilty Pleasures
CITIZENSHIP: U.S.A.
PLACE OF BIRTH: Unrevealed
KNOWN RELATIVES: Unrevealed
ALLIES: Servant of Jean-Claude
GROUP AFFILIATION: Nikolaos' Kiss
ENEMIES: Unrevealed
EDUCATION: Unrevealed
FIRST APPEARANCE: Guilty Pleasures (1993)

HISTORY: Buzz is a recently-turned vampire, undead less than twenty years, working as a bouncer at master vampire Jean-Claude's strip club, Guilty Pleasures. One of Jean-Claude's followers, he has been told not to call Jean-Claude "master," at least in front of humans, but occasionally slips; given his reaction to a gentle admonishment for so doing, it seems likely he has been harshly punished in the past for this error. He knows vampire groupie Monica Vespucci well enough to flirt with her by allowing her to feel his muscles. When she lured Anita Blake and Catherine Maison to the club as part of a plan to force Blake to investigate the recent vampire murders, Buzz knew enough about what was happening to know which table inside the club was assigned to them. Later that night Buzz returned from a break to witness a tense conversation between Blake and Jean-Claude on the front steps of the club. After Jean-Claude went inside, Blake asked Buzz to bring Monica and Catherine outside to her, but Buzz refused, citing his recent break as an excuse, forcing Blake to re-enter the club to locate her friends herself.

HEIGHT: Unrevealed but presumably tall
WEIGHT: Unrevealed; muscular build
EYES: Pale, color unrevealed
HAIR: Black
AGE: Unrevealed, presumably no more than 50 including under 20 years as a vampire.

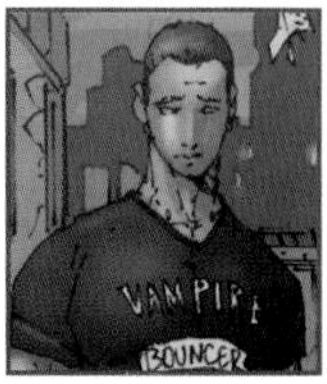

DESCRIPTION: Buzz is physically imposing, from his crew cut hair to a broad, muscular build, which suggests that even though undead, he is still pumping iron. One of the recently dead, he has yet to master the stillness of the true undead, and if he has recently fed to add color to his pale skin, he can pass for human even to a seasoned vampire expert.

DEMEANOR: Buzz clearly enjoys the shock value he gets from most visitors to Guilty Pleasures when he flashes his fangs at them, a sign that his undead status is still somewhat of a novelty to him. Since bodybuilding is inessential to maintain vampiric strength, it seems Buzz keeps up the practice partially to appear more imposing to would-be troublemakers, and largely to encourage the attentions of the mostly female patrons of the stripper bar, whom Buzz clearly enjoys flirting with.

NOTABLE SKILLS: Presumably a modicum of unarmed fighting skills.

NOTABLE ABILITIES: None demonstrated, but Buzz presumably has the standard vampiric abilities, such as superhuman strength, mesmerism, etc., though his comparative youth would suggest they are relatively weak.

BEVERLY CHIN

REAL NAME: Beverly Chin
ALIASES: None
ANITA'S NICKNAMES: Bev
CLASSIFICATION: Human
OCCUPATION: Unrevealed
CITIZENSHIP: U.S.A.
PLACE OF BIRTH: Unrevealed
BASE OF OPERATIONS: St. Louis, MO
KNOWN RELATIVES: Unspecified family members, all deceased
ALLIES: Anita Blake
GROUP AFFILIATION: Humans Against Vampires
ENEMIES: All vampires
EDUCATION: Unrevealed
FIRST APPEARANCE: Guilty Pleasures (1993)

HISTORY: Three years ago, prior to vampires gaining civil rights, Beverly Chin and her family were victims of an attack by a vampire pack. Beverly was the sole survivor. While the rest of her family was being slaughtered, vampire hunters arrived on the scene. Separated from the main group, one vampire cornered Beverly, and was about to rip the hysterical woman's throat open when one of the hunters, Anita Blake, discovered them. Blake, having already used up her gun's ammunition earlier, threw a silver dagger at Beverly's assailant; though only suffering a minor shoulder wound, this served to distract the vampire from Beverly, and it turned its attention on Blake, swiftly overpowering her. However as it crouched to feed on Blake, Beverly seized a nearby silver candlestick, and, still screaming, berserkly attacked the undead, taking it by surprise and smashing it repeatedly in the head until its skull shattered and its brains seeped out. Stunned by her own capacity for violence and loss of control, Beverly begged Anita to keep it a secret that she had slain the vampire, seemingly feeling that if no one else knew, she might be able to fool herself into believing it had never happened. Even though at this time vampire slaying was not a crime and the action was self-defense anyway, Anita told the police that Beverly had simply provided a distraction which enabled her to execute the attacking undead, and for this reason, as much as for their mutual saving of one another's lives, Beverly felt she owed Anita a debt she could never repay.

Despite this shared experience and debt, neither woman saw the other for the next three years, not avoiding one another but also not seeking them out, both wishing to put the memories behind them. Beverly, having lost control so dramatically once, worked hard to compose a controlled demeanor, and at some point joined HAV (Humans Against Vampires), a group which objected to vampires being granted civil rights. Hearing rumors within the group of death squads illegally targeting vampires, Beverly became concerned; though she felt slaying vampires should not be a crime any more than putting down a dangerous animal, Beverly also felt the group should not stoop to vigilantism. Her carefully rebuilt world shaken by this possibility, Beverly met with Blake and her detective friend Ronnie Sims, who were investigating a series of vampire murders, and largely because of her debt to Blake, agreed to see if she could find further evidence of HAV's involvement in the recent slayings.

HEIGHT: Unrevealed, shorter than 5'3"
WEIGHT: Unrevealed, petite
EYES: Unrevealed
HAIR: Black
AGE: Unrevealed, presumably mid-20s

DESCRIPTION: Beverly is a very short and delicate looking Asian woman, wearing tailored and color coordinated outfits with matching make-up.

DEMEANOR: Beverly carries herself with a comfortable ladylike dignity, working hard to maintain the façade that she has never been touched by extreme violence or lost control.

THE CIRCUS OF THE DAMNED

FIRST APPEARANCE: Guilty Pleasures (1993)

HISTORY: Presumably opened in the two years since vampires gained civil rights, the Circus of the Damned is a carnival midway housed within an old warehouse on the edge of the District in St. Louis. The sides of the building are hung with numerous large plastic-cloth sidings, similar to those you would find at an old fashioned sideshow, advertising the various macabre attractions within, and on the roof the Circus' name is emblazoned in colored lights on a large sign surrounded by giant dancing clowns; if an observer looks closely, they might realize that each clown possesses fangs. The interior mimics an old fashioned fun-fair, with the attractions held inside tents within the building, complete with carnival barkers outside loudly encouraging visitors to enter specific shows, but there is a horrific side to almost every show. The "death-defying" Count Alcourt is repeatedly executed by hanging for the entertainment of the crowd, other shows promise to let customers see zombies rise from their graves, or watch the transformations of Fabian the Werewolf. There are also more traditional fun-fair prize games, where the player can win cuddly toys, but even these show the Circus' unique twist on the carnival theme, as the toys are predators, such as soft-plush panthers, toddler-sized teddy bears, spotted snakes and giant fuzzy-toothed bats. There is a mirror-maze, a funhouse where clowns entertain the visitors, a haunted house, and even a full-sized Ferris wheel whose top nearly reaches the high-roofed warehouse's ceiling. Despite its horrific aspects, it is a popular venue, with hundreds of visitors attending, including families with young children.

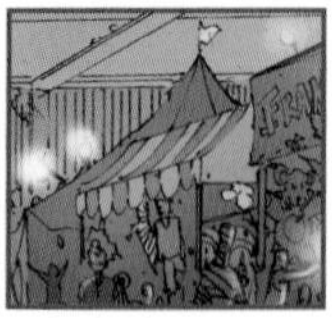

An observant visitor can detect the smell of blood permeating the venue, largely hidden beneath other, more regular carnival scents, such as cotton candy, corn dogs, snow cones, and the sweat of hundreds of people. There is an undercurrent of violence and evil about the place, apparent to those sensitive to such things. The Circus is also the lair of the Master of the City, although this fact is not common knowledge. Accessed by long flights of steps down deep below the Circus, Nikolaos has a throne room, dungeons, and her daytime resting place, which she shares with her closest coterie, including Valentine, Aubrey, Theresa, and an unidentified black vampire. As well as the stairs, Nikolaos' lair can be accessed via a labyrinthine series of tunnels known to the Wererats.

JAMISON CLARKE

REAL NAME: Jamison Clarke
ALIASES: None
ANITA'S NICKNAMES: None
CLASSIFICATION: Human
OCCUPATION: Animator
CITIZENSHIP: U.S.A.
PLACE OF BIRTH: Unrevealed
BASE OF OPERATIONS: Animators Inc offices, St. Louis
KNOWN RELATIVES: None
ALLIES: None
GROUP AFFILIATION: Animators Inc.
ENEMIES: None
EDUCATION: Unrevealed
FIRST APPEARANCE: Guilty Pleasures (1993)

HISTORY: Jamison Clarke is one of four animators working for St. Louis' Animators Inc. Though the four share both the common ability to raise zombies and their work premises, they have differing views about the undead, notably vampires. To Jamison vampires are simply people with fangs with neat powers and abilities, and he views the company's vampire slayers, Manny Rodriguez and Anita Blake as little better than murderers. Since Manny has largely retired from slaying, Jamison's main ire is usually directed at Anita, who remains active as a licensed court-appointed executioner of vampire criminals; the two argue frequently and heatedly on the topic, with Jamison accusing Anita of being an assassin and getting pleasure from murder, while Anita in return feeling Jamison is deliberately naïve and lying to himself. The vampires Jamison encounters deliberately encourage his view of them, carefully limiting what he sees of their activities.

Given Anita's attitude to vampires, when the undead Willie McCoy approached Animators Inc. with a view to hiring her to investigate the recent vampire murders afflicting the city, company owner Bert Vaughn tried to persuade him to employ Jamison instead; though Jamison was willing, McCoy insisted on asking Anita. A few days later Jamison was asked to advise Mrs. Franks, a woman whose son was considering joining the Church of Eternal Life and becoming a vampire; assuming, correctly, that Jamison would encourage this, Anita intercepted Mrs. Franks as she left the office, and tried to dissuade her. After escorting Mrs. Franks out and assuring her of Anita's bias, Jamison began a heated argument with Anita, during which he learned to his surprise that she had accepted McCoy's job offer. Unaware that McCoy's masters were coercing Anita with threats of violence against her friends, Jamison suspiciously tried to learn why Anita was willing to work for vampires, but seemingly accepted her lie that it was because whatever was capable of slaying the undead was also a threat to living humans too. Their argument was interrupted by the arrival of Phillip, whom Jamison wrongly assumed was Anita's lover, a piece of juicy gossip Anita was sure he would happily spread around the office.

HEIGHT: Unrevealed
WEIGHT: Unrevealed, but lean
EYES: Green
HAIR: Red
AGE: Unrevealed

DESCRIPTION: Jamison is a distinctive figure, with skin the color of dark honey contrasted by pale green eyes and long but curly red hair framing his face. Slender, his lean frame is the result of good genetics rather than exercise.

DEMEANOR: Jamison firmly believes vampires are misunderstood. Friendly and affable to clients, he is easily angered by Anita's undermining him in front of clients on cases involving vampires.

NOTABLE ABILITIES: Jamison is an animator, able to raise the recently dead as zombies through the use of ritual. He is not as capable as Anita, though the exact limit of his abilities is unrevealed.

THE DISTRICT

FIRST APPEARANCE: Guilty Pleasures

HISTORY: Unlike some cities, the undead community of St. Louis pride themselves on being mainstream, and a number of high visibility vampire-owned businesses have set up in the two years since Addison vs. Clark granted vampire's rights in what was formerly the city's Riverfront region, now known as the District by its inhabitants, or Blood Square by its detractors. Accessible from the 70 East Freeway, and covering an area of several blocks, much of the District comprises of older buildings, with aging sidewalks and narrow brick roads designed for horses rather than cars; the area's older residents feel it might well have been one of the things which attracted many of the older vampires. The number of human businesses has dwindled with the arrival of the vampires, and whereas formerly parking in the region's narrow streets was at a premium day, night and through the weekend, now unsurprisingly it is easy to find a space during the day.

Businesses within the District include: Dead Dave's, a bar run by a former cop, and one of the few establishments open during daylight, when it is run by Dave's human day manager Luther; Guilty Pleasures, a vampire strip club owned by Jean-Claude, and one of the District's hottest clubs; and the Circus of the Damned, a carnival midway with a macabre twist, housed within a large warehouse close to the District's edge. Unknown to most people, the Circus was also the home of Nikolaos, master of the city's vampires. The one major vampire business which pointedly does not reside in the District is Malcolm's Church of Eternal Life, which seeks to disassociate itself with the area's lurid reputation.

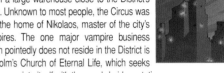

Largely due to the District, St. Louis has become a hot spot for vampire watchers. Though New York has more opportunities for the curious to see the undead, St. Louis has a lower crime rate because the local vampires deal violently with any of their own who prey too openly on normal humans. However, if only because the District is where human and vampire interaction is concentrated, the police's Regional Preternatural Investigation Team often find themselves called down to the area, and it is where the zombie animator Zachary killed all eleven of his vampire victims.

IRVING GRISWOLD

REAL NAME: Irving Griswold
ALIASES: None
ANITA'S NICKNAMES: Irving the Werewolf
CLASSIFICATION: Lycanthrope (werewolf)
OCCUPATION: Reporter
CITIZENSHIP: U.S.A.
PLACE OF BIRTH: Unrevealed
BASE OF OPERATIONS: St. Louis, Missouri
KNOWN RELATIVES: None
ALLIES: Anita Blake, unidentified wererat
GROUP AFFILIATION: St. Louis Post-Dispatch
ENEMIES: Unrevealed
EDUCATION: Unrevealed
FIRST APPEARANCE: Guilty Pleasures (1993)

HISTORY: Irving Griswold is a successful reporter for the St. Louis Post-Dispatch. He is also a werewolf. The circumstances and time when he contracted lycanthropy are unrevealed, though it seems likely to have been several years ago if his depth of knowledge of St. Louis' supernatural community and his business relationship with animator and vampire executioner Anita Blake are indicators. Irving and Anita have mutually advantageous business relationship; in return for information on cases Anita is working on for the police force's Regional Preternatural Investigation Team, Anita has supplied Irving story exclusives on several occasions, including the one which gave Irving his first front-page byline. One of the reasons Anita gets on well with Irving is that, unlike other supernatural beings, he downplays his abilities, never, for example, showing off the ability to smell a human's emotional state the way other lycanthropes do.

Irving and Anita normally maintain a level of professional distance, with the reporter calling the animator by her surname, presumably to remind her that they aren't close friends; each only contacts the other when they want something. When Anita needed to arrange a meeting with the Rat-King Rafael, she asked Irving to pass a message to Rafael through one of Irving's wererat acquaintances; for his own protection, Anita refused to divulge to Irving why she wanted the meeting. Despite being aware that he was providing assistance while a potentially huge story was being withheld from him, Irving did as he was asked, his mask of professionalism slipping long enough to tell Anita to be careful, wish her luck, and admit she was his best source for front page stories.

HEIGHT: 5' 3"
WEIGHT: Unrevealed
EYES: Unrevealed
HAIR: Frizzy brown hair with a bald spot on top
AGE: Unrevealed; however as Anita helped him get his first front page byline, he is presumably reasonably young.

NOTABLE SKILLS: Good investigative reporter.

NOTABLE ABILITIES: As a werewolf, Irving can transform from human form into that of a werewolf. In the latter form (and possibly his human one to a lesser extent), he possesses superhuman strength to an unspecified degree, rapid healing and resistance to weapons not made of silver, fangs and claws. He also possesses heightened senses of sight, hearing, taste, and smell, the latter in both forms, if other lycanthropes can be taken as examples.

HAV

CURRENT MEMBERS: Beverly Chin, numerous others unidentified
FORMER MEMBERS: None known
BASE OF OPERATIONS: Unrevealed; active across U.S.A.
FIRST APPEARANCE: Guilty Pleasures (1993)

HISTORY: While a few anti-vampire groups presumably existed prior to the undead winning civil rights, in the two years since the groundbreaking Addison vs. Clark ruling anti-vampire hate groups such as the League of Human Voters have become much more prolific and outspoken. Most people join up because either they or loved ones have been the victims of vampire attacks, others may join because their religious beliefs dictate an anti-vampire stance, and some because of simple bigotry.

Humans Against Vampires is apparently one of the largest of these groups, preaching the doctrine that vampires are dangerous animals, and should be put down, though HAV's president has stated that the organization will work within the legal system, ruling out vigilante action. Rumors persist of members setting up undercover death squads hoping to wipe vampirism off the face of the Earth. Despite the organizations name, their hatred is not limited to the undead; most members of HAV consider animators the enemy too as they raise zombies, and presumably many are anti-lycanthrope. The vampires, for their part, seem to tolerate the existence of such groups, at least at a distance, as part of the price they pay for retaining their hard won rights.

When Anita Blake was investigating the serial killings of St. Louis vampires, she had her friend, private detective Ronnie Sims, check out the possible involvement of HAV and other similar groups in the case, aware that her own animator status precluded her interacting with HAV personally. Hearing the death squad rumors, Ronnie investigated further, as Anita was reluctant to pass unsubstantiated gossip on to Nikolaos, the city's Master vampire, convinced Nikolaos would react by ordering the slaughter of all local HAV members, innocent or otherwise. Ronnie found one HAV member, Beverly Chin, willing to help, initially because she was disturbed by the possibility that the group was acting outside the law, then later because she felt she owed Anita, who had saved her life three years ago. Beverly told of other members boasting of killing vampires, and promised to learn if they were telling the truth. Her findings are unrevealed, as soon after Anita unmasked the true killer.

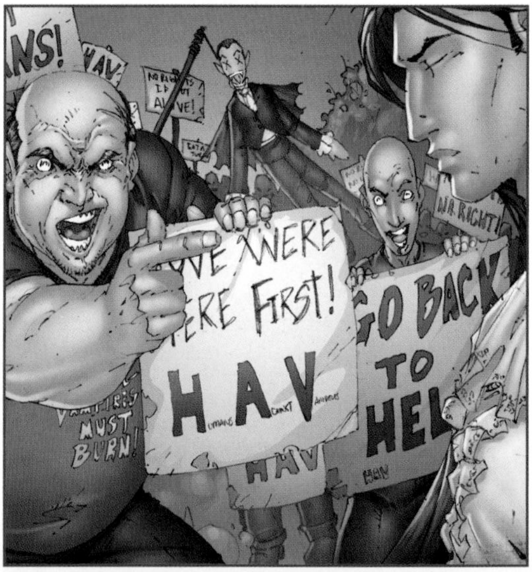
NS!
HAV
ALIVE!
WE WERE
ERE FIRST!
H A V
GO BACK
TO
HEL
MUST
BURN!
HAV

LUTHER

REAL NAME: Luther (last name unrevealed)
ALIASES: None known
ANITA'S NICKNAMES: None
CLASSIFICATION: Human
OCCUPATION: Bartender
CITIZENSHIP: U.S.A.
PLACE OF BIRTH: Unrevealed

BASE OF OPERATIONS: Dead Dave's, St. Louis, Missouri
KNOWN RELATIVES: Unrevealed
ALLIES: Anita Blake, Dead Dave
GROUP AFFILIATION: None
ENEMIES: None
EDUCATION: Unrevealed
FIRST APPEARANCE: Guilty Pleasures (1993)

HISTORY: Luther is the daytime manager and bartender of Dead Dave's, a bar located in the St. Louis neighborhood called the District by its vampiric residents. He keeps tabs on all the local gossip about the local vampires and their groupies and victims while bar owner Dave sleeps in his coffin elsewhere on the property. He knows Anita Blake as one of the regulars, and often passes information to her that he knows will sometimes get to the hands of the local police. When Blake came to him to learn the background of her informant Phillip, Luther told her what little he could about Phillip's background. He informed her of the rumor that Valentine, a vampire whose preferred prey was young boys, had often bragged that he was the first ever who had 'done' Phillip, and that the boy had loved it so much that he turned into a vampire junkie to keep getting his fix. When Blake pressed Luther to reveal the daytime resting place of Valentine so she could have a chance of stopping him before Valentine made good on his vow to kill Blake, Luther tentatively refused, fearing that the other vampires would burn the bar down in retaliation. Luther told Blake that he had to first clear it with Dave, and that if he agreed he would tell her what he knew. Blake later learned the location of Valentine's resting place from an unrelated source, sparing Luther and Dave from divulging information that many vampires would kill to prevent falling into human hands.

HEIGHT: 6'
WEIGHT: Unrevealed; fat

EYES: Brown
HAIR: Black (graying)
AGE: Over 50

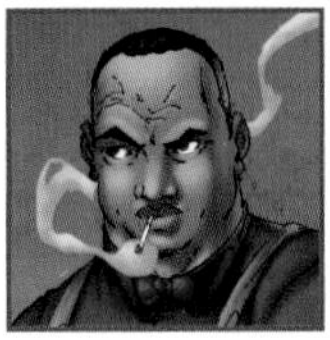

DESCRIPTION: Luther's body covered in hard fat, almost as solid as muscle. A large man, his hands are huge knuckled and his skin is almost mahogany in color. His eyes are creamy brown, but have yellow edges from overexposure to cigarette smoke; Luther is a chain smoker, never seen without a cigarette in his mouth, and he carries his own ash tray round with him. His hair is graying at the temples. His voice is deep and gravelly.

DEMEANOR: While Luther can presumably be intimidating when he chooses, he is friendly and helpful to Anita, and looks out for her, warning her if he hears anything that concerns her. He calls every man "fella" and every woman "girl."

NOTABLE SKILLS: Luther is skilled in mixing drinks and managing a business. Presumably he can physically handle drunken customers when the need arises, though this has yet to be seen.

NOTABLE ABILITIES: Luther is never sick.

CATHERINE MAISON

REAL NAME: Catherine Maison
ALIASES: None
ANITA'S NICKNAMES: None
CLASSIFICATION: Human
OCCUPATION: Lawyer
CITIZENSHIP: U.S.A.
PLACE OF BIRTH: Unrevealed

BASE OF OPERATIONS: St. Louis, Missouri
KNOWN RELATIVES: None
ALLIES: Anita Blake, unidentified fiancé
GROUP AFFILIATION: Unidentified lawfirm
ENEMIES: Aubrey, Monica Vespucci
EDUCATION: Law degree
FIRST APPEARANCE: Guilty Pleasures (1993)

HISTORY: Lawyer Catherine Maison is a good friend of Anita Blake's, one of the few people who understands her sarcastic sense of humor, and close enough to the animator that Anita is willing, however reluctantly, to buy a pink formal bridesmaid's dress with puffy sleeves to attend Catherine's impending wedding. Unfortunately for Catherine, her friendship with Anita also placed her at risk when the city's master vampire needed leverage to coerce Anita into working for her. One of Catherine's colleagues, Monica Vespucci, was a vampire groupie, and arranged a surprise bachelorette party for Catherine, consisting of just the three of them and which took the trio to the vampire strip club Guilty Pleasures. Having had minimal exposure to vampires, Catherine was sufficiently intrigued by the show to insist on staying when Anita was briefly called away on police business, and during Anita's absence Catherine was brought on stage by the vampire Aubrey. While most of the audience thought it a harmless act, Aubrey placed Catherine in a deep trance, ensuring that she would be his to call at any time and from anywhere for the rest of her life. Learning of this upon her return, Anita was told Catherine's survival was conditional on her cooperation. No longer entranced and now aware something was amiss, Catherine threatened to go to the police, but Aubrey simply erased her memories of the night, sending her home to awake the next day believing she had simply drunk too much. Luckily for Catherine, two days later she departed town for a week on a deposition, and during her absence Anita slew Aubrey, ending the threat to her friend's life.

HEIGHT: Tall
WEIGHT: Slender
EYES: Unrevealed
HAIR: Copper-red
AGE: Unrevealed; presumably 20s or 30s

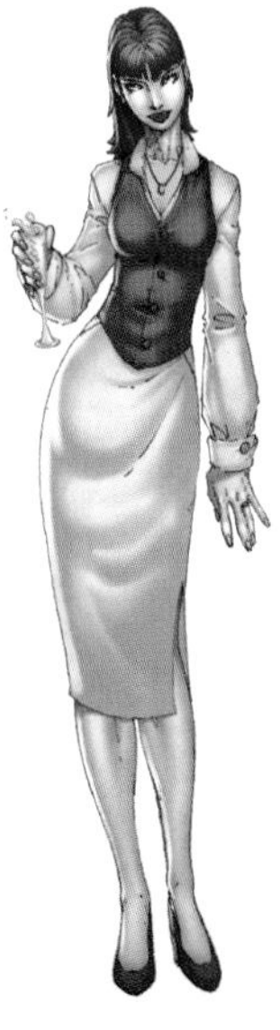

DESCRIPTION: Catherine has long, striking copper-red hair framing her freckled face.

DEMEANOR: Catherine is strong willed and refuses to be intimidated, but unfortunately her lack of prior contact with vampires made her curious enough about them to make her an easy target. She recognizes Anita's sarcasm, and can make her reign it in.

NOTABLE SKILLS: Skilled lawyer.

REBECCA MILES

REAL NAME: Rebecca Miles
ALIASES: None
ANITA'S NICKNAMES: None
CLASSIFICATION: Human
OCCUPATION: None; vampire's property
CITIZENSHIP: U.S.A.
PLACE OF BIRTH: Unrevealed

BASE OF OPERATIONS: Dogtown, South City, St. Louis, Missouri
KNOWN RELATIVES: None
ALLIES: Jack, Phillip; formerly Maurice
GROUP AFFILIATION: None
ENEMIES: None
EDUCATION: Unrevealed
FIRST APPEARANCE: Guilty Pleasures (1993)

HISTORY: Rebecca Miles is a vampire junkie, addicted to being bitten and fed upon by the undead. For five years she lived with a vampire named Maurice, treated as his property; despite this, Rebecca apparently loved Maurice, or at least mistook her dependency on him for love. They made their home in a disheveled apartment block in South City's Dogtown area and attended Freak Parties, where she would be passed around between other junkies and vampires to be used for sex and as food. However, the undead animator Zachary, needing vampire blood to maintain his life, began choosing his victims from amongst the vampires attending Freak Parties; Maurice was torn apart by Zachary's ghouls, the first of many vampires murdered by Zachary. Rebecca swiftly replaced Maurice with another vampire, Jack.

Anita went to her apartment, this time accompanied by Phillip, a vampire junkie whom Rebecca knew. Initially Rebecca believed Anita had come to slay her new lover, and hysterically attacked her, but Anita easily overpowered her. After Phillip had calmed Rebecca down, Anita questioned her, this time discovering about Maurice's attendance of Freak Parties. They left Rebecca to sleep, and seeing how her experiences had broken her gave Phillip new resolve not to end up like her.

HEIGHT: Delicate stature
WEIGHT: Unrevealed; skeletally thin
EYES: Dark
HAIR: Lifeless dark hair, shoulder length
AGE: Unrevealed

DESCRIPTION: Rebecca is thin and wasted looking, with high cheekbones on a starved face. Her body is similarly undernourished, delicate and fragile.

DEMEANOR: Rebecca's life revolves around being a vampire's pet, and she reacts hysterically to any perceived threat to that. The thought of losing another lover leaves her terrified and shaking. While she does still display other emotions around friends like Phillip, they are muted, and she is largely apathetic to the rest of her life.

EDITH PRINGLE

REAL NAME: Edith Pringle
ALIASES: None
ANITA'S NICKNAMES: None
CLASSIFICATION: Human
OCCUPATION: Teacher (retired)
CITIZENSHIP: U.S.A.
PLACE OF BIRTH: Unrevealed
BASE OF OPERATIONS: Anita Blake's apartment building, St. Louis,

Missouri
KNOWN RELATIVES: None
ALLIES: Custard
GROUP AFFILIATION: None
ENEMIES: None
EDUCATION: Teaching qualification
FIRST APPEARANCE: Guilty Pleasures (1993)

HISTORY: Edith Pringle is Anita Blake's neighbor. A retired school teacher, she now lives alone, apart from her pet Pomeranian dog, Custard, whom Anita feels resembles a wind-up toy, golden-dandelion fluff with cat feet. Fond of taking Custard for walks in front of the apartment building, Edith tends to notice those coming and going most of the time; she and Anita like each other, and Edith takes an interest in Anita's love life, or lack thereof. However Anita also strongly dislikes Custard, who seems in turn either determined to win her over or taking perverse pleasure in annoying her, constantly yapping and trying to jump up on Anita whenever she is around.

Edith had a narrow escape when she spotted the assassin Edward breaking in to Anita's apartment, believing him when he claimed to be Anita's boyfriend. Later informing Anita of Edward's visit, Edith picked up on Anita's disquiet, but was fooled when Anita claimed that she was merely unsure about giving her keys to a man; Edith counseled Anita that if she was uncertain, then he could not be the right man for her. Though Edith had not been hurt, the encounter made Anita worry about the safety of those around her given the risky life she leads.

HEIGHT: Nearly 6'
WEIGHT: Unrevealed; thin
EYES: Blue
HAIR: White
AGE: Over 60

DESCRIPTION: Tall and stretched thin with age, Edith has curious eyes which rest behind silver-rimmed glasses. She has delicate-boned hands.

DEMEANOR: Edith takes a motherly interest in Anita and her love life, and though slightly naïve, is also quick to spot when Anita is not being totally honest with her.

NOTABLE SKILLS: Former schoolteacher, able to put on an authoritarian voice at will.

RAFAEL

REAL NAME: Rafael (full name unrevealed)
ALIASES: Rat King
ANITA'S NICKNAMES: None
CLASSIFICATION: Lycanthrope (wererat)
OCCUPATION: Wererat leader, human occupation (if any) unrevealed
CITIZENSHIP: U.S.A. (presumably)
PLACE OF BIRTH: Unrevealed
BASE OF OPERATIONS: St. Louis, Missouri
KNOWN RELATIVES: None
ALLIES: Anita Blake, Louie, Lillian
GROUP AFFILIATION: Wererats
ENEMIES: Nikolaos, unidentified pro-Nikolaos factions within the wererats
EDUCATION: Unrevealed
FIRST APPEARANCE: Guilty Pleasures (1993)

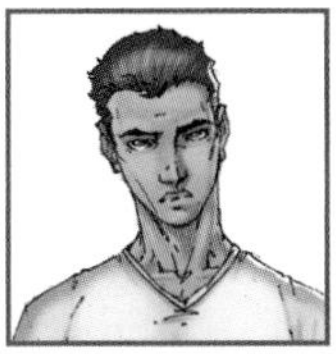

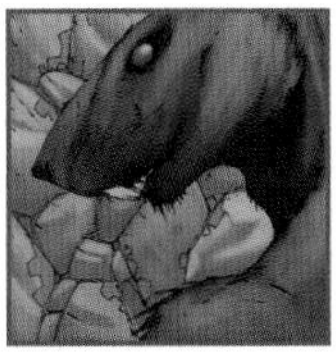

HISTORY: Rafael is the leader of St. Louis' wererats, and opposes Nikolaos' attempts to use the rats as her servants. Presumably either he or Nikolaos only came to power recently, as given her attitude to opposition, it seems unlikely this state of affairs could have lasted any great length of time. Rafael ordered his people to stay away from Nikolaos, and to resist her call as much as possible. However some in his ranks disobeyed, either through fear of Nikolaos or because they hoped to see Rafael replaced. Learning that wererats had been instructed to terrorize a prisoner of Nikolaos in the dungeons beneath her lair in the Circus of the Damned, Rafael came to the prisoner's aid, later claiming it was more to defy Nikolaos and stop his people disobeying him than out of any concern for the prisoner. After making it clear to the dissenting wererats that he would kill any who disobeyed his authority, Rafael briefly talked to the prisoner, the animator Anita Blake, and advised her to do as Nikolaos wanted in order to avoid being hurt; they connected somewhat when Anita pointed out that Rafael was not following his own advice. A few days later, Anita contacted Rafael asking if he could lead her and her friend Edward through the tunnels to make covert entry into the Circus, so she could slay Nikolaos. Though Rafael made it clear that because of Nikolaos' power over them the rats could not assist in the actual fight, he and some of his fellows agreed to Anita's request. After Anita slew Nikolaos, Rafael and his people entered the Circus, provided medical assistance to Anita and Edward, and watched as Anita slew Zachary.

HEIGHT: At least 6'
WEIGHT: Unrevealed
EYES: (Human) Brown; (rat) black
HAIR: (Human) Black, cut short; (rat) black fur over entire body.
AGE: Unrevealed

DESCRIPTION: In human form Rafael is a handsome man of Mexican descent, with dark brown skin; his voice is deep and soft, and his lack of accent suggests that despite his ethnicity he is either U.S. born or raised. He is tall, with a thin face marked with a touch of arrogance. In rat form, he appears as a tall, humanoid rat, with jet black fur, black-button eyes, and wearing cut off jeans for freedom of movement.

DISTINGUISHING FEATURES: Brand in shape of four pointed crown on left forearm, visible in both forms.

DEMEANOR: Rafael comes across as proud, suspicious and slightly arrogant, unwilling to let either himself or his people be treated as slaves or servants, not even by the Master of the City. He brooks no dissension in his own ranks, putting down opposition swiftly and brutally. However, underneath this, he appears to be a decent individual, coming to Anita's aid initially when she was attacked by rats under Nikolaos' command; though he made out this was done purely to oppose Nikolaos, his façade slipped slightly when he checked if she had been uninjured.

NOTABLE ABILITIES: As a wererat, Rafael possesses enhanced senses, able to see in dim lighting clearly, hear noises far off, and, even in his human form, able to smell normal humans' emotional states. In wererat form he possesses enhanced strength to an unspecified degree, enhanced endurance, and accelerated healing, though he is presumably vulnerable to silver weapons. He is also extremely agile and limber, able to compress and twist his body to fit through spaces much smaller than his large frame suggests.

SIGMUND/PENGUINS

KNOWN MEMBERS: Sigmund, others unidentified
BASE OF OPERATIONS: Anita's bedroom, Anita's apartment, St. Louis, Missouri
FIRST APPEARANCE: Guilty Pleasures (1993)

HISTORY: Despite her tough outer demeanor and sarcastic sense of humor, Anita Blake has one weakness. While others smoke or drink, Anita collects stuffed penguins. She now owns so many that they cover a small loveseat on the wall under her bedroom window, across from her bed, overflowing onto the floor, where they form a fluffy tide. Anita's favorite penguin is Sigmund, whom she sometimes sleeps with, taking solace from his company after especially stressful days. Anita is careful to guard her guilty secret, and even amongst her closest friends few know about her penguin addiction. The hardened assassin Edward discovered it after helping an injured Anita to bed following the painful cleansing of a vampire bite wound, but declined to comment.

Anita's penguin love extends beyond her cuddly toys; she also owns an oversized t-shirt with a picture of penguins playing beach volleyball while kiddie penguins make sandcastles off to one side. Long enough to cover Anita to mid-thigh, normally it is a sleep shirt, but she has also reluctantly worn it outside, where others can see it, when she had to conceal a gun without wearing a jacket on a swelteringly hot day.

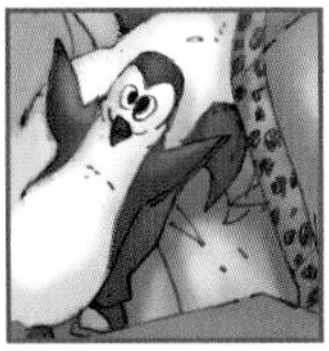

TRAITS: Anita's stuffed penguin toys come in a variety of sizes. Fluffy and plump, they serve to relax her and, in the case of Sigmund, sometimes share her bed to help her sleep after people have tried to kill her.

LENGTH: Varies
WEIGHT: Varies
EYES: Varies
SKIN: Varies, usually fluffy black and white combination.

SGT. DOLPH STORR

REAL NAME: Rudolf "Dolph" Storr
ALIASES: None
ANITA'S NICKNAMES: None
CLASSIFICATION: Human
OCCUPATION: Sergeant, St. Louis Police Department; Head of RPIT
CITIZENSHIP: U.S.A.
PLACE OF BIRTH: Unrevealed
BASE OF OPERATIONS: St. Louis, Missouri
KNOWN RELATIVES: None
ALLIES: Anita Blake, Clive Perry, Zerbrowski
GROUP AFFILIATION: Regional Preternatural Investigation Team (RPIT), Saint Louis City Police Department
ENEMIES: Zachary
EDUCATION: College degree; police academy graduate
FIRST APPEARANCE: Guilty Pleasures (1993)

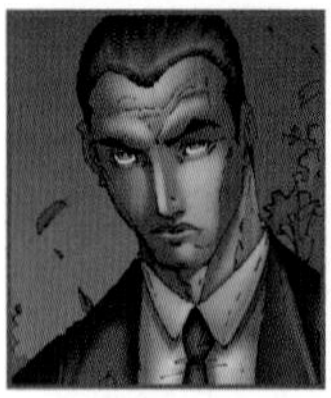

HISTORY: Dolph Storr is a career police officer who was assigned to head up St. Louis' new Regional Preternatural Investigation Team (RPIT) after the passage of Addison v. Clark, investigating supernatural-related crimes. Since the assignment was hardly considered a prestigious one, it seems likely he was given the posting because he irritated some of his superiors, but if Dolph resented his new position, he gave little sign, determined to do the job to the best of his ability. Early in Dolph's command, RPIT added Anita Blake as a supernatural consultant; Dolph recognizes his own knowledge gaps in regards to vampires and other monsters, and, as diligent in learning as he is in teaching, at each case Dolph, ever-present notebook at the ready, questions Anita thoroughly on the supernatural clues she uncovers. The taskforce's biggest recent case was the serial slayings of a number of vampires, but he was unaware that the vampires eventually took matters into their own hands, coercing Anita into investigating the case for them. Meanwhile Dolph also led the investigation into a cemetery caretaker slain by ghouls, unaware that this tied into the vampire murders. When Anita uncovered the identity of the killer, Zachary, and was preparing to confront the city's master vampire Nikolaos, she called Dolph to pass on the former bit of information, and left a letter for Dolph informing of Nikolaos' wrongdoings and coercion, to be delivered in the event Anita failed to survive her meeting with same.

HEIGHT: 6'8"
WEIGHT: Unrevealed; stocky
EYES: Unrevealed
HAIR: Black
AGE: Unrevealed

DESCRIPTION: Dolph is built like a wrestler, with close cropped black hair leaving his ears bare.

DEMEANOR: Dolph is taciturn and businesslike, dedicated to doing his job, whatever it is and however unpleasant, to the best of his ability. He is loyal to his friends, and has a teasing sense of humor, at least with those he likes.

NOTABLE SKILLS: Dolph is an excellent police officer.

MONICA VESPUCCI

REAL NAME: Monica Vespucci
ALIASES: None
ANITA'S NICKNAMES: None
CLASSIFICATION: Human
OCCUPATION: Lawyer (presumably)
CITIZENSHIP: U.S.A.
PLACE OF BIRTH: Unrevealed
BASE OF OPERATIONS: St. Louis, Missouri
KNOWN RELATIVES: None
ALLIES: Buzz, Jean-Claude, Phillip
GROUP AFFILIATION: Unidentified law firm
ENEMIES: Anita Blake
EDUCATION: Law degree (presumably)
FIRST APPEARANCE: Guilty Pleasures (1993)

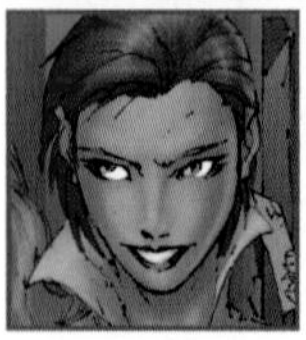

HISTORY: Monica Vespucci is a vampire groupie and regular at the Guilty Pleasures vampire strip club run by master vampire Jean-Claude. By day she works in a law firm, alongside Catherine Maison, a good friend of the state of Missouri's licensed vampire executioner, Anita Blake, a detail she presumably shared with her vampire friends. Thus, when Jean-Claude needed a way to lure Anita down to his club, he used Monica to bait the trap. On the pretext of arranging a surprise bachelorette party for Catherine, Monica called Anita, and guilted her into agreeing to be the driver for the night, then on the night itself led the trip to Guilty Pleasures. Despite swiftly realizing something was amiss and that Monica was very pro-undead, Anita reluctantly left Catherine behind when she was briefly called away on police business. In her absence, Catherine was lured on stage and placed into a deep trance by the vampire Aubrey; Monica made no attempt to prevent this, and may even have encouraged it. When Anita returned it was made clear to her that Catherine's life would be forfeit if she did not work for the vampires. Learning that Monica had willingly placed a fellow human at the mercy of the vampires, Anita promised to kill Monica if Catherine was hurt; Monica defiantly retorted that she would be brought back as a vampire if Anita slew her, but Anita informed Monica that she would cut out Monica's heart, burn it, and scatter her ashes in the river to prevent this. Clearly shaken by this threat, Monica admitted to fellow vampire junkie Phillip that Anita terrified her.

HEIGHT: Unrevealed **WEIGHT:** Unrevealed
EYES: Unrevealed **HAIR:** Unrevealed
AGE: Unrevealed, presumably 20s or 30s

DESCRIPTION: Monica takes pride in her appearance, wearing expensive clothes, a perfect health-club tan, with her short hair expertly cut and perfect make-up. She hides her bite wounds with high-collared blouses.

DISTINGUISHING FEATURES: Two old puncture wounds, nearly scars, on her neck.

DEMEANOR: Despite presumably being a lawyer, Monica comes across as ditzy and thoughtless. She is happy to do the bidding of vampires even when it means selling out other humans, friends included; it seems she finds vampirism sexually arousing, even getting turned on by mimicking vampires by licking other victims' scars and sucking on bite wounds, and she clearly enjoys being bitten herself. Apparently convinced of vampiric infallibility, Monica seems surprised that anyone can resist their mental powers.

BEATRICE
CLASSIFICATION: Human
OCCUPATION: Waitress
HISTORY: Beatrice is a waitress working at Mabel's Diner, across the street from the Animators, Inc. offices. She is a tall, brown haired woman with a tired face, but who always seems to remain cheery in spite of this. Anita often goes to lunch there, and always makes conversation with her. Beatrice was serving the day Anita went to Mabel's with Phillip, and was clearly won over by his dazzling smile.

BETTY
CLASSIFICATION: Human
OCCUPATION: Legal secretary
HISTORY: Betty is Catherine Maison's secretary. When Anita called Catherine after Phillips' death to warn Catherine of the danger she was in, Betty took the call and informed her that Catherine was out of town for the week on a deposition. She also reminded Anita of an upcoming bridesmaid dress fitting.

CHARLES
CLASSIFICATION: Human
OCCUPATION: Animator
KNOWN RELATIVES: Unidentified child
HISTORY: One of the four animators working for Animators, Inc. He is a competent corpse-raiser, but is squeamish and would be no good in a fight. He has a four-year old child.
SEE: Animators, Inc.

CRAIG
CLASSIFICATION: Human
OCCUPATION: Secretary
HISTORY: Craig is the night secretary at Animators, Inc. He's been at the company long enough to know better than to react to seeing Anita carrying guns in the office. He took Edward's call to the office looking for Anita the night she was forcibly recruited to hunt the vampire killer, and later passed Anita a message to call Irving Griswold about the meeting he was arranging for her with Rafael.
SEE: Animators, Inc.

CRYSTAL
CLASSIFICATION: Human
OCCUPATION: Unrevealed
HISTORY: A freak party regular, Crystal is a very plump blond woman in her forties or fifties. She was wearing a black negligee at the party Anita Blake attended. Overly affectionate, she literally jumped on Phillip when she saw him at the party, and began crying when Anita asked her to leave the clearly uncomfortable Phillip alone.

CUSTARD
CLASSIFICATION: Dog
OCCUPATION: Pet
HISTORY: Custard is Mrs. Pringle's pet Pomeranian, whom she likes walking outside her apartment building. Small and yappy, he annoys Anita greatly; she dislikes him with a passion, so he always tries to jump up on her.
SEE: Mrs. Pringle

DARLENE
CLASSIFICATION: Human
OCCUPATION: Unrevealed
HISTORY: A freak party regular, the auburn-haired Darlene was used by the assassin Edward to get into the same party Anita Blake attended. She knew Phillip of old, and tried to get him to spend time alone with her, but Phillip refused, uncomfortable with her licking his scars and not wanting to leave Anita at the mercies of the other, sexually predatory, partygoers.

DEAD DAVE
CLASSIFICATION: Vampire
OCCUPATION: Bar owner, former cop
HISTORY: Dave is a former cop kicked off the force when he became a vampire. He now owns a bar in the District, and though still angry at his former colleagues, provides them information through Anita Blake.
SEE: Dead Dave's.

FIELDS, RAYMOND
CLASSIFICATION: Human
OCCUPATION: Expert on vampire cults
HISTORY: Raymond Fields is an expert on cults whom Anita consults with on occasion. When trying to dissuade Mrs. Franks from letting her son become a vampire, Anita passed her Raymond's card.

MRS. FRANKS
CLASSIFICATION: Human
OCCUPATION: Unrevealed
KNOWN RELATIVES: Unnamed son
HISTORY: A tall, blond woman in her mid-forties, and from a moneyed background, Mrs. Franks learned her son wanted to join the Church of Eternal Life and become a vampire. Uncertain, she consulted Animators, Inc, and listened to the advice of the pro-vampire Jamison Clarke. As she was leaving, Anita Blake tried to hand her Raymond Field's business card, and pointed out her own vampire-inflicted scars. Mrs. Franks was briefly shaken by this, but swiftly recovered her composure as Jamison informed her that the vampires who had injured Anita had simply been defending themselves.

MRS. FRANK'S SON
CLASSIFICATION: Human
OCCUPATION: Unrevealed
KNOWN RELATIVES: Mrs. Franks (mother)
HISTORY: A slender, blond haired youth who looked younger than his eighteen years of age, the son of Mrs. Franks had expressed interest in joining the Church of Eternal Life and becoming a vampire. He accompanied his mother to Animators, Inc. when she went there seeking advice about his decision.

GRUNDICK, ALBERT
CLASSIFICATION: Zombie
OCCUPATION: Unrevealed
KNOWN RELATIVES: Unname wife, two unidentified sons
HISTORY: Albert Grundick had died leaving two conflicting wills. His wife hired Anita Blake of Animators, Inc. to raise him as a zombie to settle the question of which one he wanted to be applied.

MRS. GRUNDICK
CLASSIFICATION: Human
OCCUPATION: Unrevealed
KNOWN RELATIVES: Albert (husband, deceased), two unidentified sons
HISTORY: After the death of her husband, Albert, two contesting wills were found. Rather than spend years arguing in court over which was the correct one, Mrs. Grundick elected to have Albert raised as a zombie to get his final word on the matter.

HARVEY
CLASSIFICATION: Human
OCCUPATION: Unrevealed
KNOWN RELATIVES: Madge (wife)
HISTORY: Harvey was the host of the freak party Anita Blake attended. Wearing a leather and studded outfit, he showed immediate interest in Anita, and later spied on her and Phillip when they went to the bathroom to talk in private.

HEWITT, ESTELLE
CLASSIFICATION: Zombie
OCCUPATION: Unrevealed
HISTORY: Estelle Hewitt was born in the 19th century, and died in 1866. She was buried in her wedding dress in the Saint Charles suburbs of St. Louis. More than a century later Estelle's grave was chosen when Nikolaos wanted to test the limit of her animator Zachary's powers. With the assistance of Anita Blake, Estelle was raised as a badly decayed zombie, and promptly tormented by Theresa and the other vampires who had been monitoring Zachary's test. Unwilling to see Estelle mistreated like this, Anita begged Nikolaos to return Estelle to the grave, which Nikolaos eventually agreed to. On her orders, Zachary laid Estelle back to rest.
SEE: Zombies

JACK
CLASSIFICATION: Vampire
OCCUPATION: Unrevealed
HISTORY: Jack is the new vampire lover of Rebecca Miles. He was sleeping for the day in his dark wood coffin when Anita Blake and Phillip came round to question Rebecca about the death of her previous lover, Maurice.
SEE: Rebecca Miles

JENSEN, IRIS
CLASSIFICATION: Zombie
OCCUPATION: None
KNOWN RELATIVES: Thomas Jensen (father)
HISTORY: Abused by her father, Iris Jensen committed suicide. Thirteen years after her death, the guilt-ridden Thomas paid for her to be raised as a zombie so he could apologize to her, but she had died hating and fearing him, and refused to accept his apology. Because of this, Thomas declined to return her to her grave, keeping her for the next seven years as her mind and body both decayed away.
SEE: Zombies

JENSEN, THOMAS
CLASSIFICATION: Human
OCCUPATION: Unrevealed
KNOWN RELATIVES: Iris (daughter, deceased)
HISTORY: Having abused his daughter Iris, Thomas Jensen was overtaken with guilt when she committed suicide, and eventually had her raised as a zombie to try and make amends. She refused to accept his apology, so Thomas refused to let her be laid to rest, keeping her around as she slowly decayed. A legendry story amongst animators, Anita Blake was lured into an ambush by Zachary, who tricked her into believing Jensen was finally willing to return Iris to the grave.

JOSH
CLASSIFICATION: Human
OCCUPATION: Student
KNOWN RELATIVES: Judith (mother), Anita Blake (stepsister)
HISTORY: Josh is the thirteen year old stepbrother of Anita Blake. He thinks her lifestyle is exciting and cool.

JUDITH
CLASSIFICATION: Human
OCCUPATION: Unrevealed
KNOWN RELATIVES: Josh (son), Anita Blake (stepdaughter)
HISTORY: Judith is the stepmother of Anita Blake. She gets concerned with Anita's frequent hospital stays, and is worried that Anita is becoming an old maid because she is not yet married at 24.

LILLIAN
CLASSIFICATION: Wererat
OCCUPATION: Doctor
HISTORY: Lillian is one of the wererats loyal to Rafael, and accompanied him when he led Anita Blake and Edward into the Circus of the Damned. A doctor in her human life, she is nearly gray-haired in rat form. After Anita and Edward slew Nikolaos and her followers, Lillian treated the injuries they had received during the battle.
SEE: Wererats

LOUIE
CLASSIFICATION: Wererat
OCCUPATION: Unrevealed
HISTORY: Louie is one of the wererats loyal to Rafael, and accompanied him when he led Anita Blake and Edward into the Circus of the Damned. Small and slender with a square face, he is amiable and chatty.
SEE: Wererats

LUCAS
CLASSIFICATION: Vampire
OCCUPATION: Unrevealed
HISTORY: The second vampire murdered by Zachary, his death was witnessed by an unidentified man later interrogated by Nikolaos.

MADGE
CLASSIFICATION: Human
OCCUPATION: Unrevealed
KNOWN RELATIVES: Harvey (husband)
HISTORY: One of the hosts of the freak party Anita Blake attended. When she insulted Anita by calling her a bedwarmer, Anita returned the favor by pointing out Madge was over forty, a remark which clearly hit home. Madge later consoled Crystal after she became upset when she was told Phillip was off-limits.

MARY
CLASSIFICATION: Human
OCCUPATION: Secretary
KNOWN RELATIVES: Two unidentified sons, four unidentified grandchildren
HISTORY: Mary is the Animators, Inc. day secretary. She is over fifty, but declines to say how much over, and keeps her short gray hair in place through excessive use of hairspray. She was present in the office when Anita tried to intervene with Jamison Clarke's client Mrs. Franks, and then watched Anita meet the stripper Phillip and go to lunch with him. Mistakenly believing Phillip was Anita's lover, she silently expressed to Anita that she thought Phillip was a looker, and was embarrassed when Phillip spotted her doing this.
SEE: Animators, Inc.

MAURICE
CLASSIFICATION: Vampire
OCCUPATION: Unrevealed
HISTORY: Maurice was a regular on the freak party circuit with Rebecca Miles, whom he considered his property. He would pass her round in return for sexual favors. He was also the first vampire slain by Zachary.
SEE: Rebecca Miles

PERRY, CLIVE
CLASSIFICATION: Human
OCCUPATION: Police detective
HISTORY: Detective Clive Perry is the latest member of RPIT, although no one can figure out why, as he is unfailingly polite and soft-spoken, making it hard to believe he could have upset someone enough to be assigned to that division. He is a tall, slender black man.

ROCHELLE
CLASSIFICATION: Human
OCCUPATION: Unrevealed
HISTORY: Rochelle is a tall black woman and an apparent newcomer on the freak party scene, given her comparatively fresh scars. She attended the freak party Anita Blake went to, and was unimpressed with Anita when she upset Crystal.

RODRIGUEZ, MANNY
CLASSIFICATION: Human
OCCUPATION: Animator, former vampire slayer
KNOWN RELATIVES: Rosita (wife), unidentified children
HISTORY: Manny was the animator who trained Anita Blake, both in animating and in vampire slaying. He taught her how to combine her powers with another animator to raise older corpses, and accompanied her killing vampires, until two years ago, when he was nearly killed and spent four months in hospital. His wife Rosita convinced him that at 52 he should retire from hunting the undead, rather than risk orphaning their children. Since then he has stuck to raising zombies. He is one of four animators who work for Animators, Inc.
SEE: Animators, Inc.

RODRIGUEZ, ROSITA
CLASSIFICATION: Human
OCCUPATION: Unrevealed
KNOWN RELATIVES: Manny (husband), unidentified children
HISTORY: Rosita is the wife of the animator Manny. Two years ago, when Manny was nearly killed on a vampire hunt, Rosita begged his protégé and fellow hunter Anita Blake not to take him on any further cases, and used the well-being of their children to convince Manny to quit.

UNIDENTIFIED HUMAN ASSASSIN
CLASSIFICATION: Human
OCCUPATION: Servant of Nikolaos
HISTORY: A "two-biter" who served Nikolaos, he was told by Zachary that Nikolaos wanted Anita Blake slain. He obeyed, unaware of his actions.

UNIDENTIFIED VAMPIRE
CLASSIFICATION: Vampire
OCCUPATION: Servant of Nikolaos
HISTORY: Seemingly a protégé of Nikolaos, this black vampire was present for many of Anita Blake's encounters with the master vampire. However she never learned his name before she invaded Nikolaos' lair and found him amongst the vampires sleeping there. Anita killed him in his sleep with a silver nitrate injection.

UNIDENTIFIED WERERAT
CLASSIFICATION: Wererat
OCCUPATION: Servant of Nikolaos
HISTORY: Blond haired leader of the wererats who disobeyed Rafael's orders and tried to terrorize Anita Blake for Nikolaos. He threatened to rape Anita, but she managed to knock him off the stairs, and before he recovered Rafael arrived. When he defied Rafael, stating that the rat-king would soon be killed by Nikolaos, Rafael overpowered him and warned him further disobedience would be met with death. The blond wererat left as instructed, but his parting glance at Anita suggested he considered there to be unfinished business between them.

UNIDENTIFIED ZOMBIE
CLASSIFICATION: Zombie
OCCUPATION: Unrevealed
HISTORY: Unfortunate enough to witness the second of the vampire murders, this unidentified thirty-something man, possibly a businessman based on his clothing, was kidnapped and tortured by Nikolaos to extract the identity of the killer. Possibly because one of Nikolaos' own minions, Zachary, was the guilty party, the despairing man took his own life to end the torment, hanging himself with his belt, but Nikolaos had Zachary raise him as a zombie so they could continue the questioning. Aware that the testimony could implicate him, Zachary seemingly blocked the zombie's ability to answer, then deliberately tormented him to break his mind, leaving him useless to the investigation.

ZERBROWSKI
CLASSIFICATION: Human
OCCUPATION: Police detective
HISTORY: One of the officers of RPIT, Zerbrowski displays a locker-room sense of humor, but repeatedly finds his attempts to embarrass Anita Blake backfire thanks to her quick wit and sharp tongue.

GLOSSARY

ADDISON VS. CLARK
Groundbreaking legal case which saw vampires granted civil rights in the U.S.A.

ANIMATOR
A human able to raise the dead through a combination of rare innate magical ability and ritual sacrifice.

THE ANIMATOR
Professional trade journal for animators.

FREAK
A human who likes vampires. Usually applied to someone whose interest in vampires is excessive or sexual.

FREAK PARTY
A party where freaks may meet vampires and freely offer themselves as food and sex toys for same.

GHOUL
A corpse which rises apparently spontaneously from the grave to feed off living flesh. Unlike zombies, ghouls do not decay. They are animalistic and hunt in packs, but are cowardly and rarely attack uninjured humans.

GRIS-GRIS
A type of voodoo charm. They can provide various different powers, but the one Anita encounters must be fed by a specific substance, commonly blood, to sustain their spell, and are deactivated by another specified substance, commonly another type of blood. The one Anita encounters is sustained by Vampire Blood and canceled by human blood.

HUMAN SERVANT
A trusted human chosen by a given vampire to serve it in return for an extended life and immunity to vampire mind powers. Not all humans who serve vampires are "human servants."

LYCANTHROPE
A human who can turn into an animal, either involuntarily on the nights of the full moon, or voluntarily the rest of the time. Lycanthropy is a disease, passed on through scratches or bites from another lycanthrope. Strictly speaking lycanthropy refers to werewolves (lycanthrope is the general name covering all animals), but it is commonly misapplied to refer to all species of werebeast. Known lycanthrope types include wererats, tigers and wolves.

MARKS
The manner by which a vampire may turn a human into a human servant. Marks are given through the vampire psychically binding its life force to the chosen human, with each mark granting the human greater powers. Four marks are required to make someone a full human servant.

MASTER OF THE CITY
The ruling vampire of a given city, usually the most powerful one.

MASTER VAMPIRE
A senior vampire with greater power than most of its kind. Usually commands followers. The master of a city is a master vampire, but not all master vampires rule cities, and each city may contain multiple, rival master vampires.

RAT KING
The leading wererat in a city, who commands the other wererats residents therein.

VAMPIRE
An immortal creature, formerly human, which feeds on human blood and emotions to sustain itself. Vampires can turn other humans into vampires through unspecified means, presumably including feeding off them.

WERERATS
Lycanthropes who assume rat or rat-human-hybrid forms.

WERETIGERS
Lycanthropes who assume tiger or were-human-hybrid forms.

WEREWOLVES
Lycanthropes who assume wolf or wolf-human-hybrid forms.

ZOMBIE
The raised corpse of a dead person, restored to a semblance of life by either an animator or voodoo priest. Zombies will regain their human memories a few minutes after being raised, and can retain these for up to a week before becoming mindless once more. A zombie will normally decay unless fed raw flesh, but cannot return to the grave, however decayed, unless destroyed or laid to rest by the appropriate ritual.

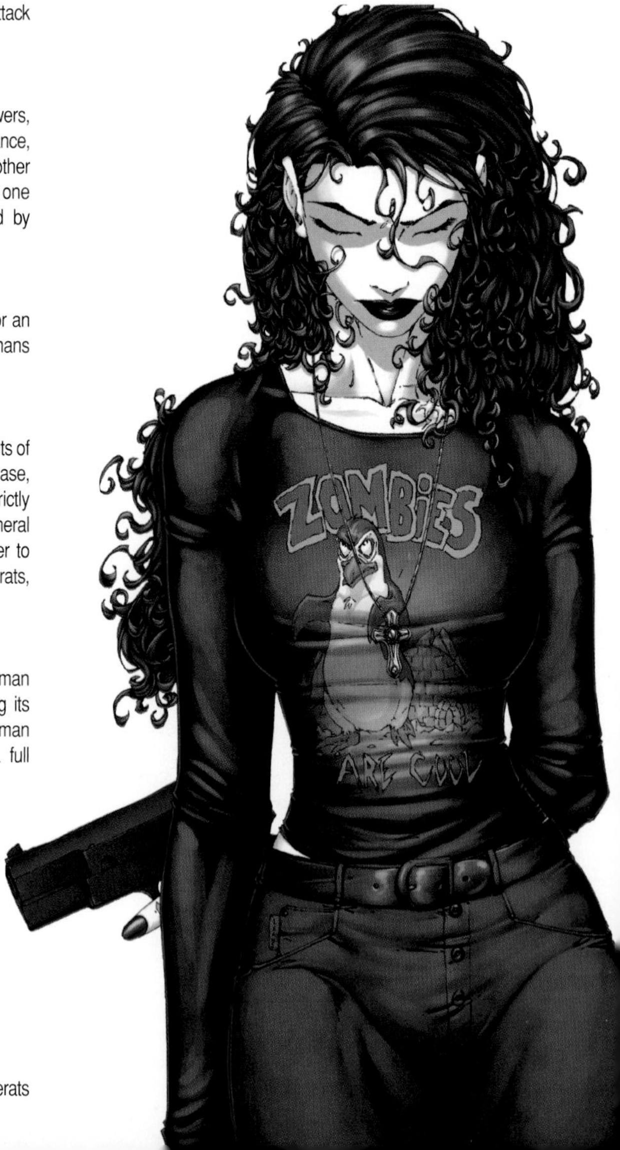
ZOMBIES
ARE COOL

#1 Cover Pencils by Brett Booth

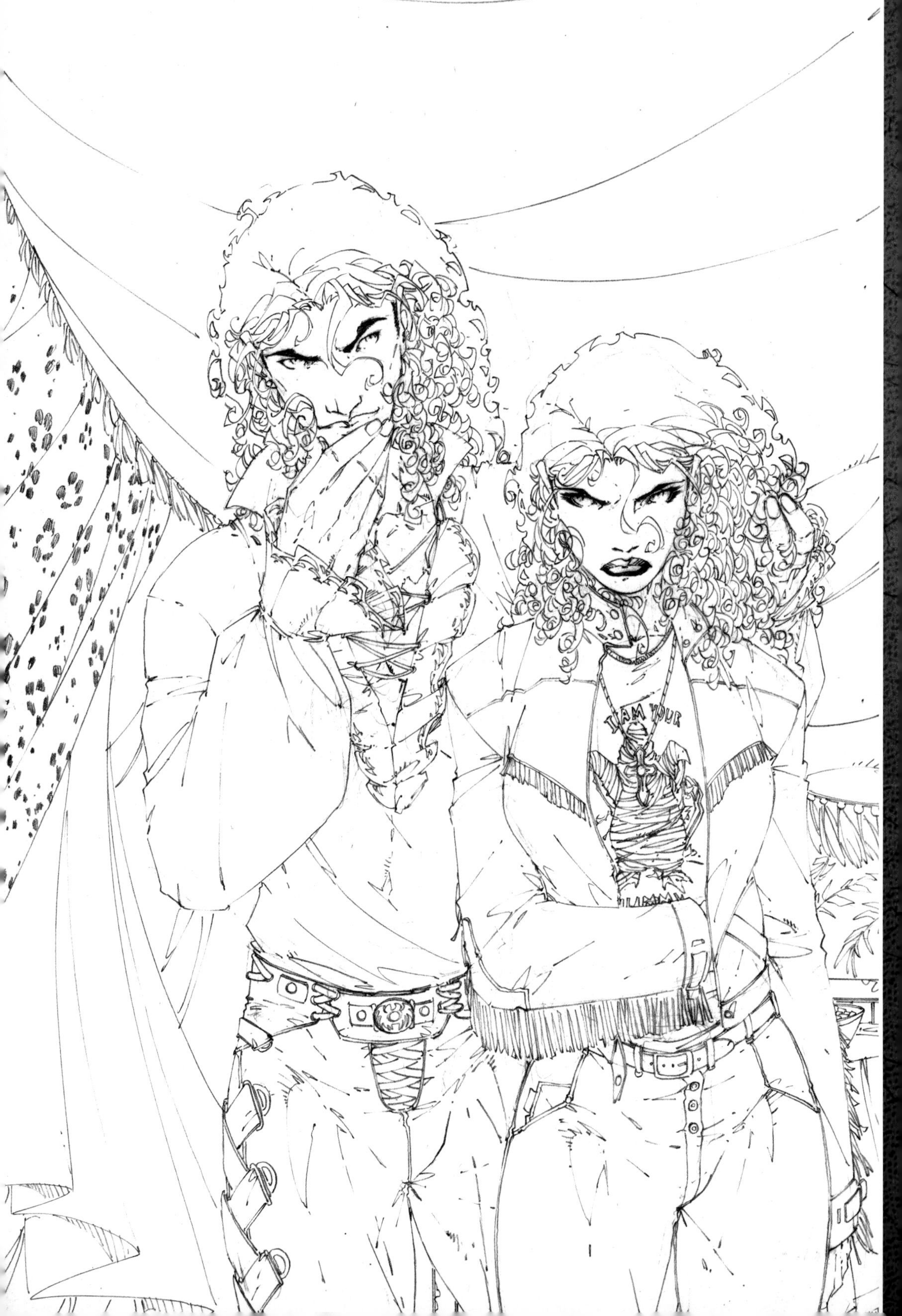

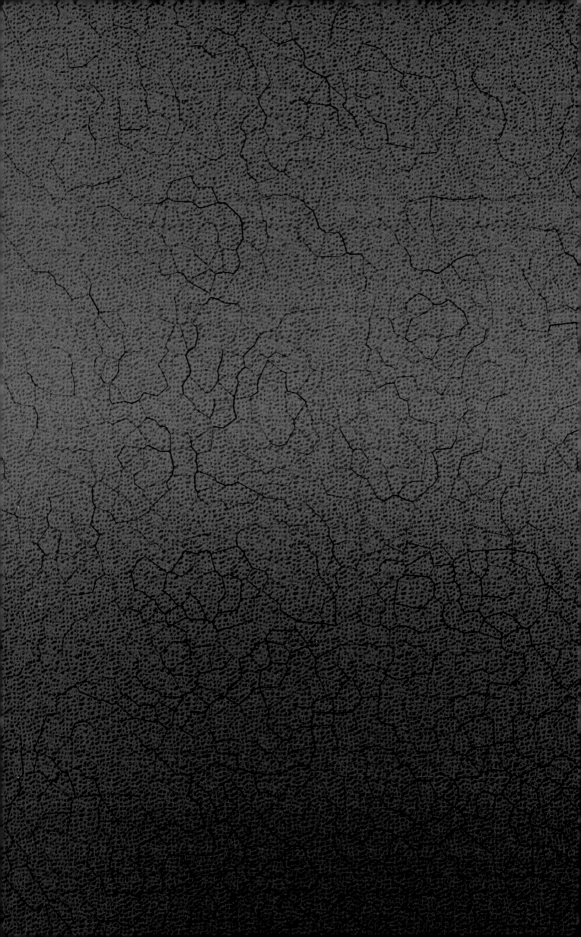